BACKYARD
STARSHIP

J.N. CHANEY
TERRY MAGGERT

LAS VEGAS, NV • PORTLAND, TN

CONNECT WITH J.N. CHANEY

Don't miss out on these exclusive perks:

- Instant access to free short stories from series like *The Messenger, Starcaster,* and more.
- Receive email updates for new releases and other news.
- Get notified when we run special deals on books and audiobooks.

So, what are you waiting for? Enter your email address at the link below to stay in the loop.

https://www.jnchaney.com/backyard-starship-subscribe

CONNECT WITH TERRY MAGGERT

Check out his website
http://terrymaggert.com/

Connect on Facebook
https://www.facebook.com/terrymaggertbooks/

Follow him on Amazon
https://www.amazon.com/Terry-Maggert/e/B00EKN8RHG/

JOIN THE CONVERSATION

Join the conversation and get updates on new and upcoming releases in the awesomely active **Facebook group**, "JN Chaney's Renegade Readers."

This is a hotspot where readers come together and share their lives and interests, discuss the series, and speak directly to J.N. Chaney and his co-authors.

facebook.com/groups/jnchaneyreaders

CONTENTS

1

THE RAIN SLAMMED down in hard, unrelenting sheets, rattling on the rental car like bullets and almost drowning out the rhythmic thump of the wipers. In one hand, I held my phone, a custom-built unit that did everything I wanted and nothing I didn't. Its screen, and the glow from the dashboard, offered the only steady light. Beyond the windows sprawled nothing but rainy gloom, split by sporadic flashbulb bursts of lightning.

My phone wasn't why I was here, though. At least, not directly. I really was just using it for light. It was the thing in my other hand that had brought me to this place, at this time, sitting in an idling car on a gravel driveway with water sluicing from puddle to puddle.

Another flare of lightning blew apart the night. Its brief crystalline glare etched the shape of a farmhouse and a fence, beyond them a barn, and beyond that the rolling fields that had been my family's land for—hell, I wasn't sure how many generations. At least four. Maybe five.

Until recently, it had all been my grandfather's. *God's green acre,* he called it, a rambling farm granted to my family by the railroad at the end of the Civil War. The tracks still ran along the west edge of the property, in fact—

Another flash of lightning. This time, my gaze stayed inside the car, on the documents unfolded in my lap. They looked important, all purposeful text and signatures and seals embossed right into the paper. They even *felt* important, much heavier than the paper alone. They bore down with the weight of *meaning.*

Of course, any document starting *...being of sound mind, do hereby bequeath...* was weighty and important. These papers were a bridge, vaulting from one generation to the next. Or, in this instance, the generation after that. In any case, they were an end, closing another chapter of my family's lineage, bringing it right up to date. But they were a beginning, too.

...being of sound mind, do hereby bequeath all property and goods and chattels above and below the surface of Blackthorn Farm, address County Road 1100, Pony Hollow, Iowa, United States of America. (Earth), to my grandson, Clive VanAbel Tudor III.

I had to smile at that last bit about *Earth.* "Just in case it got mistaken for Iowa, Mars," I said to the page. "You always were thorough, Gramps."

I killed the engine, freezing the wipers in mid-stroke. Rainwater celebrated this little victory by cascading down the windshield. I folded up the will, tucked it and the car key in my jacket pocket, and prepared to step out into the storm.

As soon as I gripped the door handle, the front door to the house opened, an island of warmly inviting golden light amid the rainy gloom. It framed a woman—small, older, tidy. Miryam Nunzio, our family's attorney, and my grandfather's friend. She was here to deal with the last wishes of a man who lived as he died—with secrets.

I popped open the car door and ran. It didn't matter, of course. Some things are simply too fast or relentless to avoid. Like the rain.

Or the future.

I POUNDED up the front steps to the house, muttering curses as water squelched between my toes. It seemed like I'd managed to slam my feet down into every puddle between the car and the porch. Miryam let me in the house, shaking her head in disapproval as I stalked past her while dripping on the ancient hardwood floor and then toed off my sodden shoes.

"You were never a clean boy. Smart as the proverbial whip, but never clean," she said, taking my jacket.

"In case you hadn't noticed, it's raining," I snapped back, but that drained all the snap out of me. I sagged a bit and smiled. "I'll take it as a compliment, though. The smart part, anyway."

A quiet pall hung over the house. I heard only the tick of the grandfather clock in the living room and the soft, irregular patter of water dripping from both me and my coat on the floor. Miryam and I found ourselves just standing, staring at each other, kneading the silence with our grief.

Although, grief is a funny thing. I missed my grandfather, but more in the way something that had just always been a part of my life suddenly wasn't. Miryam, I suspected, missed him much more. I was pretty sure this wasn't her first time in the old house on a cold, rainy autumn night.

Another second or two and the silent moment would topple into *awkward*. On impulse, I stepped forward and hugged Miryam. She hugged me right back. She *had* known me since birth, and I'd grown up with her as much a fixture in my life as my grandfather had been. She was a confidant, a friend, and sometimes even the mother I didn't have.

She finally pulled away. "You're soaking wet. And now, so am I."

"Sorry."

"Well, there's coffee on, and your room is ready. He never changed anything up there. Not since you left, anyway."

"You know, at the risk of dripping on the hardwood some more, I think I'll grab that coffee first. I took the red-eye out of Atlanta and got to spend four amazing hours enjoying a layover in Chicago."

She smiled and made a *follow me* gesture. A few minutes later, we sat across from each other at the kitchen table, steaming mugs in hand. Again, the silence fell like a shroud. But I could see Miryam struggling to formulate something, words that would break it, but in the right way.

I made it easy. I just asked.

"How?"

She nodded. "A stroke, I think, but we're not really sure. He was a big man, but at the end, he was... depleted. Small." Miryam shook her head, her brown eyes hard with sudden anger —the worst sort. Anger at circumstances, at the universe. "It's no way to go. Not for him, not for anyone." She sighed and seemed to exhale the anger with it. Tears suddenly glistened in her eyes. "*Especially* not him."

"So you don't think—"

"He was killed because of what he did? No, I don't. And believe me, I looked. I checked his room over—discreetly, of course. Had a heart-to-heart with the coroner—I know him pretty well—and he found nothing unusual either. Whatever happened to him was—it was natural. If you can call it that. All I know for sure is that no one from that life cared when he—when he went to lick his wounds and die."

Bitterness shot through Miryam's words like the lightning still occasionally pulsing through the windows. I nodded, thinking about those *wars he fought in.* El Salvador. Honduras. Bosnia. Others, places he refused to name. Dangerous places, mostly on the periphery of the headlines but sometimes not in the headlines at all.

Black ops, they were called. A sinister term, even though my grandfather insisted that they were considered black mostly because the details were kept off the government's accounting books, all of them rendered into a single, bland line item in a budget—*Non-specified operational costs, one gazillion dollars.* He'd always said it like a joke, but I never missed how his smile or laugh never seemed to quite touch his eyes. His mouth might have said one thing, but he gazed at something very different, something painful.

My father had followed in his footsteps but in a more conventional way. Instead of the shadowy, silent world of special ops, he'd chosen the exact opposite, big and showy. He'd gone Navy, fighting Iranian gunboats in the Persian Gulf and pirates off the Horn of Africa and amid the island sprawl of Malaysia, and staring down Chinese warships in the waters around Taiwan. He met an untimely end almost four years ago when a Super Hornet fighter crashed while landing on the carrier *USS Harry S. Truman* in the Indian Ocean. You didn't get much bigger and showier than that.

And then there was me.

I joined the Army, of course, with vague plans to go Airborne, or Rangers, or some such hard-assed outfit, because what twenty year-old didn't imagine they could fight bad guys with a knife clenched in their teeth. I was ninety-nine percent committed to it. The trouble was that one percent, which turned out to be my right knee. *Flexion deformity*, it was called. My knee worked just fine through a normal range of movement, but I couldn't bend it through the last ten degrees or so most people could. It was enough to wash me out of all except the most basic of military trades. But trading *Ranger* for *cook* or *vehicle mechanic* wasn't going to cut it, so I left after only four years.

And I took my bitter frustration—well, here, actually. I came to live with my grandfather, and he taught me the finer points of hunting and fishing and shooting. And all the while, he went out of his way to express how proud he was of me. My father, too. I knew both men were still a little disappointed. I could see it in their eyes. But, strangely, both seemed even more relieved that I wouldn't be following them into the service. I never asked either of them about it, and now I couldn't.

But they weren't nearly as disappointed as I was in myself. I was determined to be a warrior, and if I couldn't wage it on a real battlefield, I'd wage it in the virtual one. I jammed myself back into school and immersed myself in a sort of warfare that didn't care about trick knees—the electronic kind. Maybe, I thought, I could fight our nation's foes with weapons made of data, IP packets and route sniffers and encryption-crackers. If I couldn't stick the knife in my teeth, maybe I could support those who did from behind a monitor. Maybe I could even find solutions to burgeoning conflicts before men like my father and grandfather had to get involved at all.

So I went to war after all, but a quiet one, fought through back doors and hacked firewalls, wielding secrets and disinformation so grand that the truth was often reduced to a myth. I got very good at it and started picking up contracts—mostly the white-hat sort, but a few were grey, and one or two were as black as anything my grandfather had ever done. I rarely left my apartment, which overlooked a park in the suburbs of Atlanta. The people living around me—Janet, the guitar-playing loans manager next door, or Missus Evans with her multitude of cats across the hall—none of them knew how their lives were open books: for sale or for the taking. Either was possible for the right price.

"Hello?"

I looked up. "Sorry?"

"You were somewhere far away, Van," Miryam said.

"I was just... remembering."

She nodded. "Oh, I've spent a lot of time in this house doing that these past couple of days. Anyway, I should be going. I just wanted to make sure you got in okay and got the keys to the—to *your* house. They're over there on the counter."

"Thanks, Miryam. I really appreciate it."

I followed her back to the front door. "I'll be back in the morning. I think you pretty much know what decisions you have to make." She pulled on her jacket, then leaned up to kiss my cheek. I leaned down, in turn, to let it happen, but I was a little numb to it.

My house. Not *my grandfather's* house. Not anymore.

Mine.

I WATCHED Miryam's headlights flash as she turned her car around, then dim as she pulled away into the night. The rain seemed to have slackened, so I stuck my sodden shoes back on, jogged out to my own car, retrieved the single backpack I carried as luggage, and hurried back into the house. The oil furnace kicked on as I shut out the night behind me. I once again pulled off my shoes, considered more coffee, and decided against it. It was late, and I was tired. Instead, I squelched wetly up the stairs.

The last time I'd climbed them was-- some time ago, and I felt a pang of guilt at that passage of time. I'd gone from childhood, to an awkward teenager, and beyond in that house. For years, I'd been a kid who stayed hidden away from the world in this remote piece of the Midwest, lost in my books and the electronics workbench I kept out in the barn. That boy was long gone now. But so was my father, at least in the sense of feeling any real sort of closeness. And, of course, my grandfather, who was just gone.

My feet instinctively turned left at the top and took me to an open door. The first thing to catch my attention was a poster on the wall, pronouncing a 2011 concert date in Chicago for *Coldplay*. The music world might be like the shady world of internet security—what thrived today was obsolete and forgotten tomorrow—but I still liked that band. The hours on the bus to attend that concert had been one of the few major excursions I made off the farm until I finally left it for good eight years ago.

I sniffed and shook my head. *Left it for good*. Yeah, okay, except here I was.

"Kinda like being seventeen again, except for the acne," I said to my old room, stepping in and dumping my backpack on the bed.

It was, as Miryam said, ready. Actually, more than just *ready*. More like *utterly unchanged*. I could have just clomped up the stairs, fresh off the bus from a day of high school. A time capsule.

I undressed and draped my damp clothes over a chair I

maneuvered over the warm air register. Then, with movements made of memory and the creak of old floorboards, I brushed my teeth and readied myself for bed. Sliding under the blanket and comforter, into the coolness of the sheets, I finally let out a long, slow breath.

I'd expected grief, and there was some, sure. I missed my grandfather. He'd been more of a father figure than my father had. But if my sadness had any focus, it was less on *that* he died, but rather *how* he died. Larger-than-life men like my grandfather were supposed to have larger-than-life deaths. They were meant to end in desperate struggles against impossible odds, not the mundanity of a stroke or heart attack.

But, as I rolled over, I gave myself a mental jab. That was a boy's way of thinking about his hero. Facing a stroke or heart attack was every bit as desperate a struggle against impossible odds as a firefight. If anything, I felt bad more because Miryam had implied it hadn't been quick, the finality of a bullet. She hinted that he'd lingered, which meant that there might have been time for me to see him before he passed away. If only I'd stayed in closer touch—

Thunder boomed, truncating the thought. I nodded to the storm and its elemental wisdom. Good point. Don't go down the *if only* road—just don't, because it never led anywhere good.

I wondered what the morning would bring? What time would Miryam return? Should I set an alarm?

Nah. Screw it. Morning could wait—

Beep.

I turned back toward the door, frowning.

Beep.

Lightning flickered and thunder muttered, but more distant, as the storm rolled off to the east.

Beep.

Shit.

I levered myself out of my bed, which had started to warm up quite nicely, and planted my feet on the cold hardwood. Smoke detector, I thought. Dying battery. I'd just rip it out and risk spending one night without its dumb vigilance watching over me—

Beep.

I stopped. The sound hadn't come from above me, in the hallway, where I could see a tiny red LED glowing from the smoke detector. It had come from behind me, back in my bedroom.

2

I TURNED to face the room.

Beep.

Huh. Eight years ago, nothing in this room made any persistent *beeping* sounds. Nor had I heard it, it occurred to me, before I climbed into bed. I was sure of it. And Miryam was a careful woman, fiercely attentive to details. It was kind of implied in her job.

Beep.

So that meant two things. There was something new in my room. And either Miryam hadn't known about it or hadn't told me about it. Her deliberately not telling me about it wouldn't have even occurred to most people, but most people didn't have a grandfather who'd done shadowy things in shadowy global corners.

Was she afraid someone might be listening?

Beep.

It was entirely possible, I supposed, that someone from my grandfather's past was watching him. And now, in turn, they watched me, incidentally or not. He *had* controlled a lot of money, as well a lot of secrets. And his past wasn't *that* distant. Knowledge of the things he'd done could probably still hurt people working in the government now.

A bit of a thrill shivered through me. The thought of being watched—while standing in the doorway to my room in my underwear—was actually kind of dumb, even funny. But it was also titillating, in the way that virtually poking around in someone's computer halfway around the world, while they sat nearby, was titillating.

Beep.

I'd been waiting for it this time. The sound pulled my attention to the battered rolltop desk beside the window. It was filled with science fiction books—stories of dragons, and heroes who never took a bullet. The sound came from inside it. Left-hand side. Second drawer, I was pretty sure.

More distant thunder muttered, and I took that moment to pad across to the desk, pull open the drawer—

Beep.

—and pick up a—

A remote?

It looked like a remote, anyway, but heavier, with the polished heft of something meant to last. It rested easily in the palm of my hand. The metal—at least I was pretty sure it was metal, though it also had kind of a glassy luster to it—was cool and featureless, but a sense of hidden depths lay beneath it. On the back was a small disc, barely recessed and made to be pushed.

I hesitated. My grandfather must have left this here on purpose. In another home, I'd have just passed it off as what it seemed to be—a fancy remote. But given my grandfather's past, it might be more than that, with a purpose well beyond any apparent use.

As soon as I had that thought, though, something else struck me. It hadn't beeped since I picked it up.

And then there was that damned button just begging to be pushed.

I should just put it aside until morning.

But that wasn't going to work, and I knew it. I could be patient if I had to but, by nature, I needed to know things. I needed to see and learn. It was baked right into the mindset of a cyberwarrior whose battlespace shifted and changed by the minute.

So I got dressed in dry clothes from my backpack, went downstairs, and waited for the rain to stop. I wasn't sure why. I just had some vague sense that if something happened, I didn't want to get rained on and wet through again. So I waited thirty-eight minutes. That was how long it took for the line of squalls to finally roll beyond Pony Hollow and scud northeast to punish Garnavillo for a while, before pushing on to Wisconsin.

Less than an hour, and I was still sitting in the kitchen, trying to convince myself to push that damned button. Outside, the world dripped in darkness, the soft, steady plink of water from eaves and trees a far cry from the storm's fury when I first arrived.

I was dithering.

So I shrugged and pushed the button. It recessed, but slowly, like the mechanism was tired or old. The circular spot only sank a quarter inch or so, but it was apparently enough to cause—something. Deep blue light suddenly glimmered beneath my finger. I pulled it away to find—

"Well, I'll be damned."

My fingerprint had been impressed on the button in soft whorls of blue light, perfect in every detail. The effect lasted for a few seconds, then faded.

And that was that.

"Huh."

Whatever it was, it seemed to incorporate a biometric lock, a fingerprint reader that would only activate the device. While that was tech I understood, it was certainly not expected, and my only source of information was Miryam, who I respected too much to bother again. We were both in an hour of grief, and the remote, or object, could wait until morning. I placed it on the table with a deliberate motion, then closed my eyes as the weight of the day began to catch up with me.

Tap.

I twitched at the sound, my eyes snapping open with instant awareness.

Not a beep this time. A tap—distinct, sharp, and right in front of me on the window over the sink. I stood and moved to the glass, then realized I couldn't see a damned thing except my own reflection. It was truly pitch black outside, meaning the barn light was out, probably cooked off in the storm.

I moved to turn off the kitchen light to get rid of its glare—

Tap tap.

I jumped back. Something had indeed just banged against the glass maybe a foot or two away from my face.

What the hell?

I thought about going to the back door and walking around the house to see what was out there. But the thought of squelching through wet grass and mud in that thick gloom to find myself facing—something—didn't appeal to me at all. Instead, I did go and snap off the kitchen light, then returned to the window and lifted it.

Something large and dark immediately pushed through the opening. For the third time, I felt a pang of nervous curiosity as my eyes tried to make sense of the moving object before me. The dark shape bounced on the edge of the sink with a sharp rattle and leapt to perch on the back of a chair.

It was a bird.

But a bird wholly unlike any I'd ever seen in Iowa, or, well, anywhere for that matter. Big, the size of a large eagle, with eyes that seemed to glow golden—not from reflected light but from some place behind them. Its feathers were blacker than space, its silver talons glittered like daggers, and its beak looked as though it could shear my hand off.

I stared.

It stared back.

Finally, the bird cocked its head at me and spoke in a smooth baritone with a hint of something like wind chimes.

"You rang?"

"I—"

"You should get dressed," the bird said.

A flicker of reason finally found its way to my mouth.

"You can talk."

"An astute observation. And it doesn't change the fact that you should get dressed."

I glanced around, then scraped my finger across the corner of the kitchen counter, hard. It hurt, just like it was supposed to. *I'm awake, and aware. Good to know.*

But the talking bird didn't vanish, or even stop talking, like *it* was supposed to.

"A test to determine if you're dreaming, am I right?" the bird asked, glancing at my finger.

My voice crackled to life after a moment. "Can you blame me?"

"I suppose not. At least as long as you don't bumble around convinced you're dreaming, or crazy—oh, that'll be next, by the way, the thinking you must be going crazy part. Anyway, there are things we need to do, so please, get it all out of your system right now."

I held up a hand. "Okay, wait a second. I get it. You're a

talking bird. Like a parrot, or—I hear ravens can be taught to speak as well."

"You've never owned a parrot, or ever really interacted with one, have you?"

"I—no. Why?"

"Because if you had, you'd know that they don't actually speak. They mimic. Therefore, unless your grandfather spent a *lot* of time drilling this particular conversation into me so I could flawlessly mimic it in this particular way—" The bird cocked its head. "You're a smart guy. What are the odds of that working?"

I could only shrug. "No idea. I don't know what factors are involved, the variables—"

"Take a guess."

"Probably not very high."

"There you go. So keeping with the smart guy thing, here's the next logical place your mind should go. Maybe I'm not actually a bird at all…"

The bird ended it with a dramatically sinister flourish. All it was missing was an ominous burst of organ music.

I almost laughed. Almost. Well, if this is what going crazy is like, it could be a lot worse, I suppose.

"Okay, I'll play along. If you're not a bird, what are you?"

"Metal-ceramic composite chassis with a quantum neural net, broad-spectrum sensors, on-board fusion power-cell, and a mono-bonded feathering system that allows actual flight." The creature spread its wings—an impressive sight, as they were nearly six feet across—and promptly knocked the mug containing the last dregs of my unfinished coffee off the counter. As it banged to the floor, the bird settled them again with a tidy metallic flick.

"Sorry about that," the bird said, glancing at the small puddle of cold coffee.

"Don't worry about it," I replied, but I only had eyes for the bird. Another possibility was taking shape amid the swirling tumble of thoughts now spinning through my mind. It had been triggered by words like *metal-ceramic composite* and *quantum neural net*. Tech words. In other words, *my* language. They finally gave my thoughts some traction, letting me start arranging them back into something resembling sense.

So maybe I *wasn't* dreaming, I *wasn't* crazy, and this bird *was* real, as in a real piece of advanced military hardware that my grandfather had somehow kept under wraps here, on the farm. Whether he'd done that deliberately, which might mean he'd stolen the damned thing, or somehow just managed to die without returning it, I wasn't sure.

"See, if your grandfather had better prepared you for this, we wouldn't have to go through this whole shock and wonder step," the bird said.

"Shock and wonder——?"

"Yes. The part where you start by thinking you're dreaming, or going crazy, and then you slowly come to believe it's all real. I *told* him this would happen, but he didn't care."

This time, I did actually smile. The bird was doing a fantastic job of simulating frustrated irritation.

"That's amazing," I said, shaking my head.

"What is?"

"Well, you. You're amazing."

"Why thank you. And you don't even really know me yet. So let me properly introduce myself. Probably should have done that right up front, but it's been a while since I've paired with a Peacemaker." Now the bird actually managed to sound apologetic, even dipping his beak in contrition. A fresh rush of chill, damp air swirled into the kitchen through the open window. I glanced outside, but the night was still utterly dark.

"Yeah. Introducing yourself is a good place to start, I guess," I said, reaching over and sliding the window closed. "Along with, ah, what a Peacemaker might be. I get the sense that it means me, but I've never heard the term used for anything but an old strategic bomber."

"The Convair B-36, the largest piston-engine production aircraft ever built, in service with the US Strategic Air Command from 1949 to 1959," the bird replied matter-of-factly.

I blinked. The bird had nailed it for sure. I'd once built a plastic scale model kit of one of the giant bombers. It was probably still upstairs, in fact, on the top shelf of my bedroom closet, along with a few other kits I'd built.

"So you know about that," I said.

"I know about lots of things. For instance, would you like to know the acceptable operating temperature range for the Peacemaker's Pratt & Whitney R-4360 radial engines? The maximum dynamic shear-stress load of its main wing spar? The absolute best way to make crème brulée?"

"Not really, no." I leaned back against the counter. "Well, maybe the crème brulé thing sometime." I laughed, harder than I normally would. But I normally didn't end up talking to AI birds who could make crème brulé. I gave my hand a vague wave. "I'm sorry, but you'll understand if this is all a bit much."

Again, the beak dipped, which I guessed was a sort of cross between acknowledgement and apology. It made sense. After all, a bird-construct would be pretty limited in the emotional range it could convey. Mind you, the fact this construct could convey any emotions at all made it—

I shook my head, stunned at the elegance of the machine before me. I must have been looking at the most advanced expression of AI on the planet. And it was a bird, perched on a chair, in the kitchen of an Iowa farmhouse.

"I understand," the bird replied. "Anyway, you may call me Perry. And while the peregrine falcon doesn't have black feathers, I'm willing to take some artistic license regarding my coloration. Besides, birds are not a galactic species, but they are unique to your world. At least, falcons are." He cocked his head again. "And I like the name Perry."

"Perry."

"That's right."

I shrugged. "Sure. What the hell. Nice to meet you, Perry."

"As to what a Peacemaker might be, you've correctly surmised it has nothing to do with strategic bombers. Well, not directly, anyway. But, yes, *you're* the Peacemaker in this case. The term refers to a Galactic Knight Uniformed. But let's take this all one step at a time, shall we? So our next trip is outside, which brings me back to the fact that you should get dressed."

I glanced down at myself, then back up. "I am dressed."

"Not for going outside. It *is* a rainy night in Iowa."

"Where are we going?"

"To the barn."

"I—oh. Wait. To the barn? Why?"

"That's easier to explain in the barn than here." Perry opened his wings slightly, as though he were going to hop back to the now-closed window. I suspected he'd have no trouble opening it again. But he stopped and folded his wings back up.

"Before we go, it strikes me that you implicitly asked me a question, which I haven't yet answered—that is, who am I?"

I guessed I had, so I nodded.

"I'm a combat AI. Yours, to be specific," Perry said.

"Wait. My combat AI? Not my grandfather's?"

"I *was* his combat AI, but he's, you know, dead now. And you're his successor."

"But why do I need a combat AI? I've never even *been* in combat."

Perry's golden eyes glittered back at me.

"You will be."

3

I put on my shoes and jacket, then opened the door into the cool, rainy night. Perry leapt from the kitchen chair to the top of the short flight of stairs that led down to the back door, then paused.

"Excuse me. AI bird coming through."

I stepped back and gestured. "After you."

The bird spread its wings and launched itself into the night in one smooth motion. The wings extended just enough to clear the doorframe, then spread as it sailed off into the gloom.

I just stood, staring, shaking my head. Amazing. I had no idea AI had come so far. Or, for that matter, materials science that allowed a bird-construct to be that large but still able to fly with what appeared to be only wings for propulsion. Or power-cell technology, which had to provide it all with enough juice to keep running for—

I didn't know how long, I realized, stepping into the drizzle and closing the door behind me. Presumably, the bird had been in some sort of low-power state when I pressed that button. It had been just enough to allow it to receive and respond to whatever signal the remote control thing had produced. I expected it would need to be recharged soon. Power-source life was still the big Achilles' heel of these sorts of constructs. No matter how fancy or sophisticated they were, when they ran out of power, they were just elaborate works of high-tech art.

I squelched through mud and grass, heading for the barn. I could barely see it, just a shape in the darkness, but that was okay. My feet knew the way. It let me keep ruminating about Perry along the way.

Clearly, the bird was a piece of cutting-edge, experimental military tech. Why my grandfather had it, I had no idea. Maybe he was involved in trialing it. It did make a sort of sense, I supposed, to try out something like that in a remote corner of Iowa. But it seemed awfully strange that Gramps could just bring the thing home with him. No matter how much he might be trusted in the shadowy circles of his former profession, that just wasn't how things like that were done. You didn't simply sign out a super-advanced piece of no doubt multimillion dollar, probably irreplaceable hardware and bring it home with you for the weekend to try out. Or, if you did, then the spooky world of defense research was a *hell* of a lot more laid back in terms of its real-world security than it was online. I'd only occasionally bumped up against it during the course of my day job, and never with the intention of trying to penetrate it. But even if I had, I doubted I'd ever find a way through its labyrinthine, almost paranoid depths of protection.

But despite that, you could apparently stick super-secret tech in the trunk of your car and bring it home with you.

I wonder if Gramps had stolen Perry? But why would he? And why wouldn't the bird have its own security protocols installed, causing it to immediately try to escape to some safe place and signal for recovery? Or even just not boot up in the first place? Did the bloody thing not even have a password?

And what the hell was all that nonsense about Galactic Knights and Peacemakers?

Perry had landed just in front of the smaller, man-sized barn door. It stood open. The big roll-back ones were still closed. I glanced up at the light that should have been illuminating the barn, which looked fine but had apparently burned out. I glanced back at the house, just a few rectangles of wan light in the gloom. Yeah, I'd definitely have to replace this light. It was too dark out here.

"This way," Perry said, hopping into the barn.

I started that way, then stopped. The barn was as dark inside as out. I didn't have a flashlight, so if there were no working lights inside either, then I'd be left fumbling around in a black space full of tools and farm implements. I knew where my old workbench was, of course. Unlike my room, though, I was sure Gramps would have changed around the barn in the years I'd been gone. He had been running a working farm, after all.

But it wasn't just that. What stopped me was a sudden thrill of... anticipation? Fear? Dread? All of these things? Whatever it was, it rooted me to the muddy spot, oblivious to the drizzle, focused only on that dark doorway.

What was really going on here?

Of course my grandfather hadn't brought Perry home to trial it. That's not how these things worked. The defense research people would have been all over it, certainly once news of his death reached them. So that just made no sense at all.

And as for Gramps having stolen it, I just couldn't see it. Why? What would be the point? And again, the chances of him or anyone else getting away with something like that, for this long, were—

Small didn't begin to cut it.

A sudden gulf of *what the hell?* had opened up between me and that doorway. Whatever was happening here, I just couldn't see it being good. Or, at least, good for me. An AI construct wants to lead me into a dark, apparently powerless barn in the dead of night to *show me something*. That was creepy in ways I'd only encountered in atmospherically well-done books and movies. But this was real.

Or was it? Maybe I was dreaming, or going crazy, and I'd followed a phantasm out into the night—

"Are you coming or what?"

Perry stood in the doorway, his amber eyes two glowing points in the gloom. Like the eyes of a cat, only golden.

Okay, that sure as hell didn't help. It just ratcheted the creep factor up another notch.

"Coming why? What's in the barn that you want me to see so badly?"

"Your ship. Come on."

And Perry hopped back out of sight, into the barn.

My ship.

As if that explained anything.

Again, I glanced back at the house. Safe thing to do—go back there, wait until the hard, rational light of morning, and if any of this turned out to actually be real, then consult with Miryam. Find out just what the hell was going on. Surely she had to know.

I turned back to the barn, scowling. Curiosity had thrown itself into the mix of thoughts and feelings bubbling away inside me, like some pressure cooker about to vent—or explode.

Screw it. What I wasn't going to do was just stand here, in the rain, stuck between two imagined scenarios—one safe, the other sinister and weird, but in an admittedly fascinating kind of way.

If this had been an online mystery, I wouldn't have just walked away from it. I couldn't have resisted digging at least a little deeper.

Taking a breath, I splashed my way to the barn, stepped into its familiar stew of smells—hay, animal dung, old wood, hints of gasoline and oil and rusting metal—and immediately stopped.

"Close the door," two golden points of light said. "I'll turn on the lights once you have."

I was already reaching for the light switch. Muscle memory knew exactly where it was. "That's okay. I've got the lights," I said, my fingers finding the switch and snapping it on.

Nothing happened.

"Those lights aren't active," Perry said.

I snapped the switch a few times. "Burned out, I guess."

"No, I deactivated them."

"You... deactivated them."

"That's right. They're not necessary."

"Speaking on behalf of those of us who aren't AI constructs that can probably see just fine in the dark, they're very necessary."

"Just close the door, and I'll turn the real lights on," Perry replied. Somehow, he managed a pretty clear tone of indulgent, almost strained patience.

"How about you turn on the lights and *then* I'll close the door."

A pause—no. Wait. Had I just heard Perry *sigh*?

"Can't. The lights won't come on unless the door is closed. That's how the system's rigged to work."

Now it was my turn to sigh. This was ridiculous—

"I promise you, Van, that you'll have an answer once you close that door and I can activate the lights. You'll then have about a thousand more questions, but one step at a time."

To hell with this, I thought, fully intending to just turn around and head back to the light—and security—of the house. But that part of me that was morbidly curious was already closing the door, the metal latch sliding into place with a soft metallic rasp, then a click.

What the hell am I doing?

I tensed as I yanked the door open again—and the world turned blazing white.

I FOUND myself staring at the silvery-grey wood of the old door from about a foot away, my hand still on the latch. But a jarring dissonance hit me like a punch to the face. I'd spent many nights in the barn, working away soldering and testing circuits and electronic components, and had always needed a bright worklight to see my current project. Because otherwise, the barn was lit by a couple of middling overhead lights that lit up the space directly beneath them but mostly cast the rest into shadowy gloom.

Only this light was almost *painfully* white. Gramps must have installed a few dozen banks of white LEDs to achieve this sort of brilliance.

I turned toward Perry. Amid those last few thoughts before my universe changed forever, one stood out, utterly inane.

Gramps wasn't dead at all. I was going to turn and find him there, along with Miryam and a bunch of other people, and they were all going to yell *surprise* as soon as I turned because of some labyrinthine reason known only to a former spy. At least, that was a viable hope, if only for a moment, simply because my mind could find no plausible reason for anything that was happening to me—or what I was looking at.

I stood. And stared. For a while. Seconds, minutes, I wasn't sure.

Filling the barn, nearly from this end to the far back, and rising to just under the lofty rafters, was a spaceship.

———

"IMPRESSIVE, ISN'T SHE?" Perry said.

I might have responded. I don't remember.

"Uh, Van? Hello?"

"I—"

It was all I managed. Another indeterminate amount of time passed.

I glanced at Perry, then back at the ship.

"What the f—?"

"She's called the *Dragonet*," Perry cut in. "*Vigilant* class. I prefer the *Vigilants* over other classes of this mass. Better combination of speed, protection, and firepower, I think. Not too much of any one, but just enough of all three."

I took a step. One step. That was it.

The thing sitting in the barn looked like no spacecraft I'd ever seen. And I'd long had a passion for spaceflight, so I knew them all pretty well, from the first *Mercury* and *Soyuz* capsules, right up to the new generation ships, like NASA's *Orion*, which was only just now hitting the launchpad for the first time. This, though, was a whole different breed. Hell, it was a whole different *species*.

I figured it for a little under twice the size and bulk of a city bus. The upper section of the forward hull and the nose were enclosed in something reflective and darkly crystalline. Various protrusions extending from the hull sported what had to be thrust bells for engines of some sort. Some of these looked like they could rotate, probably through most of a complete sphere. Larger, fixed exhaust bells extended from the thing's stern. It squatted on chunky struts and landing skids, and overall had the color and luster of dark smoke. I looked for markings and saw a series of geometric shapes and dots rendered along the hull in medium grey.

"Want to step inside? Check it out?"

I looked at Perry again. "Inside?"

"Yes. Inside. You know, the opposite of outside? As in, you'll step through the airlock, and you'll then be—"

"I know what inside means," I snapped, finally getting at least some wobbly legs under the rational part of my mind. Really wobbly, newborn deer wobbly, but enough to prop up at least a few coherent thoughts.

"What the hell is going on here?" I finally asked.

"See, I told your grandfather to brief you on all of this before he died," Perry said, shaking his head with a dolorous jingling of feathers.

"Brief me on what?

"Your succession as a Peacemaker. Now, we're going to have to go through the whole process of indoctrinating you to the system instead of you just assuming your place and getting to work—"

"Okay, wait." I held up a hand. "Never mind about what my grandfather should have done, or didn't do, or whatever. Just tell me what's going on. What is a Peacemaker? What are you? And what"—I swept a hand at the ship—"the hell is *that?*"

"The Peacemakers are the enforcement arm of an interstellar organization called the Galactic Knights Uniformed. I am a combat AI, model AU-987T, serial number 18974XM6, assigned to your grandfather—and now to you—as personal guard and assistant. And this is the *Dragonet*, a *Vigilant*-class starship, used by your grandfather to perform his duties as Peacemaker."

While Perry was talking, I sat down on a hay bale and stared up at the bulk of what was apparently called the *Dragonet*. It loomed in the hard glare of the white lights, which emanated from somewhere high up in the barn's rafters. I glanced up, ready to squint and shield my eyes, but for some reason the light didn't dazzle me the way I expected it would. It was less actual light and more just a uniform whiteness that originated at the top of the barn and painted itself over everything inside. It rendered every color, right down to the green bits of grass stuck to my shoes, a perfectly saturated, almost idealized version of itself.

"So, let me see if I understand this. My grandfather wasn't actually a spec ops soldier in government service. He was some kind of galactic knight who flew around in a spaceship with his talking, intelligent metal bird, traveling between planets to enforce—something."

"The strictures and decrees of the Peacemakers," Perry said.

"Ah. Right. Of course. So have I got all of that right?"

"Well, in a really, *really* general sense, yes, you do."

I shook my head. Chuckled. Started to laugh. Laughed harder.

"What's so funny?" Perry asked.

I stopped and stared at him, tears in my eyes, then swept my hand around and laughed some more.

"This," I finally managed, wiping my eyes. "All of this. It's a thing of beauty. Scary, scary beauty. I always figured when someone went crazy, started hearing voices, that sort of thing, it was all—I don't know. Just irrational. Nonsensical. But this—"

I gestured again.

"This is amazing. It's so detailed and realistic, even *believable*. Who knew I had this much imagination in me? Hell, I *knew* I should have started writing sci fi a few years back. I'd be raking in the cash by now!"

Perry hopped to a point right in front of me. "Van, I know this is hard for you to accept, or even believe. But you're *not* imagining this. You're not going crazy. Your grandfather really was a Peacemaker. He believed, right down to the core of his being, in protecting those who couldn't protect themselves. He did that as a spec ops soldier for your military, and when the time came for him to become a Peacemaker, he kept doing it—just not on Earth."

"You expect me to believe that my grandfather was a star-faring soldier?"

"I can prove it to you."

I wiped my eyes again. "And how are you going to do that?"

"By taking you for a flight."

"Into space."

"Yes, into space."

I stood. "Sure. What the hell. I've paid the entrance fee, might as well take the whole damned tour, right?" I gestured elaborately toward the ship. "After you, my good bird."

Perry muttered something, then launched himself into the air and flew to a point about halfway along the length of the ship. As soon as he landed, a hatch slid smoothly open.

"Whenever you're ready, Van," he said, then he hopped inside and vanished.

I grinned like an idiot. "I'm ready now. To space, Perry, and step on it."

I STOPPED AT THE ENTRANCE. "Oh, wait. Something just occurred to me. A little technical problem in this, ah, adventure," I said.

I saw Perry standing just inside, in a small, bare compartment. "What's that?"

"Well, as soon as we... crash through the roof, I guess, and get airborne, we're going to be illuminated by every radar system from Chicago air traffic control to NORAD. Guess we'll be a UFO, huh?"

"Van, I'm going to turn off the lights for a moment," Perry said.

Okay, that broke through my increasingly hysterical bravado. "You're going to—what?"

"I'm going to do *this*."

The lights went out.

The ship, and Perry, were gone.

Not just gone, as in, it was too dark to see them anymore. Actually *gone*, as though they'd never existed in the first place. My night vision hadn't even been affected by the sudden cessation of the white illumination.

I sighed, long and slow. Well, that was interesting. And by

interesting, I meant the kind of hallucination that felt more real than anything I could even imagine, let alone had experienced.

I walked through the empty space that had been occupied by the—what had Perry called it? The *Dragonet?*

Nothing. I spread my arms and turned around. Just empty, cool barn air, full of the various reeks I'd long ago come to know and largely ignore.

I laughed. Alrighty, then. First thing tomorrow, I'd head to the hospital and check myself in for a psych evaluation because something was obviously very, very wrong with me—

I gasped as something seemed to grab me and shove me to one side. It wasn't physical movement, though, but more of a feeling of... displacement is the best way I can describe it. It was like those weird moments when you're drifting off to sleep and suddenly slam awake, certain you'd just fallen a couple of feet.

As soon as the feeling passed, the white light returned, and so did the ship, and Perry standing inside it.

I glanced down at my feet. I was standing exactly where I'd been when the lights went out.

"So, I guess this hallucination isn't over, huh?" I asked, looking up from my feet.

Perry gave a very human shrug that lifted and lowered his wings. "I don't know. Were you having a hallucination? Are you prone to them?"

I barked out a laugh and looked pointedly at the ship looming above me. "Apparently so."

Although it suddenly struck me that I wasn't sure if this was the hallucination itself, or if being alone in the darkened barn was part of it, too. Was I still in the house? In the kitchen? In bed asleep?

"Anyway, to answer your question—no, we won't be detected by any earthly radar or other means. The *Dragonet*, like all Vigilant-class ships, is fully stealthed against any sort of detection that doesn't involve—"

Perry paused. "How well versed are you in terrestrial theoretical physics?"

"Uh, I used to watch *The Big Bang Theory*. They used a lot of theoretical physics jargon in that. Does that count?"

"No, it doesn't. Suffice to say, for now, that any detection system that doesn't operate on principles similar to these lights won't be capable of seeing the *Dragonet*. That's why you couldn't see it, or even be aware of its existence, while the lights were off."

"But I walked right past where you are now, into the middle of the barn floor."

"Eh, yes and no. Yes you did, but the ship's stealth system shifted back to where you started the instant the lights came on. That prevents the ship from materializing superimposed on things, which would be a serious problem. Incidentally, it's also how the ship deals with navigational debris, dust, gas molecules, micrometeorites, that sort of thing, while it's in flight."

"In space."

"Or inside an atmosphere, in which case the air is shifted aside. It lets the *Dragonet* fly as though she's always traveling through vacuum."

The scientific part of me saw a problem with that. If you

simply shifted the air out of the ship's way, you'd create a zone of higher pressure around it—

That thinking didn't go very far, though. Trying to apply logical reason to fantastic illusion was a sort of craziness all its own.

"Anyway, this would be much easier to explain if you'd come aboard," Perry said.

I stared a moment longer, then shrugged. What the hell. If I was going insane, at least I was doing it in a rather interesting, even pretty cool way. I might as well enjoy the ride.

I stepped through the hatch, into the compartment. As soon as I did, the door slid smoothly and quietly closed behind me. Soft lighting came up, and a door on the other side of the compartment opened.

A new voice suddenly spoke.

"Welcome aboard, Peacemaker. Do you want to power up the ship to pre-flight status?"

4

I BLINKED AT PERRY. "Now who the hell is *that?*"

"That would be the *Dragonet*. Your grandfather called her Netty, but if you'd like to name her something else, that'd be up to you," Perry replied.

"Netty. So the ship is intelligent, too."

"From your perspective, yes," Netty replied.

I waved in mild disbelief. "Sure, why the hell not? Is the coffeemaker equipped with an AI, too? That's an actual application I could get behind—"

"No, that would be ridiculous. Why would you want an intelligent coffeemaker?" Netty asked.

That brought me up short, so I answered as plainly as possible. "I take coffee seriously. And an AI would be... useful in that regard."

"You can brew your own beans, Van," Perry said. "Netty's got more important things to do, like, you know, keep an antimatter reactor running without blowing up most of Iowa, or calculate thrust and trajectories and all that navigation stuff to get your butt from point A to point B."

I stared at the bird. There was an undertone of anger that felt too real to be mere code. Perry had emotions, and I was seeing them in real time.

"Perry," I began, then paused to phrase my thoughts more accurately. "This may surprise you, but I'm a touch stunned to find an actual spaceship in my grandfather's *barn*. You get that?"

"Yes, I get it," Perry replied. "Look, let's go to the cockpit. You can let Netty take you up for a spin, and maybe that'll at least seal the deal on all of this being real."

"Nice rhyming, Perry. I always thought you had the soul of a poet," Netty put in.

"Thank you, my dear. I'm… always, um, here."

"Now you're just trying too hard."

"Eh, I'll work on it. Anyway, Van, right this way," Perry said, turning and hopping along a corridor toward what I assumed was the nose of the ship.

I glanced back at the door that had sealed behind me. "And what if I don't want to, and I just want to get off this thing?"

The door slid aside, opening my way back into the barn.

"Okay, close it again."

It did.

"Open it again."

Again, it slid open.

Well, that made me feel a little better. I apparently had some control over this hallucination or vision or fever dream, though the reality of the ship was crowding in on any chance that I was in the middle of some high-tech fever dream.

I blew out a resigned sigh. "Alrighty, then. Onward," I said and followed after Perry.

THE CORRIDOR LED past several other compartments, all closed. I started to ask Perry about them, but he just kept hopping forward, calling back over his shoulder.

"We'll give you the grand tour later. Right now, I think the most important thing for you is to see the *Dragonet* in action."

I shook my head. "Sure, why not?"

Perry led the way into a small compartment that was mostly enclosed in—nothing, was my first thought. It was all surrounded in an empty latticework, open to the outside air. But closer inspection showed faint gleams of reflection, barely noticeable unless you were looking at just the right angle. I touched one of the apparent void spaces, and my finger stopped against something smooth, cool, and barely even visible. When I pulled my finger away, it didn't leave a print.

"Van, if you want to get settled into the place of honor, we'll get this show on the road," Perry said.

I turned to find him perched on the back of a sumptuous, padded chair facing a rectangular screen, featureless and black. Two smaller similar screens were angled toward it, left and right. I moved to the seat, hesitated and looked at Perry, then sat down.

As soon as I did, the three screens came to life. I'd expected them to be computer monitors, but these were insanely high resolution. The various instruments and displays that appeared looked absolutely real, textured and 3D. Touching one, though, confirmed it was just a 2D image on a screen.

"Okay, so I've never flown a spaceship before. What do I do? Do I have to put in a coin somewhere?"

"Netty's going to fly. She'll take us up, do an orbit, and bring us back," Perry replied.

"An orbit."

"One should be enough."

"Of Earth."

"Unless you'd prefer to go somewhere else. Netty, what's the closest planet to Earth right now?"

"That would be Mars. It's only a few days away from closest approach. Flight time would be eleven hours, seventeen minutes."

I stared at Perry, or tried to, since he still perched on the back of the chair, looming above and behind me. "We can be at Mars —*Mars*—in under twelve hours?"

"Netty's the expert. It's what she does. Most of the time, you won't have to fly the ship at all, just tell her your destination. She can even fly the ship in battle if necessary, but that's where the Peacemaker usually starts giving command inputs."

"Battle is still a pretty hands-on affair," Netty agreed.

"Battle. Wait. *Battle?* Are you telling me this ship is *armed?*"

"Twin mass drivers, and a petawatt laser."

"Holy shit."

"She used to be more heavily armed, but your grandfather

offered liens on some of her weapon systems, so the mass drivers and the laser are all that's left."

"I'm sure that means something."

"It does. For now, though, let's focus on getting you convinced this is all really happening."

"By orbiting the Earth."

"That's right."

I glanced up. "Okay, well, we have a problem then. The barn roof's in the way." I glanced back. "Unless, of course, it opens up—"

The brilliant white light vanished, and the barn roof began to slide apart, revealing ragged, patchy clouds framing bits and pieces of clear, starry sky.

"And it opens up, because of course it does," I said, sinking back in the chair. Which, I noted, was actually pretty damned comfortable. No matter how I arranged myself in it, it seemed to instantly conform and accommodate me.

"Van, the preflight checklist is complete. All of the *Dragonet*'s systems are green. Are you ready?" Netty asked.

I spread my arms at the sky. "I hesitate to say this, but… take us up."

A faint hum, underlain by a thin, rising whine rose from somewhere behind me. Some of the life-like instrument displays began to change.

And the *Dragonet* began to rise, slowly lifting from the barn's floor. I couldn't even feel the motion.

As I gaped—not watched, not stared, but gaped, wide-eyed—the barn fell away below, revealing the farmhouse, its kitchen windows still lit. Then it dropped away, and more lights appeared. Other farms, nearby towns, a smear of light that must have been Des Moines. That, in turn, all receded steadily away beneath us, more lights crawling into view as we gained altitude and our visible horizon fell further and further away.

Okay, as hallucinations went, this was amazing. I needed to find a way to record it and sell tickets. I couldn't actually believe we were flying—

Everything abruptly vanished, the view turning to a uniform deep, charcoal grey.

"What's this?" I asked. "Some sort of hyperdrive? Another dimension?"

"No, it's a cloud," Netty replied.

The *Dragonet* shuddered slightly, in a way I recognized from many flights. Turbulence. But she kept rising, punching out of the clouds, and smoothly ascending until what looked like all of Iowa, and most of the states surrounding it, came into view.

And still we ascended. At the same time, the view began to scroll, things creeping over the horizon ahead and passing beneath. Towns and villages were just points of light. Cities were larger haphazard patches of glow. And now something new slid into view—jagged darkness, like irregular sawteeth. It took me a moment to realize they were mountains.

The Rocky Mountains. The nearest of them had to be at least a thousand klicks west of the farm, but here they were, slipping beneath us. And still we gained altitude.

The next minutes, I admit, were a blur. We passed over the California coast high enough to see LA off to the left, and

San Francisco to the right. The blank, black expanse of the Pacific yawned ahead of us, but now I could see the Earth's curvature clearly. I caught a glimpse of Hawaii. Later, Australia and the multitude of islands sprawling north of it. We passed over the coast of Asia, swept past Japan and Korea and over China, and finally caught up to the sun over Eastern Europe. An explosion of light and glory lit up the Alps with gleaming snow, then laid bare the urban sprawl of Western Europe.

Something occurred to me. I reached into my pocket, where I'd stuck my phone, and pulled it out, then started tapping at it. I had no reception, of course, but I used it to take pictures instead. I snapped images of river bends, the margins of forests, the spidery traces of highways, distinctive sections of coastline.

"If you want imagery, Van, Netty can provide you with much better quality than that thing can," Perry said.

"That's okay," I replied, framing and taking a picture of an island just off the French coast. "I'm happy to collect my own."

The southern UK rolled by, then Netty announced we were starting our descent. We made a long, slow fall across the Atlantic and raced over the eastern seaboard of the States just as dawn was breaking over New York, turning the office towers to pillars of brilliant gold. We carried on across Pennsylvania, dropping steadily back toward the Great Plains and the Heartland ahead. As we did, something caught my eye. I pointed ahead and to our right.

"Uh, guys? Is that an airplane?"

Perry looked at where I'd pointed, at a big passenger plane, beacon lights pulsing, heading roughly in the same direction we were but on a slowly converging course.

"It is. A United Airlines Airbus A-320, in fact," Perry said.

"Um, aren't we worried about hitting it? Or hitting another plane? You said they can't see us—"

"Leave it to Netty. Considering some of the flying she's done, avoiding some civilian air traffic is something she could do in her sleep."

"If I slept, that is," Netty said.

We passed the Airbus and kept up our steady fall. I could make out Prairie du Chien, where the Wisconsin River met the Mississippi, then we were soaring over sprawling fields of wheat, sorghum, soybeans, and corn, most of it already harvested and fallow for the upcoming winter. Just a few hundred meters up, I saw the farm swim into view out of some mist. The barn roof opened as we approached, the *Dragonet* neatly spun and settled back into its confines, and the roof closed over top of us again.

We'd done a complete orbit of the Earth and were home, and the eastern sky was just starting to pale toward dawn.

Well, that had been one *hell* of a night, hadn't it?

I WATCHED as Miryam's car turned out of the driveway and accelerated away, trailed by a cloud of dust. The wet night had given way to a surprisingly warm, dry day. Not surprising, considering we were in that weird October period when we could have snow one day and blistering heat the next. It was as though summer and winter were duking it out, even though the outcome was inevitable.

And speaking of inevitable outcomes, I thought, turning and looking at my phone and laptop, which were sitting on the kitchen table. There was one right there. At least, the conclusion seemed like the inevitable outcome of my spur-of-the-moment photo session from orbit the night before.

I'd taken twenty-one pictures, all of really specific river bends, headlands, forested hills, stretches of coastline, and islands, mostly across western Europe. A few, though, caught bits of the Eastern Seaboard of the States. I'm pretty good with my geography, but there was no way I could memorize every wiggle of coastline or turn in a river's course. And yet, I had been able to match every single feature I'd recorded to its corresponding place on the map. Twenty-one pictures, twenty-one exactly corresponding places on Google Earth. When I switched to satellite photo view, the concurrences were even more clear.

I walked to the computer, opened a window, and stared at the image. It depicted an island in the English Channel, taken from at least a couple of hundred kilometers up. But that wasn't the satellite photo. That was a picture currently residing on my phone.

Which meant I had taken it.

And that had led to a stunning line of thinking.

I hadn't been hallucinating, or tripping balls, or dreaming, or any other such thing. The only other conclusion seemed insanely unlikely to be true. And yet, there it was. It made me think of Sherlock Holmes's pronouncement regarding this very thing.

Once you eliminate the impossible, whatever remains, no matter how improbable, must be the truth.

In other words, I had actually orbited the Earth in a spaceship last night, in the company of two sentient artificial intelligences.

And now, here I was, staring at a picture of an island in the English Channel, Jersey, apparently, that I'd taken last night from orbit.

I closed everything up and headed outside. I mucked across ground still wet from the previous night's rain, passing goldenrod and dandelions sprouting among the yellowing grass. It had become a fine, warm day, and I was sweating by the time I stepped into the cool gloom of the barn.

I opened my mouth. Closed it again. This felt stupid. Of course there'd be no answer. I *couldn't* have orbited the Earth last night.

Once you eliminate the impossible…

"Perry?"

Silence. I started to think, ah, there, see, it really was all some sort of dream or imagining. That lasted right up to the moment Perry descended with a softly metallic flutter of wings from somewhere in the rafters and landed to perch on the edge of an empty horse-stall.

"You rang?"

I stuck my hands in my pockets. "Okay, then. You *are* real."

"Last time I checked I was."

"Right." I sniffed and shook my head. "This is—it's unbelievable."

"And yet, here we are."

"So now I decide if I want to do this, take over from my grandfather as a—what did you call them? Peacekeepers?"

"Peace*maker*. There's a difference. Peace*keeper* assumes there's a peace to keep. Your job would be to *make* that peace in the first place."

"So, what, I fly around Earth, troubleshooting all the nations' conflicts and troubles?"

Perry gave me a steady, golden stare. "No, not at all."

"What then?"

"You fly around the *galaxy*, troubleshooting conflicts and troubles among the stars."

5

I stared back. "The galaxy."

"That's right."

"Even at the speed of light, it takes four years to get to the closest star to Earth. Sounds like I'd be doing a *whole* lot more traveling than peacemaking."

"Why would you travel at the speed of light?"

"Because it's as fast as anything can go?" I held up a hand. "No. Wait. You're going to tell me you have some sort of warp drive or something, aren't you?"

"Well, technically, it's a twist drive, in that it twists space to bring two distant points momentarily together. The *Dragonet* just kind of nudges itself from one point to the other. But Netty takes care of all of that. You just have to tell her where you want her to go."

"A twist drive. I—"

I stopped. I wasn't sure why this, of all things, was something to get caught on. Backyard spaceships and late-night Earth orbits, yes, but dodging around the cosmic speed limit set by light in a vacuum, I was having trouble with.

I finally shook my head. "Do you have any idea how much money that would be worth?"

"Vast amounts, I'd imagine. Same with the *Dragonet*'s weapons, and her antimatter drive, and inertia limiters, life support systems, scanners—"

"Yeah. I mean, holy shit. And yet, you and Gramps were able to keep this under wraps here, in Iowa, for—how long, anyway?"

"About twenty-five years."

I shook my head. "Twenty-five years—"

I stopped, as though I'd just slammed headfirst into a concrete wall.

"Wait? Twenty-five *years?*"

"Almost. Twenty-four years, ten months, eight days—"

"I don't care exactly *how* long," I said with some heat, raising a hand as the full realization of what Perry had just said slammed into me like a speeding truck. "That means you were here, in this barn, the whole time I was out here, in this barn, working on my electronics stuff, weren't you?"

"It does indeed. Both Netty and I are actually quite familiar with you and have been for some time."

My mind raced back over the years. Apparently, I'd walked through this barn, walked right through the *Dragonet*, being displaced, or shifted, or whatever the ship's stealth system supposedly did, without even realizing it. I'd buried myself in electronic projects, tinkered with old motors and gas engines, built things out of wood and even metal, all within arm's reach of a freakin' spaceship. And I'd never known it.

I rubbed at my face, thinking of something beyond awkward. "You saw me hide—"

"Your adult magazines, pilfered from various older relatives? Naturally, and may I say you have excellent taste. Since some of the older issues are worth quite a bit of money, I've been careful not to damage their hiding place, over there behind the feed bin."

I looked up to the ceiling, a mild flush on my cheeks. "Glad to hear you approve of my collection. Perry, a question?"

"Go ahead."

"If I were to order you to never mention this topic again, what are the chances that gets followed?" Van asked.

"To answer your question, to the extent that your orders to us don't conflict with the Peacemakers' Charter or various generally recognized interstellar laws—and there aren't many of those—or certain other policies and procedures, yes, we're bound to obey you," Perry said.

There were a bunch of things to unpack in that one statement. The Peacemakers' Charter? Interstellar laws? And certain other policies or procedures—like what? But I shoved all that into my rapidly filling mental junk drawer to deal with later on. Right now, I wanted to make good and sure of one thing.

"Okay, fine. I am ordering you guys to wipe all memories of my, ah, collection. You can do that, right? Just delete the data?"

"And there's one of those policies, right there. We're not allowed to excise memories," Perry said.

Netty cut in. "Doing so can lead to processing issues, which can affect our performance. And I'm assuming you don't want my performance to be affected while I'm, say, in the middle of a whole bunch of twist-drive calculations."

"It's also just not allowed. Our memories have to remain intact in case they're ever needed for review by the Council," Perry said. "And before you ask who the Council is, rest assured, you'll get a full briefing as soon as we begin our first op. That's when you formally assume your role as a Peacemaker Initiate. Until then, suffice to say that it's the governing body of all Peace-makers—more or less."

I waved it off. The list of things I didn't understand, and questions I needed answered, was already so long that another wouldn't matter. "Then allow me to *suggest* we keep my teen years hidden, like an unpleasant historical document. Oh, and my choice in clothes, too. I'm not proud of my selection in jeans."

"Neither am I. I'm only too happy to do so, within the limits of my protocols. Human fashion swings from simple to trashy, if I may say, and you needn't worry. Only Netty and I will ever be aware of the fact that you wore jeans with rhinestones."

"That was *one pair*."

"Understood. It's as good as in a vault," Perry said smugly.

"What happens now?"

"Now, we confirm your outfitting with a b-suit and sidearms," Perry replied. "Then, we activate your title, and you formally become a Peacemaker Initiate."

"And then the fun begins," Netty added.

I could only shake my head. "I'll bet it does."

THE B-SUIT TURNED out to be a battle suit—a sleek, midnight blue and black rig that covered me from neck to toes. A light pair of boots, made of something that resembled a cross between vinyl and butter-soft leather enclosed my feet. It had a helmet, too, which apparently allowed for vision all the way from near ultraviolet to far infrared, could generate radar and ultrasound imagery in no-light conditions, and made an airtight seal with the suit's collar, allowing the whole rig to be used as a space suit.

I stared in appreciation at the form fitting lethality of it all—at the supple suit, and the sinister helmet—it had a smooth, blank faceplate which, to anyone seeing it, was as black and featureless as a visored motorcycle helmet.

"This is badass. Not gonna lie," I muttered. At Perry's urging, I stripped down to my underwear, then slid myself into it. It seemed to conform to my body even as I donned it, and sealed itself up the back as soon as I pushed my fingers into the linked gloves. I frowned at that.

"Can't I remove these gloves? So I can use my hands?" I asked, lifting my right and splaying my fingers out.

In answer, Perry picked up one of my shoes in his beak and tossed it to me. I instinctively caught it, my frown deepening. What had been the point of that?

But it hit me while I was holding the shoe. I could *feel* it, as though I held it in my bare hand. The glove was definitely *there*, but as far as my sense of touch was concerned, it didn't exist at all.

This technology would be worth—hell, *billions* to NASA, or Space-X, or the ESA, the Chinese, or anyone else hurling people into space atop chemical rockets.

"And you said this is armor, too?"

"It's designed to stop all small-caliber projectiles and fragmentation effects of explosives up to a certain energy level. I'd give you the numbers, but it's probably easier to understand this way. In terms of terrestrial weapons, it will stop any pistol round or grenade fragment completely, instantly distributing the kinetic energy over much of the suit's surface area. Rifle caliber rounds *might* penetrate, but even if they don't, they're going to hurt. It also offers protection from brief pulses from directed-energy weapons, is effectively radiation proof, and is immune to the effects of corrosive and toxic chemicals."

"Holy shit. What *can't* it do?"

"It's weakness is heat. What it can't do is simply make your body heat go away. It can store it for brief periods of time, but you would eventually cook in the thermal energy given off by your own body."

"I'll say it again. *Badass.*" I snapped my fingers, frowning. "About the heat, though--"

"Radiant system in place. Under no circumstances will you be allowed to roast," Perry said with great confidence.

I replied with dignity. "Thank you. I prefer being medium-rare, at most."

Perry managed a snort, then next took me to the armory, which was really just a locker mounted inside a utility compartment full of ship components. When it opened, I jumped back as something moved inside.

"Sorry, I should have warned you that this is where Waldo lives," Perry said.

"Who—or *what*—the hell is a Waldo?" I asked, watching as a chunky thing I'd taken as just another part of the *Dragonet* suddenly unfolded spider-like legs and disengaged itself from the opposite bulkhead.

"Waldo is the *Dragonet*'s maintenance bot," Netty said. "I use him to conduct routine maintenance and on-the-spot repairs of the ship."

"So there's a *third* AI aboard?"

"Waldo's definitely got the A-part down, but he's a little light in the I-part," Perry said.

The spidery construct turned a crystalline eye on me, stared for a moment, then folded itself back up and plugged itself back into a receptacle on the bulkhead.

"Waldo has only limited autonomous function. Think of him as more of an extension of the ship, and of me," Netty said.

I shrugged. "Sure. Why not?"

Perry hopped into the compartment and revealed the armory. My standard sidearm, it seemed, was a handheld mass driver called a light slugger. Essentially a handheld rail gun, it could drive a three millimeter slug to some fantastic velocity—enough, Perry claimed, that it could penetrate the armor of some older terrestrial tanks. The armory also contained a heavy slugger, a long-arm variant of the light version that was heavier and bulkier but with more penetrating power. A goo gun, a non-lethal sidearm that could fling out a short-ranged gout of adhesive foam to immobilize a target, rounded out the ranged weapons.

There was also a short knife with a vibrating blade that could cut through most materials like the proverbial hot knife and butter. But the thing that really intrigued me was a sword. An actual sword. The geek in me recognized it as a short sword, generally similar to a Roman *gladius*, a short, broad-bladed stab-bing weapon. I picked it up and hefted it. It was surprisingly light for its size but otherwise seemed kind of... mundane was the first word that came to mind. Compared to all the other technological marvels that had just poured into my life, this seemed strangely out of place.

I turned to Perry. "There's got to be a story to this. Like, did Gramps run around with it on his hip, stabbing people he couldn't just, you know, blow to bits or vaporize at a distance?"

"Yes."

I blinked. "Really?"

"That is the Moonsword, and it's your badge of office as a Peacemaker. However, both ancient custom and formal protocol require you to reforge the Moonsword by your own hand in order to gain status as a Peacemaker Acolyte."

"I thought you said I just had to launch on my first actual mission to become a Peacemaker."

"A Peacemaker *Initiate*, yes. That means you're both covered and bound by the terms of the Charter, but your powers under it will be limited until you earn higher ranks."

"In other words, you'll be a noob," Netty put in.

"Look, you guys are going to have to explain this Charter, and my powers and stuff—"

"We will, in due course," Perry said. "Too much information all at once isn't going to do you much good."

"Well, neither are these weapons, honestly. I can shoot pretty well, sure, or at least I could. I wasn't in the Army all that long, and I've done a fair bit of hunting and target shooting, but—" I picked up the light slugger, a vicious-looking little weapon. "But as for shooting at other humans, I don't know."

I was a cyber-warfare expert. My weapons had been keyboards and mouses, processing power and relentless patience. I'd never fired shots in anger at, well, anyone, outside of FPS video games, anyway. And I was pretty sure that things like *Border-lands* or *Call of Duty* didn't really count.

"Well that's no problem, then," Perry said.

"How the hell do you figure that?"

"Because you won't be shooting at many *humans*."

I TOURED the remainder of the *Dragonet*. Perry and Netty explained briefly how the ship worked as I did. I frankly didn't understand most of it, since it was based on tech that, until a day ago, didn't exist for me outside of science fiction. This included the drive, which was powered by the mutual annihilation of matter and antimatter. That provided the juice both for the n-drive, or normal-space drive, and the t-drive, or twist drive, that could supposedly fling me between stars. But the AIs' description revealed a catch. A big one.

"The amount of antimatter required to power the twist drive is significant. With its current fuel stock, the *Dragonet* can only make a single twist," Netty said.

If I understood this, that was a serious problem. "So I could go to, say, Alpha Centauri or Betelgeuse or wherever—" Even as I said those things, I realized they were just words, because the actual concept of traveling to such places simply didn't fit inside my brain. "Anyway, I could go somewhere far away but never be able to get back?"

"Not without refueling, no. There'd still be enough fuel to maintain the *Dragonet*'s essential systems functions and operate the n-drive, though," Netty said.

"So what happens if we twist drive to someplace light-years away where we can't refuel?"

"Then one of your distant descendants will eventually make it back to tell the story," Perry said. And although he had a beak, I could swear he somehow grinned as he said it.

"That would kind of require a woman, wouldn't it? To even have descendants? Or do you guys have an answer for that, too, like cloning or something?" I shot back.

Netty cut in. "The whole discussion is academic anyway. Even if you could produce progeny, asexually or otherwise, a more direct one would likely die in deep space when the antimatter fuel *was* finally exhausted."

I scowled. "So am I missing something here? Or does it just

seem incredibly stupid to have a ship that can only twist one way? I mean, how the hell did my grandfather deal with that?"

"Ah, well, that's where it gets complicated," Perry replied. "When your grandfather died, certain components of the *Dragonet* were claimed by other Peacemakers who had liens on them. That's how business among Peacemakers is handled."

"Liens. So you're saying another Peacemaker came here, to the farm, took some pieces off this ship, then flew away as part of some business arrangement?"

"Yes. Unfortunately, that included extended-duration fuel cells, which are quite highly prized among Peacemakers."

"Among many others," Netty added.

"So how do I get them back?"

"Well, you could buy them, but they're rare on the open market and really, really expensive on the black one. And you don't have enough wealth in the first place."

"Hey, Gramps was pretty well-off."

"Unfortunately, terrestrial currency has little value beyond, well, Earth," Perry replied. "Your grandfather has also bequeathed you the full value of his account in the Quiet Room, but even that's not enough."

"Wait. Are you telling me I have money in some intergalactic bank?"

"Well, unless you intend to scribe all of your bonds onto certi-chips and stash them under your mattress, yes, that's where your account is."

"Okay, let me guess. I can earn more—bonds? Is that what your money is called?"

"That's right. It's the standard galactic currency," Perry replied.

"So I can earn more by doing Peacemaker jobs?"

"You can. There are contract payments, bounties, a stipend from the Council, plus any funds you acquire in a more—let's call it a more *creative* way."

"So, stealing it."

"I prefer my description."

"You can also enter a covenant with another party," Netty put in. "That's usually another Peacemaker, but it doesn't have to be. Essentially, you provide something of value and get something of value in return."

"And that's how Gramps had liens on parts of his ship. He owed them because of covenants he had that involved them."

"Exactly. He offered a lien on the *Dragonet*'s extended-duration fuel cells in return for the services of another Peacemaker. He'd intended to pay off the covenant over time and discharge the lien, but he still owed bonds at the time of his death. Accordingly, the lienholder came to claim his compensation. It's all perfectly legal," Netty replied.

"Yeah, I'm sure it is. It also sounds like I need to keep a lawyer on board. An accountant, too."

Perry aimed his golden gaze directly at me. "You have both."

"You?"

"Among my many talents, yes."

"A mechanical bird who claims to be a combat AI, a legal expert, and a financial guru? Sure, why not."

I realized that I had a whole lot to learn. And I still hadn't even stepped into the actual role.

Which brought me circling back to a question I'd been constantly pushing aside until *later*. Except *later* had finally become *now*.

Did I even *want* to be a Peacemaker?

———

THAT EVENING, I sat down at the kitchen table with a shot of whiskey over ice and stared out at the barn. How many evenings and weekends had I spent in there, piddling around with what I'd taken, at the time, to be cutting edge electronics—when all along there was a hyperdrive *spaceship* sitting close enough to touch?

It made me wonder what else was hidden away from everyday sight?

But I brushed that aside as interesting, though not especially important musings. I fixed my mind on what did matter.

Did I want to be a so-called Peacemaker?

Perry and Netty had revealed some of Gramps' missions to me, or at least the parts of them they could. Apparently, the Galactic Knights Uniformed, the body that oversaw, or regulated, or actually owned the Peacemakers—I wasn't sure of the details —had a host of rules and policies that precluded revealing some mission information, even to me. But it didn't matter. I got the idea quickly.

Gramps, as a Peacemaker, had essentially been an interstellar troubleshooter. He'd participated in a wide range of missions, in a multitude of different places. Some had been clearly military operations, but others were more like law enforcement, or even resolving contract disputes and disagreements over trade. And a few had taken place on relatively low-tech worlds, the most primitive of which seemed to roughly correspond to Earth's early medieval period. Apparently, the whole primary, non-interference directive thing was real. Low-tech societies were supposed to be left alone, and if they weren't either by accident or design, the Peacemakers might be called on to fix it.

So fly among the stars in the *Dragonet*, fixing problems and generally trying to keep the peace. Or—

I glanced out the window at the sprawl of corn and soybean fields receding to the horizon, under an overcast, autumn sky. With most crops harvested, the greyish light only managed to render the drab yellows and tans and browns into even more drab yellows and tans and browns. I sniffed. I had enormous respect for the people who could be successful farmers. It takes something that I knew I didn't have.

That's probably why I ended up in cyber-ops, my current day job. The pay was decent, and sometimes excellent, but it mostly involved long hours staring at a monitor, running various tools to crack security, and then either extract, alter or plant data. It had none of the frenetic keyboard-pounding, heated action portrayed in pop culture. It was really more like daytrading, or even just ordinary coding, but with different sequences of key-presses and mouse-clicks—

I stood. Did I want to be a Peacemaker?

Not particularly, no, was the honest answer. But it also wasn't the right question. The right question was, *did I want to pass up the chance to give it a try?*

And the answer to that was easy. No way in hell would I miss this chance.

6

I MADE myself more comfortable in the *Dragonet*'s pilot's seat and looked down. Far below me, the Horn of Africa scrolled slowly past, giving way to the northern part of the Arabian Sea. Yemen, Oman, and Saudi Arabia sprawled off to my left, the Indian Ocean to my right, and the coastline of India and Pakistan straight ahead.

I shook my head, taking in the dapple of sunlight on the Arabian Sea.

"Okay, so according to, uh——" I studied the instruments that Perry and Netty had started explaining to me. "That. That thing, right there. That's telling me I'm in a stable orbit, right?"

"That's right. As long as that little spaceship icon is centered in the circle, your orbit is stable. You apply thrust to raise it or lower it," Netty replied.

"Okay, so——" I stopped. "Where, exactly, do we need to go? I told Miryam I had to travel on urgent business for a few days, so it's not like I've got a massive time crunch here, but I'm not even sure where we're going."

"Your first stop would be the starport at what you would call Ross 248," Perry said.

"*I* would call it that? More like I wouldn't call it anything because it's not a place I get to all that often." I flashed Perry a grin. If he appreciated my attempt at being glib, he didn't show it.

"For our purposes, we use standard terrestrial star-catalog references. Other races use different names. For instance, to the Capians, Ross 248 is known as—"

I winced as Perry spat out something that crossed an old computer modem trying to connect with a wailing cat.

"Seriously? That's a language?"

"A Capian would probably say the same thing about English."

"Okay, but if all of these other races—and, I mean, this is sinking in now, that there are other *races*—anyway, if they all speak different languages, how the hell am I supposed to under-stand them?"

"Don't worry, we've got you covered, Van," Perry said. "Check out the compartment in your left armrest."

I did and found it contained a number of gadgets, including one that looked like a small flashlight. I extracted that one and held it up. "What's this? Some sort of weapon?" I had visions of using it to blow holes in walls or vaporize buildings.

"It's a flashlight," Perry replied.

"Ah. Oh. Okay. Nice to have a flashlight handy, I guess." I put it back, and Perry had me retrieve, instead, a small cylinder made of foam, like a single earplug. He told me to slide it into my ear, so I did. It conformed itself perfectly to my ear canal.

"This is some sort of translator?"

"That's right."

"So talk to me in some other language."

"I am," Perry replied. "I'm speaking Capian right now."

I didn't hear any of that modem-cat racket, but I did notice Perry's mouth moving out of sync with his words. Well, huh. Just another bit of tech that would be worth millions, probably billions down in—

I glanced down and saw the sun gleaming off snow-capped Indian mountains. So, India, but anywhere else on Earth, for that matter.

"You can get rigged up with an implant for permanent, real-time translation if you want," Perry went on. "I'd recommend that as a nice goal, though, rather than a must-do. You've got more important uses for your time and money. For now, the ear bug should be enough. Netty and I can translate for you, too."

I extracted the bug and put it away. "Okay, so what's next?"

"Next, we break orbit," Netty replied.

"We can just twist, or whatever it is, from here?"

"In theory, yes, we could. But the more gravity is affecting it, the harder it is to twist space. You need a bigger, more powerful twist drive to do it. So a big battlecruiser might be able to twist right out of orbit, but I'm afraid the *Dragonet's* just not up to it."

"So we have to fly away from Earth first. How far?"

"Straight up from the ecliptic plane for about twelve hours

should be enough to lower the gravitation to within the twist drive's operating range."

"And what would happen if we just tried to twist from here?" I asked.

"We'd burn a lot of fuel, go nowhere, and probably break the twist drive. If Perry and I can't fix it, then you'd have to call for recovery and pay for that, plus parts."

"You'd start your career as a Peacemaker deep in debt. I wouldn't recommend it," Perry put in.

"Let's not do that."

Netty talked me through the process of breaking orbit. It turned out to be as complicated as I wanted it to be. I could just say, *Netty, take us to a safe twist distance*, and she would. Or, I could fly the *Dragonet* manually, right down to firing individual thrusters, if I wanted. As tempting as it was to try my hand at it, I settled on the former, for now.

A faint rumble vibrated the *Dragonet*, and India began to slowly fall away, before finally disappearing from view. Ahead of me lay nothing but black emptiness, punctuated by a few, bright stars.

"Congratulations, Van," Perry said.

"For what?"

"You just joined an exclusive club. You're one of only a small tribe of humans who've ever left low Earth-orbit."

I frowned at that. I could think of twenty-seven, the astronauts of Apollo 8 and 10, and 11 through 17. Oh, and Gramps, so twenty-eight. I made twenty-nine.

I told Perry that, which just raised another question. "Are there any others?" I asked.

"Yes."

"Well, spill it. How many?"

"I can't say."

"You can't, or you won't?"

"At least one of those is correct."

My frown hardened into a scowl. "Why the sudden evasiveness?"

"Reasons, Van. I'll answer every one of your questions that I can, but we're occasionally going to run into some I can't, for legal, policy, or other reasons."

"Or because you don't know?"

"*Pfft.* I suppose, though it's unlikely."

I gave up and settled back into the pilot's seat for what was going to be, I gathered, about the next twelve hours. But I couldn't help wondering who those other humans who'd apparently left Earth had been—and why Perry couldn't, or wouldn't, say.

I FILLED the next hours with a more detailed tour of the *Dragonet*, including some basics about her operations. Netty took care of the vast majority of working the ship, assisted by Waldo, and sometimes by Perry. Gramps had apparently gotten in on the act, too, eventually coming to do a lot of the ship's routine maintenance himself. For now, I was content to leave it to the experts and focus more on the amenities.

The *Dragonet* sported two small crew compartments, each including a bed and ample storage for personal effects. A tiny galley and a compartment that combined the functions of sink, toilet, and shower into one space rounded out the crew habitat. There was, however, one more compartment, spartan in the extreme, whose purpose was more somber.

"Prisoner transport. We call it the brig," Perry said.

I just nodded. Prisoner transport. I tried to imagine carrying someone locked up in here, to wherever they needed to go. It was an unsettling thought and probably the first time the more unpleasant implications of being a Peacemaker crept into view.

Perry was talking me through the intricacies of my battle suit, the form-fitting armor I'd briefly examined before, when Netty interrupted.

"Van, there's a ship falling toward the Inner Solar System."

"*Toward* the Inner Solar System. So it's like us? Not from Earth?"

"Look who's suddenly *not from Earth*," Perry put in, sounding smug.

"It isn't from Earth, no. It's a standard *Fornax*-class workboat, modified to class six threat status."

"I'm sure that means something," I said, starting back toward the cockpit.

"The *Dragonet* is class eight. That means we can reasonably expect to deal with any vessel ranging from class one through class seven. Eight and higher are best avoided."

"How high do these classes go?"

"Class one hundred is the highest recognized threat status."

I clambered into the pilot's seat. "Holy shit. What would a one hundred even look like?"

"No idea, since there isn't anything that powerful known to exist. The highest class on the scale I'm aware of is class sixty-seven, which is an orbital mega fortress located in a classified location."

I could only shake my head. "Sure, okay. So what would be class one?"

"A rock. Or a wreck."

"So class six is no threat to us, is what you're saying."

"No, I'm not saying that at all," Netty replied. "If you fly into a rock, it's still going to hurt, even if it's technically just class one."

"A class six can pose a significant threat to us, actually," Perry said. "If it got the drop on us, ambushed us, that sort of thing. The threat rating is more a comparison of a straight-up fight."

I scanned the instruments, then curled my lip. "Alright, which of these tells me all of that?"

"Tactical is directly ahead of you, top of the display. But when we go to alert status, you'll also get a heads-up display projected right onto the canopy, like this," Netty replied.

Luminous bits appeared all around me. The most eye-catching was a circular icon, like a bullseye, that highlighted the other ship. A small window alongside it held a magnified image and some other data. It looked not too different from the *Dragonet*, maybe a little chunkier, but about the same size and mass.

"So… I am actually looking at an alien spaceship right now."

"Insofar as it's not from Earth, that's right," Perry said.

"Huh. The truth really *is* out here." I narrowed my eyes at the tactical data displayed alongside the icon. "What's this red bit here, where it says *No Transponder?*"

"That, Peacemaker, is the problem. Under the terms of interstellar law, all non-military vessels, and all military ones outside of specified exclusion zones, are required to broadcast a transponder code."

"I'm assuming this means they're up to no good?"

"Well, that, or they're suffering a transponder malfunction. But it's almost always *no good*."

"Okay, so what do we do? Intercept?"

"Ordinarily, yes. But this is literally your first flight, and you're not actually operational yet. That's the whole point of going to Ross 248," Perry replied.

I stared at the image of the other ship. "Do we know where they're going?"

"They're currently on a course to intercept the NASA *Newton-1* probe, launched last year for detailed survey of the Jovian moons, especially Europa," Netty said.

"Why would they be interested in a NASA probe? I doubt that any of the tech is useful to them, right? Isn't it primitive by comparison?"

"Oh, very much so. They'll be more interested in some of the materials used in it, especially its plutonium power cells. Plutonium fetches a good price on the markets, both the open and black ones," Perry answered.

"So they want to strip that probe for parts? For plutonium? Won't that give them away?"

"Not at all. An EMP burst to knock the probe's systems offline would do it. From NASA's perspective, they'll just have lost contact with the probe."

I thought about the various space missions that I knew had failed. Since humanity had started launching things out of orbit, there'd been more than a few. How many had been legitimate malfunctions, and how many had been greedy, opportunistic aliens?

I glared at the image. "I just have to let them go and plunder that probe, and I can't do anything to stop them?"

"Well, technically, under GKU policy, you can intervene, but you're not obligated to. However, if you're injured or the *Dragonet* is damaged, you may not be eligible for duty subsidies," Perry said.

"Wow. Is space ever bureaucratic."

"You've barely started down the officious rabbit hole here, Van, believe me."

I pulled my lower lip across my teeth, a habit from long hours of studying tedious computer code. "I really don't want these assholes just swooping in and plundering that probe." I drummed my fingers on the armrest. "Can we talk to them?"

"We can hail them, sure," Netty replied. "There's no guarantee they'll answer, though."

"What the hell. Let's give it a try." I turned to Perry, who'd perched on the copilot's seat, which I gathered was his accustomed place. "Is there some formal protocol stuff about what I should say?"

"Allow me. Netty, open a channel, if you please, my dear."

"Done."

Perry's voice suddenly rang with authority. "Unknown ship, this is the GKU ship *Dragonet*, registry PM109879. Please identify yourself and state your business in this system."

I waited.

Silence.

"Looks like they're not interested in—" I started, but a staccato burst of speech cut me off.

"This is the free trader *Klrgzt*. We're having some problems with our transponder. Sorry about that. As for why we're here, well, we're—"

I heard another voice mutter in the background.

"—archaeologists. We're here to do, um, archaeology."

I raised a finger, and Netty suspended the channel. "Okay, I'm new to this space stuff and all, but seriously, these guys are lying. And they're doing a pretty piss-poor job of it, too."

Perry lifted and lowered his wings. "Very astute."

"What do we do?"

"Well, standard protocol would be to board them and conduct an inspection, pursuant to the Treaty of Spica, Section Two, paragraph nine."

"Am I going to have to learn all of this legal stuff?"

"That's why you've got me. But it wouldn't hurt."

"Did my grandfather know it all?"

"Nobody knows it *all*. Well, except for me, of course," Perry replied.

I had to smile. A combat AI, a legal expert, a financial guru—and an ego.

I opened my mouth, but Perry cut me off. "Before you go ahead and say sure, let's board them, I'd point out that they're likely armed and would quite happily kill you."

"Are you serious?"

"The galaxy is a cold and hostile place, Van. You're a lone Peacemaker in a remote system. It would be a long time before you were missed."

"Even longer, actually, since you're not fully registered with the GKU," Netty added.

"Way to make me feel special, guys. So what do you recommend we do, here?"

"Order them to leave the system until they have a working transponder," Perry suggested.

"Okay, so they go off and fix it, then come back and strip that probe anyway."

"You asked for my recommendation, and you got it."

I considered the situation. I knew I was way out of my depth here. But it didn't seem like a very auspicious way to start a potential career as a galactic Peacemaker, turning what amounted to a blind eye to a crime. Even under pretty much any Earthly law, stealing a probe would still be stealing—even if it were happening somewhere near Mars.

"Open that channel again, Netty," I said.

She did, and I prepared to make my voice as officious as possible.

"Free trader—" was as far as I got before realizing I didn't remember the name, which had sounded like a nonsense word anyway. I held up a finger for Netty to cut the channel again and looked at Perry.

"They identified themselves as free trader *Klrgzt*."

"What the hell is a *Klrgzt*?"

"It's a Saparan word, but it doesn't have a direct English translation. It sort of means, *as free as a bird recently released from a cage where it was being held against its will*."

"A bit on the nose for my taste, but then again, criminals are rarely subtle." I signaled for Netty to resume the channel.

"Free trader *Klrgzt*, by the power vested in me by the, um, Galactic Knights Peacemakers, I hereby order you to leave this system, never to return." I glanced at Perry, who just stared back.

"Close," he said.

"This is free trader *Klrgzt*. We've got a valid flight plan to do this archaeology we came here to do. And what's with trying to order us to *never return*? You can't do that."

I glanced at Perry and gave a helpless shrug. He took over.

"Free trader *Klrgzt*, pursuant to the provisions of the Treaty of Spica, Section Four, paragraphs six through eight, your operating without a valid transponder signal invalidates your flight plan. Please withdraw from this system immediately, or you will be boarded for inspection pursuant to the Altair Protocols, specifically Protocol Three, section—"

"They have just launched two missiles at us and are accelerating away on a diverging course," Netty cut in.

Perry shook his head. "Assholes."

"Woah, wait a second. Did you say they launched missiles? Like, they're *shooting* at us?"

"They are. And they must really want that probe because those missiles aren't cheap, at fourteen hundred bonds apiece," Netty replied.

I gaped. We had some sort of ordnance streaking toward us, and both Netty and Perry seemed pretty *meh* about it, discussing dollar—or bond, or whatever—values.

"Guys, shouldn't we *do* something about those missiles?" I asked, watching the tactical overlay. It now clearly showed a new icon, rapidly closing on us. The heads-up projected on the canopy sent the same message, only in an even more stark way, by highlighting exactly where the inbound missile was.

"Van, do we have your permission to engage this target with lethal force?" Perry asked.

"You have to ask?"

"Yes, actually, I do. AIs aren't allowed to use lethal force without approval by a recognized sentient race."

"Aren't AIs like you sentient, though?"

"Do you really want to take *this* particular moment to delve into some specific points of interstellar law?"

"In case anyone's interested, those incoming missiles are forty-two seconds out," Netty put in.

"No, I don't. Do whatever you have to do so we don't get blown up," I said with as much calm as I could muster.

"Well, we were going to do that regardless," he replied. "Self-defense is always authorized. Anyway, Netty, can you slave the ship to me?"

"Done."

Perry didn't seem to do anything, but the starfield suddenly rotated, and that dull thrum vibrated the ship. Displays flickered and changed. I tried to make sense of it all, but just as I'd figured out what was going on, something new was happening.

One display was pretty clear, though. It showed the missiles less than twenty seconds away.

"Guys, how about those missiles, huh?"

"Stand by," Netty said.

"For what?"

A couple more seconds passed, then Netty spoke again.

"This."

One of the missiles abruptly lit up, as though suddenly caught in the beam of a powerful floodlight. I could actually *see* it, a hard point of light flaring against the stars. An instant later, it vanished into a dazzling shower of sparks. Even as they faded and died, the second missile got the same treatment, obviously hit and destroyed by the *Dragonet*'s laser.

The other ship had turned its tail to us and started to run. Perry ran them down, though, taking advantage of the *Dragonet*'s superior acceleration to relentlessly close in.

"Free trader *Klrgzt*, kill your engines and prepare to surrender to lawful Peacemaker custody," Perry said.

The response was another missile. This time, it only had about ten seconds of flight time to close. Netty destroyed it uncomfortably close to the *Dragonet*, which swept through the glittering sparks of its debris.

I let out a breath. "I guess that's a *no*, huh?"

"In the Peacemakers, we have a specific term to describe refusing to surrender by using force," Netty said.

"What's that?"

She said it, and I raised my eyebrows. "Huh. I spent a few years in the Army, and even I don't remember hearing anything quite that, um, colorful."

"You can always just condense it down to *up yours*."

"Or translate it into Latin. Everything sounds way more legal and scholarly if you translate it into Latin," Perry offered.

I chuckled but it came out short and sharp. I couldn't pull my eyes off the overlay, which I was starting to understand. Based on it, the flight time of another missile from the other ship would be just over five seconds. My stress level ratcheted up another notch or two, but I was oddly separate from the threat. Watching missiles seemed more like a game than warfare.

"Close enough," Perry said, then the *Dragonet* shuddered. I didn't see anything fly away from our ship, but the aft end of the other ship erupted with a searing flash and a shower of spinning debris. It immediately stopped accelerating, which meant we overtook it in seconds. As we raced past, Perry fired one of the rail guns again, neatly blasting a cluster of feathery antennae off the top of the other ship's hull.

"That leaves them with no engines and no comms," Perry said.

I glanced at him. "So now what?"

"Now, we resume our way to Ross 248."

"But what about the other ship? The Kirg—whatever the hell it was. Do we just leave it here?"

"They're not going anywhere."

"Yeah, but they're stuck, right? Aren't they eventually going to run out of air, or food and water?"

"Eventually."

"So—"

"Their location is marked," Perry cut in. "When we get to Ross 248, we'll notify a collection team to come and take them into custody."

"Yeah, but only if they're still alive. They might even be injured or dead now!"

"They might. Of course, if we hadn't taken action, then you might be the injured or dead one, right?"

I drummed my fingers on the armrest. "I suppose."

Perry leaned toward me. "Van, what did I tell you about the galaxy?"

"That it's a cold and hostile place."

"Attaboy, Peacemaker. It's the one law that trumps all others. Don't ever forget that."

7

THE TWIST, when it finally happened, was anticlimactic. Netty announced she was about to spool up the twist drive. When she did, it was over after a brief instant of disorientation. Nothing seemed to have changed.

I glanced at Perry. "I was expecting something more dramatic," I said and waved a hand at the view beyond the canopy. "It doesn't look like we've moved at all."

"Well, when we were leaving Sol, you had the sun to your back. Let's see what's back there now."

The starfield abruptly pitched and spun, then something massive slid into view.

"Oh. Holy shit. What is *that*?"

"That, my friend, is Ross Starport, aka Crossroads."

I stared. When Perry mentioned a station, I'd expected something like one of those big rings once portrayed in sci-fi books and movies, or maybe something like the ISS. What I *hadn't* expected was a haphazard sprawl of spheres, cubes, prisms, struts, girders, and myriad other components. Some of them looked brand new, still gleaming, while others had a haggard, worn character to them. At least a dozen other ships clustered around it, some underway, others motionless, apparently parked. The whole thing had to be as big as a dozen city blocks. Beyond, the red dwarf star called Ross 248 shone with a dull, ruddy gleam that lit everything orange-brown.

I sat and took it all in. And for that moment, Perry and Netty just let me.

Eventually, I took a breath and shook my head. "Okay. Well. That really brings it home, doesn't it?"

"Brings what home?" Perry asked.

"That we are not alone."

"Who? Humans?" Perry actually laughed. "Ah, sorry, Van, we never get tired of hearing that. You humans are all so ponderous and philosophical about your place in the universe and all that—as though you're actually going to have this much stuff, filling this much space, and the only living things that would *ever* occur in it are you guys."

"We especially like the UFO stuff," Netty put in. "You've built a whole popular culture around the damned things."

"So what are they?" I asked, my gaze still locked on the jumbled spectacle of the station apparently called Crossroads. "UFOs? Are they real?"

"Half the time, no, they're not. They really are just natural phenomena."

"What about the other half?"

"Scientists, cultural anthropologists, those sorts, studying you and your planet. Early spaceflight cultures are always interesting to watch—especially the *will they or won't they nuke themselves* part," Perry said. "And some are just assholes out to—what's the human term? Troll? They're trolling you?"

"*Trolling* us? By flying around in spaceships and deliberately letting themselves be seen?"

"You think humans have a monopoly on being tools?"

"We're being called by Crossroads traffic control," Netty cut in. "We've been cleared to dock at port two alpha, in the Peacemaker zone. I'm taking us in."

That slight thrum rippled through the *Dragonet*, and Crossroads began to loom larger and larger, filling the view ahead.

THE PEACEMAKER ZONE turned out to be one of the newer, sleeker modules making up Crossroads. I stepped out of the airlock, into the station, clad in my form-fitting armor, then stopped and began taking stock of just what the hell I'd gotten myself into.

The airlock opened into an atrium three floors high. Or maybe decks was a better term. I'd expected something utilitarian, more like the images from the inside of the ISS—consoles, conduits, pipes, equipment, tie-downs, storage lockers, that sort of thing. What I hadn't expected was what amounted to a tidy greenspace, lined with hydroponic troughs laden with drooping foliage. The air was breathable, but only just, which necessitated me wearing a rebreather that resembled the nasal tubes used by hospitals to administer oxygen. Perry had explained that most species needed oxygen, just varying amounts of it, and it was easier to supplement a low-level than to reduce a higher one. It didn't stop me from inhaling a green, wholesome smell that reminded me of fresh-cut grass on a warm summer day.

"Uh, Van? You're blocking the airlock," Perry said from behind me.

I stepped aside. "Sorry. Just a little overwhelmed here."

"Understood." Perry hopped past me and flung himself into the air, soared up to a few meters height, then dropped back to perch on a nearby railing. As he did his little aerobatic display, I noticed a woman—a *human* woman—garbed much like me, approaching. I had to admit that the form-fitting aspect of the uniform did more for her than it did for me. But she strode up amid a cloud of brusque purpose, making it clear that this was business about to unfold.

"Initiate Tudor?" Her voice was, like her manner, all clipped efficiency.

"Please, it's Van," I said, sticking out my hand.

She looked at it as though I were offering her some dead thing I'd found on the way here. "No, it's Initiate Tudor. I'm Adept Santorelli. My first name is Gabriella."

"But, let me guess—it's Adept Santorelli."

She gave a thin smile that flicked on, then off. "You learn fast. That's good because we don't have a lot of time."

"For what?"

"For you to prove that you can be a Peacemaker."

I glanced at Perry, who just lifted and lowered his wings in what I took to be a shrug.

"Oh, yeah. The admission trials. Did I forget to mention those?"

SANTORELLI, it turned out, was one of four human Peacemakers, but the only one currently aboard Crossroads. The other Peacemakers were aliens, which brought me smack into a head-on collision with yet another stunning reality.

There were actual *aliens*.

It had been implicit, of course, in the whole spaceships, space battles, and space stations thing. Perry had even mentioned some alien races by name. But, until I finally came face to face with one, aliens had remained an abstract concept, just something kind of *out there somewhere.*

But then Santorelli took me to a quiet office and introduced me to a creature that seemed a combination of something vaguely octopus-like, with a lower body shaped like the back end of a massive slug. It wore its own version of the close-fitting, blue-black armor. I noticed a series of three concentric circles emblazoned on the uniform in gold. It represented rank, apparently, as Santorelli introduced him—or her—anyway, *it*, as the Chapter Master of the Galactic Knights Uniformed for the region of space that included Earth. Its name translated to something long and descriptive in English, but the alien made it simple.

"You can call me Gus."

"Gus."

"Yes. It's what your twice-spawn called me."

"My twice-spawn?"

Santorelli leaned in. "Your grandfather."

"Gramps called you Gus."

The alien actually nodded, or I assumed that's what the sudden wobble of the top end of its body meant. "He said I reminded him of someone he knew back on Earth."

"You're kidding."

"I am not."

"You're not."

"I wasn't aware your species was given to mimicry."

I blinked. "I—what?"

"So far, this conversation has consisted mainly of me making statements and you echoing them back to me."

I shook my head. "Yeah, sorry. It's just that—well, you're the first alien I've ever seen in the, er, flesh."

"I'm not the alien. *You* are," Gus said.

I just stared, then the creature began to vibrate, making an audible hum. A look of alarm must have flashed over my face because Santorelli leaned in again. "He's laughing."

"And this is why we pair Initiates with Adepts of their own species," Gus said. "It reduces the natural friction resulting from cross-species culture shock."

I nodded at that. "Probably a good idea, yeah."

"Now, what's going to happen is that Adept Santorelli is going to give you an orientation session to acquaint you with the amenities and restrictions of the Peacemaker module. You'll then have a rest period, and following that, the first battery of tests will begin."

"Okay. Can I look around the rest of this—Crossroads, right? That's what this place is called?"

"Yes, it is, and no, you cannot. You aren't ready for that."

"As an Initiate Peacemaker, you'd be the perfect target for any number of criminal sorts," Santorelli said.

"Criminal sorts? What do you mean?"

Santorelli flashed that on-off smile again. "Criminal sorts like the Unbound. They're similar to the mafia back on Earth. Let's call it *very* organized crime. In any case, in order to advance past a certain level in the Unbound, you have to kill a Peacemaker."

"And it doesn't matter if it's a grizzled Adept or a brand-new Initiate," Gus put in.

"What they're saying is that if you step foot outside this module, you're probably going to be very quickly dead, Van," Perry added from the back of the room.

Now, I might have a stubborn streak in me, but I'm not stupid. Two Peacemakers and an AI were telling me just how bad an idea it would be for me to treat the rest of the station like a shopping mall in some new city. I got the message and turned to Santorelli.

"Well, then, let's orientate away, shall we?"

She gave me a bemused look. "Yes. Let's."

IT TURNED out that the Peacemakers had a nifty trick for teaching you what you needed to know. They *injected* it into you.

I stared at what amounted to an elaborate hypodermic, mounted on the end of an AI-controlled arm and filled with a murky fluid. "So you're telling me that you can give me all the skills I need just by sticking that into me?"

"It's a little more complicated than that," Santorelli said. "First, we need to establish your achievement level in whatever area we're working on. The system will then tailor the nanobots to deliver the appropriate biochemicals, memory RNA, that sort of thing to enhance that area, to bring it up to a minimum standard."

"It's basically the Peacemaker version of boot-camp," Perry said, from across the spartan, rather sterile room. "By the time you're done, you'll be good enough in each of the ten basic skill sets to perform the basic duties of a Peacemaker."

"And what are these ten basic skill sets?" I asked.

"Spaceflight; atmospheric ship combat; extra-atmospheric ship combat; ranged personal weapons; melee combat; zero-g combat; stealth and subterfuge; information systems; laws, policies, and procedures; and diplomacy," Santorelli replied.

"Okay, well, I know information systems," I said, giving her a sheepish smile. "I guess it's a start."

She nodded. "Actually, it is. According to your dossier, you're especially skilled in the use of information systems, including intrusion and counter-intrusion."

"You guys know about that?"

Santorelli flicked that smile at me. "We know a great deal

about you, Initiate Tudor."

"Well, that sounds ominous."

"Not at all," she replied in a tone that was *entirely* ominous. "But... we're going to start with your obvious strength." She gestured at the hypodermic contraption. "We've already established that you're at the maximum untrained baseline, so this will just be an enhancement. Basically, once it's done, you'll have a good understanding of extraterrestrial computers and info systems."

"Huh. And what are the risks?"

"There's a one-half percent chance you'll have an adverse reaction to the enhancement."

"And what, exactly, constitutes an adverse reaction?"

"Death or various things that aren't death."

I forced a smile. "You've got one hell of a bedside manner."

She picked up something that looked like a clipboard but was apparently a fully functional portable computer called a slate. "I need you to authorize what we're about to do to you. All you have to do is state your concurrence."

"I'm curious—what happens if I don't?"

"Then you'll be returned to Earth with your memories suitably altered to make all of this seem unreal, like a dream or hallucination."

"I wonder how many supposed UFO abductees are really washed-out Peacemaker candidates," I said. I'd meant it as a joke, but this time Santorelli didn't smile.

"Wait. How many of them are failed Peacemakers?"

Now she smiled. "Are you going to authorize this or not?"

I looked at the slate. At the hypodermic. Back at the slate.

"I guess this is my last chance to back out, huh?"

"It's your last chance to voluntarily leave the Peacemakers. You could still prove to be unsuitable and simply be rejected as a candidate."

"And go back to Earth with a memory gap or worse?"

She said nothing and held the slate toward me. I briefly considered just calling it quits right here. This was, after all, a —*big step* didn't even begin to describe it.

But who was I kidding? I stood with my toes on the brink of a whole universe of things and stuff I'd never even imagined existed. Was I really going to turn away from it?

Moreover, the orientation session—assuming it hadn't all been lies, but I had no reason to believe it had—made it pretty clear that the Peacemakers were an agency of, if not *good*, then at least law and order. Gramps and my father had both described their jobs to me in a similar way when I was making that transition from insular child to more outward-looking teenager. I actually remembered Gramps' words about it.

"I work with people who try to stop bad guys from doing bad things."

"So you're a good guy?"

"Most of the time, yeah, I am."

I hadn't really appreciated that *most of the time* part until the moral grey of the world started seeping into my own life.

And now I could be a good guy most of the time and stop bad guys from doing bad things.

I touched the slate where she indicated, leaving my thumb

print, and read aloud the passage glowing above it.

"I, Clive VanAbel Tudor III, do hereby concur with the provisions of, and accept the risks associated with…"

The text went on at some length. It was somehow surprising, comforting, and discouraging all at once that lawyers seemed to be as fundamental a part of the universe as the Higgs Boson.

When I was done, Santorelli instructed me to stick out my arm. The robotic hypodermic hissed as it injected the cloudy fluid into my arm and then—

Nothing happened.

I looked at Santorelli. "Uh—am I supposed to be feeling something?"

"Ideally, no. But you do have to give it a few minutes." She took the slate and turned for the door. "I'll be back in about half an hour. Just stay here and don't move around too much. The training system will keep an eye on you for adverse reactions."

With that, she left.

I turned to Perry. "She seems nice."

"Adept Santorelli has personally disrupted two major criminal syndicates, made forty-one arrests, intervened in three major trade disputes—oh, and has eleven recorded kills."

"Oh. Huh. So she's actually kind of terrifying then."

I spent the next few minutes discussing things that had come up during the orientation with Perry. He eventually worked the conversation around to my own background. "Tell me, Van, what would you say is the most complex computer system you've ever worked with?"

I frowned at the question. "Oh, probably one of the top end

systems made by the Druzis Amalgam. They use an organic component to their computing substrate that allows for a sort of encryption that most other systems…"

I trailed off. What the hell was I talking about?

I stared at Perry. Blinked.

I knew all kinds of things about information systems I'd never actually used. Processing architectures, data storage and retrieval methods, encryption schemes, interface protocols—I knew the specific operational details of dozens of computer systems, and I knew them well—intimately, even. All of the memories were right there, as clear as a clean blue sky. And yet, if I tried to trace any of them back to where I'd learned them, where they'd come from, there was nothing. It was like having the complete knowledge of a college course but no memory of ever attending class.

Perry cocked his head. "Interesting effect, isn't it?"

"That's—" I shook my head. "Holy shit. I mean—" I shook my head again and gestured at the terminal sitting on the table near the robotic arm. "I know how to *use* that, how it *works*. And I know it as well as I know the rig sitting on my desk back in Atlanta. And I built that myself, to my *own* specs."

"Congratulations, Van. You just ticked off the Information Systems box on your admission record. Only nine more to go."

I leaned back and thought about the architecture underlying both Perry's and Netty's artificial intelligence. It was so elegant, so artful in its fundamental simplicity, and I understood it in nearly every respect—and it was based on principles and technologies I hadn't even realized existed until a few minutes ago.

I shook my head a third time, looked back at Perry, and said the only thing that came to mind.

"Badass. *Definitely* badass."

I LINED up the shot and snapped out a round, taking the target squarely in the middle of the face. Bits of debris were still spalling from the impact when the second target popped up, and I had to hip-shoot that one. My slug clipped the edge of the target, and I fired again, scoring a lethal hit.

A chime sounded, announcing the end of the run. The lights came up. I immediately stopped and unloaded my weapon, making it safe. My arms and fingers once again amazed me by flicking and snapping through all of the requisite motions, using muscle memory I hadn't even possessed until about an hour earlier.

Santorelli, who'd been following me through the fifty meter shooting course, stared over her slate. She pushed up her lower lip and nodded. "Not bad. Your average score for the three runs is eighty-nine out of a hundred. More to the point, it climbed a little each time."

She inspected my weapon to ensure its safety, then took it and returned it to the support bot, a roughly humanoid construct named Cecil. He was one of three AI-controlled bots that did everything from overseeing weapons and ammo storage, to assisting with local security, to keeping the Crossroads Peacemakers' module clean and tidy.

"I'm no stranger to shooting," I replied. "Between the Army

and Gramps' insistence on teaching me target shooting and taking me deer hunting, I've put a lot of bullets downrange."

"And it shows," Santorelli said, glancing down at the slate. But her grey eyes flicked back up. "It shows in your melee combat skills, too. Not been in a lot of fights, have you?"

I shrugged. "I was never much into bars or otherwise had much occasion to beat the shit out of people—or them out of me. My bad, I guess?"

Santorelli tucked the slate under her arm. "Take a one hour break, then we'll resume."

"What's next?"

"Diplomacy."

"Ah, well, this oughta be good. After all, we computer nerds are known for our people skills."

Santorelli said nothing and just nodded toward the crew lounge, then turned and walked away.

"I don't think she likes me," I said when she was out of earshot.

Perry, who'd been watching, landed beside me. "What makes you think that?"

"Just her whole deal. It's not very—I don't know. Very friendly, I guess."

Perry looked straight at me. "Well, it could be that, or it could be that she's a professional, doing her job, which is assessing you as a potential Peacemaker."

I glanced at him, then looked back to where she'd disappeared through a door. "Good point. Maybe my people skills aren't all that great after all."

"It could just be that you're an ordinary man who's been plunged headfirst into a vast, complicated world he didn't even realize existed until just a few days ago."

"You really have a way of cutting through the bullshit, don't you?"

"Pretty much right at the top of my job description, Van."

IT WAS funny how Santorelli emphasized the need to take care of yourself, including eating right and adequate rest—and then subjected me to a barrage of trials and tests that spanned two entire days. I probably managed about five or six hours of sleep the whole time, and not in a single stretch, either. I finished the last one, an in-depth quiz about specific points of law, policies, procedures, and protocols, at what my body was telling me had to be the wee hours of the morning of my second day on Crossroads. That was after bouts of unarmed combat, flying a simulation of the *Dragonet* through all sorts of gyrations, followed by fights against other ships, and, most nerve-wracking of all, donning the full uniform and stepping into zero-g vacuum.

It all ended up involving a lot of flailing around on my so-called baseline trial—I got the virtual shit beaten out of me, lost control of the *Dragonet* and crashed it, and literally flailed around helplessly in zero-g. But it had allowed the teaching system to craft appropriate payloads to deliver into me via injection, each of which brought me up to an acceptable standard. I could at least hold my own in a fistfight. I could perform essential maneuvers in the *Dragonet* and put up a decent fight against adversarial ships, and I could prevent myself from floundering around and crashing into walls and things. I suddenly had "experience" in all of these things, albeit experience that came out of a syringe.

I sat with Santorelli in the conference room where she'd run the test. It turned out that was another universal constant, like gravitation. Conference rooms in space were the same bland, slightly soul-crushing places they were on Earth; there was no limit to what public spaces could do with variations of beige. This one could as easily have been in some hotel or convention center in Miami or Cleveland, as aboard a sprawling spaceport light years from either of those places.

"So how'd I do?" I asked her when the last question was done. Or I meant to, anyway, but I managed the *How'd* part before losing the rest in a yawn.

"Well, considering your understanding of basic legal principles before your enhancement fell somewhere deep in the *sucks* category, your performance after enhancement is quite a bit better."

"So, I sucked less, you mean?" I said, offering her a tired smile.

"Let's not get too generous," she replied, and I grinned at what I'd taken to be a rare joke. But Santorelli wasn't smiling.

I deflated. "That bad?"

"Your performance managed to get all the way up to adequate. A piece of advice—don't stray too far from Perry, especially if there are any legal issues involved. Oh, and you should get that knee of yours regenerated. It held back some of your scores, especially in that melee combat category."

"Okay, how do I do that?"

"By paying for it."

"Naturally." That was becoming a common refrain. Peacemakers were members of a large organization that was either chronically broke or just damned cheap. Either way, it seemed to leave individual Peacemakers on the hook for a lot of their own expenses. It also incentivized them to make money whenever they could.

I wondered how big a problem corruption was among Peacemakers. But it didn't seem like a very diplomatic subject to broach, so I just left it.

Instead, I sipped at what passed for coffee, at least here on Crossroads. It was apparently some ground root thing imported from some planet called Nether Reach. It was brewed like coffee but tasted like a mix between bitter cherries and boiled turnips. But it also contained something that acted like caffeine, and that was good enough for me, despite the delicate floral notes of dead flowers harvested from the bottom of an abandoned building.

I was lowering the cup again when I froze. "Wait. Don't stray too far from Perry?"

"You have a problem with that?"

"No. It's damned good advice, actually. But it also implies that I'll be spending time with Perry. Does that mean I'm in?"

Santorelli offered her first genuine smile. "Based on your performance in orientation and subsequent trials, yes, you qualify as a Peacemaker Initiate."

I laughed and shook my head. "Really? You said I sucked at the legal stuff, but honestly, I thought I sucked at almost all of it."

"You did. But that's not really the point, because very few Initiate Probationals are any good in more than one or two of the ten subject areas. What's more important is your potential. The systems assess whether it's even worth injecting you with the enhancements. In your case, it was."

"Huh." It hadn't really struck me until that moment that I'd somehow just assumed this was all a brief flight of fancy. Of course I'd never actually qualify to be a Peacemaker. Gramps was a Peacemaker, but Gramps was also a larger-than-life, almost heroic figure, a hard, skilled spec ops soldier. I was a computer nerd from Atlanta who'd somehow stumbled into the coolest vacation ever—and when it was done, I'd still be a computer nerd in Atlanta.

But now, apparently, I was a Peacemaker Initiate—

Wait. I gave Santorelli a puzzled look. "I thought I was already an Initiate."

"No, you were a Peacemaker Initiate *Probational*. Once you're invested, you lose the Probational part."

"Oh, okay. And what does that mean? I can zip around and do Peacemaker things now while oozing bravery?"

"Well, technically you have no powers or authority of your own as a Peacemaker Initiate. You'll draw them from your Senior, a Peacemaker Adept, essentially acting as their deputy."

"Oh. Alright, makes sense, I guess. And my Senior would be?"

I braced myself for it to be Gus or some other alien creature

—a blob, or maybe a sentient swarm of insectoids, which was apparently a thing. Santorelli smiled again, but she'd gone back to the thin, mostly humorless version.

"That would be me."

I raised my eyebrows and started to grin, but she raised a hand.

"Before you think I requested to be your Senior because you're just so damned good or whatever, it just worked out that way. As a matter of policy, we prefer to match new Initiates with a Senior of their own species. I happen to be the only human available."

"The way you say that has a definite *tolerating this, not loving it* vibe to it," I said.

"There's a reason for that. I don't look forward to babysitting an Initiate while trying to stay on top of my own job."

"Well, I'll do my best to avoid soiling my diapers."

Santorelli picked up her slate and stood. "And yet you will anyway. But there it is. Now, an hour break and then we'll do the Investiture. Gus will officiate. And then, work."

"I'm looking forward to it."

Santorelli just studied me for a moment, then leaned in. "I'm not. Oh, and by the way—no, I *don't* particularly like you, Clive VanAble Tudor III."

She straightened, flashed that on-off smile one more time, then left.

For a while, I just stared at the door that had closed behind her.

Well, this was going to be fun.

8

I LET Perry take the *Dragonet* out of dock, not wanting to try out my brand new piloting skills so close to the vast collision hazard that was Crossroads. As he backed the ship away from the airlock with deft puffs of thrusters, I contemplated the thing sitting in my lap.

It was a gun. Or, more correctly, two guns, a weapon called a pulse gun, with a more conventional underslung projectile weapon. The first fired a coherent pulse of energy that could be tuned from a non-lethal stun effect, to a very lethal blast effect. The second fired, well, a projectile, but not simply a bullet. It fired either a flechette round that launched four vicious darts at its target, an armor-piercing penetrator, or an explosive round that would detonate like a small grenade. A built-in folding stock allowed it to be wielded as either a pistol or a bulkier, but more accurate, carbine.

It was called The Drop, as in, getting *the drop* on someone.

And it had belonged to my grandfather.

Following the Investiture ceremony—an affair I'd expected to be mostly an officious, bureaucratic exercise, but which turned out to be surprisingly solemn and ceremonial—Santorelli led me into another conference room, gestured at a terminal, and indicated for me to sit. When I did, she placed The Drop on the table in front of me, tapped a control on the terminal, and quietly left.

The screen lit with an image of Gramps. He wore the close-fitting uniform of a Peacemaker and had three concentric circles emblazoned over his heart. That put him on par with Gus, meaning he held a fairly senior rank in the Peacemakers.

"Hello, Van. If you're watching this, then I guess I'm dead—and I'm speaking to you from beyond the graaaaavvve. . . " He laughed and waved a hand. "Sorry, couldn't resist. Anyway, you watching this means you've made it to Crossroads and have passed the orientation trials to become a Peacemaker." His eyes bored out of the screen, right into mine. "I'm proud of you, Van. I always have been. I know you thought your dad and I were disappointed that you didn't pursue a career in the military. We weren't. Or, maybe we were, but we were disappointed *for* you, not *in* you."

Gramps went on to give me what amounted to a pep talk, the sort of thing I frankly usually find hokey, but it left tears in my eyes. He then went on to bequeath The Drop to me, saying, "She's served me well and gotten me out of more than a few scrapes. And in case you're wondering why I didn't leave her on the *Dragonet* for you to find on Earth, well, I guess I wanted to make sure you'd decided to become a Peacemaker first. Leaving it here with Gus seemed like a good way to do that. I'm handing you over, in a sense, to good people—people in my trusted circle, of superior quality. You'll fit with them because that's who you are, Van. It's your core, and it's the reason why I go into the beyond knowing that you're going to succeed, and more."

Gramps had glanced down, then up again, his eyes bright with emotion. "Anyway, I'll end with this. Trust Perry and Netty. The three of us were a team, and you should consider them that way, too. They're family now, just as they were to me." He sighed. "And that's it. When I end this recording, I'm also ending my career as a Peacemaker. My health isn't getting any better, and even if I could afford all the regeneration therapies, I probably wouldn't. You just reach a point where it's time to stop and say enough. Take some time to sit and—sit. That's it, just sit."

He ended with a tired smile. "Take care, Van. I love you, kid. This is your Gramps, signing off."

It had taken a while then before I could get my eyes to stop stinging. Now, sitting in the *Dragonet*'s pilot's seat, The Drop in my lap, I had exactly the same problem.

"Van?"

I wiped my eyes and turned to Perry. He lowered his head.

"Yeah, I miss him, too," he said.

"Me too," Netty put in.

I made myself smile. "Thanks, guys. Anyway, Perry, you wanted something?"

"Yeah. A destination."

"Uh—I thought Santorelli was going to upload some cases she wanted me to start working on."

"She has, but there's one problem. Fuel. You can get *to* any of these cases, but that'll be the end of the line, unless you can earn some bonds to refuel the *Dragonet*."

"Don't the Peacemakers cover any of that? Like, don't I get an expense account or something?"

"You get a stipend, based on your rank and record. And you did. Your first installment arrived only a couple of hours ago."

"Alright. So what am I missing here? We've already got money, right?"

Perry cocked his head. "We did. And we used it to refuel the *Dragonet* so you can leave Ross 248."

"So I'm broke again."

"Pretty much. You could probably pay for a pretty decent dinner."

I sighed. I had a sinking feeling that finances were going to prove to be an ongoing headache. "So what do you suggest?"

"Perry and I recommend heading for Procyon. There's a Quiet Room on a moon orbiting the fourth planet. Your grandfather kept his main account there," Netty said.

Just a couple of days ago, I would have needed that all explained to me. However, thanks to the neural enhancements, I simply knew what Perry was talking about. The Quiet Room was, in effect, a bank, with branches scattered throughout known space. They were a neutral organization, existing apart from every other independent star system, interstellar state, guild, syndicate, or corporate body, that underwrote and regulated the standard currency, the bond. And, just to make things awkward, bonds had no digital format. They were physical tokens that could be exchanged like good old US dollar bills, British pound notes, or any other Earthly currency in pre-internet times.

On the face of it, it seemed like a massive step backward, considering how advanced all this extraterrestrial technology was. But it actually made good sense. If there were anything resembling an interstellar internet, it was a hodgepodge of mismatched computer systems of wildly varying sophistication, tech-level, and security flung across hundreds of light-years of space. There was simply no way to ensure the integrity of electronic transactions transmitted through such a chaotic mess, and across the gulfs between stars, at that.

I put The Drop aside, then turned my attention to the *Dragonet*'s controls. They made sense to me now. Netty still did most of the routine flying, which generally involved long stretches of keeping the ship traveling in a straight line. And she or Perry had to, by regulation, perform all docking and undocking maneuvers within one hundred klicks of a licensed station or facility, at least until I got properly certified.

Properly certified. To fly a spaceship. I chuckled and shook my head.

"What's so funny?" Perry asked.

I looked at him. "Life. The universe. Everything. I mean, there are seven billion people on Earth who struggle with the big questions, including, are we alone? Or is there life out here?" I chuckled again. "It turns out there is, and it can certify you to dock at space stations if you pay the requisite fees and pass the required tests. It's like, I don't know, finally clawing your way off the surface of Earth and flying into the boundless, awesome mystery of space—and finding out the DMV is already there, issuing freakin' permits."

WE WERE ABOUT three hours out of Crossroads, and I was taking the opportunity to fly the *Dragonet* myself for the very first time. In fully manual mode, without any assistance from Netty, it was like trying to control a speeding sled on glare ice, except the sled and the ice existed in three dimensions, and you had a dozen different inputs that could shove you in virtually any direction. The first time, I managed to put the ship into a sort of corkscrewing spin that Perry claimed even an experienced pilot would find it hard to duplicate.

I took my hands off the controls and let Netty get us back under control. "Okay, that's nothing like the simulator. Who the hell uses fully manual mode to fly anyway?"

"Two types of pilots," Perry replied. "The ones who have no choice because of damage or systems failures or whatever, and the ones who choose to do it anyway because if you manage to get good at it, it makes you a *really* dangerous opponent in battle."

"That's why most pilots routinely use semi-auto mode. You make the control inputs, and I interpret them to accomplish what you want," Netty said.

We tried it, and what a massive difference. Now, if I used the side stick to indicate a course change to the left, Netty fired all the necessary thrusters, in all the necessary sequences and with all the necessary timings to result in a smooth, arcing turn to the left.

I nodded. "Okay, that's way better—"

"Van, we have a bit of a problem," Netty suddenly cut in.

My gut knotted up. A *bit of a problem* in a spaceship could get very deadly, very fast, something I knew from my recently injected experience as a pilot. That same experience had me sweep my gaze across the three display panels and the heads-up, looking for cautions and alarms. I found only one, though, a power-control display that glowed yellow instead of green.

"We're, uh… losing some power it looks like?"

"That's right. The ship's systems are demanding a certain amount of power from the reactor, but slightly more power than that is actually being drawn," Netty replied.

"Oh." I considered that, but none of my brand new memories seemed to cover it. "So what does that mean? Do we have to go back to Crossroads?"

"The difference is only zero-point-eight percent, so it's within acceptable limits. But it shouldn't be there at all. I'm trying to narrow down where it's happening."

I let Netty resume complete control of the *Dragonet*, and just waited. As I did, I glanced at Perry. "Maybe I broke something?"

"Not likely. The *Dragonet's* actually a tough little ship. What she lacks in internal space and amenities, she makes up for in durability."

"Good to know."

Netty spoke up. "I've deployed Waldo to check over some

components, and they're all fine. It seems like the power's being drawn through a ground-port on the exterior of the ship."

A ground-port. Right. The *Dragonet* could draw power through umbilical hookups when she was docked, and she had several external ports for just that purpose. Netty flashed up a stylized schematic of the ship, highlighting the balky port. It was left-side—or, rather, port side—rear.

"It's almost like there's something out there that's tapped into that port and is drawing power from it," Perry said.

"Are you saying someone attached something to the *Dragonet*?" I asked.

Perry lifted and lowered his wings in that shrug of his. "Maybe. But there were no security alerts. Moreover, we were docked on the Peacemaker module, which is probably the most secure part of Crossroads to begin with."

"And, yet, here we are," I said.

"Yup, here we are."

"So, Netty, what do you recommend we do?" I asked.

"An external examination of the ship makes the most sense."

"Sounds good."

A moment passed, but nothing happened.

"Netty?"

"Right here."

"Are you doing that external examination you mentioned?"

"No."

"Uh, why not?"

"Because I can't. We don't have any external maintenance remotes."

My gut had mostly unclenched, but it lost a bit of ground as an uneasy feeling started to take hold. "What about Waldo?"

"He's not equipped for external work. He'd just drift away."

I looked at Perry. "Oh, shit. Are you guys saying that *I* have to go out there?"

"We're not saying anything, Van. If you're content to leave whatever's out there, well, out there, doing whatever it does, then there's no problem, right?"

"I've got a little over one hour in zero-g and vacuum, and half of that was spent proving just how good at handling it I *wasn't*. How come there isn't some system to do this—like that maintenance remote thing Netty just mentioned?"

"There is. The *Dragonet* had just such a system installed, in fact. But your grandfather—"

"Let me guess. He offered someone a lien on it, and they came and took it when he died."

"You're catching onto this pretty fast," Perry said.

I slumped back in the seat, glancing down at The Drop as I did. As much as I appreciated Gramps bequeathing me the old and trusty weapon, I was starting to think a fat bankroll would have been a lot more useful.

I allowed myself a sigh of disgust, then unharnessed, grabbed my helmet, and headed for the airlock. My body went through all the motions like clockwork, thanks to the enhancements. But those same enhancements did nothing for my gut, which had now knotted knots around knots at the thought of stepping into that airless void.

I GRIPPED A HOLD-ON, a small metal half-loop protruding from the *Dragonet*'s hull. "Hey, this isn't as bad as I'd expected."

Perry answered. "Really?"

"Yeah, really. It's way, *way* worse."

I ended with a nervous laugh and contemplated the next hold. It was, by design, close enough for me to reach, but it looked to be a million klicks away. Beyond it, the *Dragonet*'s hull formed a sort of miniature horizon where it curved back toward the rear end of the ship. It left me inhabiting a tiny world about ten meters across, surrounded by—nothing. Absolutely nothing.

The zero-g course back on Crossroads hadn't really prepared me for this. It had been an enclosed space, but there was nothing *enclosed* about this. Everywhere I looked that wasn't the *Dragonet* was an endless plunge into infinite blackness. And by plunge, I mean *plunge*, because no matter what direction I turned, it felt like down. Vertigo buzzed around the back of my mind like an unseen hornet. Any second, it would sting me with nauseating dizziness, and I'd be stuck out here, disoriented and helpless, until I either got control of myself or ran out of air.

I took a breath, loud inside my helmet, and muttered away to myself. "Okay. Okay, Van, just grab that next hold. That's it. That's right. Hand out, fingers closing—there, you got it. Now, pull yourself to it and start concentrating on the next one—"

"We don't really need the running commentary, Van," Perry said, his voice crackling over the comm.

"I'm not doing it for you," I hissed, turning and making sure my tether wasn't fouling on anything behind me. There was that. I was tethered to the ship, so the worst that would happen would be a slow drift until the tether went taut. My brain knew that, at least. My gut, not so much.

About a thousand years later, I finally reached the balky port. Right away, I saw something that was *wrong*. A small, roughly rectangular box not much longer than my hand, was inserted into the port. Placed the way it was, and colored the same medium grey of the hull, it was virtually invisible to casual inspection. My helmet camera transmitted the image to Perry and Netty.

"Any idea what this thing is?" I asked.

Perry answered. "It's a box."

"No shit."

"Sorry, Van, but we can't really be more specific. It's literally a box. Whatever's inside it is something we'd have to find out by opening it."

"You can't, like, scan it or anything?"

"The *Dragonet*'s scanners aren't meant for that sort of work. There are portable rigs that could do it, but we don't have one of those aboard—and no, we didn't have one your grandfather bargained away. They're just pretty damned expensive."

"So I get the sinking feeling I'm supposed to retrieve this... this *box*, and bring it back inside with me."

"Either that, or we ignore it and let it continue doing whatever it's doing, or you remove it and just throw it into space, or you destroy it in place. I think that about covers the options, right?" Netty said.

As we'd been talking, I'd pulled myself closer to the device, so now it was just a couple of meters away. I was actually starting to get the hang of this zero-g thing. I had to admit that the enhancement I'd been given worked pretty well. Without it, I'd be a blubbering mess out here. With it, I wasn't quite blubbering *or* a mess.

"So we have *no* idea what this thing is," I said.

"If I had to guess, I'd say it's probably a data tap. It's probably recording information about our course, flight data, all that stuff, and it might even be able to sneak itself into our comm traffic," Perry said.

"Not a very good data tap, though, since we detected it," Netty put in.

"Might be defective, or it wasn't installed correctly."

I cut in. "So, what you guys are telling me is that it's probably not dangerous."

"That's right," Netty said.

"Well, unless it's a bomb," Perry added. "In that case, it would be really dangerous, of course."

I'd been reaching for it but now yanked my hand back.

Big mistake.

The movement spun me around the hold-on I was gripping, twisting my wrist free. And the resulting motion of that started me slowly sailing away from the *Dragonet*. I flung out a desperate hand, trying to hang on, but that only started a slow spin.

"Shit I lost my grip shit—!"

Perry spoke up. "Van?"

"Can't reach oh shit this is—!"

"Van!"

I flailed around, saw something sweep across my field of view, grabbed at it—

And it went taut, bringing me to a dead stop about ten meters away from the ship.

The tether.

"Oh. Well then. Okay, the tether stopped me."

"Which was just what I was trying to tell you," Perry replied.

I took a moment to let my breath and heartbeat slow from machine-gun fast to something not *quite* machine-gun fast. Then I grabbed the tether and pulled myself, hand-over-hand, back to the ship.

"Well, there's a year or two from my life I didn't need," I said, finally grabbing the structure of the *Dragonet* again. Strangely, though, I no longer felt quite so near-panicky out here in the yawning void. That stark burst of terror seemed to have burned a lot of it away, leaving me wrung out but also feeling more in control.

"So we were talking about that being a bomb," Netty said.

I pulled myself back to within arm's reach of the device. It meant nothing to me, but somehow, it being a bomb didn't feel right. Given the available tech, a bomb shouldn't need to be externally powered. Hell, even an Earthly bomb could run off batteries. I explained my reasoning to Netty and Perry, and they both agreed. As much as they could, anyway.

Netty had more information to share now, too. "While you were off doing your little spacewalk, I was able to establish that the thing isn't just drawing power, it's also tapped into the data port in the umbilical receptacle. It's firewalled against intrusion pretty well, but I don't think it's a weapon."

I glanced at the status display on my suit's heads-up. I still had over ninety minutes of oxygen left. So, for the next twenty minutes, I sat tight and took in the breathtaking view of nothing but impossibly distant stars and waited while Netty carefully probed the device more fully. Finally, she pronounced her assessment.

"I'm virtually certain it's not a bomb."

"*Virtually* certain?"

"That's as good as it's going to get, Van, sorry," Netty replied.

I stared at the device for a moment, then shrugged.

"To hell with it," I muttered, then I grabbed it and yanked it out of the port.

"Okay, Van, the first thing you should do, before you even touch it, is to examine it for any markings or writing," Perry said.

I looked at the device, firmly clutched in my gloved hand, and started to laugh.

I WAVED a hand at the device, sitting on the deck inside the airlock. "You said it *wasn't* a bomb."

"No, I said I was *virtually certain* it wasn't a bomb," Netty shot back.

Perry cocked his head at it. "It might also have *contained* a bomb to prevent tampering."

I put my hands on my hips. I stood clad only in shorts, in dire need of a shower to strip away the sticky, anxious sweat. But I also wanted to resolve the mystery of the enigmatic device.

I finally settled on a shower, reasoning that if Netty couldn't penetrate its firewalls, then there was likely nothing I could do that she couldn't.

For now, anyway. As I learned more about how all this tech worked, I'd definitely revisit this.

I stashed the device in a storage locker, turned toward the tiny lavatory, and paused. "Who would have done that, I wonder?"

Perry did his head cock at me. "What? Attach that device to the *Dragonet*?"

"Yeah. I'm a Peacemaker, sure, but I've still got that new Peacemaker smell." I looked down at my still-unshowered self, sniffed, and wrinkled my nose. "Actually, it's more of a ripe, sweaty Peacemaker smell. But still—who'd be interested enough in me to bother?"

"No idea. Whoever it was, though, was able to bypass both Netty's local security and the security measures of the Peacemaker module. That implies someone with skill, resources, or more likely both."

"Maybe it's not you they're interested in. Maybe it's your grandfather," Netty suggested.

I nodded. That was certainly a possibility, too.

I blew out a long sigh and finally headed for the shower. It was a mystery that was just going to have to wait because I had to fly off in my powerful, armed spaceship to a distant star system—

To do some banking.

9

PROCYON BLEW Sol away in nearly every way. It was bigger, heavier, and much brighter, its light a searing white. A small white dwarf companion star was lost somewhere in the glare. Like Sol, the system had nine planets—two of them were Earth-like, one skirting the inner edge of the Goldilocks Zone, the other slipping around its outer limit. The next planet closer to the star likely could have been Earth-like if its surface hadn't been scoured to the bedrock by heat and stellar radiation. One of the remaining planets was a gas giant, and a big one at that, one and a half times the size of Jupiter, and the rest were barren hunks of rock.

So that was all the technical stuff about the system. What left me sitting in the *Dragonet*'s cockpit, staring dumbly at the approaching star, was the simple fact of the place. Crossroads had been stunning in its own way, but this was different. These were other Earths. Whole planets, with atmospheres and oceans and complex ecosystems. And two of them, at that. Somehow, it left me awestruck in a way that Crossroads hadn't.

"There's plenty more where that came from," Perry said, and I just nodded. I'm sure there was.

Netty flew the *Dragonet* along the approach trajectory given to us by The Quiet Room's traffic control AI. Apparently, the Quiet Room was more than just a bank. It functioned like a nation-state in its own right, handling its own traffic control around its facilities, seeing to its own defense, and even possessing its own police force and military assets. I was starting to get a picture of what the Quiet Room was all about, and it made me a little uneasy. They did control essentially all of the money, after all, which made them immensely powerful. It was as though one of the low-key tax havens back on Earth had suddenly acquired superpower status. To me, that just screamed out the potential for abuse and corruption.

Not that it mattered right now. Today, I just wanted to withdraw some money. Netty neatly landed the *Dragonet* on the largest of two moons of the fourth planet, the more distant of the two Earths. The ship settled onto one of six large circular pads which, once the engines were shut down, began to sink beneath the surface. When we reached bottom, a good fifty meters down, huge doors irised closed over the top, and the big space pressurized over the course of the next ten minutes.

I'd cleaned myself up and was wearing my Peacemaker uniform without helmet. The arrival message from The Quiet Room had made it clear that all weapons had to be kept locked up aboard visiting ships, so I went unarmed. Perry hopped along beside me as we walked away from the *Dragonet*, his talons hitting the floor with a rhythmic, metallic *ting-ting-ting* as we went.

Ahead of us, a door slid open and someone stepped out. I braced myself for tentacles and eyestems and the like but found myself facing a very human-looking woman, red-haired and handsome, with a somewhat severe edge, probably in her late thirties or early forties. Her blue eyes fixed me with a penetrating stare.

"Welcome to The Quiet Room, Position 61," she said, her voice smoothly cultured, obviously honed after a multitude of greetings and dealing with clients.

"Can I ask you to confirm your identity, please?" she asked.

"Uh, Clive VanAbel Tudor III," I said, then glanced down at my uniform. "Oh. Right. Peacemaker Initiate." I shrugged and smiled. "I'm still getting used to that."

A faint smile played across her lips. "You're new to this, aren't you?"

"How'd you guess?"

She answered by holding up something that looked like a slim cell phone. "Can I get you to speak your full name again? We need to do a biometric confirmation of your identity."

I did as she asked, and the device beeped. She glanced at it, nodded, and looked back at me.

"Peacemaker Tudor, I'm Dayna Jasskin. I'll be your customer service representative for your business today. Please follow me," she said and turned back to the door through which she'd entered the bay.

Perry and I followed her along a corridor to a hub-like junction. The walls were colored in various pastel shades, which I gathered meant something. We followed baby blue to a cozy office, one of whose walls offered an amazing, panoramic view of—

"That's Zagreb, in Croatia," Dayna said. "My hometown."

For a moment, I stared at the cityscape. I gazed out from a fourth or fifth story vantage point, over a bustling street busy with pedestrians and start-and-stop traffic.

"That's just an image, right?" I asked.

She smiled. "Well, since we're beneath the surface of a moon, orbiting a planet about twelve light-years from Earth, then it's not likely to be the real thing, now is it?"

I turned to her with a shrug. "You said it yourself—I'm new to all this. You could have told me that was a portal straight back into your office in Zagreb, and I'd have probably believed it."

"Fair enough," she said, gesturing for me to sit in a remarkably comfortable chair across the polished wood desk from hers. "Now then, what can we do for you today?"

"I'd like to withdraw whatever funds I've got here."

"So are you closing your account?"

Perry interrupted. "No, he's not. Rather, he would like to withdraw eighty percent of the funds he has here and then transfer the remainder to a Quiet Room Position as yet to be determined," Perry said.

I glanced at him, then shrugged. "What he said. He's the expert."

Dayna smiled again, then touched a glowing spot on her desk. "Chensun, would you come in here please?"

A moment passed, then a door behind and to one side of the desk slid open. Another—person—entered. Humanoid, but obviously not human, Chensun stood at least a few centimeters taller than I did and had skin pale enough to almost rate being called white, a strikingly long and thin nose, and blue-tinged black hair in three braids. I had no idea if Chensun was male or female or, for that matter, if that even applied to—I settled on *them* as a pronoun.

"The Peacemaker wants to withdraw eighty percent of his current funds account and place the remainder in a transfer token, destination yet to be confirmed," Dayna said.

Chensun looked at me for a moment, as though I were some new item on a familiar menu. Finally, they shook their head. "This individual has no account here."

"It was my grandfather's. He bequeathed it to me—*dammit.*"

Dayna raised an eyebrow. "Problem?"

"It just struck me I never brought along his will, or any sort of legal paperwork." I turned helplessly to Perry. How was I going to prove what I was claiming? This was a bank, after all, and one thing banks *didn't* tend to do was take the word of strangers off the proverbial street that some of the money in their vault just happened to be theirs, now, and could they please have it?

Perry, though, was ready for that. "I have transfer certificates, signed off by the relevant and competent authority of the Galactic Knights Uniformed, confirming that Clive VanAbel Tudor III is the beneficiary of his grandfather's estate in its entirety, including the funds held here."

If someone had told me only a few weeks ago I'd be sitting in an office light-years from Earth, ready to kiss a mechanical bird right on his alloy beak—well, here we were.

Perry must have done some sort of data transfer while he was speaking because a little rectangle popped open in mid-air, just above Dayna's desk. She and Chensun both examined it, then Dayna nodded. "This seems to be in order."

"Peacemaker Tudor has six thousand four hundred and sixty-one bonds in his account. He is requesting to withdraw five thousand one hundred and sixty-two, with the balance being placed in a pending transfer token," Chensun said, then turned their mild gaze on me. "Might I recommend the funds be placed into a high-interest investment account until the transfer token is activated? This will generate a more favorable return for you. Or, as an alternative—"

Chensun went on to rattle through several options, all of which seemed to involve either investing or locking-in my money in various ways, for various interest returns, over various periods—

There was a reason I'd always tended to stay away from the financial side of cyber-ops. I wouldn't call myself irresponsible with my money, but I'd always had a, *here's money, here are things I need or want to spend it on, done* sort of approach to finances. I turned to Perry as Chensun was speaking and gave him a helpless look.

He spoke up again. "A high-interest investment account is fine. We don't want to lock up those funds because we're going to need them."

I glanced back at Dayna. "I'm new to this."

"You don't say."

"Yeah, well, it also means that I don't really have a grip on how your money policy works."

"Or any actual income, for that matter," Perry put in.

I glanced at him, a little surprised he'd just blurt that out. Of course, maybe not talking openly about your finances was an Earth thing. In any case, he wasn't wrong, so I just turned back to Dayna with a shrug. "That's kind of at the top of the to-do list—start earning money. I'm coming to realize that flying around the galaxy fighting evil ain't cheap."

Dayna actually laughed, then shook her head. "Sorry, I don't spend much time around humans these days—especially brash ones, charming in their own sort of naïve way."

Charming? She thinks I'm *charming*?

Nice.

Dayna glanced up at Chensun. "Would you excuse us, please?"

The alien nodded once, then quietly withdrew.

"They seem nice," I said, but Dayna surprisingly shook her head.

"The Vela are many things, but I wouldn't use the word nice. They're efficient. More to the point, they can handle numbers and calculations the way you and I might approach walking upright—it's just something they naturally do. Even better, they have no actual interest in money beyond its numeric properties."

"Walking calculators with no interest in cash? They sound like the perfect bankers."

"Indeed they are. Anyway, Peacemaker—"

"Please, it's Van."

"Alright, Van, I have a thought regarding your lack of income," Dayna said.

Perry leaned toward me. "Don't accept any liens on the *Dragonet*, or anything else," he hissed.

Dayna smiled. "I wasn't thinking of borrowing. Although, if you're interested, we do have a range of financial solutions available, assuming you've got the required collateral—"

"I'll stick with my financial expert's advice here, thanks. Borrowing money isn't really going to work."

"A good choice, but hey, I'm a banker, I'm supposed to try and sell our services, right?"

I nodded. "Naturally."

"However, there is another way you could earn some income, by leveraging your particular talents and status as a Peacemaker."

"Oh. I'm listening. What's the job?"

"Van, you might want to hear the details before you accept it," Perry said.

I glanced at him, then back to Dayna. "Again, I'll go with my advisor here."

Dayna chuckled. "This job is perfect for you, a brand-new Peacemaker. Essentially, we have a debt that needs to be collected."

Once more, I glanced at Perry, but he said nothing. Dayna went on.

"It's an in-system job, so you won't have to deal with extra-system costs like fuel. I can provide a mission file with all of the details, but what it amounts to is this. There's a man on Sunward

—that's the next terrestrial planet located, well, *sunward* of this one—named Wil-Stur."

"Wil-Stur. Okay. And what's his deal?"

"He acquired a weapons printer, whose cost was underwritten by The Quiet Room. It's part of some scheme he has to reclaim his birthright, some orbital fortress or something like that in a nearby system. Anyway, he stopped making payments on the printer some months ago and has essentially ignored every communication from us since then." She smiled sweetly. "We would like the money he owes us, plus owed interest, or the printer itself."

"Back on Earth, you'd just send someone to repossess it."

"Yes, but imagine that we were back on Earth and the thing we wanted to repossess was in the hands of some terrorist group. You don't just send around some bored magistrate with some repo paperwork, right?"

"Yeah, I guess not," I said, frowning a little at the idea of facing something Dayna was describing as a *terrorist group*. "So why hasn't anyone else picked up this job?"

Beside me, Perry stretched out a wing and tapped my arm. "Way to ask the right questions, Van."

I glanced at him, wondering if this was sarcasm. But Perry was a mechanical bird, and trying to figure out if a mechanical bird is being sarcastic is, unsurprisingly, not easy. That said, though, he didn't follow up with anything, so I took it as sincere and got a little burst of pride from it.

"Frankly, the job doesn't pay all that well for the amount of work involved. The fee is twenty thousand bonds, with five thousand upfront, and the balance payable on return of either the printer or the full value of the outstanding account."

Twenty thousand bonds. It sure seemed like a lot until I actually took a moment to think it through. The twist drive had consumed just over four thousand bonds in antimatter fuel to get here. And those words, *terrorist group*, still loomed pretty large.

"If it makes you feel better, the issue is probably less one of actual danger and more one of aggravation," Dayna added.

I raised an eyebrow at her, and she sighed. "Wil-Stur, not to put too fine a point on it, is a raving nutcase, mixed with a healthy dose of complete asshole. I said terrorist group, but I should have said delusional, wild-eyed crazy person. His *army of the revolution*, as he calls it, consists of about a dozen people, half of them crazy themselves, and the other half just opportunistic leeches siphoning off his family's remaining fortune."

"He has a family fortune?"

"He did. When his father died, he became obsessed with recovering his family's ancestral seat of power—that would be the old space station a system or two away. Over the three years since, he's taken a large sum of money and turned it into a small sum of money and a lot of crazy talk and really bad decisions." Dayna leaned on her desk. "Bottom line—no one wants to deal with this guy."

"Why the hell would you loan someone like that money to begin with?" I asked.

"Good question, but my predecessor would have to be the one to answer it. He would be the one currently without a job."

"Ah." I turned to Perry. "Any reason we shouldn't take this on?"

"Yes. Lots of them. And were you an established Peacemaker with a healthy bank account and regular income, I'd definitely tell you to pass, it just isn't worth the effort for twenty-K bonds. But you're not, and you don't, so it's this or hope you can find something better before the money runs out."

I tugged at my lip, thinking. My available funds left the *Dragonet* able to make one twist, maybe two. And if I hadn't found some income by then, I'd be spending some time—maybe *lots* of it—in whatever system I ended up in.

I turned back to Dayna. "What the hell. Collecting a debt from a crazy guy isn't exactly the stuff of epic legend, but you gotta start somewhere, right?"

10

WHILE NETTY MADE the flight from Outward, on whose moon The Quiet Room was located, to Sunward, the innermost of the two terrestrial planets, I reviewed the file Dayna had provided. It basically recapped what she'd already told me.

Wil-Stur was twenty four years old, so a little younger than me, the scion of a wealthy family who'd made their fortune through several generations of mundane but lucrative, interstellar trade. Wil-Stur, upon his father's death, had inherited this fortune and immediately proceeded to blow it on a succession of wild schemes to reclaim the old space station orbiting Luyten's Star only a few light-years away. It turned out his family had briefly owned the station before Wil-Stur's grandfather had apparently sold it—at a tidy profit, at that—to some corporation. Based on the file, it had all been on the up-and-up. No one had stolen anything from Wil-Stur's family.

But the man himself—and he was a man, another human— simply couldn't or wouldn't accept that. He emptied the family coffers in increasingly insane schemes to take the station back, involving spies, mercenaries, and even an alleged attempted assassination. The latter had been decisively thwarted when it turned out the target, a regional executive probably entirely unaware of Wil-Stur's existence, had died two years previously from natural causes.

"This guy, Wil-Stur, has loser written all over him," I said, looking up from the slate.

Perry bobbed his head. "He's far from the most aberrant case I've ever heard of, but he's definitely up there."

I thought through the legal ramifications, based on my newly acquired knowledge. "Since I'm doing this as a private contract on behalf of The Quiet Room, I don't have the full powers of a Peacemaker, right? I still need a warrant if I want to, ah, arrest the guy."

"That's right," Perry replied.

"So what if he just tells me to piss off? Doesn't that leave us kind of stuck?"

"Yes and no. Yes, because ordinarily, as a Peacemaker, and especially as an Initiate working freelance, your powers would be quite limited. You could apply for a warrant, if one hadn't already been issued. But you'd have to get Adept Santorelli to sign off—"

"And she probably wouldn't."

"For something like this? Probably not."

"So you said yes and no. What's the *no* part?"

"The Quiet Room. They've effectively hired you to do this job. They carry a *huge* amount of clout, and as long as they're willing to back you, you're probably in the clear."

"Good to know."

I settled back in the seat and watched the planet called Sunward grow first from a faint dot to a shining point, and then to a distinct disk. Wil-Stur had apparently hunkered down on an orbital platform he still owned, sitting in geosynchronous orbit about fifty thousand kilometers above Sunward's equator.

I had to smile at that. Fifty thousand klicks. That was about ten thousand klicks more than the circumference of the Earth. Not that long ago, I'd have considered it an unimaginably vast distance. Now, though, it seemed like nothing, just a quick jaunt.

It was funny how quickly you could get used to changes in your perception of the world around you—even if those changes involved essentially rebooting your understanding of the whole freakin' universe.

We flew on a while longer, then Netty spoke up.

"Van, just as you asked, we're on an approach trajectory to Wil-Stur's orbital platform, which, incidentally, he's named the Sanctum of Righteous Fury."

"The Sanctum of Righteous Fury? Really?"

"I kid you not." The central console and its tactical display flicked to an image of the surrounding volume of space. Sure enough, among the little icons representing other ships presumably going about their business, and sundry other satellites and orbital platforms, one stood starkly out.

The Sanctum of Righteous Fury.

"Does it actually show up as that on the official charts?"

"It does. He's actually trademarked the name, and done all of the legal paperwork to have it formally recognized."

"This guy really *is* a nutcase."

"And a belligerent one," Netty went on. "The Sanctum has lit us up with fire-control scanners."

Thanks to my implanted knowledge, I knew exactly what that meant. It was a markedly hostile act and immediately authorized me to use lethal force in self-defense.

I shifted in the seat. On the way here, I'd focused on the *crazy* aspect of Wil-Stur and not paid too much attention to the *dangerous* one. I shoved aside the complacency and made myself sit up.

"Okay, Netty. Let's—ah, shit. Let's see. I've got this." My mind raced through the possible responses. I could have just asked Perry or Netty for their recommendations, but I wanted to start doing this on my own. They seemed content to wait.

"Okay. Let's switch the laser into autonomous defensive fire mode," I said.

"Done," Netty replied.

"And now, let's try out my mad new diplomacy skills. Netty, send a message to Wil-Stur. Let's try this. This is Peacemaker Van Tudor, acting on behalf of The Quiet Room. I've come to recover the weapons printer you have, or the money you owe for it, plus interest. I look forward to resolving this situation amicably—"

"Van?"

"Just a second, Netty. I'm on a roll here. I look forward to resolving this situation amicably and hope that we can—"

"Van."

I glared at the tactical display, which seemed as good a place as any to make my displeasure at being interrupted known to Netty. But the tactical display glared right back at me, showing a launch alert. Wil-Stur's *Sanctum of Righteous Fury* had just fired a missile at us.

"Well, shit. He's shooting at us."

"Which is what I was trying to tell you," Netty replied, sounding a little annoyed.

"Yeah, my bad, sorry about that." I was still getting used to interpreting what the tactical display was telling me, but it seemed to show the incoming missile behaving pretty erratically. It would accelerate, then coast, change course, coast some more, accelerate again, and once more change direction. The overall result was that the missile's initial flight time to reach us had gone from six minutes, to just over five.

"At this rate, that missile's going to run out of fuel long before it reaches us, isn't it?"

"It is. I'd suggest that it's a clever ploy, but it's frankly not," Netty replied.

"It suggests that either its guidance AI is malfunctioning, or Wil-Stur is flying the damned thing manually," Perry added.

I snorted derisively. "Well, he is a nutcase—"

"I have an incoming transmission from none other than the man of the hour, Wil-Stur himself," Netty cut in.

"This oughta be good. Go ahead and put him on," I said.

An image popped open of a man with tousled blond hair, a chubby face, and eyes of such a pale blue they appeared more off-white, a disconcerting color for human eyes. He leaned into the image.

"Spare me your counter-revolutionary lies," he spat. "Minions of the authoritarian despots are not welcome here."

I held up a hand. "Okay, woah. Let's back up here a bit. My name's Van Tudor, and I'm a—"

"Peacemaker, yes, I know. A pawn of the autocrats that seek to control all of known space. Tell your masters that I have seen through their plan to seize the property of hardworking citizens, and I won't have it! I won't!"

I just stared. *Nutcase* was spot on.

The missile was now just under four minutes out, on a trajectory that would see it miss us by at least hundred klicks. Netty kept tracking it with the laser, just in case, but I decided to ignore it.

"Look, how about we just talk," I suggested. "I'll come aboard your Sanctum of Righteous Fury, alone, and we'll talk, see if we can work something out."

Wil-Stur's eyes narrowed. "Why should I trust you?"

"Not saying you should. But you shouldn't automatically distrust me either."

"You're an agent of the galactic oppressors."

"Actually, I'm a brand *new* agent of the galactic oppressors, who's more interested in keeping his ship fueled up than doing any, ah, oppressing."

Wil-Stur stared back at me, eyes still narrowed. I decided to try and seal the deal.

"Hey, look at it this way. If you can work things out with me, just a lone Peacemaker and his AI bird, then you won't have to worry about the galactic oppressors sending bigger forces down the road. That way, you can stay focused on restoring your family's ancestral property instead of fending off the autocrats or whatever, right?"

Wil-Stur stared a moment longer, then nodded once. "I suppose it's not an unreasonable suggestion. I have one condition, however."

"What's that?"

"That I be allowed to make my case to you, and that you, in turn, commit to bringing my grievances before your masters. I want them to understand just what is at stake here."

The man's disturbing pale eyes seemed to bore out of the image at me. I nodded.

"Agreed, as long as you call off that missile you shot."

Wil-Stur answered by reaching for something off-screen. A moment later, the missile vanished with a dazzling flash.

"He successfully destroyed the missile—which, I might point out, was armed with an illegal fusion warhead," Netty said.

I sighed. "One thing at a time, guys. One thing at a time."

THE SANCTUM OF RIGHTEOUS FURY turned out to be a disused traffic control platform, long-since supplanted by a more modern, distributed system of AI-controlled satellites. The platform had been sold off as surplus, picked up by Wil-Stur's family for some purpose now lost to time, and remained one of the few assets he held.

After exiting the airlock, we entered a dimly lit corridor with muggy, stale air that reeked faintly of ozone and oil, with a whiff of hot insulation. Perry had urged me to bring my helmet, clipped to the back of my belt, and now I understood why. Sudden decompression of the decrepit station seemed like a definite possibility.

We were met by a small bot on balloon tires. It instructed us to follow it in a tinny, mechanical voice. Perry actually sniffed.

"Second-gen AI at best. It's probably worth money as a collectible."

As we fell in behind the bot, I glanced down at him, hopping along with me, and offered a wry smile. "So there's a pecking order among AIs?"

"Pecking order? Is that supposed to be a joke?"

"Well, no, but now that you mention it—" I grinned. "If the beak fits and all that."

"Ha ha, no, stop it, Van, my sides are starting to hurt from laughing so much. Anyway, yes, you're damned right there's a pecking order among AIs. I'm an eighth-gen. State of the art."

"Is there a ninth-gen?"

"Why would there be? I mean, seriously, how could you improve on *this*?"

He spread his wings. I rolled my eyes.

The old bot led us through a labyrinth of dark, reeking corridors, past compartments that were either stuffed with junk or completely empty. A few had exposed power conduits and skeins of optical cable dangling from racks and mounts where equipment had been removed. That oily, slightly acrid stink still lingered, and in a few places the air seemed slightly hazed with a fume of—something.

"I grew up with ideas of spaceships being all clean and tidy, mostly white, covered in gold foil," I said, eyeing some viscous fluid dripping out of an open pipe. "This is more like a bar I used to hang out in during my college days, right after closing time. Throw in a couple of fistfights and someone staggering around in their underwear, and it's a perfect match."

The bot stopped at a door, extended a mechanical gripper, and rapped on it, loudly. A moment passed, then the door scraped partially open. Wil-Stur's face appeared in the gap.

"Are you alone?"

I glanced around. "I don't know. I can only see Perry and your little bot thing here, but I'm not sure if there's anyone else around. Why, are you expecting someone?"

Wil-Stur's mouth opened and closed a few times. Finally, he opened the door fully and waved me in. He almost caught Perry's tail slamming it shut.

"Excuse me, but that's carbon-nanosheet reinforced, layered alloy-composite back there, and it ain't cheap," Perry snapped.

Wil-Stur ignored him and strode back to a desk, it and a chair being the only pieces of furniture in the compartment. One wall was hung with a tattered paper star chart, covered in lines, scribbles, and a few crude military symbols. I saw the weapons printer squatting in a small compartment opening off to one side.

But all of that registered in the time it took me to flick my gaze over it, then my full attention landed right back on Wil-Stur.

He wasn't wearing any pants.

A tunic, looking like a piece of an old military uniform, a little threadbare, but still tidy, covered him up top. And he wore shiny black combat boots on his feet, grey wool socks protruding from them partway up his shin. But in-between the two was nothing but hairy legs and pale blue boxer shorts.

"Looks like we've found your *guy staggering around in his underwear*," Perry muttered. I shushed him, but it didn't stop me from giggling.

Wil-Stur turned and leaned on his desk. "Welcome to the revolution, my friends. The shackles of oppression have been cast off in this room, and the freedom that follows will soon spread across the stars."

I blinked. "Uh, okay. Anyway, as I said on the comm channel, I'm—"

"An agent of the counter-revolution, an instrument of oppression, and a mouthpiece for the jack-booted foot crushing the throats of those would stand up against the oppressors, yes, yes, I know." He waved a dismissive hand as he spoke.

I frowned and decided to try a different approach. "You know, maybe I am those things, certainly to some people, anyway. But I'm not here to be an instrument or a mouthpiece or whatever. I'm really just here to collect the amount you owe to The

Quiet Room on that printer over there, or else recover it for them."

Wil-Stur looked at the printer. "That device is the only means I have to properly outfit the forces of the revolution. I can currently arm... five thousand troops. Perhaps six thousand. But I have purchased all of the weapons I am able, so I have to produce my own, if I'm going to reach my goal."

"Which is?" Perry asked.

Wil-Stur drew himself up. "To arm and equip one *million* revolutionaries so we can spread freedom across the stars!"

I looked at Perry. He looked back. Even in his glowing, mechanistic eyes, I could see he was thinking the same thing I was.

This man isn't just crazy. He's bat-shit, over-the-top, needs-a-straight-jacket insane.

I turned back to him. "Alrighty, then. If you want to keep the printer, that's fine. I'll need to collect the amount owed in back payments, plus interest—"

"Interest? *Interest?* Interest is just usury, a penalty inflicted on the downtrodden to keep them in their place while enriching those bastards sitting in their high seats of power." He shook his head. "No, I will be paying none of your *interest.* Now, if that is all, then leave, and take my message of contempt back to your masters, you mewling lapdog."

Out of all of that, for some reason, my mind caught on that last bit. I'd never been called a *mewling lapdog* before. Had anyone outside of breathless fiction or social media?

But I shook my head. "I'm sorry, but that's not going to be sufficient. The Quiet Room—"

"Are the oppressors! How can you not see that! They control the money! All of the money! They control everything, lurking behind the curtain, reaching out only to manipulate events to suit their sinister agendas." He lowered his head, looking down at the disheveled piles of paper on his desk, and shook his head again, hard. "No. No. There shall be no more money pressed into those hidden palms."

He looked back up. "Now, get out. My patience is at an end."

I had to admit, so was mine. "Okay, look—"

Snapping a curse, Wil-Stur reached down and started fumbling open a drawer.

"Weapon!" Perry shouted, then flung himself at Wil-Stur in a storm of beating metallic wings. Then it was my turn to curse and rush in, trying to prevent Wil-Stur from shooting Perry, Perry from harming or killing Wil-Stur, or either of them from catching me in the middle of it. A blur of shoving, punching, cursing, and flapping wings followed, culminating in me smacking Wil-Stur over the head with the butt of a pistol I'd managed to snatch out of his grip. He slumped against the desk, then toppled to the floor, moaning.

I glanced at the pistol, my enhanced memories recognizing it as a nano-jet, a weapon that fired a stream of nanobots that could be programmed to do anything from causing a persistent, mild irritation to whatever skin they contacted, to acting as a lethal toxin. I snapped out the ammo-capsule and stuck it in a pocket, then stuck the weapon itself into my belt.

"And there was your fistfight," Perry said, perching on Wil-Stur's desk and staring down at the groaning heap of revolutionary zeal. "If anyone pukes on the floor, it's a complete imitation of your college years."

I smirked, but it unfortunately had felt more like a bar-room brawl than any sort of controlled takedown. "We've got to work on coordinating our efforts. Those wings of yours are like knives," I said, heading for the printer.

"Bah. They won't cut through your Peacemaker armor."

"Which would be fine, except without my helmet, my face, eyes, throat—you know, delicate squishy bits—are right *there*."

Perry bobbed his head. "Good point. I got used to working with your grandfather. I guess I need to recalibrate my behavior."

Wil-Stur groaned again. I glanced down at him, then started unplugging cables from the printer. "Yeah, well, let's worry about that later. While the pantless wonder is down and out, let's grab this damned thing and haul ass out of here."

We were stopped once by a human woman in heavy combat armor, cradling a power rifle. Perry and I both froze, me clutching the bulky printer in both arms. Okay, this was a problem.

Except it wasn't. The woman just stepped aside to let us pass.

"You guys need a hand?"

I gaped at her. "Don't you, like, work for Wil-Stur?"

"Yup. Vawna Sander, Blackstar Security." She glanced down at herself, then shrugged. "I usually carry a card, but I'm out."

"Don't worry about it," I said, lugging the printer past her. She made no effort to stop us. I finally had to stop and turn back.

"Doesn't Wil-Stur pay you to, I don't know, stop people from doing this? Taking stuff from him?"

Perry tapped my leg with a wing. "Van, let's not keep the nice lady from her business," he hissed.

She shrugged. "I suppose." She suddenly brightened. "Hey, you didn't happen to kill him, did you?"

I shifted the printer. "No, of course not!"

She actually deflated at that. "Oh. Okay, whatever."

"You *wanted* him dead?"

She nodded.

"Okay, I'd say that Wil-Stur is definitely *not* getting his money's worth out of you," Perry put in.

"He dies, the contract ends, and I get to haul off this shithole and away from his crazy ass. Otherwise, I'm stuck here until this cursed contract's done."

"Ah. Okay. Well, don't want to keep you from your work," I said and turned away, rolling my eyes at Perry.

"Yeah, whatever," Vawna Sander replied and wandered off the other way.

WE REACHED the *Dragonet* and undocked without incident. About five minutes out from the platform, Wil-Stur came on the comm. Needless to say, he was displeased.

The first fifteen seconds or so of his transmission probably violated broadcast standards against gratuitous profanity. I let him get some of it out of his system, then raised a hand.

"I'm sorry that we had to resort to force, but I'd point out that you were the first one to reach for a gun," I said.

"So that I could kill you and preserve the revolution!"

"You had me at the kill you part. Anyway, I think our business is concluded here, so—"

"Oh, not by a longshot it's not," he snapped, his tone a menacing growl—or as menacing a growl as a man not wearing pants could manage. If he'd just sat down at the desk, it would have been fine, but he was standing, apparently trying to loom and be all intimidating. It just meant my attention kept being pulled back to his baby-blue boxer shorts.

"The station has just launched three missiles," Netty said.

My attention immediately went to the tactical overlay. None of the missiles were projected to come anywhere near the *Dragonet*.

"I will hunt you to the ends of the universe, you so-called Peacemaker," Wil-Stur spat.

"You do that, big shooter. Just do me a favor first and put some pants on."

11

THE STACK of bonds Dayna Jasskin accepted from Chensun and handed to me had a reassuring heft. I now had enough money to cover my near-term expenses and still make two or three twist jumps. But Perry and Netty had already put forward some other uses for the money, all of which seemed sensible, and together made the stack of bonds suddenly seem a whole lot smaller as I thought about them.

Netty advocated for upgrades to the *Dragonet*. She had a list. Extended-duration fuel cells and a dedicated point defense battery were at the top of it, and although I didn't have enough funds to outright purchase either, I did have enough for a down payment on one of them. Perry, on the other hand, suggested that I invest in reforging the Moonsword.

I furrowed my brow at that. "Why? Isn't a sword a little

archaic given that we've got, like, spaceships and things like The Drop?"

"The Moonsword is more than just a weapon. It's a symbol. It's your badge of office. And the more you upgrade it, the more credibility you'll have as a Peacemaker."

"I thought that came with working up the ranks."

"Internally to the Peacemakers and the GKU, it does. But to the universe at large, your Moonsword is your calling card. Your grandfather had reached the point where just showing the sword was enough to get him into private meetings with very influential, very powerful people."

While Perry had been talking, I'd made my way to the weapons locker and extracted the Moonsword. It didn't look all that impressive, more like a reproduction of a Roman gladius than anything especially unique. "It sure doesn't look like much."

"That's because this is just its basic substrate. Each Reforging adds a new layer, which makes it more useful and powerful. And, more to the point, makes it *obviously* more useful and powerful."

"So what happened to Gramps' upgrades to it? They didn't get seized under some lien scheme too, did they? That just sounds dumb."

"No, they didn't get seized, but they did get removed. When a Peacemaker dies or retires, the sword is restored to its basic substrate before it's given to their successor."

"So how do I get it Reforged?"

"By taking it to Starsmith."

"Let me guess—and pay for it."

"Of course."

So now I eyed the stack of bonds, pondering what to do with them. Dayna smiled at my obvious uncertainty.

"It only gets more complicated from here," she said.

"Yeah, I'm starting to realize that." I started to turn back to the money, but something that had been nagging at me made me look back at her.

"So you're a human."

She lifted an eyebrow. "Last time I checked."

"And so was Gramps, and it turns out Wil-Stur was human too, and he has human mercenaries on his payroll. There seem to be an awful lot of humans out here among the stars."

"Well, the first humans actually left Earth shortly after we invented radio," Dayna replied.

"Radio? That was over a hundred years ago."

"It was. But radio brought humanity to the attention of the interstellar community. It meant humans had potential—and, even better, they were cheap to employ."

"In fact, the first human recorded to have left Earth was a mister Nathan Buckley, an inventor from Providence, Rhode Island, in 1911," Perry said. "He was contacted by a delegation from the Arkosian Autonomy and offered a position as a consultant."

I stared. "A consultant? From 1911 Rhode Island? What the hell could he consult on? Buggy whips? Wagon wheels?"

Dayna shrugged. "The Arkosians are known for playing the long game. They're now the biggest employer of humans in known space and have Nathan Buckley's great grandson on their Central Committee."

"In fact, it was him—Galen Buckley—and his father before him who advocated for admitting humans to the Peacemaker Corps," Perry put in.

"So there are generations of humans out here that aren't from Earth?"

"There are. I'm one of them. My grandfather came from Russia. He was a *spetsnaz* special forces soldier, recruited by a mercenary company based out of Teegarden's Star. My grandmother was a British nurse working in Bermuda. She got hired on by a medical research consortium located on Outward, the planet around which we're currently orbiting."

I turned to Perry. "You told me only a handful of humans had ever left Earth."

"That depends on what you consider a handful. In comparison to the total human population, I'd argue that a few thousand people is just a handful."

"A few *thousand*?"

"Now you know why I was being evasive. That's the sort of knowledge we like to keep from would-be Peacemakers until they've graduated from Initiate Probational to full Initiate."

I turned back to Dayna. "So aliens just come to Earth and—what, *hire* people? To go offworld?"

"Pretty much."

"How has that not gotten out?" I asked, but as soon as I'd uttered the question, I realized it had, after a fashion. Just as some UFO abductees were washed-out Peacemakers, others were no doubt people who'd been approached and, for whatever reason, had turned the offer down.

Dayna confirmed it. "Ask any UFO enthusiast. They'll give you all the 'proof' you want that spaceships are flying around Earth all the time."

"But they're right, as it turns out."

"That's what makes it so funny."

I shook my head. Aliens buzzing around Earth, head-hunting talent, while generations of humans were being born and living their lives in space. Not to diminish the accomplishments of the likes of Yuri Gagarin, Alan Shepard, Neil Armstrong, and all the men and women who came after them, of course. But I wonder how they'd all have felt knowing that, while they strapped tanks of noxious, volatile chemicals to their butts and used them to fling themselves out of the Earth's atmosphere, other humans were twisting around the galaxy, going about their everyday business.

Okay, I had to admit, it *was* kind of funny.

"In any case, I do have another possible money-making opportunity for you," Dayna said.

I narrowed my eyes slightly. "Does it involve crazy men without pants?

"What?"

"Never mind." I glanced at the stack of bonds. "Anyway, what's this new job?"

"Carrying a passenger."

"Why do I suspect it's not as simple as it sounds?"

Perry intervened. "I'd also point out that Peacemaker ships aren't certified or insured for simple carriage of passengers. Now, if this were someone in need of an escort, that's a different matter."

"In other words, we can't just fly people from point A to point B. We have to fly problematic people from point A to point B," I said.

"That about sums it up, yeah."

"I'm well aware of the restrictions on Peacemaker ships," Dayna said coolly. "I wouldn't have suggested this otherwise."

"So who is this troubled passenger that's in need of a gallant escort?" I asked.

"Her name is Torina Milon. Her family is currently locked in a dispute over property rights on a resource-rich moon in the Van Maanen's star system."

"Van Maanen's Star is a white dwarf, with virtually zero energy output. Who would locate there?" Perry asked.

"Someone who wanted to make a fortune off of helium-3. I don't understand all the details, but something about the moon orbiting the third planet there has accumulated some of the richest helium-3 deposits in known space," Dayna replied.

Perry cocked his head. "How was I not aware of that?"

"Because the really rich deposits have only recently been located, at considerable depth in the moon's bedrock. Like I said, I don't pretend to understand the science behind it. Anyway, Torina's family already had helium-3 mining rights there, and have for about thirty standard years. Up until just a couple of months ago, they were making decent money mining some middling-grade deposits. When they discovered the rich stuff, well, things changed."

I nodded. "Suddenly, they find themselves sitting on a fortune, and now other people are interested in it."

"And Torina's family is in the spotlight, a place they do *not* want to be. There are at least a couple of big corporations, a few mining consortiums, and about a thousand other parties that want a piece of that action. But Torina's family has it all locked down," Dayna replied.

"Lucky them."

"Well, except for the death threats, sure."

I frowned. "Death threats? Really? Can't they report them to the police?"

Perry leaned over. "Van, you *are* the police."

I blinked at him, glanced at Dayna, then looked back to him again. Perry was right. Individual nations, planet-states, and even star-spanning political entities all had their own internal law enforcement. But when it came to problems and disputes that crossed borders, or involved unregulated systems like Van Maanen's Star, then the Peacemakers were it—

Wait.

"What's The Quiet Room's interest in this?"

Dayna maintained that cool, neutral look. "What makes you think we have one?"

"Well, unless you're moonlighting as some sort of job broker, I presume that you'd only bring this little task to my attention if The Quiet Room had some sort of stake in it. And you don't strike me as the moonlighting type."

Dayna opened her mouth, but I raised a finger. "Let's see if I can work this out. Van Maanen's Star is an unregulated territory. It falls under the... um, Seven Stars League, as a protectorate territory." I glanced at Perry. "Right?"

"Bang on, Van. You're on a roll, keep going."

"Okay, so whatever permits grant Ms. Torina's family the mining rights must have come from them, the Seven Stars League. But if the helium-3 deposits are really that rich, then the League would have probably expropriated the moon by now and paid out Torina's family. They haven't, which tells me that someone powerful enough to prevent it stopped them, probably because they have a sizable interest in the deposits. How am I doing so far?"

Dayna grinned. "You might be new at this, Van, but you're pretty good."

"Well, if I am, it's thanks to the memories and knowledge that the Peacemakers injected into me."

"Even so, you've reasoned that out pretty well," Dayna replied. "Yes, The Quiet Room has a significant interest in the helium-3 deposits now being developed on Damon, which is the name of the moon in question. We'd like to retain that interest, free from interference from other parties."

"So, it would be me, Perry, and Netty, my ship's AI, against a bunch of corporations and consortiums and the like? Sounds a little lopsided, don't you think?"

"All you'd be asked to do is make sure Torina makes it home to her family in one piece. They've got other assets they're bringing into play—they've damned well got the money for it—but that's going to take time."

"So I carry Ms. Torina to Van Maanen's Star? That's it?"

"And for that you'll be paid twenty-five thousand bonds."

I glanced at the twenty thousand bonds sitting on the desk in front of me. Doubling it, and adding another five thousand to the stack seemed like a damned good idea. It would take the financial pressure off for a while. And this little escort quest didn't sound too onerous for what Dayna was offering.

Except for one thing.

I raised my eyes and looked back across the desk at Dayna. "I'm assuming there's probably some sort of commercial travel service Ms. Torina could use, correct?"

"Several, in fact," Dayna replied.

"And I'm assuming none of them would cost anywhere near twenty-five thousand bonds."

"Probably a tenth of that, at most."

I smiled. Dayna knew where this was going. "So for a bank to be willing to lay out that kind of money just to escort someone on a one-way trip home, there's got to be some pretty serious risk."

Dayna steepled her fingers and returned my smile. "Cute *and* smart. You've got it all going on, don't you?"

"Never one to turn down a compliment—or point out that it doesn't answer the question."

Dayna laughed. "Yes, there's some risk. Someone—and we're not sure who, because it's buried under geological strata of holding companies and subsidiaries—has hired a pretty, um, let's call them a ruthlessly efficient private security company owned by a man named Marcus Pevensi. He has a reputation for giving his clients their money's worth."

I glanced at Perry. "Have you heard of this guy?"

"Pevensi? Oh, yes. He's something of a celebrity among the thuggish sociopath set. He formed his company, Falling Star

Security Services, a couple of years ago, and has been loosely implicated in a few unpleasant incidents since."

"And he's another human."

"He is. No one knows much about him before he popped up on, well, everyone's radar, not just the Peacemakers. There's a rumor that he was already doing some pretty nasty stuff in a few recent hotspots back on Earth, and that someone up here took notice and specifically recruited him. Digging any hard information out about him, or any of his backers or employers, has proven pretty tough."

I glanced back at the stack of bonds, then back to Dayna. Again, she knew what was coming from me.

"I'll do it, but make it *thirty*-five thousand bonds."

Chensun, who'd been quietly standing nearby, lifted an eyebrow. It was the most expressive display of emotion I'd yet seen from them. Perry just turned to look at me.

Dayna laughed again.

"You're actually trying to haggle with The Quiet Room?"

I shrugged. "Gramps told me once, you don't ask, you don't get."

"The Quiet Room doesn't haggle, Van."

I nodded, scooped up my bonds, and stood. "Let's go, Perry. I'm sure Dayna here has some work to do. You know, finding someone else to protect Ms. Torina from a mercenary thug who seems to be somewhere in the upper parts of the Peacemakers' most-wanted list."

And I walked away.

"Thirty thousand," Dayna said.

I stopped and turned back. "I thought you said The Quiet Room doesn't haggle."

"It doesn't. But I do. Only with people I like, mind you."

I grinned. "So you like me?"

"Van, I absolutely *adore* you. You're a man who's suddenly been thrown into the deep end of reality, you're woefully out of your depth, and when someone throws you a lifeline, you've got the balls to stick your head back above the water and say sorry, but I want a longer one."

I walked back to the desk. "Thirty sounds more than long enough, thanks. Is there some paperwork we need to do?"

It was Chensun who answered, and for the first time, he looked happy. "There's *always* paperwork to do."

I MET Torina Milon at the *Dragonet*'s airlock. We'd had to make a flight back to Sunward—giving Wil-Stur's creaky orbital platform a wide berth as we did—and pick her up on the planet's surface. It was my first time on the actual surface of an alien planet, albeit one pretty Earth-like overall. Its sun, the star Procyon, wasn't the right color, being whiter than familiar old Sol. It was also noticeably brighter. Moreover, Sunward's gravity was a little higher than Earth's. As soon as I stepped outside of the effect of the system that maintained the interior of the *Dragonet* at a comfortable one g, I sagged slightly. It was, I thought, like wearing the bulky body armor I'd lugged around during my stint in the army. The air had a higher oxygen content, though, so I could add a pinch of oxygenated euphoria to the mix.

I shaded my eyes against the glare of Procyon and took in the panorama surrounding the star port. Rolling fields swept off to every horizon, dotted with clumps of dark trees. Straight lines that I took to be roads bisected the landscape, and I could make out the distant gleam of buildings, some standing alone, others in small clusters.

"Kinda looks like Iowa," I said, glancing at Perry.

"You sound disappointed."

"Well, this *is* an alien world. I guess I expected it to be more, you know, *alien.*"

"You'd prefer going somewhere with a corrosive and toxic atmosphere, crushing gravity, and seas of liquid ammonia? Because Netty and I can certainly arrange that and introduce you to the—"

A burst of noise erupted from Perry's beak, a cross between an angle grinder, an old dial-up modem, and words that roughly sounded like *argle-blarg.*

I winced. "What the hell was that?"

"The race that lives on the planet I just described. What they call themselves, along with the entire rest of their language, doesn't directly translate into English," Perry replied.

"Or any other languages, really," Netty put in. She was able to listen in and participate in conversations by means of a vox, a small communication device built into the Peacemaker outfit.

"Sounds like they're hard to do business with," I replied.

"They work through an intermediary, a biomechanical hybrid

race that somehow seems able to communicate with them. They're actually very nice people—well, they're pretty much amorphous blobs, but they're still very nice," Perry said.

"Van, there's a vehicle approaching. It's probably our passenger," Netty put in.

Sure enough, something about the size of a standard sedan had separated from the cluster of buildings that served as the star port's terminal. It rolled across the blast-scarred tarmac of the port on fat balloon tires. It was, in fact, almost the only activity that I'd seen here since we arrived, aside from some figures moving around another ship squatting a few hundred meters away. I already knew the reason for it; this particular star port was reserved for VIP and other special traffic. The unwashed masses arrived and departed Sunward through two other, more plebeian star ports elsewhere on the planet.

Still, this seemed like an awful lot of real estate to eat up this way. The *Dragonet* and the other sole ship grounded here used up maybe a tenth of the available space. "This place seems as dead as heaven on a Friday night," I said. "Which is another thing it has in common with Iowa."

"Because of The Quiet Room's influence here in Procyon, both Outward and Sunward are considered pretty much neutral ground. So a lot of diplomatic meetings happen here, a lot of summits and peace talks, and a lot of treaties getting signed," Netty said.

"In fact, it's about a five minute flight from here to one of the ritziest, glitziest resorts in known space," Perry added.

"Huh. Wouldn't mind checking that out sometime."

"Van, all the money you've got would barely cover the valet fees."

I shrugged. "I did say *sometime*, like, when I'm fantastically wealthy."

The car rolled up and stopped. A door slid smoothly open, and Torina Milon stepped out.

My first impression was *brusque efficiency*. Without waiting for her baggage, being unloaded from the car by a robotic attendant, she strode toward the *Dragonet*. She wore a brimmed hat and expansive sunglasses that hid much of her face, but I figured her for late twenties or early thirties, a little on the willowy side, but making up for it with a lithe, purposeful sort of grace.

She stopped. Her sunglasses threw back tiny, distorted reflections of me and the *Dragonet*.

"Peacemaker Tudor?"

"At your service—"

"The bags are right behind me," she said, then breezily walked by and entered the *Dragonet*.

I gaped after her and glanced down at Perry. "Uh—"

"That about sums it up, yeah."

I saw to her baggage—only two pieces, and one of them more like a backpack than a suitcase—then clambered into the ship with Perry. Netty sealed the airlock behind us. I found Torina Milon in the cockpit, already strapped into the copilot's seat.

"Hope you don't mind, but I took the liberty," she said, gesturing at herself neatly strapped into the seat.

I smiled and shook my head. "No, ma'am. Unfortunately, the

Dragonet doesn't offer much in the way of creature comforts, but—"

"Not an issue, Peacemaker Tudor. I've traveled farther in worse."

"Please, it's Van."

She removed her sunglasses and gave me a cool smile that ended somewhere well below her eyes. "And you can call me Ms. Milon."

I just nodded and strapped into the pilot's seat. Great. Wealthy and arrogant was always an appealing combination.

"Okay, Netty, let's get this show on the road, shall we?" I said. Netty acknowledged, and the low thrum of the *Dragonet*'s thrusters spooling up vibrated through the ship. I glanced at Ms. Milon, but she'd already leaned her head back and closed her eyes.

I curled my lip. If she wanted to sleep for the whole trip, that would be fine with me.

12

THE MESSAGE ARRIVED for Torina when we were about an hour shy of the twist to Van Maanen's Star. Her eyes flicked open the instant Netty announced it, and she began to deftly unstrap herself from the copilot's seat.

"I'll go figure out where my cabin is."

"And I'll just stay here and do pilot stuff," I said.

She glanced at me, offered me another smile that apparently wanted nothing to do with her eyes, and left.

Perry hopped up on the copilot's seat when she was gone, his accustomed place.

"She seems nice."

"In a robotic sort of way, yeah. Which I guess you'd find appealing with, you know, you being all robotic yourself."

"Frankly, Van, to the extent I find anything appealing or not, I find biological organisms of all sorts kind of disgusting. All those secretions and gaseous emanations—and don't get me started on the casual shedding of dead cells and hairs and things. That's just rude."

"Sorry, Perry, but it's how we biological organisms roll. We were kind of made that way—"

Torina abruptly returned to the cockpit, pushed her way back to the copilot's seat—forcing Perry to evacuate it—and sat down.

I decided to take another stab at being friendly. "That was quick."

Torina nodded, snapped her harness back into place—

And began to cry.

ONE OF THE things I liked about mostly dealing with people online was the sterility of it. Perry, in his own way, had actually hit the proverbial nail on the head. People were messy, and not just in a shedding-dead-skin-cells sort of way. They were messy emotionally and had mental states that could whipsaw from one extreme to the other, sometimes almost instantly. Dealing with them online put a comfortable, almost sterile barrier of electronics between me and them, meaning I didn't have to often worry about any of that.

But I hadn't been a hermit, either. And while my three serious attempts at starting up a relationship had ultimately gone nowhere, they'd given me enough practice at dealing with upset and unhappy people that Torina's abrupt collapse into tears was only mildly surprising. I'd suspected there were some depths hidden behind those sunglasses, and it turned out I was right.

So I opened my mouth to offer some great words of comfort and understanding.

"Uh—"

That was as far as I got. Okay, so much for comfort and understanding. Let's try practicality.

"Is there anything I can do?"

Torina didn't answer immediately. She continued to weep for a moment, then wiped her eyes. "I'm sorry. This is so unseemly."

Unseemly. Now there was a word you didn't hear very often.

I waved it off. "No need to be sorry," I said, then left it at that and gave her time to compose herself. Finally, she slumped back in the copilot's seat.

"My family. They're gone," she said.

I turned to her. "Gone? Oh. Oh, no. I'm so—so *sorry*—"

"Oh, not gone like that. At least—" She shook her head. "I don't know. I mean that they're literally gone. As in vanished." She paused to wipe her eyes again. "That message I got was from my uncle. He'd twisted into the Van Maanen's system and was immediately warned off by two ships with no markings. He challenged them, but they actually fired warning shots at him. Before he twisted back out of the system, he tried raising my father. He got nothing but dead air."

She looked at me. "He also told me that my family's holdings there are now up for sale for an exorbitantly high price. That includes the mining rights, of course. My father supposedly put them on the market, but—" She leaned back again. "He didn't. He wouldn't."

I could only shake my head. "That's awful. Whoever did this—"

"Pevensi. It was him. I can't prove it, but I know it was him."

"Fine. Pevensi. That bastard needs to be stopped. Have you contacted the—who was it? The Seven Stars League? They're the ones that issued the mining permits and all that, right?"

"The Seven Stars League is so corrupt I'm sure they've got a whole department of their government that just oversees bribes and kickbacks. If Pevensi—or, really, whoever's backing him because he's just a hired gun—anyway, if they've greased the right appendages, then the League won't do a damned thing," she replied.

I clenched a frustrated fist. I wanted to help this woman, but what could I, a lone Peacemaker, do—?

I caught myself. Perry had said it back in Dayna's office.

Van, you are *the police.*

This was precisely the sort of thing the Peacemakers were intended to do. If the Seven Stars League wouldn't intervene, then the Peacemakers had to. It was their—*our*—reason for existing.

I nodded. "Okay. Then it looks like we're going to have to handle this. Perry, how many other Peacemakers are available? How soon can they get to Van Maanen's Star?"

Perry didn't answer.

I turned around to look at him. "Perry?"

His amber eyes stared back at me. "Van, there aren't any other Peacemakers available."

"What? What do you mean? There are *hundreds* of them —er, us."

"There are. Hundreds. Seven hundred and sixty-two, in fact, per the last update I got. And those seven hundred and sixty-two Peacemakers have to deal with the problems and issues of roughly one and a half trillion sentient beings divided among nearly one hundred and thirty planets and moons, and another thousand or so orbital or deep-space installations."

"Shit."

"Right?"

"So we're on our own."

"Pretty much. There are some categories of operation that will involve multiple Peacemakers. Some will even pull in actual military units from the Galactic Knights Legion. The biggest one ever, in fact, engaged forty-four Peacemakers and three companies of the Legion in locating and recovering a classified experimental device."

"What sort of device? What did it do?"

"Let's put it this way. If it were ever activated, none of us would be here to talk about it. And by none of us, I mean literally none of us, anywhere, ever."

"Holy shit!"

"Again—right?"

I let out a breath. "So there's no way we're going to get even one other Peacemaker to help with this."

"Afraid not. All due respect to Ms. Torina and her family, but—"

"But we're not important enough. Who actually ends up mining and selling that helium-3 doesn't really matter in the big picture," Torina said, a rueful, bitter smile tightening her face.

"What she said, unfortunately," Perry replied.

"What about The Quiet Room? They've got a vested interest in this, right? Kind of why they hired me in the first place?"

"First, you just answered your own question—that's why they hired you. Second, don't let Dayna's easy charm fool you. The Quiet Room is hedging its bets. If you and Ms. Torina here can't sort this out, then they'll just shift their business focus to whoever the new owners end up being," Perry replied.

"They're probably already putting out feelers about that now, in fact," Torina added.

I looked out the *Dragonet*'s forward canopy, at the stars. "Okay. Fine. Then it's just me. Or, actually, us. Me, Perry, and Netty. Fine. Ms. Milon, we're going to put this right."

Her smile actually turned genuine. "How gallant. Unrealistic, even stupid, but gallant."

"I guess this is the part where I say something truly noble and start us on the road to inevitable victory." I gave my own rueful smile. "Trouble is, I'm not even sure where to start."

"I have a suggestion," Netty put in.

"I'm all ears, Netty."

"You're a Peacemaker Initiate, with limited resources and almost no money."

"Thanks for pointing that out. I hope your suggestion

amounts to more than how woefully unqualified I am to actually do this," I shot back.

"It does. You need new and better capabilities, and you need them quickly, and you need them to be ones you can afford. My suggestion, therefore, is to travel to Starsmith and begin the process of having your Moonblade reforged."

"A sword. That's your suggestion."

"Not just *a sword*, Van," Perry replied. "The Moonblade. It's a lot more than just *a sword*."

"Yeah, yeah, I know, it's my traditional badge of office as a Peacemaker—"

"It is, but it's more than that. It's also a weapon. And by weapon, I don't simply mean a blade you swing in combat. The more overlays you have forged onto it, the more capable and powerful it becomes. The first overlay is almost always the same for all Peacemakers. It's called Solitude, and it gives the sword the ability to disrupt communications systems of all types."

"Oh. Yeah, okay, that could be handy. What comes after that?"

"After Solitude, the overlays become more and more attuned to the specific Peacemaker. When your grandfather wielded it, for instance, the successive overlays became more and more about stealth and subterfuge."

"So you guys are recommending that we go to this place called Starsmith and get the first overlay forged onto that sword, the Moonblade. How long is that going to take?"

"Including transit time to and from, and the time you'd likely have to spend waiting for the reforging to be done, from four to six standard days is probably a reasonable estimate," Netty said.

I turned to Torina. "Is there any way you, your uncle—someone, anyway—can block the sale of your family's property for about a week?"

She just stared back at me. I saw her gaze drop, then lift again. She was sizing me up. Deciding if I could really help her, or if I was just engaged in a deluded bit of wishful thinking. The longer the moment went on, the more I became convinced she was just going to pass and find someone better suited to the task of taking on Pevensi, his mercenary thugs, and whoever was paying them. I couldn't really blame her.

But she finally nodded. "I think so. That's the nice thing about the sort of corruption you find the Seven Stars League. If they'll do it *with* you, then they'll also do it *to* you. I'll call up my uncle and have him do some appendage greasing of his own."

Huh. She was game. Go figure.

I nodded. "Okay. In the meantime, where would you like me to take you?"

Torina actually laughed, though it still rang with a bitter edge. "Home. But you can't. So I guess this escort mission is just going to continue until you can, since that's what you're being paid for."

I stared. "You mean, you want to stay on the *Dragonet?*"

"Unless you're kicking me off."

"What? No, no, of course not."

Torina gestured at the stars ahead. "In that case, shall we?"

I stared a moment longer, then smiled. "Okay, then. Netty, do your magic. Take us to the Starsmith."

THE STARSMITH WASN'T JUST a place. It was also, Perry explained, a person, an actual artificer skilled in the forging of the Moonblade. And it was, more philosophically, an idea, a concept that could be summed up in a single line.

The nearer the hand, the deadlier the strike.

"Sorry, I don't quite get it," I said to Perry. Torina had gone to her little cubicle cabin in the back of the *Dragonet* and was talking to her uncle.

"What it's saying is that the closer you are to your foe, the more likely you are to defeat him," Perry replied.

That made me frown. "Really? Blasting someone to molecules thousands of klicks away is less deadly than fighting them with a sword?"

"It's not meant to be taken literally, Van. It's metaphorical. It's—" Perry stopped. "You know what? I'll leave it to Linulla to explain."

"Linulla. Is that the Starsmith's name?"

"It is. He's a Conoku."

I initially drew a blank on the word Conoku, but then my enhanced memories kicked in. The Conoku were a squat, arthropodal race that resembled large crabs. Their origins were unclear, their homeworld unknown, and they were superlative engineers. Their involvement in any sort of crafting or construction project was highly prized, so much so that the handful of them who freelanced commanded correspondingly high fees.

That gave me a moment. I narrowed my eyes at Perry. "Wait.

Conoku don't come cheap. Will I even be able to afford this Linulla's rates?"

"To reforge the Moonblade? Yes. For over three hundred standard years, the Galactic Knights and the Starsmiths have had a firm agreement in place that governs things like fees. In fact, technically, when you pay Linulla, you're not compensating him for his services. You're actually making a tribute to the Starsmiths as a whole."

"But it still costs me money, right?"

"It does."

Not long after, Netty announced that we were ready to twist to Struve 2398, a binary pair of red dwarf stars known for their tendency to suddenly and unpredictably increase in brightness, before fading again. Such so-called "flare stars" weren't great candidates as habitable systems. That was why, despite having two Earth-sized planets, Struve 2398 was classified as uninhabited. In fact, it wasn't, because that was where the Starsmith was, located on Struve 2398-Beta, the outermost of the two planets. But Struve 2398-Beta didn't exactly roll off the tongue, so the planet, and by extension the whole system, was simply called Starsmith.

And only a moment after Netty said we were ready to twist, Torina returned to the cockpit.

"My uncle is pretty sure he can get a week, maybe even eight or nine standard days," she said, settling back into the copilot's seat. "So you've got that much time to—do what, exactly?"

"Ah. Yes. The plan. I was getting to that part."

Torina stared.

I stared back.

Finally, I just shrugged and smiled. "Oh, so you don't have one, either."

I braced myself for Torina to curse me, decide I was a waste of her time, and write me off. Instead, she smiled back and then laughed a genuine laugh. It ended with her head back against the seat's headrest. She rolled her head toward me, then shook it.

"What the hell have I gotten myself into here?"

"Van's got a lot of potential," Perry put in.

She curled her lip in a peculiar way. "A newborn baby's got a lot of potential, too. But I don't see any around, so I guess it's you or nothing. Just go live out my days with my uncle."

"We're not going to let that happen," I said. "I might not have an actual plan, but here's what I'm thinking. Once we're done at Starsmith, we'll go back to your home and find out exactly what the hell is going on. And then—we'll do whatever comes next."

"That sounds as good as anything I'd come up with."

"And more than you'd get out of a newborn."

That lip curl again. "I guess we'll see."

13

STRUVE 2398 was not a habitable system. That became clear when we finished the twist, and an alarm immediately chimed. I gaped at the instruments for a minute. I knew this—

Right. High external radiation. The meter actually had to recalibrate, rescaling itself by a factor of ten to show the true reading.

"That doesn't seem good," I said, glancing at Perry. I was waiting for either him or Netty to react. But Perry just raised and lowered his wings in that shrug of his.

"Bah. Flare stars do this. The rads here are always bad." He flicked his amber gaze at the instruments. "Not usually this bad but still nothing the ship can't handle."

"Just don't go outside," Netty put in.

"Wasn't planning on it. So if the radiation in this system is this bad, how do the Starsmiths put up with it?" I was cycing the data Netty had cobbled together about the two planets here. The inner was a write-off, a radiation-scoured rock. The outer, Starsmith itself, wasn't much better.

"Underground," Torina suggested. "It's all probably subterranean."

"Bingo," Perry replied.

We settled back and let Netty fly the remaining distance, catching up with the world called Starsmith, falling into orbit around it, then spiraling down to land on a flat, barren plain. Like the inner planet, this one's atmosphere had been largely blown into space by the constant gusts of stellar wind from the binary red stars. A few stubborn wisps of heavier gases was all that remained. The result was blank, fissured stone under a perpetually black, starry sky. By day, everything was lit crimson by the twin suns. By night, it was just black. We'd arrived late in the day, so the two suns sat low in the sky, one touching the horizon, the other about the width of my hand above it. Everything cast two sets of mauve-brown shadows.

I peered out the port in the airlock. "So this place is either pitch-black, or everything's the color of blood. Nice."

A single silvery dome and a few smaller boxy structures scattered around it were the only signs of anything that wasn't rock. Netty had grounded us about a hundred meters away. Perry assured me that the armor would protect against the radiation during the brief walk. Fortunately, the *Dragonet* carried a second spare set. I'd opened the locker to show it to Torina, then left her and moved to the airlock so she could change. I left Perry to help her don the suit, its harness, and various bits and pieces, assuming it would take a while. Only a couple of minutes later, though, she stepped into the airlock behind me, fully suited up.

"That was quick."

"Sorry. Next fit, I'll take my time," Torina replied.

Okay, so she'd obviously had some experience wearing suits similar to armor. That was a good sign. I'd been starting to worry about having to try and protect her on top of figuring out how to crack her case. But she seemed at least somewhat able to take care of herself, albeit under a cool exterior that bordered on disinterest. I gave her another sidelong glance, just to see if she was secretly French.

I decided she was not but reserved the right to change my mind based on further evidence.

We exited and crossed the barren expanse of rocky ground. It was an eerie experience, like walking through some vast, empty auditorium, lit only by a pair of red floodlights. The rad meter on the suit's heads-up gave a bright red, alarming number to describe the radiation currently sleeting around us. But it also offered a reassuring *RESIST 99%* beneath it. I took the suit's word for it, and we made our way to the dome.

Where we found someone waiting for us. Outside. Without any sort of suit at all.

The Conoku were described as crab-like. That pretty much nailed it. The creature squatting outside an open hatch in the dome did, indeed, look like a giant crab, but with a much more humped and rounded shell, and more limbs, ranging from nimble little arms no longer than my forearm to a pair of massive claws.

Four beady eyes stared at us from a bony ridge set just above a beak-like mouth.

I stopped. *Now this is an alien.*

A voice suddenly crackled through the suit's headphones.

"Haven't seen a lot of aliens yet, have you?"

The voice was a smooth baritone. I could imagine it carrying a pretty good tune in karaoke. I blinked and shook my head.

"Not really. I mean, don't take this the wrong way, but a few weeks ago, I'd have considered you a monster."

"If it makes you feel any better, I still consider you a monster. I mean, all that exposed flesh, no shell—ugh. Gives me the creeps. I'm Linulla, by the way. And you must be Van's grandson."

"Uh—"

"He's having trouble getting past the whole *monster* thing. I'm Torina Milon, and Van here is my big, strong hero who's going to save the day."

"I—" I stopped and shook my head. "Sorry. Yeah. Van Tudor. The Third. Pleased to make your acquaintance." I automatically stuck out a hand without thinking about how Linulla would shake it. But he didn't and instead extended one of his smaller appendages to fist-bump me.

I'd just been fist-bumped by a giant talking crab. On the dead surface of a barren planet lit by two dim, red suns. Eleven light-years from Earth--a distance which I'd covered aboard an intelligent spaceship, accompanied by an AI bird and the heiress to a helium-3 mining fortune.

It would make one hell of a good sci-fi story.

Linulla was actually one of seven Starsmiths present, each a master craftsman—craftsbeing?—in a particular field. Linulla himself focused on the forging and reforging of blades and edged weapons. The others were involved in various other esoteric pursuits, including one Starsmith who actually did most of its work off-planet, somehow reforging lighter elements into heavier ones, but without using nuclear fusion or a particle accelerator or anything similar to do it.

"Xnsas has managed to produce stable atoms of element 120, but only in experimental runs," Linulla was saying as we walked along a catwalk enclosed in a transparent tube. Xnsas—which apparently somehow had a *q* sound stuck in the middle of it—breathed a mixture of methane and ammonia, so his lab was mostly hidden by billowing greenish vapor. At one point, something like a massive Portuguese Man of War slipped into view out of the bilious mist. It had dozens of tentacles dangling from what looked like a huge, pulsating brain.

"Hey, Linulla. Got some new customers, I see?"

The voice, a rich bass that reminded me of Barry White, seemed to come from all around us.

"I do. Xnsas, this is Van Tudor and Torina Milon. Van's a Peacemaker Initiate, here for his first reforging."

"Ah. Well, Van—may I call you Van?"

"Sure. Why not."

"Anyway, Van, I'd say you're in good hands with Linulla, but—"

"I don't have hands, hah hah," Linulla finished. "Xnsas, don't you ever get tired of that damned joke?"

"Nope. Anyway, nice meeting you, Van, Torina."

And with that, the giant floating tentacle-brain vanished back into the mist.

"Is it a good sign that I'm getting used to seeing things like that?" I asked, directing it at no one in particular.

"It is. The real test, though, is going to be when you end up facing the *really* weird stuff," Perry said.

"Really weird—? Actually, never mind."

We carried on to Linulla's lab, a huge, circular chamber hacked into the planet's crust. Workbenches, tables, and all manner of components and purposeful-looking bits and pieces were strewn about the periphery, while the middle of the expansive space was dominated by a hulking, flattened sphere. A maze of pipes and conduits splayed away from it, vanishing into the walls and ceilings.

"My friends, welcome to my forge. Now, I'm going to assume that you're in a bit of a hurry, so I'll get right to work." I handed over the Moonblade, which I'd strapped to my armor's harness, to him.

"Well here's an old friend," Linulla said. "I've lost count of the number of times I've had this blade heating up in my forge."

"How many—overlays, right? How many did you do for my grandfather?"

"Five. But this blade goes back way past your grandfather. He was actually its sixth wielder. You make lucky number seven."

"Oh. Huh. I had no idea it had that much history behind it."

Linulla held it aloft. Its blade, unremarkably and dully metallic, barely even gleamed in the hard lights mounted around the forge. If anything, it looked more like lead than steel. It wasn't, of course, and actually seemed both preternaturally sharp and hard. So I'd assumed there was more to it but hadn't even considered it might have a lineage.

"The Moonsword was originally forged from metal discovered in a rogue comet—oh, it must be nearly four hundred standard years ago now. The origin of the comet is unclear, but it seems to represent a fragment of some larger body that slowly accreted dust, gas, and ice over, well, who knows how long. Millions of years for sure. Maybe billions. Anyway, it's mostly iron and nickel, with some cobalt and a few other minor metals, but it's the other impurities that make it special."

"What other impurities?" I asked, eyeing the blade with a newfound and increasing respect.

"That's the thing. We're not sure. They're elements we recognize, like calcium and fluorine and so on, but they're arranged in a crystalline structure we've never been able to duplicate. Either it was a one-off natural phenomenon, or somebody a long time ago knew a lot more about metallurgy than we do."

"Which is saying quite a bit, since Linulla here probably knows more about metallurgy than any other living being," Perry said.

"Oh, stop it, Perry, you're making me blush. Or you would be, if I—"

"Could blush. Yeah, I get it. I see that Xnsas isn't the only one who likes his dumb jokes."

Linulla vibrated for a moment, apparently engaged in a bout of the Conoku version of laughter. When he was done, he held up the blade again.

"Anyway, there was supposedly only enough of this alloy—which we call star steel, by the way—to make three blades. The Moonblade is one of them. The Sunblade, carried by another Peacemaker, is another."

"And what about the third?" I asked.

"No idea. Whatever happened to it is lost to the ages."

"Okay. So, how long is it going to take you to reforge, or overlay, or do whatever it is you do to the Moonblade?"

"One overlay, and the first? A day and a few hours to do testing and any final refinements."

"So, I'm curious—how many overlays can you do?"

"I can keep doing overlays until you run out of money. Or die, of course."

I smirked. "Of course. Well, hopefully the first will happen well before the second does."

"Hopefully."

We left Linulla to do his work. As we turned to leave, to return to the *Dragonet* and wait there, I saw Torina examining something on a workbench. Perry and I joined her.

"Amazing, isn't it?" she said.

She was looking down at a fantastically complicated filigree of some silvery metal. It didn't seem to have any obvious purpose, but it likewise didn't seem to represent anything. It was just apparently random loops and whorls, tendrils, and swirls, all rendered in chrome-bright alloy. It was, I thought, as though someone had made a sculpture of the wind.

It was absolutely stunning.

I turned back to Linulla. "What is this?"

"Oh, that? I haven't decided yet. I just work on it when inspiration comes to me, add a bit, tweak a bit, change a bit." He paused. "Come to think of it, I don't think I've done anything to it in, oh, sixty years or so now."

"Sixty *years?*"

"Hey, what can I say? Inspiration knows no schedule."

LINULLA DELIVERED THE SWORD, as promised, the next day. I'd spent much of the waiting time inside the Starsmith, getting tours of the various labs, forges, and other facilities. I even got a detailed walk-through of Xnsas's forge lab. That one was a little nerve-wracking, knowing that even a single breath of the greenish fog would turn my lungs to goo. But the armor quite happily did its hermetically sealed thing, and I came out with lungs intact. I also gained a new appreciation of the work being done here.

Xnsas had actually managed to stabilize an element with an atomic weight of 120. Such an element wouldn't even exist in nature and would only last minute fractions of an instant in the most powerful Earthly particle accelerator. But Xnsas was able to let me hold a nugget of the stuff, barely the size of a pencil eraser. It pressed down against my palm like I was holding a heavy book.

"What's it used for?" I asked.

"Right now, for impressing visitors to my lab. It doesn't have any applications yet since you're holding the only known instance of it in the universe."

Perry, who was unsurprisingly unfazed by the toxic atmosphere, spoke up from a workbench on which he'd perched. "Lots of niche uses but important ones. The *Dragonet*'s artificial gravity system and parts of its twist drive both use tiny amounts of these exotic metals to do their thing."

We returned to the *Dragonet*. Torina had stayed there, apparently intent on alternating between brooding over her situation and calling up people she knew to rally support for her cause. I'd left her to it, not wanting to intrude. But as soon as I stepped back into the ship, I could feel the gloom.

I found Torina sitting in the copilot's seat, head back against the rest, her eyes closed. I thought she was asleep and started to extract myself from the cockpit. But her eyes flicked open, and she gave me a tired smile.

"How's it going?" I asked.

"Awful, but thanks for asking."

I turned back and settled in the pilot's seat. "Anything I can do?"

"I hope so. I mean, isn't that what this is all about?"

"No, I mean, is there anything I can do right now?"

She shook her head. "Whoever's after my family's properties has done a pretty damned good job of locking down whoever else might be able to help me. I've talked to a dozen different people, and they all have reasons they can't, or won't, get involved."

"I'm sorry."

Torina shrugged. "The universe is a harsh place."

I glanced at Perry. "So I've heard."

"I did manage to learn a bit about what's going on at Van Maanen's Star, though," she said. "Netty, can you show Van that flight manifest?"

An image popped up on the tactical panel. It showed several long, looping trajectories, all of which converged on a single point. It was the moon hosting the Milon family's holdings.

"A friend was able to provide this. These are the schedules and trajectories of robotic ships that have apparently already started to haul helium-3 concentrate out of the system. There are only three ships doing it so far, but it's started." Her face turned as hard as alloy. "Bastards. They're not even pretending to wait until it's been sold."

Her voice ended in a tremble. I would have offered her sympathy, but my attention was snagged on the image, like clothing caught on barbed wire.

"Huh."

Torina's eyes had gone downcast. Now, I felt them lift back up to me. "Huh? *Huh*, what?"

"Huh, as in I have an idea." I turned to her. "Remember that plan you were asking about? I think I might just have one."

14

It turns out that spaceships aren't easy to find.

We twisted into the Van Maanen's Star system, but instead of getting underway, Netty kept the *Dragonet*'s drive powered down. She also reduced every power level she could, keeping only life-support fully operational.

"With passive scanners only, the drive not running, and the transponder off—which, I might point out, is a violation of Inter-system Traffic Control protocols, as defined by—"

"Yes, I get it, Netty, we're not supposed to switch off the transponder. Consider me duly chastened," I said.

"Your chastening is noted. Anyway, with all those measures in place, our chances of being detected are minimal. If someone happened to scrutinize this region of space in visible or infrared, they'd likely see us—but space is big."

"Yeah, I noticed." I turned to Torina. "Well, that's step one. We're here. Now for step two. Perry, you're on."

Perry had linked with the *Dragonet*'s comm system and now waited to get a firm fix on the location of one of the robotic freighters carrying the plundered helium-3 away from Torina's homeworld—or, more correctly, an empty freighter deadheading back for another load.

"Okay, I've got one, Van," Perry said as a red dot appeared on the tactical board. It hadn't been hard to find because the freighters *were* running with their transponders happily pinging away. It spoke to the arrogance of whoever was behind this sleazy little operation.

"Alright." I slid a keyboard and track-ball combination out from where it was normally kept stowed, beneath the left-hand instrument board. I tapped at it, clearing the tactical board, and replaced it with a command screen for the *Dragonet*'s operating system. I hit a moment of strange dichotomy—I'd only seen glimpses of this OS, and never actually used it, and yet I knew it well. Once again, the Peacemakers' knowledge in a syringe came to the rescue.

"Okay, Perry, go ahead," I said.

A moment passed. Perry activated a laser comm beam and directed it at the freighter. Our hope was that it would receive the incoming beam and send a query back, asking for ident and clearance data. Assuming it did, and I was able to convince it that we were legit, then I should get some level of access to the freighter's various systems.

For the first time in days, I felt less like a passenger on some great joyride of an adventure and more like someone actually in control. This was cyber-sneaking. This was hacking. This was my element. The specific commands and protocols and other bits and bobs might be different, but the principles were essentially the same.

Given the distance, there was a delay of almost a full second each way. Still, five seconds had passed, and then ten, and still the freighter hadn't responded.

"It might not have a comm beam receiver. Or it might have one, but it's broken, or pointed away from us, or—" Perry stopped. "Or, it could be responding right now."

Sure enough, the screen lit up with a query from the freighter's AI. It was, Perry and Netty had assured me, not an AI in the way they were—more emphasis on the artificial and less on the intelligent. It didn't take a sophisticated system like either of them to run a plodding freighter.

I tapped away at the keys, entered commands, and waited. Provoked a response, then responded to it—and waited. Got further queries, responded, waited. Did it again.

"This is taking a long time. Is there something wrong?" Torina asked.

I shook my head. "Nope. Contrary to popular perception, hacking is about as exciting as watching paint dry." I tapped at the keyboard. "I'm trying to insinuate myself into its operating system without triggering any countermeasures or intrusion alarms. Right now, it thinks it's talking to its power plant manu-facturer, and that I want an update on some performance specs."

Torina curled her lip in that way. "Whee."

I smiled but kept working. Less than five minutes later, I had what I wanted. The freighter's AI had allowed me to run diagnostics on all systems connected to its powerplant—so all of them—as part of a potential recall issue. I'd long since learned that anything with liability implications for not cooperating cracked open a lot of doors, or at least cracked them a little wider.

"And—there." I leaned back, sighed, and stretched out my fingers. "As far as that freighter's concerned, the *Dragonet* doesn't exist."

"Well done, Van," Perry said. "Hacking wasn't your grandfather's strong suit by any means. He was more of a sneak in and shoot things kinda guy."

"But won't the freighter's computer have recorded all of that? Or did you wipe its memory?" Torina asked.

"It will, and I didn't," I replied. "Once you start erasing data outside of normal operating system reads, writes, and deletions, you dramatically increase the chances you're going to be detected."

"So you've left a record behind."

"I have. And as soon as some maintenance tech reviews it, they're going to see it." I waved a hand at the keyboard. "But the last time anyone logged into that freighter's maintenance logs was almost two months ago, so I'm not going to sweat it."

I pushed the keyboard back into its stowed position. "Okay, Netty, time for step three."

The power immediately came back up, and the drive thrummed to life. The *Dragonet* accelerated, its course converging with that of the freighter.

Step three was tucking ourselves in as close to the freighter as possible, then accompanying it on its inbound journey. Step four was—

Step four was whatever came after step three.

"Easy there, Van. Just nudge the thrusters—shit! Netty!"

Netty immediately took control of the *Dragonet* and stopped us from colliding with the freighter, a looming bulk now only a couple of hundred meters away. She deftly brought us to a relative stop with the big ship and kept us there.

I glanced at Perry. "I've never heard you swear before."

"Sorry, but when I'm staring my impending fiery destruction in the face, curse words kind of slip out."

I looked at Torina. "That bad, huh?"

She nodded.

The freighter, now utterly blind to our existence, happily sailed on toward Van Maanen's Star, allowing us to approach and snuggle in close as we did. We'd make the rest of the approach to the star and, more importantly, to Torina's homeworld, tucked right in against the huge ship. This would merge our much smaller scanner returns with its much more prominent ones. But that meant getting in really close; Netty suggested less than five hundred meters, and ideally less than three hundred. I decided to take this as an opportunity to try out my flying skills. It shouldn't be hard, right? Just nudge the *Dragonet* in close, then fly in a straight line.

Except it wasn't that simple. The *Dragonet*'s thrusters turned out to be a lot more potent than I'd realized, a fact that only became clearer as I tried to ease closer to the freighter. All of my previous flying, the entire few hours of it, had been done in open space, well away from any collision hazards. Errors of a few hundred meters were irrelevant out there. Here, they were the difference between *fiery destruction*, as Perry put it, and—not that.

The result had been a terrifying series of frantic maneuvers, the *Dragonet* heading toward the freighter much too fast as I applied too much thrust, then veering away again as I applied too much opposite thrust. For some reason, I just couldn't seem to get the thruster controls right.

I sank back in my seat, much of my buoyant satisfaction of having successfully gotten us here gone, left behind us in the *Dragonet*'s convoluted wake.

Torina spoke up. "Netty, can you give me control, please?"

"If Van authorizes it."

I turned and gave her a curious look. She responded with a lifted eyebrow.

"Are you about to say something like *I didn't know girls could fly spaceships?* Because, if you are—"

"No, no, it's not that. I guess I just assumed, you know, you come from a rich family, so you probably get chauffeured around. If there are space chauffeurs, that is." I frowned. "Are there?"

"Yes. They're called *pilots*. And I did my first flight, dock to dock, when I was sixteen. Now, would you like my help or not?"

I sat up. "Sure. Netty, she can have control."

We spent the next half-hour easing the *Dragonet* to about a klick away from the micrometeorite-scarred hull of the freighter, then snuggling back in close again. Torina did it the first couple of times, her fingers tapping lightly at the controls, moving the ship at what amounted to no more than a quick jogging pace back and forth. I flubbed it again on the first try, but Torina crouched alongside my seat and reached for my hands.

"And if you interpret this as anything other than me trying to help you—" she started, but I raised a hand.

"Don't worry. I wouldn't—" I began, then stopped. "Okay, this is going to sound hokey, but I don't know. I think this Peacemaker thing, this uniform, means something. That I'm a professional and should damn well act like one."

Torina stared at me for a moment, then made an impressed face and smiled. "So chivalry really *isn't* dead. Okay, then."

She put her hands on mine—a nice sensation, I'll admit—then showed me exactly how the thruster controls responded to varying degrees of pressure and press time. By the time the half-hour was up, I was neatly moving the *Dragonet* away from the freighter, then closing it back in, actually bringing her to a gentle stop just over a hundred meters away from the towering cliff of alloy.

"You're a pretty damned good teacher, you know that?" I said. Even to me, there was open admiration in my voice. I didn't care.

She shrugged. "I have an incentive to be. Like Perry, I'm not a big fan of experiencing a fiery death."

WE USED the freighter to cover our final approach to the moon, whose official name was given in the star catalog as *Van Maanen's Three-Alpha*, marking it as the first moon of the third planet orbiting Van Maanen's Star. Torina called it Milon Estates, although its legal designation under the auspices of the Seven Stars League was Helso. And, unlike what I thought of as a moon—that is, either an airless rock like the Earth's Moon, or something toxic, frozen, or volcanic, like many of the other moons in the Solar System—Helso was actually almost Earth-sized and orbited a Jupiter-like gas giant.

The result was, as we closed the final distance, an increasingly breathtaking panorama of Helso backdropped by the vast, sweeping curve of the gas giant, all stripes and whorls of pastel colors. Both Helso and its planet gleamed as pale half-circles, one vastly larger than the other, in the wan light of Van Maanen's Star, a dim white dwarf.

I was still feeling my way around things like planetary physics. I knew pretty much what any well-versed science nerd back on Earth would know. It was enough to tell me that Helso should be far too cold to have a breathable atmosphere. The white dwarf produced far too little heat, and the air should be just deposits of snow and ice on the moon's surface. But it clearly did have an atmosphere because I could make out both clouds and bodies of water.

Perry had the explanation. "The moon undergoes tidal stretching as it orbits the gas giant. This heats up its interior, which in turn heats up its surface enough to keep the atmosphere, well, being an atmosphere instead of glaciers."

"It's a delicate balance," Torina put in. "And we still need to bundle up and put on rebreathers when we go outside. But it's home—"

She stopped, and some of that self-assurance she'd shown while helping me pilot the *Dragonet* slipped away.

"It's still home, Torina," I said. "You've just got a pest problem, like cockroaches or termites." I raised my head slightly. "And I'm the exterminator."

Torina stared at me for a moment, then burst out laughing. "That has got to be one of the most ridiculous things I've ever heard."

"Hey, I was just trying to make you laugh," I replied, which was a lie. I'd actually been trying to come across as dramatically noble.

Note to self—no more attempts at dramatic nobility. It didn't play well in Iowa. Or space.

"THIS IS AWFUL," Torina said.

I had to give a glum nod in agreement. We'd made it down to the surface intact, mainly because I'd let Netty handle the complex problem of keeping the *Dragonet* in close company with the freighter as it plunged into Helso's atmosphere. I was quite content to rest on the laurels of not smashing into things I'd earned during the approach to the moon. We'd landed a short distance away from where the freighter had touched down. And we'd apparently managed it undetected, thanks to Perry's assertion that deep space scanners were largely ineffective at ranges of less than a few thousand klicks.

Now, Torina, Perry, and I stood a short distance away from the *Dragonet*, which Netty had grounded just behind a ridge to block any direct view from Torina's actual estate. We'd crested the ridge, so I could just make out her home, a cluster of stout buildings and domes about three klicks away. Between there and the ridge upon which we stood, a lush forest of a native species of tree, which Torina called syrupwood, sprawled.

Or it had. Most of the forest had been stripped away, trunks and branches respectively piled to dry out, prior to being sold. Apparently, dried and ground up, syrupwood made a popular— and profitable—export. In the meantime, robotic diggers chewed away at the exposed bedrock, extracting it, pulverizing it, and conveying it to another freighter, grounded alongside the mining operation. More pulverized rock poured out of a pipeline extending from the freighter in a slurry, further polluting the landscape with grey sludge.

Torina's voice suddenly hummed over the helmet's headset. I'd already braced myself for tears. Hell, I felt a little like crying myself at the wanton destruction. But Torina's voice was anything but teary. If hard, cold ice were turned into a voice, this is what it would sound like.

"Bastards. The helium-3's not enough for them. They have to strip away our forests, too."

"It makes sense," Perry put in. "If they need to remove the trees anyway, they might as well—what?"

He'd stopped when he'd noticed both Torina and I glaring daggers at him.

"Oh, right. That was pretty insensitive, wasn't it?"

"Little bit," I shot back.

Torina pointed at a spot on the far side of what was once a lush forest. "Right there. Under a big syrupwood tree shaped like a tuning fork. His name was Davon. His father was my father's chief financial advisor. Under that tree, it was the very first time I'd ever—" She stopped and gave me a sidelong glance through her visor. "The first time I'd ever been kissed."

I was going to commiserate, offer her condolences, a shoulder to cry on, whatever she needed—but I was also about to remind her that the longer we spent here, the more likely we were to be discovered. That proved unnecessary, though, when Netty suddenly cut in.

"Folks, we've got a ground vehicle incoming. It just crested a ridge about five hundred meters away."

I PUT one hand on The Drop, which hung from one hip, and the Moonsword, hanging from the other. I'd tested the Moonsword when Linulla returned it to me, complete with its first reforged overlay, and found that by drawing it, it would disrupt comms across an area about fifty meters in diameter. It had also become even sharper than before. It was the first capability that interested me right now.

We could see the vehicle, a ground-effect car, slowly approaching. I drew the sword but held it down along my side.

"Netty, do you know if these guys sent out any comms messages? Alerted anyone?"

"No, sorry, I don't know for certain. They didn't broadcast anything, but that doesn't mean they don't use comm lasers, microwave beams, that sort of thing," she replied.

I gripped the Moonsword's hilt. "Okay, then. These guys are going to want to know what we're doing here and how we even got here without them knowing about it. Suggestions?"

"Oh, I've got a suggestion alright," Torina hissed.

I glanced at her. "Any suggestions that don't involve violence?"

Silence. It wasn't surprising. There really was no way of making our presence here appear innocent. *Sorry, sir, we just managed to avoid your scanners and land alongside your illegal forestry and mining operations and, oh yeah, I'm a Peacemaker, and this is the heiress to the family fortune you usurped? Nothing to see here, move along?*

I unclipped The Drop's holster but didn't draw it. Yet.

The car stopped about twenty meters away, and two humanoids with shockingly pale skin dismounted. They were tall, gangly and with offensively long arms ending in fingers that were even longer and *more* offensive to my human perception. Both were clad in non-descript grey coveralls that had all the personality of wet toast, and each wore a rebreather mask. Both were armed with nasty looking sidearms, and one had a rifle of some sort slung on their back.

They both moved to the front of the car and stopped. One began talking into a device. The other just waited.

Torina began walking directly toward them.

"Torina, what are you—"

She cut me off with a raised hand. I sighed and started after her. Perry flung himself into the air and immediately climbed up to a good thirty or forty meters.

The one speaking into the device gave it a frustrated shake. The Moonsword, it seemed, delivered when it counted.

The other one drew their sidearm and pointed it toward Torina.

"Close enough. Who are you?"

The voice was clipped and mechanical, the obvious product of some sort of synthesizer. Torina just kept walking.

Shit. She was going to get herself killed. I made to draw The Drop—

"Pevensi is *not* going to be pleased that we were able to get this close without being detected," she snapped, continuing to close the distance.

I saw both of the security guards stiffen and exchange a look. "Wait. What? Pevensi sent you?"

"To test security, yes. I've also brought along this Peacemaker who's looking for a deal with Pevensi."

The two now radiated confusion like a beacon. The one who'd been trying his comm unit returned to it, speaking urgently and shaking it, then speaking again.

I had no idea what Torina intended to do. She was only a few paces away from the two security guards now. Sure, she'd bluffed them this far, but then what? Her against both of them?

Which is exactly what it was. When she'd reached three paces, Torina suddenly hurled herself at the two guards.

I drew The Drop, ready to open fire, mindful of Torina's presence so I could avoid hitting her. But by the time I'd even started to assess where my first round would go, Torina had already taken things into her own hands.

The next few seconds were a study in stylish brutality. Torina kicked the first one back, knocking him off balance, and seemed to shift the direction of her attack in midair, then she slammed her other foot into the second one's face. She'd landed and spun, chopping the first on the side of the neck, then whirled around and knocked the second's leg out from under him before slamming an elbow on the back of his neck as he toppled forward. I lost track of her next few moves, a blur of arms and legs.

It was as though someone had crossed ballet with an MMA cage fight.

And then it was done. Torina stood over her two fallen opponents, the only sign of her brief explosion of lithe violence being her breathing a little harder.

I stood, gaping. So did Perry, who wheeled and landed beside me.

I blinked a few times. "That was—" I just shook my head.

Perry bobbed his head. "It sure was."

Torina beckoned me over. "Would you like to put that new sword of yours to use?"

I glanced down at the two fallen aliens, then back at her. "Oh, no. They're out cold. Killing them would be—"

"Oh, for—no, not to kill them. Here, hand me your sword."

I glanced at Perry. "Can I do that? There's no rule or anything against it?"

"Do you mean, does the Moonsword have an inherent spirit that will be offended if you let another hand wield it?"

"Uh, yeah."

"No, it doesn't."

I offered the Moonblade, still in my hand, to Torina. She took it, bent down, and deftly cut off the longest and thickest of the braids hanging off the alien's head. It only took her one quick pull, and the blade cut through the mass of hair and the metal ribbons binding it up.

"These two are Salt Thieves," she said, standing and glaring down at the unconscious aliens. "They actually started out probably three hundred years ago as literal salt thieves, on a planet where salt was a scarce commodity. Since then, they've grown into one of the biggest and baddest guilds of assassins in known space."

"Baddest? You just took down two of them in less time than it would take me to tie my shoe."

"Caught them on their back foot, fortunately. But if they come at you deliberately, at a time and place of their choosing, well—" She shrugged. "Let's just say they put the *brute* into *brutal*. Anyway, their braids denote their membership in the guild and their status. This one"—she nudged the first one she'd attacked with her foot—"is some middle-grade rank. The other's lower ranked because he's got the shorter braids."

She stepped over the first and bent down toward the second. "And they're about to get even shorter than that—"

"Hang on a second, Torina," I said, then took the Moonblade back from her. I knelt and grabbed the thickest of the alien's braids.

"You know, I once went to a grey-hat crackers' conference in Prague," I said. "There was this one Russian douche there, an arrogant, mouthy son of a bitch that kept dropping hints that he'd been involved in some big cyber attacks, ransomware shit, that sort of thing. And if anyone tried to call him on it, he just fired a barrage of threats back at them." I glanced up. "Long story short, he was an asshole and a bully. He also had a ponytail."

I pulled the Moonblade through the braid. It literally felt like pulling the proverbial hot knife through butter.

I stood, the braid dangling from my hand, and looked at Torina. "I *hate* bullies."

Which was all great but left us facing a huge question.

What now?

I asked Torina that very thing as we stood watching the mindless excavators keep up their relentless mechanical chew into the bedrock.

"We've come this far, I feel like we need to see this thing right through," I said.

Torina stared at her birthright, slowly being ground down to pulverized rock and billowing dust.

"Someone's behind this, and it isn't the Salt Thieves," she said. "Whoever they are, they have a *lot* of money and the sort of arrogance that lets them think they can start up an operation like this on land they don't even own yet. But none of this is theirs. It's *mine*."

She almost spat out that last word—mine. But then she stopped and looked at me. "Actually, Van, some of it is yours. You've earned it."

"By giving you a ride here, during which *you* taught *me* some things about flying? Then landing and watching like a wallflower while you kicked ass?"

"Are you trying to argue yourself out of being paid a handsome bonus?"

I grinned. "You couldn't have done it without me."

Torina laughed. "Anyway, The Quiet Room only paid you to bring me, and you have. So, technically, you're done."

"She's right, Van. You've fulfilled your contractual obligation to The Quiet Room," Perry put in.

"But here you are, asking what's next. That means a lot to me."

That made me a little red in the face. "Okay, well, I sure ain't earning anything just standing here. So, I'll ask it again—what now? Where to next?"

Torina glanced back at the two aliens, still sprawled alongside their hover car. "Let's go find the Salt Thieves. Somebody hired them, and I want to know who."

15

We left Helso in a much more conspicuous way than we'd arrived, by simply lifting off and hurtling ourselves back into space. Torina even asked Netty to burn the drive extra hard as we exited the moon's atmosphere, just to make our presence abundantly clear in the form of a spectacular exhaust plume.

"I want those bastards, whoever they are, to know that we were there," she said, watching Helso recede behind us with a face like glacier ice. "Despite all their precautions, we were there, and they never knew it."

"It means they're probably going to up their security, in case we decide to come back," Perry said.

Torina just nodded. "Good. It'll cost them more money and make them just that little bit more paranoid." She turned to me. "The more we force whoever's behind this to react to us, and force more moving parts into their plans, the more likely they are to screw up."

I nodded. That made perfect sense.

Once we were clear of Helso, Torina excused herself from the cockpit. She'd already given us our next destination, a space-port called Dregs, in the Epsilon Eridani system.

I lifted an eyebrow at that. "Dregs? Because it's, what, scummy?"

"Very."

"Name's a little on the nose, isn't it?"

Torina smirked. "Hey, if the smelly, dirty shoe fits."

She headed back for the cubicle that served as her cabin. When she was gone, Perry hopped onto the copilot's seat.

"Netty and I have been talking," he said.

I grimaced. "Uh-oh."

"It's nothing onerous, Van. We just think Torina's a good match for you."

I shot him a glare. "Not really looking for matchmakers, thanks."

Perry returned a steady gaze. Netty spoke up.

"Not like that. Honestly, neither Perry nor I have any interest in with whom or what you exchange genetic material."

"Who or *what?*"

"Hey, it takes all sorts to keep the galaxy spinning. Which, by the way, was one of your grandfather's sayings."

"What we're getting at, Van, is that you could learn a lot from her," Perry said. "She seems able to move in the high-class circles, but she also knows the galactic underbelly pretty well."

"And she's a damned good pilot," Netty put in.

"And she kicks ass in a fight," Perry added.

"Yeah, okay, I get it, guys. And you're right. I'd already kind of concluded the same thing, in fact. It's part of why I want to see this case—I guess it's a case, right? Anyway, why I want to see it through."

Perry cocked his head. "Part of why? What's the other part?"

I looked out the cockpit at the star-speckled view. "I like her. And, just to be clear, what I mean by that is that I genuinely like her. She's getting a raw deal, and she doesn't deserve it."

Perry bobbed his head. "No argument here."

EPSILON ERIDANI WAS the most Sol-like star we'd visited yet. It was a lot younger than Earth's sun, though, and smaller. But what it lacked in size it made up for with youthful enthusiasm, pouring out a lot more energy than Sol. It was enough to make three planets habitable, although one of them, the innermost, was only barely so. Its day-side surface temperature was essentially an unrelenting heat wave, while a blizzard of stellar wind scoured it of any life more complex than microorganisms living in the soil. But it also offered rich mineral resources and had about a thousand mining operations tearing away at its surface.

The other two more distant planets were much more like Earth. Our destination, Dregs, was a starport on the outermost of the two, a planet called Simon's World, after—someone named Simon, I assumed. Dregs sat in a broad, flat salt plain, similar to the

Bonneville Salt Flats back in Utah, only much, much larger. The starport itself was actually five separate ports, arrayed around a rambling settlement like the spokes of a wheel around its hub. The reason for this quickly became apparent: the sky was full of ships.

It looked to me like dozens of ships were in varying states of ascent from, or descent to, the port. In fact, Netty clarified that there were twenty-six, the maximum number that could safely occupy the airspace over Dregs. We actually ended up stuck in a parking orbit, waiting in a queue for our turn to land.

"What's the big draw here?" I asked. "I see the port, Dregs, and then a whole lot of nothing. For that matter, there doesn't even seem to be much habitation on this Simon's World."

Torina had just slipped into the copilot's seat, displacing Perry back to his spot behind and between the two seats at the back of the cockpit. "There isn't. The Eridani Confederacy—which, by the way, is just this star system—maintains Simon's World as an open world," she said.

Open world. As soon as she said it, my new memories provided the context. An open world, under interstellar law, was one accessible to any party that wanted to land on it. Most inhabited planets had restrictions, ranging from draconian, in the case of the more xenophobic ones, to mild, in the case of the more tolerant. But few planets were open. It meant that the Eridani Confederacy didn't enforce any rigorous customs control over the planet. Open worlds tended to be havens for all sorts of things, ranging from bases for freedom fighters from other planets seeking to cast off what they saw as shackles of oppression, to outright criminals dealing in all of the worst sorts of goods and services.

Interestingly, there was a bit of an editorial memory attached. The Galactic Knights, and therefore the Peacemakers, were generally okay with open worlds. Yes, they were cesspools of crime and villainy, but they were *known* cesspools of crime and villainy and provided a vital sort of back channel for the Peacemakers, plugged straight into the galactic underworld.

Of course, no customs controls didn't mean no controls at all. The Eridani Confederacy didn't care much who came to Simon's World, but they *did* care about what they brought with them. Cargos were subject to inspection, and excise fees were payable based on their value. The Confederacy also collected a surcharge on landing fees.

In other words, the Eridani Confederacy squeezed as much money as they could out of Simon's World while turning a blind eye to most of what went on there.

"We've been given landing clearance," Netty announced. "Incidentally, you'll be happy to know there's a neat little clause in the open world treaty that exempts Peacemakers from paying any landing fees or being subject to any sort of customs or excise inspection."

"Yeah, that doesn't sound like something that might get abused," I said, rolling my eyes.

"Oh, not at all, Van. The large amounts of money that can be earned by Peacemakers running uninspected cargo into open worlds doesn't tempt anyone at all."

Torina leaned over to me. "Perry's totally *not* suggesting you do this," she said, her voice a theatrical whisper.

"Actually, I'm not. Peacemakers aren't supposed to break interstellar laws, a principle in which I place a good deal of faith and respect," he replied, sounding a little miffed.

Torina just grinned. I glanced at Perry. "So Gramps never did anything below board like that?"

"Once. And he smuggled in medical supplies to bypass a corrupt warlord who was just seizing everything coming in from off-world himself to resell on the black market. Yes, it was technically illegal, but in that case—"

He just lifted and lowered his wings in a shrug.

I smiled and turned back to watch the spectacular light show that would be our atmospheric entry. As the first tendrils of plasma began to stream around the *Dragonet*, I thought about my grandfather's illegal smuggling.

Medical supplies?

Good for you, Gramps.

WE GROUNDED at Pad Complex Four, the most southwesterly of the five. Netty landed the *Dragonet* on our designated pad, between a hulking freighter and a sleek, gleaming ship Torina informed me was a yacht. It had the name *Spica's Flame* emblazoned on it.

"Cool name for a ship," I said, stepping out of the airlock and shading my eyes against the oppressive glare of the early afternoon sun.

"It's not a ship," Torina said. "It's a musical group."

"Spica's Flame is a band?"

She nodded. "And a famous one. They had one performance hit the top of most charts around known space a few years back. Considering how many cultures that involves, that's pretty rare."

I made a *huh* noise. I'm not sure why I'd assumed that popular bands were just an Earth thing, but they clearly weren't.

"They should add Earth to their tour list if they're that good," I said, only half-joking.

Torina gave me a look. "So the first official contact with humans should be an alien band?"

I shrugged. "Hey, it's got to be someone, right? Might as well be culture instead of missiles."

Any further conversation was cut off by the roar of a ship lifting a few klicks away. Watching it rise on a pillar of incandescent fury was, I had to admit, awesome even among all of the awesome things that had suddenly crashed into my life. It made me wonder how the hell I ended up *here*. Was this even real, or was it all just some grand delusion after all?

"It's real, Van," Perry said.

I shot him a sharp glance. "What, you can read my mind now?"

"Nope. I just recognized the signs. Your grandfather went through the same thing. First disbelief, then acceptance, followed by occasional bouts of more disbelief. Those eventually go away."

"Which might just mean I've finally and totally retreated into a fantasy world," I offered back.

"It's an entertaining one, though, right?"

"Can't deny that."

A speedy little ground car swept toward us, pulling a trail of whitish salt and grit along behind it. It stopped about twenty-five meters away, and a squat creature that seemed nothing but a torso atop four jointed legs came striding toward us.

Okay, I recognized it. It was called a Qygil, or something like that, but they were commonly known as Symbots, a riff on both symbiote and robotic. Symbots were an organic life-form that were born from some complex biological process my new memories didn't specify and were then implanted into a mechanical, AI-assisted body for the rest of their lives. Symbots had a reputation for almost ruthless efficiency and were, as far as anyone knew, the only species in known space with no sense of humor whatsoever. Unsurprisingly, this made them the perfect bureaucrat.

The Symbot stopped facing me. I noticed that it had a small plate bearing the insignia of the Eridani Federation welded to its hull. "You're Peacemaker Van Tudor, human, pilot of *Dragonet* registration GKU-08975?"

My natural tendency would be a smart-assed reply like *last time I checked,* but I held my tongue and stuck to formality.

"I am, yes."

"Your landing fees are waived in accordance with—" The Symbot went on with chapter and verse of the relevant legislation. It would be interesting, I thought, to see the Symbot and

Perry go head-to-head over some obscure matter of interstellar legalese.

Well, as interesting as what amounted to two machines debating the law could be, anyway.

"What is the intended duration of your stay?" the Symbot asked.

"Um, not sure. Depends how long it takes us to find what we're looking for."

"That response is insufficiently specific. I need you to specify a duration for your stay."

I frowned. "Why?"

Torina smoothly cut in. "Because your ship is taking up a revenue-generating landing pad, without you having to pay any fees for it. They want to get us out of here as soon as they can so they can bring in a paying ship."

I smiled at the Symbot. "We will be here conducting specific Peacemaker business until we're specifically done. Is that sufficiently specific for you?"

The Symbot said nothing for a moment. I started to wonder if something had gone wrong or we'd somehow broken it. But it finally uttered one line, then turned and stalked back to its ground car.

"Enjoy your stay," it said—which would have been a nice sentiment if it hadn't been offered in the most insincere tone I think I'd ever heard.

Which was actually a remarkable achievement for a mechanical voice.

16

WE TOOK a mag-lev tram from the landing pad to the settlement of Dregs itself. It wasn't a long trip, less than ten minutes, and was far smoother than any other train I'd ever experienced. A working mag-lev system like this one was just another in the burgeoning catalog of wonders I'd simply fallen into taking as, *oh yeah, that's pretty cool.* It wasn't that I was bored, it was more that I was simply saturated. It reminded me of a visit I made to the Uffizi art gallery during a conference in Florence, Italy. By the time I was about halfway through, I'd become numb to all the artistic splendor. I actually reached a point where, if I looked at any more great masterworks, I was going to scream or puke or— something. It turned out that this isn't just common, it even has a name, Stendhal Syndrome. The unending barrage of wonders I'd experienced since pressing the button on that remote-like device back in Iowa wasn't inducing nausea or panic, but it was leaving me feeling at least a little deadened about it all.

Stepping off the tram in Dregs sure didn't help.

It was, I thought, like stepping off a train into the bustle of any big city. I'd been to New York, London, and Tokyo, so the sudden chaotic flood of sight and sound wasn't new to me. What *was* new was a chaotic flood of sight and sound erupting from a crowd that was, with a few exceptions, not composed of human beings.

I was immersed in a crushing multitude of beings, ranging from pretty much amorphous blobs to things that vaguely resembled giant, anthropomorphic wasps, to things with tentacles, or fronds, or segmented legs, things with chitinous carapaces, bony exoskeletons, things partly made out of metal—

Things. Many, many *things.*

I turned to make sure Torina and Perry were still with me. They were, giving me somebody to whom I could direct my next statement.

"Holy. Shit."

Torina grinned. She had to raise her voice over the racket. "A little overwhelming the first time, isn't it?"

"A little?"

We moved on, Torina leading because she seemed to know where she was going. Despite the press of creatures bustling about the square—which seemed to combine a platform for the arrival and departure of the mag-lev trams with a public square and open-air market—we made our way through it with surprising speed. It took me only a moment to figure out why.

"They're making way for us, aren't they? Because I'm a Peacemaker," I said to Perry.

"They're making way for you—hey, watch it, mechanical bird here!" Perry snapped at what a baby elephant might look like if you gave it a much more humanoid head and an extra set of arms ending in wriggling tentacles. It turned and yowled something straight at Perry, making me reach for The Drop's holster. But Perry warned me off.

"He was just apologizing, Van," Perry said. "Anyway, they're making way for *you*, because *you're* a Peacemaker. You can bet that"—he paused while we veered around a cart trundling slowly along on balloon tires, laden with sacks and boxes and with no apparent driver—"that half of these people are involved in something criminal, and the other half want to be."

"It's basically one big shared guilty conscience," Torina said.

"So I just have to hope one of these... people? Is that even the right word?"

"What would you call them?" Perry asked.

I opened my mouth but just eased it closed again. Maybe I was stunned at the stark reality of being among a throng of aliens, but I had to keep reminding myself that, to them, I was an alien, too. It was a sobering thought.

I turned back to my companions. "So I just have to hope that none of these people have a score to settle with the Peacemakers."

"Now you're starting to *think* like a Peacemaker, Van. Well done," Perry replied. I just shrugged back, though.

"People having scores to settle with me? I'm used to it. I was a cracker, remember? I broke into bad guy's accounts and siphoned off all their money, that sort of thing, and I generally did it in ways that left people so pissed they threatened to burn down the world. Anger, I can handle, and I guess I'm just now coming to grips with being an outsider."

"You're not an outsider, Van. You're a Peacemaker," Perry chided.

"You know what I mean, Feathers."

"Sassy, but fair. Didn't know you had it in you."

We reached Torina's destination, a seedy bar on the far side of the bustling square. A glowing 3D sign hovered in midair just above the door, proclaiming the place to be called *Hiatus*. At least, I assumed that was its name and not just a commentary of some sort. Torina was accosted by a holographic image of a strikingly handsome man clad in a shimmering bodysuit that didn't extend below his elbows or knees. It offered to be her companion inside, but she waved it away. I had a correspondingly lovely image of a woman in a thong—no top—sidling up to me to tell me that she *loved a man in uniform*. Just as Torina had, I waved her off.

"And the AI bird gets no love," Perry said.

"They're crass advertising, Perry. A lot higher-tech than I'm used to, of course, but still—they just want to entice you inside. What would do that for you? A pretty AI girl bird?"

"Just saying it would be nice to be asked. Mild accosting makes me feel wanted." Perry sniffed. He was quite good at being wounded.

We entered the bar, a cool, dim, and relatively quiet place that was a sudden and wrenching transition from the brightly sunlit racket outside. I figured there were about a dozen patrons, making the place about one third full. Torina led us to a table, which neatly configured itself into seating for two humans.

I settled into a surprisingly comfortable seat, pausing to adjust a bulky pouch clipped to the back of my harness. It contained a hood, an alternative to lugging around a full helmet for the armor. It provided most of the same functionality as a helmet, including an airtight seal and a heads-up, but at the expense of reduced protection. I questioned why we needed to bring the damned things along in the first place, because they just seemed like one more thing to carry.

"SOP, Van. Standard Operating Procedure," Perry replied.

"Yeah, but we're on the surface of a planet with a perfectly good atmosphere."

"Peacemaker Operation Regulations, Section Five, Extravehicular Deployments, Sub-Section Four—"

I held up my hands in surrender. "Fine, we'll bring the stupid things."

Torina grabbed her helmet. "Better to have it and not need it and all that."

I looked around the bar. Except for the, um, *unusual* clientele, it wouldn't have looked too out of place on Earth.

I made an impressed face. "This place actually is pretty nice —" My own feet cut me off, crackling as I peeled them off the floor. "If you ignore all the dirt and... whatever that is sticking to my heel, that is. They ever clean this floor?"

Torina shrugged. "Some of the patrons naturally exude, ah, let's call them substances."

"Is that supposed to make me feel *better?*"

"Don't worry. Most of them are non-toxic." Before I could say anything else, Torina turned and tried to get a server's attention.

I decided that the less I dwelt on the floor, the better, so I focused on something else instead. "Do they sell human drinks here, too, or am I going to get stuck drinking a methane fizz or something?"

Perry gestured toward the bar with his head. Among the sprawl of containers inside a transparent lockup behind the bar were a few bottles I actually recognized. Hell, there was one of them in the cupboard over the sink back on the farm in Iowa.

"Now wouldn't those distilleries be gobsmacked to know just how far their stuff has traveled," I said, shaking my head.

"What makes you think they *don't* know?" Perry replied.

I stared. "What, they're deliberately exporting their booze to the stars?"

"Let's just say there are a few businesses back on Earth whose brands you'll come across out here. And they make good money doing it, although the conversion from bonds to terrestrial currency is a pain in the ass."

So Earthly businesses were surreptitiously profiting off exports into outer space. That explained a few things and tickled my interest in trade. "I wonder if twinkies would sell out here? Or cookies? What's the galactic demand for empty calories that bring a flash of joy followed by a sugar crash and regret?"

"Exactly the same as on earth," Perry said. "Rabid."

Torina had been scanning the crowd, apparently looking for

someone, and finally found them. She called over a—waiter, I guessed, although what arrived was just a metallic box traveling on a nifty set of horizontal screw shafts that let it deftly move in any direction.

"That Cetan at the table near the back wall. I want to buy him a drink. Make it a Celestial Fog," she said.

"Understood, ma'am," the box said before engaging its screws and nimbly scampering off.

"Someone you know?" I asked her, eyeing the creature for whom she'd bought the drink, apparently a Cetan. All I saw was a hulking figure with four muscular arms and no apparent head, just a protruding bulge where a neck would start. It wore nothing but a grey vest-like garment.

"Not at all. But he's wearing grey, which means he's the gatekeeper."

"I'm sure that means something."

Torina smiled. "I offer to buy him a drink, which is a signal that I want to speak with his boss."

I wondered about the Celestial Fog thing, if it had some significance or specific meaning as well. Torina shook her head. "Not particularly. They just make a damned good Celestial Fog here."

The Cetan—I'd say *stood up*, but it was really more a case of *unfolded itself*—and lumbered through a door in the back of the bar.

"That's our cue," Torina said, standing. Perry and I followed her, walking straight into a billowing cloud of vapor that smelled like an unholy mix of skunk and strawberries. It emanated from a pair of aliens mostly consisting of frond-like appendages. They sat at a table, waving their fronds through the smoke, which wafted up from a small brazier.

I coughed and waved the vapor away. "How do I know some alien isn't going to be smoking, I don't know, cyanide or something?"

"You can only smoke cyanide in a designated lounge," Perry said, hopping along beside me. I glanced down at him but couldn't tell whether he was joking or not.

We passed through the door after the Cetan, who stood down a short hallway, holding another door open. Torina nodded to him as we passed, so I did likewise. The creature rumbled something that meant nothing to me. I glanced at Perry again.

"Remember your musings about people around here who don't like Peacemakers? He's one of them," Perry said.

"Did he call me a name or something?"

"Something like that. And no, you don't want to know what that name was."

"I'll choose intellect over valor this time," I said, looking back at the Cetan with meaning. "This time."

We followed Torina into a second smaller, more intimate bar with a half-dozen tables. If anything, it was dimmer and smokier than the main bar had been, despite there being no patrons at all. Its sole occupant was a large, pale, worm-like creature, glistening and segmented, with a fan of squirming tendrils around a mouth that was nearly identical to mine.

It wasn't a good look.

"Torina Milon, it *is* you. You going through another *slumming it* phase? I thought you'd be past all that by now," the creature said, its voice clipped and mechanically flat. The little translator bug in my ear seemed to be working overtime, trying to keep up with what it was actually saying, which sounded like a stopped-up sewer finally starting to drain.

"Sorry, Flagas, but my wild days are behind me," Torina said.

"Too bad. She was quite the life of the party," the creature, apparently named Flagas, said. "Of course, now she's traveling with a Peacemaker, so yeah, I guess those glory days are gone." Flagas extended himself over the bar, looming close. He smelled like mildew and rust. The galaxy was going to make me invest in nose plugs, among other things. "That means this must be business then."

"You might say that," Torina replied, reaching into a satchel she'd carried off the *Dragonet*, extracting the braids we'd cut off of the Salt Thieves, and tossing them onto the bar.

"Ah. I see that you've had dealings with the Salt Thieves," Flagas said.

"Brief, violent business, yes. It came out in our favor."

"Congratulations. That isn't an easy outcome to achieve when it comes to them. Was that all?"

"We didn't just come here to brag, Flagas," Torina snapped. "I want to know who hired the Salt Thieves to take over my family's estate on Helso. And if you want to know who hired who to do what sordid, nasty thing, you're the go-to guy."

Flagas reared back, his tendrils writhing. "Now now, Torina, you know better than that. Some business dealings simply aren't meant for public consumption."

"Flagas, look. I want to know—"

"I'm sure you do. But, the fact is, you're pretty much—what's the Earthly term for the benefit of our human Peacemaker friend? *Persona non grata?*"

Torina stopped, staring. "According to whom?"

"According to *the word*. You know, *the word?* That indefinable sort of messaging that permeates our particular social stratum?"

I saw Torina sag a little, some of her bravado drained away. It seemed that she'd intended to trade on her family's wealth, reputation, or maybe both to get what she was after. But if someone more powerful had put a cordon around her, then that approach could be closed off. I was familiar with it, because it happened in hacker and cyber-war circles back on Earth. Word would be spread that a particular cracker or hacker might be compromised, and they became hands-off.

Which didn't help Torina, but I had an idea for something that might.

"Come on, Torina. Let's go. Since Flagas here doesn't want to assist, we'll use my other method. I'm more suited to it anyway. Don't like chit chat and dancing."

With that, I turned and walked away.

Torina, to her credit, followed me. I glanced back and saw nothing but frustrated confusion on her face, but she was playing along.

Perry got into the act, too. "Van, you sure that's wise? If it doesn't work, and you get caught—"

"It always works, and I never get caught," I cut in, then carried on back to the door and reached for it—

"You do realize that this little performance you're putting on isn't going to work, right?" Flagas asked.

I turned back to him, smiling. "It already has. You could have just let us leave, but you didn't. You want to know what this *other method* we've got might be."

"Why would I, since this *other method* is entirely fictitious?"

"Okay, then. I guess you've got nothing to worry about," I said, turning back to the door.

"You're giving too much credence to your uniform, Peacemaker. It doesn't impress me."

Again, I turned back. "You know what? Me neither. See, I've spent most of my adult life doing things that the authorities would consider, ah, let's say *problematic*. Now, I'm new to this Peacemaker thing and still not all that great at a lot of it. But there is one area in which I can claim expertise. See, I specialize in intruding into computer systems. Very, very secure computer systems. I slip in, get what I want, slip back out, and so far, I've done it without being caught."

I let my smile widen. "If you have any secrets out there in cyberspace that you don't want known, Flagas, you'd better go and get rid of them. All of them. Flush that cesspool, friend, because there's nowhere you can hide them from me when I get my hooks inside that joke you call a security system. No, don't interrupt me—doesn't matter how much you pay for your walls. They're nothing more than an irritation to me, and when I peel your secrets away, I'm not keeping them. I'll take each and every number, account, and crime—and broadcast them like shitty reality television. For your convenience, reality tv is—"

"I know what it is, you insolent ass," Flagas gurgled.

"Good for you." I turned and started to open the door.

"Wait."

For the third time, I turned back, still smiling.

"For the record, I'm doing this only because I don't need the aggravation. If you want to find out what the Salt Thieves are up to, you want to speak to Koba. He pilots a shuttle up to their orbital platform, a former military setup that got declared surplus and sold off."

"Koba. Shuttle pilot. Got it. And if this works out, then I'll spend my scarce time rooting through other, more deserving people's lives. If not—"

I shrugged, opened the door, and left, Torina and Perry right behind me.

"For a slug, he catches on quickly," Torina said.

I snorted. "That's the only thing he does fast."

ONCE WE WERE OUTSIDE, Torina gave me a genuine smile. "Pretty impressive, Van."

"I was just going to say that," Perry added, eyes flashing.

"Hey, it just does me good to be more than a tagalong," I replied. "Anyway, now we have to find this Koba. We've got a name, so let's get him."

Perry spoke up. "Already got that covered. The Eridani authorities publicize updated transit manifests every few hours to help pilots, loadmasters, and mercantile types plan their shipments. There's a Koba running a regular shuttle service to one of the major orbital platforms, where ships that can't enter an atmosphere dock."

"That doesn't sound like a disused military platform," I replied.

"It's not. But Koba has filed three variant flight plans in the past week that take him to another location in a higher orbit. The destination isn't specified. It should be, but that smells of someone in traffic control being bribed."

"Well, then. Let's go book passage with Mister Koba, shall we?" I said, and this time I let Perry lead the way since he knew Koba's regular route.

KOBA'S SHUTTLE operated out of Starport Two, to the northeast of Dregs. Another of the mag-lev tramways took us there and deposited us in a terminal that seemed almost as busy as downtown Dregs itself.

"Starport Two handles local orbital traffic, so it does a higher volume of business," Perry explained. "Anyway, Koba's pad is this way."

He hopped off through the throngs, while Torina and I hurried to keep up. Just as it had in Dregs itself, the crowd automatically parted ahead of us and closed back in behind. It made me feel creepily conspicuous but also a little important. As we progressed, I noticed more than a few backs quickly turned, faces hidden, and conversations hushed.

"There must be a few dozen illegal things going on here," I said as we slalomed our way among kiosks hawking all sorts of stuff, most of which I didn't recognize and, in the case of food stalls, I didn't want to.

"A few dozen going on within earshot, more like," Torina said. "Probably hundreds, all through the terminal."

"And almost none of them worth your time pursuing," Perry put in, turning his head completely backward to look at me while continuing to hop straight toward the parting crowd.

"Or, to put it another way, you could spend your whole career running down crimes in this one building and still never get ahead of it," Torina added.

I just nodded. I'd realized long ago that a lot of law enforcement was about being pragmatic. There were always going to be way, *way* more crimes than there were cops, so they had to pick their battles.

We reached Koba's pad after a long walk, a few minutes on a moving sidewalk thing, and a brief trip in a smaller version of the mag-lev tram. His pad was right on the periphery of Starport Two, with nothing but barren, rolling hills beyond the perimeter fence, covered in patches of something scrubby, rust-colored, and generally grassy.

"Charming, if you like the tundra," I muttered.

I stepped off the tram and watched as ships thundered skyward from all five ports, only to be replaced by others thundering in to take their spots. This remote pad seemed lonely by comparison, well away from the action.

Which is how Koba sort of liked it, I guess. Torina confirmed it when I mused about it as she walked toward the small, bunker-like hut squatting near what must have been Koba's shuttle.

"Oh, these isolated, out-of-the-way pads fetch a premium price for sure," she said.

As we approached, a figure detached itself from the building. It might have been human, except for its almost skeletal proportions, skin textured like beef jerky, and a face concealed by dark goggles and a breathing mask hooked up to a canister hanging from its belt.

"Koba Transit Incorporated, at your service." The voice was tinny and distorted but decidedly male. "Do the charming lady and her companions need transport to High Port? Or some other destination in orbit above this lovely planet?"

"Option two, thanks," I said.

"Ah. And where are we off to today?"

"We're off to see your boss in the Salt Thieves, whoever that might be," Torina replied, her voice flat.

Koba straightened from a dramatic bow. "Salt Thieves? I'm sorry, who are they—?"

I cut him off. "Stow it. Let's dispense with the little dance where you pretend not to know what we're talking about until we come up with the secret password or whatever? We know you carry people up to meet with the Salt Thieves. And you *know* that we know. Right now, we have no interest in you. We just want tickets for a trip to see your boss."

Koba crossed his arms. "Still have no idea what you mean, sorry. Now, I'm a busy guy—"

"Perry, what's my jurisdiction here as a Peacemaker?"

"Under the provisions of various legal instruments pertaining to interstellar commercial law and enforcement, you could open a case with the Eridani Federation authorities, who would be obligated to investigate and report their findings to you," Perry replied.

"And can I impound ships and cargo in the process?"

"If you could show exigent circumstances—for instance, if you had valid reason to believe a crime under those instruments I mentioned was being committed, or was about to be, or if evidence of such a crime were in danger of—"

"Okay, never mind, I get it," Koba said, holding up a skeletal hand. "Last thing I need is my ship impounded on bullshit charges." His goggles loomed at me. "Just know that I'm going to let certain parties know about this, and they aren't going to be thrilled that a Peacemaker—"

"Yeah, yeah, blah blah threats, blah blah you'll be sorry, blah blah. Got it."

Torina smiled. Much of her cool demeanor had returned.

"Now, about those tickets?"

IT STRUCK me that Koba's shuttle was only the second spacecraft I'd ever traveled in. It made me miss the *Dragonet*.

As we lifted, the shuttle's engines roared in a way that made my teeth vibrate. The ship shook and rattled. Something came loose from the top of the compartment and clacked against the deck a few centimeters from my right foot. Torina and I were strapped into a circular compartment lined with acceleration couches around its circumference, facing inward. Again, the *Dragonet* had spoiled me. This clunky old shuttle didn't include any sort of gravity system, so I got to experience some of what Earthly astronauts must have when they launched atop a chemical rocket.

The teeth-chattering roar went on for almost ten minutes, then stopped. The big, invisible hand that had been pressing me into my seat abruptly relented, and now I felt nothing, no weight at all.

A hatch opened at the top of the compartment, or what had been the top, anyway. I thought it was Koba who'd come through, but it was another similar alien, who introduced himself as the flight engineer named Balo.

"You folks need anything?" he asked, pulling himself along the wall and stopping to just drift a couple of meters away.

"So you're the flight engineer *and* the flight attendant," I noted.

"And the chief mechanic who keeps this old bucket flying, and the guy who handles all the logistics, like fuel and new filters for the air scrubbers—"

"Which seem to need changing, judging from the smell," Torina put in, wrinkling her nose. The air *did* smell vaguely of hot electronics mixed with a bathroom drain.

"It's on my list," Balo said. "Anyway, we're about twenty minutes from docking. If you need anything, just hit the intercom."

With that, he pulled himself back to the hatch and vanished through it.

There was a sudden pulse of acceleration as a thruster fired. Something creaked, followed by a sharp ping as one piece of metal striking another split the fetid air.

I scowled. "Is it just me, or does this thing seem like a—"

"Piece of junk?" Perry offered. "Yes, it is."

"But it's been certified as safe, right? Like, there are regulations about spacecraft, basic standards, that sort of thing."

"There are."

"And… they get enforced, right?"

Perry and Torina looked at one another, then both answered.

"Sure."

"Let's go with that."

Great.

Still, it seemed like an uneventful flight, and when it came to spaceflight, I didn't have to be a veteran astronaut to know that uneventful was good.

That is, right until the moment the alarm went off.

17

THE SUDDEN BLARE of a klaxon made me jump so hard I'd have been flung out of my seat, flailing around, if I hadn't been strapped in. An angry red light began to flash, and the hot electrical smell intensified. The compartment began to fume up with hazy, blue smoke.

The hatch swung open, and Balo reappeared, urgently beckoning us.

"This way! We've got a fuel leak, and the whole ship might blow! The crash pod's up here!"

I didn't need to be told twice. I unsnapped my harness and launched myself out of my seat, then stopped with a stanchion on the wall and made sure Torina and Perry were on their way. I urged them past me.

"Ladies and mechanical birds first!"

Torina shot nimbly past. So did Perry. It turned out that in zero-g and in an atmosphere, Perry's maneuverability was unparalleled. With no atmosphere, he had to rely on four small thrusters, each with about thirty seconds of propellant.

The situation didn't seem to be getting any worse at least. The next compartment up was all pipes, cables, conduits, battered storage lockers, and a small airlock outlined in red. Crimson lights flashed around it, making it easy to find even in smoke or darkness. I urged Torina into it, then Perry. Next I turned to Balo.

"Where's Koba?"

"Still at the helm! He'll keep things together long enough for us to get away, then take his own pod! Hurry!"

I turned and slid through the opening. As I did, something caught my eye.

I spun around. Balo was starting to close the hatch behind us.

"What about you?"

"I'll go with Koba! You just sit tight. You should be rescued by the Orbital Crash Team in an hour or so—"

I reached out, grabbed the alien, and yanked him into the pod with us.

"Hey—!"

"You come with us. Just to be safe."

He tried to resist, but Torina, apparently picking up on there being something up, deftly grabbed and pinned him. I reached back and slammed the hatch shut.

It locked with an ominous clack.

A few seconds passed, then a voice crackled over the intercom, loud in the cramped confines of the pod. It was Koba.

"Yeah, sorry, folks, false alarm. Well, for me and Balo, that is. For you, I'm afraid it's a very real alarm. By the way, pro tip: don't bother trying to hold your breath. You'll just burst your lungs when the air pressure hits zero. Anyway, hope you enjoyed your flight—well, this far, at least."

Balo squirmed frantically in Torina's grasp, the long fingers of one skeletal hand reaching desperately for the intercom. He came up about half a meter short.

"So how does this work exactly?" I asked him. "You sell passage to people, then kill them with a fake evacuation and dump their bodies?"

"Please, the air—!"

"Is going to be gone soon, yeah, I figured."

"But you'll die!"

"Wasn't that the plan, though?"

Torina smirked. "Well, except for the part where you pulled Balo in here with us," she said, then looked at me. "How did you know?"

I pointed back at the hatch. "This crash pod is welded to the shuttle. I happened to notice the weld seam as I was coming into what was apparently the place I was going to *die*." I almost spat the last word into Balo's face, then glared at the shabby surroundings. "I've got shitty news for you, Balo. After an incident a few years ago in a New Orleans dive bar—"

"A wh-what?"

"A bar where dreams go to die and the glasses aren't clean, but that's the point, asshole. Anyway, after an incident in which I saw my life flash before my eyes because of a misunderstanding with a woman named Doralise—redheads, am I right? Anyway, she—"

"Please, we'll all die!" Balo choked.

"Don't interrupt my story, it's rude. Anyway—"

"PLEASE!"

I reached back and yanked the hood out of its pouch on my harness. "I won't. And Torina won't because she's got one of these, too. And as for Perry—"

He lifted and lowered his wings. "Mechanical bird. What can I say." He turned his amber gaze to me. "Now, about those SOPs you find so annoying—"

"Later." I opened my mouth to say more, but a hiss cut me off. My ears popped. "Oops. Time for the hood. Anyway, Balo, I'd say it was nice knowing you, but it really wasn't."

He flailed and floundered in Torina's grasp. "Please! Anything! Name your price!"

"Who employs Koba?" I asked.

"I—shit. If it tell you that, I'll—"

"What? Die?" I grinned and started to put on the hood. "Torina, Perry and I will take care of him while you hood-up."

"Okay—shit. His name is Steedu! Now—"

"Where?" My ears popped again, and dull pain flared behind my eyes. The effects of anoxia would soon start to kick in. Torina knew that too because she shot me a worried look over Balo's shoulder.

"I don't—"

"Where? And you've got ten seconds to tell me, then we're

putting on our hoods and you're going to fall unconscious and die."

"He's on a ship. The *Vagabond King*. It travels from system to system, pretty much randomly—that's all I know! I don't know where he is now, I just—"

Balo stopped, licking his lips. The panic began to fade from his face.

I felt lightheaded too. I nodded to Torina, and she and I both donned our hoods. Then I reached over and punched the intercom.

"Hey, Koba. It's Van here. You know, your paying Peacemaker passenger? You should probably repressurize this capsule, or your buddy Balo here's going to be submitting his resignation in about, oh, I'd say two or three minutes."

Balo's head lolled forward. I turned back to the intercom. "Better make that one minute, maybe less."

A long pause, then Koba's voice crackled through the speaker.

"What do you want?"

"Well, for a start, an atmosphere would be nice."

"THEY SHOULD both be flung into space themselves," I muttered, tapping my thumb against the slate where Perry indicated, signing off my report.

"Gotta be pragmatic, Van. The greater good and all that,"

Perry replied, moving aside to let Torina settle into the *Dragonet*'s copilot seat.

I could take some satisfaction at least in knowing that Koba and Balo would be going into an Eridani prison for at least the next twenty standard years. Considering that they were responsible for the murders of at least five people, killed during their little fake emergency scam, they deserved far worse. And just to add insult to fatal injury, they'd concocted an especially vile way of monetizing their lethal little scam. Buried in the fine print of the ticket they sold was an agreement to purchase flight insurance. Thanks to having a well-placed and profoundly corrupt middle-level manager in the insurance provider being on the take, the payouts went to a fake beneficiary. Later, Koba and whoever else was part of his wicked little scheme would divide up the proceeds. The price for Koba's life had been his and Balo's full cooperation with the Eridani Federation authorities in unwinding all of their insidious corruption.

Which was good, but still. At least five people were dead. And, considering that people went missing on Dregs all the time, the chances of it being tied back to Koba were pretty remote.

Which did leave a big question, though.

"Why did they even try it with us? I'm a Peacemaker, Torina's heiress to a fortune, and you're immune to vacuum," I asked Perry.

He did his wing-shrug thing. "They panicked."

Torina nodded. "You bludgeoned your way aboard their ship and were forcing them to take you to the Salt Thieves. They were more afraid of them than they were of us."

"Don't let them get to you, Van. Believe the talking bird when he says that their brutal thuggery is amateur stuff compared to the real criminals out there."

"One of whom is apparently this Steedu." I looked at Torina. "Do you know him?"

She shook her head. "I've never heard the name before. Which means that he's just another link in the chain that started with Pevensi."

"Well, there's one way to find out, I guess, and that's find the *Vagabond King*."

Perry cut in. "Actually, Van, I have a suggestion. Now would be a good time to take a trip to Anvil Dark."

"What the hell's an—" I started, but once more, my implanted memories kicked in.

Anvil Dark was the primary Peacemaker installation, the hub of the organization's activities in known space. It was located in a peculiar and very specialized orbit in the Gamma Crucis system, also known as Gacrux, about ninety light-years from Earth. Gacrux, the closest red giant to Earth, had one large planet named Mesaribe and several smaller, barren ones known only as numbers. Anvil Dark, a massive, heavily fortified orbital platform, had been parked in one of the Lagrange points around Mesaribe, the point where its gravity, and that of Gacrux itself, essentially canceled out. As the planet orbited its star, Anvil Dark orbited with it, remaining perpetually in Mesaribe's shadow.

"You really should make a trip there, Van, and relatively soon," Perry said.

"Is it a requirement? Like, is there some regulation some-where that means I have to do it?"

"No. It's just a really good idea. You've done great work by getting this far, but before you start on the trail of this Steedu, you should go and do some research, find out what you're getting yourself into."

I looked at Torina, but she just nodded. "Perry's right. It probably would be good to find out what the Peacemakers know about Steedu before chasing after him. You're further up the criminal food chain now, and that's when the predator starts getting really hungry—and dangerous."

I nodded back. If both Torina and Perry thought it was a good idea, who was I to say otherwise? "Okay, let's go to Anvil Dark. Netty, a course, if you please?"

"Already calculated and uploaded into the nav system. There is one thing I should point out, though," Netty replied.

"What's that?"

"After we twist to Anvil Dark, we'll need to refuel. And, as far as I know, you don't have the money to fully refuel the *Dragonet* again."

"Well, hell. She's right." I turned to Torina. "Any chance I could take out a loan?"

She sighed. "Actually, you can have it all. All of my money. Which, I should note, is only the bonds I actually have with me."

I blinked a few times. "What happened? You still have a family fortune, right?"

"We do. At least, in theory. I spoke to my uncle while you were tied up disposing of Koba and his minion with the Eridani authorities. Most of our accounts have been frozen, pending investigations related to supposed fraud."

"Oh. Those scum. That sucks."

She shrugged. "We've apparently gotten closer to whoever's behind all this than they're comfortable with, so they're upping the stakes."

"But your family hasn't been involved in any fraud." I glanced at her sidelong. "Right?"

"What do you think?" Torina snapped back at me.

I raised a hand. "All due respect, Torina, but as much as I trust you, I don't know anything about the rest of your family."

She deflated a bit. "Fair enough. Anyway, the long and the short of it is, I've got about forty thousand bonds to my name."

"Enough to refuel the *Dragonet* once," Netty said. "So we can get to Anvil Dark, and we can go somewhere from there, and then—"

"And then we need more money," Perry finished for her.

I gave a glum nod. "Don't suppose the Peacemakers at Anvil Dark will hook us up with a free refueling? Since I'm, like, a Peacemaker too?"

Perry spoke up. "That's not how it works, Van, sorry. The Peacemakers have already invested a bundle in you, between unrestricted use of the *Dragonet*, my eminently pleasant company, and a host of other costs related to certification and keeping you accredited. Just ensuring your Peacemaker status remains recognized in essentially every system costs a small fortune."

"Your memory enhancements back at Crossroads cost another small fortune," Netty put in.

"The theory is that if they cover all of that, *and* they let you essentially keep whatever money you can earn, then the least you can do is gas up your own ship," Perry added.

I shook my head. "Sounds like a recipe for massive corruption."

"You'd think so, but it's really not. Corrupt Peacemakers lose all those certifications and accreditations I mentioned. They'd also send Netty and me recall codes, so you'd lose us, too," Perry replied.

"Peacemakers are well aware that it's far from a perfect system, but all agree that it's the least terrible one that the GKU *could* be using," Netty said.

Perry leaned forward. "There is one consolation. Fuel at Anvil Dark is discounted for Peacemakers."

"Great. Do I get bonus reward points when I gas up, too? Maybe a free travel mug?"

Torina smiled. "Don't fight the system, Van. Your enemies are the ones out there *not* wearing that uniform."

I sighed. "Yeah, yeah, I get it. Hate the players, not the game."

Perry bobbed his head. "Words to live by, Van. Words to live by."

GACRUX—THE name an amalgam of its actual name, Gamma Crucis—was a spectacular sight, a glowing crimson disk that seemed to fill half the space-scape. It was actually one of the stars in the Southern Cross, the Earthly constellation. I had to shake my head at the memory of a beach party just outside Sydney, Australia a year or so ago. I had been following another of the plethora of hacker/cracker conferences that ran every year, a drunken trip out to a beach for a fire, more booze, and the obligatory guy with the guitar. I'd been sitting close to a dangerously stunning brunette named Cait. I pointed out the Southern Cross to her, which was only visible in the Southern Hemisphere.

She'd been vaguely fascinated and briefly mused about *what it was like out there* before lapsing into a complex discussion about whether or not her car—a custom street racer—could achieve escape velocity with the new modifications she'd made to it. To say I was smitten was an understatement, but I shook off the memory of her long, black hair to stare in awe at the sight before me.

I was now looking at the Southern Cross from the *inside* and felt a lot more qualified to answer that question. *Cait, wherever you are—it's more beautiful than you can imagine.*

Anvil Dark, it turned out, was just as ominous looking as its name. Three massive rings stacked around a central hub wheeled with sinister majesty in the perpetual shadow of the super Earth called Mesaribe. Once, something over a billion years ago, it would have been quite Earth-like, with oceans and forests and a breathable atmosphere. Of course, its surface gravity was also almost twice that of Earth, so it still wouldn't have been that hospitable. But more so than it was now, essentially a cinder of a planet, anything resembling a volatile compound scoured away when Gacrux swelled into the red giant it was currently. The burnt-out planet now swung in a tidally locked orbit just beyond the point at which its surface would start to melt. But while it was fiery on the far side, on this one, it was ice, trapped in a cheerless frozen darkness.

It did make a handy sun shade for Anvil Dark, though.

I saw other *Dragonet*-style ships approaching Anvil Dark, parked near it, or jetting away. I also saw a few larger, more imposing ships. They were Dragons, ships with actual crews, captained by senior Peacemakers, each with the firepower of a cruiser. Dragons were reserved for especially hazardous missions, where the speed and agility of a *Dragonet*-class just wasn't enough.

"So only Peacemakers are allowed access to this place?" I asked.

"Them and other members of the Galactic Knights, plus certain dignitaries. Anyone else who enters the Shadow of Mesaribe without clearance is subject to attack," Netty replied.

I could hear the capital letters in that phrase, the Shadow of Mesaribe. It was steeped in Peacemaker lore and had levels of significance to it I didn't understand, and wouldn't, unless and until I rose higher in the ranks. But that was an issue for another day. Today, we just needed to ensure we were clear to dock.

"Okay, so are they going to recognize us, or do we need a key to get in?" I asked.

"You need a key," Netty said.

"Alright. And that key would be…?"

"It would be me," Perry said.

Both Torina and I looked at him. "You?"

"In the metallic flesh. Allow me to demonstrate."

Perry went still, and his eyes glowed. At the same time, data sluiced across the comm system. A few seconds passed, then data sluiced back. And a few seconds after that, a message appeared on the nav screen.

CLEARANCE GRANTED. ASSUMING REMOTE FLIGHT CONTROL IN THIRTY SECONDS.

"This is the part where I get to be a passenger, too," Netty said as Anvil Dark took control of the *Dragonet* and maneuvered us among the bustling traffic before finally bringing us to dock at an airlock in the middle ring of the three. We were offered a slot in an actual hangar, but that would have involved the *Dragonet* entering through a massive airlock, which had to be depressurized and repressurized—for a not insignificant fee. The external airlock, on the other hand, was free, which was definitely in my price range.

The last of a series of thumps and clunks, then a green signal —and we had a solid dock. We'd arrived. Torina and I unstrapped and headed for the airlock. Anvil Dark and the Peacemakers waited just beyond it.

18

IF THE PEACEMAKERS had a home anywhere, it was Anvil Dark. Headquarters, logistics base, fortress, workshops, business center —for *thirteen hundred years*, it had been all of these things and much, much more. Most fundamentally, though, it was the place where Peacemakers could gather, simply hanging about to experience one another's company, get together in small groups to seek or provide assistance to one another on especially challenging cases, form alliances, or even assemble formally. These latter events, called Conclaves, were rare. The last Peacemaker Conclave, which had summoned all active Peacemakers to Anvil Dark, had happened nearly twenty years ago.

I got it. In that sense, Peacemakers were like hackers and other cyber operatives. Cyber-ops was a solitary profession, involving long hours sitting alone behind a terminal, often waiting for programs to execute and produce results. Since that could happen a minute from now, or an hour, or maybe many hours, it meant you had to wait for things to happen. It was, not to put too fine a point on it, often lonely and boring. That's why there were so many cyber-security conferences, hacker gatherings, and the like. It gave people who normally labored in tedious solitude a chance to spend time with others who *got it* because they lived the same lifestyle themselves.

It was the same here at Anvil Dark, which was essentially a permanent Peacemaker conference. And it made sense. An organization like the Peacemakers, whose members were normally scattered over literally hundreds of light-years of space, needed a touchstone, a place to call home, even more than Earthly hackers did. Whether it was to have a damaged *Dragonet* repaired, seek legal advice on some particularly thorny case involving many overlapping jurisdictions and often implicating powerful parties, or just take a break from the rigors of the job, Anvil Dark provided it. And it provided it in the company of people who *got it*.

And then some.

As we'd been making our final approach, I'd just stared and shaken my head. Thirteen hundred years. So at about the time this station had been built, back on Earth, the Moors had crossed the Straits of Gibraltar, seized the Iberian Peninsula, and stormed into present-day France until they were stopped by Charles Martel at the Battle of Tours. Gunpowder technology wouldn't even arrive in Europe for over five hundred more years.

Holy shit.

Now, we wandered along a soaring concourse leading around

the circumference of the middle of the three massive rings. It was, I thought, not too different from one of the big shopping malls back on Earth, although without the shrieking kids and a lot darker. Anvil Dark was literally dark. Perry explained that the station was routinely kept dimly lit through most of its interior because it was easier for beings used to brighter light to see in gloomy conditions than the other way around.

Which underscored another reality of the Peacemakers, one that I'd known but without actually knowing I knew it.

Not all Peacemakers were human.

I'd known it, of course, because I'd already met one—Gus, the head of the Peacemaker installation on Crossroads. But I'd somehow let myself assume he was an aberration because the only other Peacemakers I knew were Gabriella Santorelli and, of course, Gramps. But most Peacemakers were not, in fact, human. I saw many Peacemaker uniforms around me as we made our way along the concourse, but none of them enclosed a human being.

That only caught me up in a moment of natural conclusion. As we wended our way among the crowd—sparser, quieter, and definitely more disciplined than the throngs back on Dregs—something else struck me as much more of a disconnect. I glanced at Perry, who was hopping along between Torina and I.

"Perry, I thought you said there were fewer than eight hundred active Peacemakers."

He glanced up at me. "That's right."

I looked pointedly around. "Well, I see about fifty Peacemaker uniforms right now. And this station is huge. So, unless almost all of the Peacemakers on board just happen to be here, on this concourse, where I can see them, then there has to be more than that."

"A lot more, I'd think," Torina put in.

Perry bobbed his head. "You're right. There are."

"So you made a mistake? Lied to me?"

"Nope. I said there were just under eight hundred *active* Peacemakers. At any given time, there are probably another couple of hundred involved in training, getting their ships repaired or upgraded, that sort of thing. Then there are another four hundred or so assigned to desk jobs—dealing with legal matters like warrants and writs and the like, providing adminis-trative support, and generally making sure things are running—well, I'd say smoothly, but let's face it, any organization this big and far-flung is never going to run *smoothly*. Let's say they keep it running *at all*."

I nodded my understanding. Okay, that's where the hacker analogy broke down. There was no overarching global guild or association or other similar sort of corporate body for hackers.

We ambled past a kiosk selling interesting electronic doodads. I veered that way. A lot of this concourse seemed to be devoted to businesses operating out of storefronts along one side, with the other a vast, curving expanse of windows opening onto the bustling starscape. Cast in the pall of Mesaribe's shadow, the ships and shuttles hustling purposefully about outside were marked mostly by their strobing anti-collision beacons. The view reminded me of warm summer evenings on my grandfather's farm, walking through the apple orchard beside the barn and watching the fireflies flicker and twinkle amid the gloom.

But the electronic gizmos had caught my eye, pulling my attention away from a breathtaking view. I recognized a few variations on the data slates we had aboard the *Dragonet*, and things similar to other devices onboard. The rest of the inventory meant nothing to me. I started asking the shopkeeper, a small alien, slender and grey with big, black eyes, questions. For the moment, I forgot about Torina and Perry and lost myself in a whole new world of techno-babble. I picked up one item, a universal decryptor, then turned it my hand and studied it.

"You have a good eye. That can break any encryption rated Cosmic Four and below," the little alien said. "And it's guaranteed to do it in real time for Cosmic Three and less, and in no more than ten standard minutes for Four."

I sniffed and shook my head, looking at the little device. "Must be some sort of quantum computing rig."

The alien nodded. "Exactly right."

"Amazing. Imagine how much this would sell for on Earth. I don't even know what sort of encryption levels we use back home."

"Earth? Pfft. They're just starting to nibble at the edges of Cosmic Two."

I raised an eyebrow. I'm not sure why it surprised me that the little alien knew about Earth, but—

I narrowed my eyes. "Wait a minute. All due respect, but you look exactly how aliens are usually envisioned on Earth. You know, grey, big eyes, that sort of thing."

The alien shrugged. "We've had a few interactions with Earth, sure. Mostly keeping an eye out for new potential markets. If your people would, to borrow one of your own phrases, *get off their asses* and develop real spaceflight, we could do some serious business."

I put the decryptor back down. "Okay, so I gotta ask—what's the deal with the abductions and cow mutilations and stuff?"

"Oh, for—that was *one* weirdo, and we put a stop to him a long time ago. Don't tell me your people are still going on about that?"

"Let's just say that you made an impression."

We carried on, past more shops selling an astonishing array of stuff, from ship components, to armor, to various types of injected enhancements, to weapons—holy crap, the weapons. Putting together everything for sale in that concourse, I swear there was more firepower than the entire US military.

And I could afford exactly none of it.

"This is frustrating as hell, you know," I said. We'd reached a bulkhead lined by a bank of elevators. I turned back and looked along the broad, curving sweep of the concourse. "I'm the kid in the candy store, except all the candy is super amazing, and it all costs way more than I can afford."

"It's like anywhere else, Van. You have to work to pay the bills."

I scowled. "Whatever happened to that post-scarcity economy thing that sci-fi has been promising me? You know, where you tell a machine what you want, and it creates it for you on the spot?"

"That would be the fiction part of science fiction," Torina

said, then gestured expansively around. "And this isn't science fiction, Van. This is the real deal."

Yeah, well, the real deal was starting to feel like kind of a raw one.

———

PERRY SUGGESTED that I make the trip to the Upper Ring, where the Keel was quartered and maintained its offices. It was customary for new Peacemakers to present themselves to The Keel, the Peacemakers governing body. It was a group consisting of the seven most experienced and accomplished members of the organization. One of them held the title of High Master and was nominally in charge of the entirety of the Peacemakers Chapter of the Galactic Knights, and also a high-ranking Galactic Knight themselves.

My new memories told me, though, that it was actually a lot more complicated than that—of course, because nothing was ever simple. While the Masters were technically in charge of the Peacemakers, they really only dealt with broad matters of policy and mostly let their far-flung subordinates—such as Station-Masters, like Gus on Crossroads—interpret it. And even then, most Peacemakers ended up applying policy and regulations as they saw fit, given their immediate situation.

It made sense because the political, social, cultural, and economic conditions in one region of space were likely very different from others. Even more than that, though, individual Peacemakers came to develop their own style, their particular way of approaching a case. The inevitable result was a sprawling, tortuous hodgepodge of widely varying approaches to the Peacemakers' duties across known space. Given a particular case, one Peacemaker might insist on a subtle, more diplomatic approach to its resolution, while another might immediately rush in, guns blazing, and sort things out afterward. A third might decide to employ subterfuge, perpetrating espionage in the name of justice, and a fourth may decide the potential benefits weren't worth the time and effort and simply ignore it altogether.

Which, to me, seemed really dumb. How could you run an organization that might unleash all sorts of lethal violence to deal with a case in one place but would sidle up to the parties involved in a patient display of quiet diplomacy to solve the same case in another? How could that have any credibility?

I asked both Torina and Perry that very question as we took an elevator to the Upper Ring.

Torina pursed her lips. "Well, you made a living breaking into computer systems back on Earth. Did you ever break into one to further a good cause? Say, to help dissidents organize and rally against an oppressive government?"

"Yeah—and I see where you're going with this. Your next question is going to be, did I ever break into a system to help a government take action against subversives, terrorists, that sort of thing. And yeah, I've done that too. And, yeah, I get it. In the first case, I might help them by providing some high-end encryption, and in the second, bust through their encryption and wipe out files. Same guy, two very different approaches."

"If you're going to answer your own questions, Van, you don't really need Torina and me, do you?" Perry asked.

I offered a rueful smile. "Only as long as I lob softballs to myself. I need to keep you guys around for the hard stuff."

The elevator stopped, and we exited into a plush lobby that would have done justice to the swankiest hotel back on Earth. Thick, soft carpet invited you to yank off your shoes and socks and just enjoy the pliant feeling underfoot. A fountain tinkled away in a shallow basin ringed by brightly flowered plants, most of which I absolutely didn't recognize—not that I was any sort of expert in botany, but I knew the basics, and none of this foliage fit them. For instance, I didn't think there were any terrestrial plants that looked like they were made of spun glass. Chairs and couches were opulent studies in the word *upholstered*. Elaborate, vibrant tapestries draped the walls, some depicting specific scenes, others apparently just intricate, fractal-esque patterns.

"Wow. This is… plush."

Torina quirked her lip into a sardonic smile. "Yeah, it's tough at the top."

We padded across the lobby, sinking so far into the carpet I started to wonder if there was actually floor beneath it. The only other exit was a set of doors emblazoned with the Peacemaker logo in what looked like real gold. Blocking the way to it, though, was a semicircular desk, behind which sat—

It took me a moment to figure out *what* sat there.

Imagine a squid. Now, imagine that squid has a torso that splits into tentacles at both ends, with one set of them ending in clusters of—eyes, I guess? The other set divided, and divided again, into a multitude of writhing tendrils. Now, imagine that wearing a Peacemaker uniform. Needless to say, it was tailored a lot differently than mine.

I slowed on instinct, my primitive monkey hind-brain reluctant to get any closer to the, um, person. But Perry just hopped up on the desk with a metallic clack of his claws.

"Yo, Max, how're you doing?"

One of the clusters of eyes swiveled around and locked on Perry. The others remained fixated on a variety of documents and screens, while most of those writhing little tendrils tapped away at consoles and keyboards.

A voice that sounded like several, perfectly harmonized, replied. "Hey, Perry, long time no see. Doin' alright there, Feathers—oh. Right, you're not with Mark anymore. I was sorry to hear about that."

"Yeah, well, we all end up eventually being deactivated. Anyway, this is his grandson, Van. He's following in his granddad's footsteps. Or he's starting to, anyway."

One of the eye clusters swung toward me. And the whole time, the creature, which was apparently named Max, kept working away at a half-dozen different workstations.

"Very pleased to meet you, Van."

"I, uh—"

"While Van is remembering how to speak English, this is Torina Milon," Perry said.

She smiled and offered her hand outstretched, fingers splayed. Max extended a tentacle and touched each of the tips of her fingers with a fleshy tendril.

"Pleased to meet you, Torina. Have we met?"

"I don't think so. But my family has one of your Communes overseeing our business administration, so you might be picking up psychic echoes from them."

"Ah, yes, that must be it. What is that Commune's designation?"

"Pearl."

"Oh, yes, I know Pearl. That would explain the echoes."

I just watched the conversation between Torina and the fleshy, tentacled blob named Max bounce back and forth. I understood the words but had trouble making sense of the context. Commune? Designation? Psychic echoes?

"So, Van, have you remembered how to talk yet?" Perry asked.

"Uh—"

"Apparently not. Van's new to pretty much everything."

"Don't you worry about it, Van. Your grandfather, Mark, took a bit of time to get used to it all, too," Max said.

While Max was speaking, the doors behind the desk slid open. I waited to see what kind of life would come slithering or oozing out of it this time, but it was a human, a man, probably in his sixties, judging from the greying hair and beard. He wore a Peacemaker's uniform but with many more patches and braid than I'd seen before.

"Did I hear someone mention Mark? Do you mean Mark Tudor?" he asked.

"Yes, sir. This is his grandson, Van," Max replied.

The man strode around the desk, extending his hand. "So

you're Mark's grandson. I heard you were on your way here."

He took my hand and shook it. I stared.

"Van has forgotten how to speak," Perry said.

Torina chuckled.

I shook my head. "Uh, no. No, I actually haven't. I'm just a little—"

"Overwhelmed," the man said, grinning. "Tell me about it. When Mark and I first stood right where you are, I think we forgot how to talk for a bit, too." He glanced back at Max. "Part of it is just Max's radiant beauty. But part of it's their psychic aura, too. If you're not used to it, it can fill your brain with static."

"I—yeah. Okay. So, you knew my grandfather?"

The man nodded. "I did. Very well. In fact, the first time I met him, he tried to kill me."

THE MAN, whose name was Petyr Groshenko, also turned out to be one of the Masters. He led us back through the doors, along a corridor lined with more doors, and into a soaring space dominated by a massive, triangular table made of some rich, ruddy wood with grain that seemed to slowly writhe and change, like a really sluggish lava lamp. One corner of the triangle had been truncated, and there was a voluminous cushion, like a queen-sized mattress only more plush, set there. Each of the sides of the triangular table had two more places laid out to sit, although only two of them were what I would call chairs. More tables and various types of seats were arrayed around the perimeter of the room.

"You're really fortunate, Van," Perry said. "Most Peace-makers don't get to see the Keel until well into their careers. Some never see it."

Groshenko smiled and gestured to one of the chairs at the big table. "Here. Sit."

I stared. "What?"

"Sit. Please."

"But—"

Groshenko just waved me over. I glanced at Torina and Perry, both of whom shrugged, then walked to the chair and sat down.

"There. I finally managed to get a Tudor to sit at this damned table," he said, grinning again.

I shook my head. "I'm sorry, I don't understand. And what did you mean, my grandfather tried to kill you?"

Groshenko leaned against the table and laughed. "Your grandfather and I played the same game. We just played for different teams. And we ended playing on the same field—oh, at least three times, I think, or maybe it was four—"

He shrugged. "Anyway, we crossed professional paths several times. That first time was in Africa, during a border war between two countries that never happened. Your grandfather got the drop on me. The drop—it became a joke. He even named his sidearm after it."

"Yeah, I know. I have it locked up on the *Dragonet*," I said. I got it, now. My grandfather and Groshenko had both been involved in the shadowy, spooky world of spec ops. They'd obviously been opponents, enemies, who somehow became friends. Friends who then somehow ended up Peacemakers.

I looked at Groshenko. "There's a whole lot of story behind you and Gramps that I'd love to hear. But what did you mean, you finally got a Tudor to sit at this table?"

"Bah, your grandfather was a stubborn asshole. He was eligible to be a Master. He earned it. Hell, he *deserved* it. But the obstinate old fool refused. He *refused* the title of Master. He's the only Peacemaker ever to have been known to do that."

"Why?"

"Because being a Master isn't a job, and it's not even a life*style*. It's a life. You give up everything else. As far as anyone on Earth who knew me knows, I died long ago. I haven't even been near Earth in, oh, has to be ten years now." He smiled at me. "Mark didn't want that. He didn't want to just vanish, officially missing, and eventually be assumed dead. He had more important things in his life, like his grandson."

I just stared.

Groshenko scratched behind an ear. "Mark told me all about you. He told me how your father was away for most of your life, and how you finally lost him completely to that accident on that aircraft carrier. And he told me how you lost your mother as well—"

I held up a hand, and he nodded and just went on.

"Anyway, he wanted to be there for you. And he wanted, or hoped, anyway, that you'd be his Successor as Peacemaker when the time came. And here you are. So, yes, I've finally persuaded a Tudor to sit at the Keel.

I sat there, staring at the remarkable wood and its languidly flowing grain. Gramps had turned down becoming a Master so he could be there for me during those awkward, wonderful, terrible years between child and man. He'd actually tried to balance an incredibly demanding, not to mention totally bizarre career with taking care of his teenage grandson. He was literally commuting light-years back and forth to be there for me.

I had to look away for a moment and try to swallow the sudden hurtful lump in my throat. Groshenko, Torina, and Perry all became interested in other things, giving me that moment. Because I needed it.

I finally stood. "Well. Okay. There are about a thousand things I'd like to hear about you and Gramps—like, how he tried to kill you in a war that never happened. And how the two of you both ended up as Peacemakers. But—"

"But you're on a case after our friend, Steedu," Groshenko replied.

I frowned. "You know about that?"

He laughed and waved a hand. "Don't worry. Perry told my AI when you arrived here."

But he crossed his arms and turned serious. "Steedu isn't the worst the galaxy has to offer by any means, but he's still pretty bad news. He hasn't been operating this long, this successfully, without managing to stay out of the Peacemakers' reach. You might want to consider something a little less, um, challenging for your first major outing."

"On the other hand, Van is basically unknown as a Peacemaker, so he won't be on Steedu's radar," Torina said.

"Ah, yes. Miss Milon. I'm sorry to hear about your troubles. I also understand that Pevensi's involved." He glanced at me. "Now that is a man you definitely *don't* want to run afoul of.

I glanced from Groshenko, to Torina, and back to Groshenko. "I appreciate the advice, but I think I'll stay the course with Torina here."

Groshenko barked out a laugh. "I knew it! As soon as I saw you, I thought he's going to be as stubborn as that old mule of a grandfather." He sighed. "Well, I can't say it surprises me—and honestly, I'd love to see Steedu taken down a peg or two. To that end, I have a present for you."

"Really? Oh, and here I didn't bring you anything."

Groshenko gave me a hard smirk. "You've got Mark's sense of humor, too."

"Is that a good thing?"

"Sometimes," Groshenko replied, returning to that easy grin of his. I could see why Gramps liked this man. They weren't all that different.

"Anyway, my AI's going to upload some instructions and clearances to Perry. You're going to take that *Dragonet* of yours into a nice, cozy hangar and get some armor upgrades installed. It's my way of saying welcome to the Peacemakers—and to do something in memory of the man I considered my best friend."

That lump came back again. I just offered my hand to Groshenko, and he shook it with a smile that could have come from Gramps himself.

19

THE *DRAGONET* actually felt more solid. The armor upgrade, modules of applique armor custom fit to the ship and fastened to the hull in strategic locations, would dramatically increase the *Dragonet*'s survivability. At least, that's what the lumpy shop foreman had told me.

"You won't be able to go toe to toe with a cruiser or anything, but all your vital bits have extra protection now."

I smiled. "Protecting my vital bits has always been a priority for me."

Apparently, the foreman's race had no concept of innuendo. He simply took what I said as agreement, so I left it at that.

"Solid joke there, Van," Perry muttered.

"I thought so. Hate wasting good material."

"Tell you what. Use it again sometime, and I'll act surprised."

"You're a team player, Perry. Thanks."

"Don't mention it."

As we departed Anvil Dark in the uparmored *Dragonet*, which Groshenko had also supplied with full provisions and a refueling, Perry pointed out just how generous the Master had been.

"He gave you about one hundred and five thousand bonds worth of stuff."

That raised my eyebrows in surprise. Torina sniffed and smiled.

"It's good to have friends in high places," she said.

But Perry came back with a word of warning. "Just be careful, Van. The Masters aren't exactly the most innocent lot of beings. You don't rise to that rank in the Peacemakers—any organization, for that matter—based on your charm and good looks."

Torina nodded. "He's saying that as fond as you are of Groshenko, he's a creature of politics and no doubt has enemies. So friends of his—"

"Are enemies of *his* enemies, yeah, I get it. But a hundred-odd thousand bonds worth of stuff goes a long way to take the apprehensive edge off, if you know what I mean," I said.

Torina and Perry both nodded.

"So where to, boss?" Netty asked.

I looked at Torina. "Good question. Any idea where this Steedu might be?"

"No, but I think that's the point. He follows a more or less random path for a reason."

I turned to Perry. "How about the bird? Any ideas?"

"I've exchanged data with all of the other combat AIs that were on Anvil Dark, and—no. Sorry. The best I got was his last registered comm log, which was back at Crossroads, two days ago. But where he went from there is anyone's guess." Perry cocked his head. "On the bright side, I did learn about a whole pile of paying jobs available, just in case we can't run Steedu down right away."

"So there's money to be made."

"More out there than we could ever spend. Of course, that's not the real question, though, is it?"

I exchanged a bemused glance with Torina. "Okay, I'll bite. What *is* the real question?" I asked.

Perry's amber gaze stayed locked on mine. "The real question is, how many mistakes can you survive?"

WE RETURNED to Crossroads since it was the last hard location we had for Steedu. The trouble, it turned out, was that from Crossroads, he could have twisted to just about anywhere.

"Isn't there a maximum distance or something?" I asked as we made lazy circuits of a holding pattern. As far as I knew, there wasn't, but I wanted expert confirmation.

"In theory, no," Netty replied. "If you use enough energy, you could twist together two points on opposite sides of the universe."

"But energy means fuel, so fuel's the limiting factor."

"That's right. All we know about Steedu's ship, the *Vagabond*

King, is what's available in ship registry databases and some data in Peacemaker intelligence archives. None of that includes actual performance data, but the *King's* twist drive is rated to handle enough power that it could go anywhere in known space."

"Which means we have to assume he could be anywhere in known space," Torina said.

"That is, unfortunately, the inescapable conclusion," Netty agreed.

I drummed my fingers on the armrest. "Okay. So he was here two days ago. Since then, he could have gone—as far as we're concerned, anywhere. And that's all we know." I sighed and glanced at Torina. "Been here before, except in cyberspace. There's nothing quite like that sinking frustrated feeling when you realize you've traced a contact as far as you can and… "

My voice trailed off as a thought came to me. Torina glanced at Perry.

"Do I smell burning insulation?" she asked.

Netty responded with an indignant sniff. "Not on board this ship, my dear. Everything's in perfect running order—"

"I'm sure it is, Netty," Torina said, smiling. "I was talking about Van's brain."

"Oh. Well. Then sure, and probably some smoke, too."

I scowled. "If you two are finished badmouthing me while I'm sitting *right here*, I have an idea. When I lost the trail of someone I was trying to run down in cyberspace, my go-to was to work backward, looking for clues that might mark the way forward again." I turned to Perry. "Can we find out where Steedu came *from* to get *here*?"

Perry cocked his head. "Crossroads is a busy place, and it runs on a pretty rigid schedule. Peacemakers can come and go as they please because we have our own module with its own airlocks. But the unwashed masses are given windows of time to use specific locks and hangars, and get slapped with a serious surcharge if they go overtime. Even parking space around Crossroads is controlled and subject to usage fees—of course."

"Guess being a Peacemaker has its privileges. But, all that said, Perry, what's your point?"

"My point is that ships usually request approach and docking clearance in advance before they even arrive here. They're given a window of time for it, which determines their schedule. So you don't want to be late, but you don't want to be early, either."

"Okay, so you're suggesting Steedu might have requested docking clearance before coming here."

"And that would mean he'd sent a comm message ahead of his arrival to book clearance," Torina said.

"And a comm message would be logged, with its location of origin," Perry finished.

I reined in my sudden enthusiasm. Just as I was no stranger to losing trails, I was no stranger to dead ends, either. "So the jackpot question is, how do we get access to those comm logs? I'm sure they're pretty well-protected. I mean, I can probably hack them, but—" I frowned. "Wait. Wasn't there something in Steedu's Peacemaker dossier about an outstanding writ?"

"There is. He was involved in a civil dispute over ownership of some salvage a few years back. He had a judgment rendered against him *in absentia* since he never bothered to show up for the hearing. The matter was referred to the Peacemakers, and we issued the writ. But all it says, Van, is that if we encounter Steedu, we can order him to make payment on what he owes. If he doesn't, we can seize property equal to the amount outstanding. But all he'd have to do is make payment, and he'd be clear."

"Not exactly the most gripping Peacemaker case, is it?" Netty put in.

"No, and another dead end," Torina said, frowning.

But I shook my head. "Not necessarily. Correct me if I'm wrong, Mister Legal Eagle—"

"Not an eagle," Perry said.

"Noted. Anyway, my spiffy new memories are telling me that an outstanding writ gives us legal justification to, um, access such data and information as may be necessary, to, uh—"

"As may be necessary to ensure execution of that writ," Perry finished for me, then bobbed his head. "And you're right. We'd need Gus to sign off on it, though."

"Perry, put the wheels in motion. Let's start following the breadcrumbs to our friend Steedu."

"What if he didn't actually leave breadcrumbs?" Torina asked.

I smiled. "Everyone always leaves breadcrumbs, my dear. They usually just don't know it."

WE LEARNED a lot about Steedu once we were able to get that first peek beneath his rock. It turned out there were lots of squirmy things wriggling away under there. Steedu, however, seemed to be pretty good at knowing just how far he could push the law, so while everything we found fell into the unethical or immoral categories, and usually both, very little was illegal. Based solely on what we were able to learn once we dug into his comms trail, there wasn't much to give us any traction.

We did, however, manage to find a message to a customs broker suggesting his next port of call after Crossroads was Wolf 424, a binary red-dwarf system with only two intact planets—both gas giants. Some ancient cataclysm had smashed three or four one-time rocky worlds into debris, forming a complex series of asteroid belts that were chock full of rich mineral deposits. The Lupine Agglomerate, a loose collection of small corporations and independent belt miners, oversaw the system. But they had as much interest in enforcing the law as you'd expect any motley group of miners to have when all that united them was the sole goal of not having to outright fight one another for mineral rights. It meant Wolf 424 was a pretty lawless place and would be as much a haven for criminals as Dregs, if there were anything actually there.

"Really, the only reason anyone goes there that doesn't actually have anything to do with asteroid mining, is clandestine meetings, ship to ship, in deep space and away from prying eyes," Torina said. The way she said it hinted at it being more than just general knowledge on her part, as though she'd had some experience with it. I didn't pry, though.

"So Steedu went there to meet someone," I said.

"And that is where it gets interesting," Perry replied. Torina and I both turned to look at him.

"The advantage of being able to do trillions of calculations a second is that I can find patterns in things pretty quickly," he went on. "I've run through all of Steedu's historical comms traffic, using the writ to justify dipping into the archives of five other systems. Steedu travels between them in a seemingly random way. But it's not random."

I glanced at Torina. "I think this is the dramatic pause."

Perry bobbed his head. "You're damned right it is. Steedu's flight path seems random because he periodically meets up with another ship, the same one every time. It's called the *Dust Mote*, and it's registered to a company based out of Ad Leonis. That's the home system for the Leonides, Steedu's species."

"Koba and Balo were both Leonides," Torina said.

I thought back to the skeletal Koba and his sidekick, Balo, who'd tried to space us back on Dregs. "Birds of a feather—oh, sorry, Perry."

"What is it with you humans and your avian sayings? Birds of a feather, bird in the hand, bird brain—oh, and I take particular exception to that one."

"Focus, Perry. You were telling us about Steedu's meetings with this ship, the Dust Bunny."

"Mote. Dust Mote. Anyway, the Dust is captained by one Felun, a female Leonide with whom Steedu has, let's call it some passing familiarity."

"Ah, now this *is* starting to sound interesting. Go on."

"Well, based on public records, Steedu and Felun spent many

of their formative years together, during which he was on a cross-creche exchange. And now you're going to ask me what that means, and I'm going to answer that it boils down to the fact that Leonide society is rigidly divided vertically, not horizontally, like in a traditional caste system. Creches are the fundamental Leonide social unit, and there's very little interaction between them. In fact, it's pretty much taboo. The closest they come is an exchange between creches, like the one involving Steedu."

A slow smile spread across my face and Torina's, as we both immediately got it. "So you're saying that Steedu is paddling in some forbidden waters, here? He's meeting up with Felun from time to time to do some more, ah—"

"Cross cultural exchange?" Torina put in, offering a suggestive leer.

Perry bobbed his head. "Sure looks that way, doesn't it?"

"Well well, looks like we have a new weapon on board, one as powerful as any missile or laser," I said.

Torina quirked her head at me. "And that would be?"

I smiled. "Shame. Trust me, it can be more powerful than an exploding sun."

EVERYONE MAKES MISTAKES, even powerful, self-assured criminals. Steedu's biggest one was overlooking the fact that, while the movements of his own ship weren't public, those of the *Dust Mote* were. In fact, since it was a freighter that relied on cargo haulage to generate revenue, its movements were pretty much advertised.

By telling known space where the ship would be, and when, it makes planning cargo pickup and delivery by potential customers much easier. So now that we could track the *Dust Mote*, all we had to do was figure out when and where it would next rendezvous with the *Vagabond King*.

Just following it was an option, but a poor one. We'd burn fuel with every twist, so even a few hops along after it would cost us a fortune. But there was a better one. The Dust Mote was scheduled for another stop at Wolf 424 in just over two days. It was unusual because it took the freighter off of a more lucrative route between bigger markets.

"You'd think her employers would have something to say about that, going on little side jaunts," I said.

Torina sniffed. "I'm sure Steedu is making it worth some dispatcher's while to make it all look legit."

"We officially have a hard lead on Steedu now." I looked out the cockpit for a moment, at the starfield, then turned to Torina. "So, I have to ask. Once we catch up with Steedu, what then?"

"We find out the truth. Then we make him pay."

"With?"

"Well, see, that's where you and I are different, Van. You're a shame first, resort to violence later kind of guy. I'm the opposite. Violence often *is* the answer."

I remembered her swift and ruthless efficiency in taking down the two Salt Thieves and made a mental note to stay on her good side. "So you'd make him pay with, like, his life?"

Her reply was immediate, and delivered with flat dispassion. "Sure."

Perry leaned in. "And his ship. Or at least, some of the armor and guns from it. The Peacemaker writ does give you powers of seizure if he fails to pay up, remember."

I glanced at Perry, then back to Torina. "Miss Vicious and Mister Pragmatic. You two are a killer combo."

20

THE PLAN WAS SIMPLE, as the best plans are. We arrived at Wolf 424 and eased our way into one of the asteroid belts, then Netty had us station-keep in place, in low power mode, with our passive scanners listening in all directions for the *Dust Mote's* transponder signal. Hopefully, the freighter wouldn't arrive on the far side of the system, which would necessitate us making a high acceleration and pretty obvious approach. But when the *Dust Mote* twisted into the system, it appeared only about a fifth of the way around our own orbital circumference from us.

Slowly, Netty started working us toward the freighter. We stayed in low-power mode, though, and Netty did her best to make us look like just another of the many prospecting and mining ships poking around among the asteroids.

Steedu's ship, the *Vagabond King*, arrived about four hours later and immediately set course for the *Dust Mote*. Even that didn't seem unusual, though. During our wait, we'd seen three other discreet rendezvous happen between ships, possibly for innocent reasons, but probably not. The *Dust Mote* and *Vagabond King* were just another of many navigational pairings.

I frowned at the image of the *Vagabond King*. I'd expected something larger and more grandiose. But she only massed about three times as much as the *Dragonet*. She was, however, well-armed for her mass—two laser batteries, two missile launcher arrays, and a potent but short-ranged weapon called a proton cannon. The latter was just as the name described, a weapon that spewed an intense stream of charged particles down the length of an annular magnetic field. But the field could only be projected a few thousand klicks, meaning the weapon could only be used at pretty much point-blank range. According to Netty, though, within that range, the thing was deadly as hell.

"We need to claim that under the writ if we get the chance," Perry said. "Proton cannons are rare and *really* expensive."

"Yeah, well, let's figure out how we're going to get at Steedu without finding out just *how* good that proton cannon is first-hand," I replied.

Torina shrugged. "Customs inspection."

I glanced at her. "What?"

"Customs inspection. As far as we know, the *Dust Mote* does legit-imate runs with legitimate cargoes, right? Her being here isn't illegal in any way, and it's not unusual for Peacemakers to do contraband searches. And if her crew has nothing to hide, they won't object."

"Well, sure. But Steedu might."

But Torina shook her head. "I don't think he will. You have the advantage of being a brand new Peacemaker Initiate. You'll come across like some enthusiastic new guy out to impress the boss with your dedication to duty, upholding the law, blah, blah. I think Steedu will just hang back, let you do your thing, and wait until you're gone before completing his, um, rendezvous."

"Yeah, but he might just turn tail and run."

Torina smiled. "Never underestimate the power of a space boner."

I smiled back. "Truer words."

"MY CUSTOMS DOCUMENTS are in order, as are my shipping manifests. It's all attached to my ship's transponder broadcasts, if you'd bother to check," Felun said. I couldn't see her face beneath the goggles and mask that Leonides apparently needed to withstand oxygenated atmospheres, but I knew it would be pinched in frustrated anger. She only expected to spend a few hours here, doing whatever it was Leonides did during forbidden trysts, and then needed to be on her way. But I had become an officious interruption.

"I understand that, Captain. But pursuant to Article Four of the Inter-System Commercial Charter, paragraph three—"

"Yes, I know. You can board and conduct a verification inspection. Of machine parts. Because that's all I'm carrying."

I was actually glad she'd cut me off. Perry had coached me,

but I couldn't remember if the particular bit of administrivia I was leaning on here was in subsection three-A or three-B.

"The excitation chamber of an x-ray laser is a *machine part*, Captain."

"And it would be illegal to be carrying those because they're restricted goods, yes. That's why I'm not. I've got pumps and reverse-osmosis filters for water purifiers—*which*, I might add, are badly needed on Tigon's World."

"Oh. Well, I'm surprised you're here then and not rushing to the aid of the thirsty people there."

That caught her off-guard. Perry muttered *attaboy*. I heard Torina, out of sight just outside the cockpit, giggle.

Felun sighed. "Fine. How long is this going to take?"

I looked at my instruments. The tactical overlay put us well within range of the *Dust Mote*. But the *Vagabond King*, hanging silently nearby, was just coming into range now. Through my ear bug, Netty spoke up.

"Another fifteen minutes of closure should be enough. The *Dust Mote* is only ten minutes away, though. You need to come up with an excuse to dawdle," she said.

I smiled at Felun. "From the time we get to you, probably no more than an hour or so, if you have people available to help us out."

"I'll see to it personally," she snapped and signed off.

I stared at the screen, which was showing the Peacemaker logo. "Well, that was rude."

"Van, I don't think we're going to be able to knock out all of

Steedu's weapons before he can return fire," Netty said. "If we try, I'd estimate less than a fifty percent chance of success."

"What do you recommend?"

"The surest way to disable his ship is to fire on his engineering section and try to force his reactor into safe mode. He'll still have power cells for life support and basic functions, but he'll otherwise be dead in the proverbial water."

"Uh-huh. So what's the catch?" I asked as Torina clambered back into her seat beside me and Perry took his place behind and between us.

"We'll have one opportunity, with about a seventy percent chance of success."

I glanced at Torina, who shrugged. "Better than under fifty percent."

I sighed and nodded. "That it is. Let's do it. Netty, I'll let you handle the targeting."

The next minutes passed in silence. We veered away from the *Dust Mote*, angling closer to the more distant *Vagabond King*. Felun came back on the comm.

"Hey, Peacemaker. In case you hadn't noticed, we're over here," she said, her voice full of scowl.

"Understood. But we need to do a circuit of your ship before docking. It's Peacemaker Policy, Regulation Four, Section Three—"

"None of you have ever done that before."

I shrugged. "New regs. What can I say."

"Just hurry it up," she snapped and signed off again.

I looked at tactical. "Netty, how long?"

"Another minute."

"So now you're making up regs, eh, Van?" Perry asked.

"Is that a problem?"

"Oh, no, not at all. It's just that it took your grandfather a few months before he felt comfortable enough to start making shit up. You've only been doing this for days."

"What can I say? I'm a fast learner when it comes to lying."

"I sense a New Orleans story in there somewhere," Perry said.

"Fort Lauderdale, too, but that's for later."

The final sixty seconds crawled past with agonizing slowness. Netty started us on the beginning of a slow arc, as though we were about to complete a circuit of the *Dust Mote*. I saw the targeting reticle on the tactical overlay suddenly highlight the *Vagabond King*, as Netty locked our laser battery onto it. The view zoomed in, and the reticle shifted squarely to the middle of its engineering section.

"Laser's charging. Firing in five seconds," Netty said.

I gritted my teeth. If this didn't disable Steedu's ship, then we were going to have to run like hell. And if that happened, our chances of getting close to him again would run away right along with us.

The laser fired.

A half-second delay, then the drive section of the *Vagabond King* lit up so brightly that the image had to automatically darken. The dazzling flare lasted a good five seconds, then died.

And so did the *Vagabond King*. Its running lights and other emanations went dark, while its transponder snapped to distress mode.

The comm immediately lit up with incoming messages, this time from Felun *and* the *Vagabond King*. I opened the first.

"Just what the hell do you—"

"Captain Felun, I'm going to say this once, and once only. You are to get underway and get the hell out of this system. You are not to ask any questions or even think about looking back. Otherwise—"

"Who do you think *you* are to tell me—"

I pressed on, raising my voice. "*Otherwise*, I will have to report back to the Leonide authorities that you were interfering in a Peacemaker investigation of Steedu, your, um... compatriot. That will probably bring your relationship with him under scrutiny. Is that *really* what you want? Think carefully before you answer."

Felun sputtered, then went silent. A moment later, she terminated the comm. And a moment after that, the *Dust Mote* began to accelerate away.

"There goes one frustrated lady," Torina said. "Her libido is showing up on the scans as force-five disappointment."

"Good. The scumbag deserves more than just forced celibacy," I growled and turned my attention to the stricken Vagabond King. "Yup. Now, let's go see her even more, ah, *frustrated* boyfriend."

NETTY NEATLY LINKED us with the disabled *Vagabond King*, thanks to a universal docking adapter or UDA that was the standard under interstellar law. Every ship was supposed to be equipped with at least one, mainly to facilitate rescues and evacuations. Ours clunked and bumped into place, locked, and threw a green "hard dock" signal.

Torina and I had suited up fully, wearing not just helmets, but also the armor overlays. These were essentially an extra vest and short trousers made of ballistic weave interlayered with supercon-ductive foil that added another layer of protection to the basic Peacemaker armor. The damned things turned the light, form-fitting armor into something that reminded me of the bulky flak jackets and similar stuff I'd lugged around in my army days, so they definitely weren't day-wear.

"Van, I'll go first," Perry said, hopping in front of the airlock.

I glanced at Torina, then frowned down at him. "You sure? They're probably waiting for us over there," I said, nodding my head at the hatch.

"Of course they are. That's why I'm going first. *Combat* AI, remember?" He flicked his golden gaze at me. "I'm not just another pretty face."

I wasn't sure about this. Perry was a slick piece of tech, but he didn't seem sturdy enough to lead the way into what might be a pretty hostile reception. I knew that I sure wasn't happy about it. But we couldn't raise Steedu on the comm, so either we'd knocked them out, or he just wasn't talking. It was still an unnerving sign.

But Perry was a long veteran of this sort of thing, so I bowed to his wisdom, stepped back, and drew The Drop. I kept the Moonsword, on my other hip, sheathed. Torina brandished a light auto pistol, a wicked little weapon that fired three-round bursts of tiny, 2 mm sabot rounds. She'd test-fired it into the tank, a box filled with gelatinous goo kept just inside the *Dragonet's* airlock for that very purpose, test-firing small arms before deploying. The Drop had punched a frangible slug into the goo with a throaty boom, followed by a snap of plasma bolt from the underslung projector. The sludge happily swallowed both. Her burst actually blew some droplets of the stuff back at her, making Perry mutter something about *spaceship hulls* and *explosive decompression.*

I nodded to Perry. "Everyone ready?"

"I am," Torina replied.

"The bird's good to go," Perry added.

I hit the airlock control, and the hatch slid open. So did the outer hatch on Steedu's ship which, again, was required to be operable from outside by law—and by common freakin' sense. There weren't many laws that everyone, even the most nefarious types, almost universally accepted, but the UDA was one of the few. After all, *anyone,* no matter how law-abiding, might need to be rescued.

We entered the *Vagabond King's* airlock. Netty closed the *Dragonet's* outer hatch to protect the ship from intruders, while I cycled the lock of Steedu's ship closed. Because we'd never depressurized the airlock, the inner hatch was immediately ready to open.

I hit the controls.

As soon as the hatch slid open, Perry launched himself into the interior of the Vagabond King, his eyes suddenly ablaze with radiant emission. He poured out energy across the whole EM spectrum, flooding the radio, visual, infrared, and even UV bands with noise. It was directional, though, so while Steedu's people were suddenly buried in garbage EM emissions, Torina and I weren't.

Yeah, I got why Perry had insisted on going first. He'd told me about this capability but not how well it worked. We heard shouts and cries from beyond the wall of EM noise, ringing with alarm and confusion.

Torina didn't waste any time. She lunged forward, shouting, "Perry, shut it down!"

He did, leaving Torina facing three of Steedu's crew, one human and two aliens, armed with handguns and boarding axes, nasty melee weapons combining the function of axe and hammer. But they might as well have been armed with nukes for all the good it did them. Blinded and disoriented by Perry's EM light show, Torina had taken two of them down by the time I caught up, and the third while I stood and watched.

She glanced at me. "Sorry, didn't mean to hog all the action."

I spread my arms. "No, please carry on. I'm quite happy to supervise."

We pushed into Steedu's ship, a slick vessel with an awful lot of shiny new components. Steedu was obviously doing well in the ill-gotten gains department. Perry and Torina took down five more crew members along the way, and I dropped a sixth. A human, he lunged out of a side compartment as we were passing it, and I just reacted. It turned out that if I literally didn't think about the moves and just let them happen, my implanted hand-to-hand combat skills were pretty damned good. My feet and legs turned and braced, my arms and hands punched this, chopped that, then grabbed and flung—and I was standing over a fallen man groaning and making gestures of surrender. With a hiss of satisfaction, I shook my hands out, the shock of impact leaving them in seconds. I'd hit the bastard *hard*.

"Not bad," Torina said, smiling.

I snapped a pair of plastic cuffs on the man and glanced up. "Think I need to practice that."

"The *Dragonet*'s a little cramped for sparring, but I'd be up for giving you some pointers."

I stood. "You just want to beat the snot out of a Peacemaker."

She laughed. "Not at all. That would be the result, sure, but I don't *want* to do it."

We passed two more crew who just meekly stepped aside and made way for us. A third actually stepped to block our way but with his hands up. He was another Leonide.

"Steedu's locked himself in the bridge. I'll get you in there, but I want a favor," he said.

I narrowed my eyes. "I'm listening."

"I, uh, might have an outstanding warrant with you guys—"

"Two, one for conspiracy to steal property, in the form of a shipment of entertainment consoles on Crossroads, and one for trafficking in illicit chemicals on Zhago," Perry put in.

"Oh, yeah, I'd forgotten about that one. Anyway, if you could overlook those—"

"I'll overlook one of them, your choice," I said. I had the power to clear a Peacemaker warrant, probably for situations just like this one. Another triumph of pragmatism over justice, but there you go.

"Since I forgot about that Zhago one, how about you do so as well?"

"Considering that dealing drugs on Zhago is punishable by ten lashes a day with a chain whip for thirty consecutive days, it's probably a good choice," Perry said.

The Leonide led us to the bridge, punched a code into a terminal beside the imposing blast door, and it slid open.

Torina leapt in and landed in a ready crouch.

"Honey, I'm home," she said.

I glanced at Perry. "Is everyone in known space really that into the dramatics?"

"Actually, yes, pretty much."

"Huh."

I stepped in behind Torina, The Drop at the ready. "Here's Johnny!"

I found both Torina and Steedu staring back at me. She had her needle gun trained on him, and he had his hands up.

"Your name's Johnny?" Steedu asked.

I glared back at the Leonide. "No. It's—" I shook my head. "Never mind. I'm Peacemaker Van Tudor, and you are under arrest, Steedu, for… lots of shit, probably."

Steedu slowly lowered his arms. "Look, I don't know what you think I've done, but you'll find no outstanding warrants—"

"What about the writ against this ship?"

"I'd be happy to pay the outstanding balance right now." He

spread his arms in a shrug. "That was all just a miscommunication anyway."

Torina scowled. "I don't give a damn about your writ or your ship. What I want is answers."

Steedu frowned. "Who the hell are you?"

"Torina Milon."

I couldn't see Steedu's features under his mask and goggles, but I saw him stiffen in a way that told me he recognized the name.

"Okay, look. I'm a really, really junior partner in that particular venture. And I'm just about to get out of it anyway. Tell you what, I will give you my share, a gift—"

"You're offering to *give* me part of my own family's property? Really?"

"Wait. Wait. That came out wrong. I—" He shuffled his feet. "Wait."

I scowled. "Steedu, how about we talk about your reason for being here, at Wolf 424, in the first place. You know, your little liaison with Felun—"

I guess that touched a particular sensitive nerve because Steedu stared at me for a second, then muttered something and reached for a sidearm. I snapped out a single shot from The Drop, the frangible bullet slamming into his upper right arm and shoulder and shattering into a multitude of fragments. None should have gone deep enough to do life-threatening harm, but it still dropped Steedu like a bag of rocks.

Torina immediately snapped a curse. "Van, if you killed him, then we've just turned this into a dead end."

"Shit. I'm sorry, Torina, but—"

"No, he's alive," she replied. "He won't be talking for a while, but he's alive." She immediately began to administer a first-aid spray to his wounds. Perry, in the meantime, hopped up on a bridge console and plugged in. His eyes flickered for a moment.

"You'd think a criminal would have better encryption than this," he said, then paused. "Ah. Well. That's good news. For us, anyway."

"What's that?" I asked.

"Even if Steedu can't talk, I think we've got everything we need right here in his ship's data core. And lots more besides." Another pause, then Perry lifted his wings slightly.

"Oh wow, Steedu. You've been *very* bad, haven't you?"

21

STEEDU'S SHIP turned out to be far more lucrative than I'd realized. By executing the outstanding writ, the Peacemakers were able to seize the ship in its entirety, haul it back to Anvil Dark, and strip out anything any decent, law-abiding ship wouldn't need—like a proton cannon. That weapon was quickly claimed by someone higher up the food chain than me, but I didn't really mind. I didn't have to participate in the feeding frenzy around the *Vagabond King*'s illicit upgrades. As the executor of the writ, I was entitled to thirty percent of its cash value when it was resold back into the open market as a simple freighter, armed only for self-defense.

It was a *lot* of money.

It also gave me a boost in my cred as a Peacemaker. I was hardly a household name, but I did see a few Peacemakers on Anvil Dark recognize me, and a couple even congratulated me on a good score. But no sooner had my well-wisher ambled off along the concourse than Perry hopped in close beside me.

"Don't let all the smiles and appendage shakes fool you, Van. For every Peacemaker genuinely impressed and glad for you, there are three or four who are going to be envious, bitter, resentful, or some combination thereof."

"I suspect you've also put yourself on the scanners of some of the more ambitious ones," Torina put in. "You were a nobody, and now you're suddenly a somebody. And somebodies can be a threat."

I looked from one to the other. "You guys couldn't just let me bask a little longer in it all, huh?"

Perry shrugged his wings. "Nope."

THE *DRAGONET* WAS ABOUT to get an upgrade.

The logical evolution was to build it up into a *Dragon,* a much bigger, heavier class of ship. Thanks to the foresight of their ancient designers, the *Dragonet* and *Dragon* were both modular vessels, the latter essentially the same as the former, but with more modules plugged in. But I was still a long way from being able to afford such an extensive refit. So the more modest upgrade I'd decided to purchase with my prize fees from the *Vagabond King* added hardpoints for up to four more weapon systems or external stores, although the only ones I'd purchased for now was a second laser battery—reconditioned, not brand new—and a close-defense package.

The latter was a nifty add-on, and I'd gotten a good deal on it, too. It was based around a rapid-fire point-defense cannon, reminiscent of the Phalanx close-in weapon systems used by the US and allied navies for anti-missile protection. Netty controlled and fired it autonomously. But it also sported an electronic-countermeasures suite to jam incoming ordnance and a glitter bomb launcher. And by *glitter bomb*, I meant just that. It could cough out roughly a garbage-can sized projectile that when detonated just a few klicks away from the ship quickly spread a scintillating cloud of highly reflective glitter intended to diffuse and weaken incoming laser shots. As long as the ship didn't maneuver, it would sail along with its protective cloud of glitter, at least until it finally dispersed. I'd heard of something vaguely similar during World War Two back home, under the code name *Window*, but that was ribbons of reflective material. Candidly, the idea of a glitter cloud was a touch hilarious.

"What's so funny?" Torina asked. We stood near the ship, looking at her hull with a critical eye, but I was fighting a laugh.

"The glitter bomb. Makes me think we should play club music when we launch a round," I said, grinning.

"You make music with clubs? How simple is your culture, Van? I mean, music should be more than thump, thump, thump—"

"Not—no, not with a glorified stick. A place where people go to dance, and drink, and engage in the age-old pursuit of booty."

"Booty? What the hell is going on down on Earth?" Torina asked, alarmed.

I sighed. "Booty is—you know. Physical acts. With another person."

"Ahh."

"Yes. Ahh. And club music is more like—" I thought for a second and then did my best impersonation of every European DJ I'd ever heard. "Like *nnn-tst-nnn-tst-nnn-tst*."

"Oh! We call that Asterlille songs," Torina said with a laugh.

"Beautiful word. What's it mean?"

"Translated, it means *songs for those who love to look at themselves*."

I snorted. "Then you *do* understand club music. And it goes hand in hand with glitter bombs."

"I'll make a note to find some for our exterior speakers," Torina said with some dignity, then we were both looking over the schematic of my ship's newest features, and the gravity of my job came rushing back in like a tide. Being a Peacemaker was about justice.

It was also about details, because it was a business.

Case in point—the *Dragonet* changed names, thanks to a decision I alone made.

Dragonet was the class name of the ship, officially distinguished only by the combination of its hull number and my Peacemaker ID code. That was boring. I ran through the names I knew of fictional dragons, decided to avoid possible copyright infringement, and settled on *Fafnir*, a dragon from Norse mythology.

"You do realize that Fafnir was killed by Sigurd, right?" Netty said in response. "Do you really want to name your ship after a dragon that ultimately failed?"

I shrugged. "Aside from *Puff, the Magic*, can you name any major literary dragons that *didn't* end up dead?"

"Good point. *Fafnir* it is."

This did lead to a couple of other issues, though. The first was a question, which I posed to both Netty and Perry.

"Why didn't my grandfather ever upgrade to a *Dragon*?"

Netty answered immediately. "Because his barn wasn't big enough."

That left me staring, then made me chuckle. Oh, Gramps, you bastion of practicality, you.

But Perry added a little more to the answer. "Your grandfather preferred to work alone. That isn't uncommon among Peacemakers. Some spend their entire career in a *Dragonet*, with no one but their combat AI for company. Others are just the opposite, hauling around whole retinues of deputies, legal advisors, spacecraft engineers, even mercenaries, aboard their *Dragons*."

And that opened the way to the second issue. I had no particular designs on building a retinue, partly because I wasn't ready to ride herd on yet more people, and partly because the *Fafnir* could really only accommodate two people in anything resembling comfort. But Perry made a suggestion, as Torina and I toured the newly refitted ship.

"It strikes me that you intend to see through Torina's case to its end. And, Torina, it seems to me that you plan to stay with Van until that's done. So, Van, why don't you hire her as your Second?"

I stared at Perry for a moment, went, "Huh," and turned to Torina. A Peacemaker's Second was their chief deputy and derived actual, legal authority from the title. They were also adjunct members of the Peacemaker's Guild, the organization that included Peacemakers everywhere. "What do you think?"

"What do *you* think?" she replied. "You're the one who needs to see value in it."

"Well, let's see. I've seen you kick serious ass, twice, without breaking a sweat. I've seen you fly a spaceship like a pro, I've seen you navigate the scummy criminal underworld as well as you can no doubt navigate big business and big money. I'd say that there's value in it, sure."

"Okay, then. I accept—boss."

I grinned. "Boss. I like that."

"I was kidding."

"So was I."

"But I do have a—I don't want to call it a price because that isn't worthy of what's really a generous offer. Let's call it a favor."

"What's that?"

"The damage done to my home is, well, it's catastrophic. It's going to be really hard to repair. So I'd like your help once we've sorted my legal issues and we've got our family estate back in procuring a team of Synergists from Arminsu-el to restore it to what it used to be and get it all balanced again."

I could only shrug. "Sure. I'll do what I can. But let me guess —it costs money."

"It does."

"More money than we have."

Perry actually laughed at that, an odd, tinny sound that

vibrated his beak. "Oh, hell yes. Far, *far* more money than you have."

Something about the way Perry said it made me narrow my eyes at him.

"Of course it does. And—I'm just taking a wild guess, here—there's a job that will pay for it, and that job has already been suggested to you by the Guild, right?"

Perry laughed again. "Hey, it's almost like you were there in the meeting. Or you're psychic. Tell me, what am I thinking now?"

"That I'm doubtful even a psychic could read the mind of an AI?" I smirked. "Also, that this job is going to involve crossing swords with someone or something unstable, even dangerous?"

"First, some psychics can, though they're rare. Second, I'm actually starting to think you are one. Van, let me tell you about the cult known as the Arc of Vengeance."

I REMEMBERED Tau Ceti being in the terrestrial science news, about ten years earlier, for having evidence of super-Earth type planets—as many as four of them, in fact. It was a big deal because Tau Ceti was the closest star to Earth that was similar to Sol and apparently had potentially habitable planets. Being the geek I am, I'd read the article on whatever science news blog I'd found it on and moved on. At no point had I thought, *hey, maybe one day I'll go there.*

And yet, here I was. We'd twisted the *Fafnir* into the edge of the Tau Ceti system and now hung out in the Oort Cloud, planning our next move against the Arc of Vengeance.

Despite their sinister name, what they were was a group of five families that had banded together to become pirates. Tau Ceti was one of the busiest systems in volume of traffic in known space, having those four super-Earths inferred back on the original one, plus no fewer than nine more planets. There were seven rocky worlds, one ice giant similar to Neptune, and a colossal gas giant bigger than Jupiter, which Netty informed me was pushing the boundary between *planet* and *star*. This amazing assemblage of worlds boasted just over one hundred and twenty moons as well, for a total inhabitable space many times that of Earth. According to Perry, there might be as many as five hundred billion people living here, divided into sixteen major political units. The system had no overarching authority, aside from a Council similar to the Earthly UN that provided an illusion of cooperation.

Meanwhile, back on Earth, people mused that there might be as many as four planets here, meaning there might even be a chance for extraterrestrial life. They had absolutely no idea how right they were.

"So how the hell, in a system this busy, do pirates manage to function at all?" I asked, eyeing the tactical overlay and the bustling multitude of ships painted onto it. Everything from grubby little tramp freighters, to luxury liners and yachts, to darkly sleek, massive warships plied their way into, around, and out of the system.

Netty provided the answer. "It's because it's so busy they can get away with it. Take note of the thick, dense asteroid belt between planets seven and eight that crosses partway across the orbits of both. That leaves two planets subject to frequent, large impact events, meaning there's a whole swath through the middle of the system that's a dead zone, just empty space. Ships traveling between the inner and outer parts of the system either have to traverse it or take a long detour above or below the ecliptic plane."

"A long and expensive detour, no doubt," Torina put in.

"Indeed. The amount of crew time and fuel makes it prohibitively expensive. And the Arc is very good at knowing just how much piracy they can do, without spiking the costs up too high and making the detours worthwhile."

"They're a massive pain in the ass," Perry said.

"Okay, so why haven't they been reined in before this?" I asked.

"Because they've greased enough appendages to keep the authorities, including the Peacemakers, off their backs. But they've obviously pissed someone off, someone who can afford bigger bribes, or at least bigger strategically placed bribes. Anyway, that's why this is suddenly a thing."

I nodded. The job sounded relatively straightforward. The Arc of Vengeance was known to use robotic transfer shuttles to move stolen cargo through progressively more legitimate layers of shell and holding corporations until it came out squeaky clean and ready for market at the other end. This didn't stop all sorts of black and grey market activity along the way, of course, but the Arc apparently made most of its money legitimately. Perry had explained it was easier to launder the goods than the money, thanks to the vigilance of The Quiet Room.

"So the robotic transfer shuttles are their weak link. Nab one, prove it's carrying stolen goods, and use that to justify deploying a Peacemaker Cohort here to take out the Arc once and for all," Perry said.

Torina sniffed. "So some other group of scumbags can just move in and take their place."

"One group of scumbags at a time, my dear. It might as well be the motto of the Peacemakers."

I nodded again. A Cohort was a temporary task force, assembled and deployed by the Peacemakers to conduct large operations. They had no fixed organization and could even include military assets from the other Chapters of the Galactic Knights, military forces from other political units, or even mercenaries. The largest ever constituted, my installed memories told me, comprised half of the Peacemakers in known space, a full Company of the Galactic Knights Resplendent, and a brigade of planetary assault marines underwritten by The Quiet Room. And that's all I knew. The details, and even the location or locations of the operation that had required all of this force, were still classified. Even Perry wouldn't divulge anything about it because of locks built into his programming.

But that was down the road. The immediate problem was finding, and then seizing intact one of the Arc's transfer shuttles. They normally ran without transponders, or would spoof legitimate ones. That made them extremely hard to find amid the bustling traffic in the Tau Ceti system.

I quirked my lip at Netty, puzzled. "So why run some of these things with no transponders, and others with fake ones?"

"The ones running without transponders likely never leave the confines of the asteroid belt or enter shipping lanes. If they did, they'd become a navigational hazard."

"And that could attract all sorts of unwanted attention, some of it from corporations and other parties rich and powerful enough to care. The Arc relies on staying *below* the radar to operate, and that means not pissing off the wrong people," Perry put in.

"So the ones running with fake transponders are trying to pass themselves off as legit," I said.

"Temporarily. The AIs that run traffic control are mostly concerned with preventing ships from, you know, smashing into one another. Unless they're told otherwise, as long as a ship is broadcasting a legit transponder code, they don't care who or what it is," Netty said.

Torina was nodding along. "The Arc probably aren't the only ones up to no good in this system, and they're probably not the only ones faking the codes." She smiled sweetly. "Remember, when you turn over a rock, you expose *everything* underneath it."

I nodded back. "Yeah, okay. So, is there some way to check the codes of all the ships currently flying around this system? See if any of them don't make any sense?"

A pause. Perry broke it.

"Van, that's actually a really good idea."

IT WAS A REALLY good idea that worked, too. It took time, but Netty and Perry, working together, tested the transponder code of every ship in the system—all three hundred and sixty-odd of them. Three or four entered or left the system every minute, but the Arc's shuttles only worked in-system so we could ignore those. By comparing all of those transponder codes to various traffic control databases and ship registries, the two AIs were able to narrow the field down to four possible targets. These were ships that realistically couldn't be at Tau Ceti.

We then did a casual meander through the system, but took advantage of a feature of Peacemaker transponders to do it. We could switch it to undercover mode, which meant it would portray us as just a generic workboat registered to a shell company owned by the Peacemakers for that very purpose. Perry admitted it was legally grey, and cautioned that I'd have to do a bunch of paperwork to justify it when I returned to Anvil Dark.

Paperwork. The true universal constant.

Two of our candidates turned out to be military vessels, up to who knew what. We gave them a wide berth and left them alone. The third was a luxurious yacht, bearing a corporate logo that made Perry emphatically shake his head.

"Nope. Stay away from that one, unless you want to get one of the wealthiest families in known space pissed at you."

Torina looked at him. "Do you mean the—" She frowned. "But I thought they got divorced."

"They did. But the two females and the hermaphrodite threatened to reveal—"

"Uh, guys? Little focus here? You two can swap celebrity gossip later, okay?" I said.

The fourth target was a hit. We'd found one of the robotic shuttles, en route away from the asteroid belt to a cargo transfer station orbiting Tau Ceti Nine. We just shadowed it on a parallel course for another hour, while I wormed my way into its scanner controller and carefully blinded it to our presence. I slumped back in my seat when I was done. It had been a *lot* harder than hacking the clunky freighter back at Van Maanen's Star, and I'd needed more help from Netty and Perry to break various layers of encryption.

Now, we paralleled the shuttle, about five hundred meters away. That led to our next problem.

"How do we seize control of the damned thing?" I asked.

"Can you just, ah, *hack it* and take control of it?" Torina asked.

But I shook my head. "It's one thing to tweak software to do one specific thing, like ignore the *Fafnir*. But to take full control, I'd have to dig right into its AI, and I don't think my hacking skills are quite there yet."

"In that case, Van, you've got two choices," Perry said. "Board it and seize control of it, or disable it by shooting at it. The first means a spacewalk. The second risks destroying it, because our weapons just aren't that surgical."

Which meant I really only had one choice, and now, here I was, puffing little jets of gas from a maneuvering unit, an MU, strapped to my back, while unspooling a tether back to the *Fafnir*.

And it was no fun at all. Netty had brought the *Fafnir* to about a hundred meters from the shuttle, as close as she was comfortable going. But I still had that hundred meters to cross, and as soon as my own ship was behind me and out of view, I had only the shuttle as a visual reference. If I looked in any other direction—

Let's just say that I now understood what the word *vertigo* means. Just like the rest of my skills, I definitely needed to work on this whole space-walk thing.

With the shuttle doggedly fixed in my sights, I slowly finished the crossing. I reached the other ship, grabbed a stanchion on the hull, and took my first breath in—well, a while.

"Van, you okay? Sounded like someone just punched you in the gut," Torina said.

"That was just me, gasping in terror. Gimme a second."

When my heart had slowed to something less *hummingbird* and more *human being*, I pulled myself to the shuttle's airlock. Being below a certain mass, and not certified to carry a crew anyway, the robotic ship had no UDA. There was just a flat hatch, with a handle beside it marked MANUAL OPEN.

Okay. I grabbed the handle and twisted it.

But sometimes timing is everything.

No sooner than I had, Perry came over the comm. "Van, before you open that—"

That was all he got out before the universe exploded.

FOR THE FIRST TIME, but probably not for the last, the armor saved my life. When the hatch exploded outward, right into my face, my supple armor went rigid and absorbed most of the impact. I was flung in one direction, the hatch sailed off in another, while shimmering motes of frozen air twinkled and danced all around. The stars became a whirling kaleidoscope, spinning so fast they turned into curved arcs of light.

"Van!"

I yanked myself out of a stunned dumbness, whereupon my mind snapped from neutral to high gear, and started to race.

"OH SHIT!"

"Van!"

"SHIT, I'M OUT OF CONTROL—"

"Van, press the Recover switch!"

"PERRY—"

"Van, press the damned Recover switch!"

His voice burned through the sudden detonation of panic. I fumbled a moment, then found it, the Recovery switch on the MU's control panel. The thrusters immediately began to fire in staccato ripples, quickly stopping my wild tumble and bringing me to a halt relative to the *Fafnir*.

I took stock. Despite the trauma of taking a big alloy hatch in the face, then spiraling out of control into the void, everything seemed okay. My suit systems were all green, and my only injury seemed to be my right arm, which had taken the brunt of the impact and was probably going to be bruised. Without the armor, though, I'd likely have broken bones, or worse. I now hung about fifty meters away from the *Fafnir*, a little less from the shuttle.

I sucked in one more breath, then let it out. "Okay, what the hell just happened?"

"As I was about to say, Van, sometimes these asshole bad guys cut through the hinges and overpressure the airlock. If anyone tries to bust in—well, you don't need me to tell you what happens," Perry replied.

Torina spoke up. "Van, are you okay?"

"More or less." I sighed. "I just have to drag my ass back to that shuttle, I guess, and—"

"Actually, Van, that probably isn't going to work," Perry cut in. "When that hatch blew, it probably triggered some security protocols. The airlock's inner hatch will be sealed, so you'd have to cut through it. And the AI probably started a timer, so if it doesn't receive a clearance code in a given time, it'll shut down the magnetic bottle in the reactor and just blow the ship."

"Oh, for—you're telling me we either have to try and disable it with our weapons and quite likely destroy it and the evidence on board, or else wait for it to blow up and destroy all the evidence on board."

"You might as well come back in, Van," Torina said. "You don't want to be out there when it explodes."

I glared at the shuttle. So damned close. If we only had some way of quickly cutting into it without the brute force of a laser or a missile, and disabling it...

My thoughts trailed off into an idea. "Screw that. I'm taking this shuttle home. Netty, is there a schematic available for this thing?"

"It's a standard class two workboat. Assuming it hasn't been altered, this schematic should apply." A schematic diagram of the shuttle popped onto my heads-up. "Why?"

I toggled the MU and started back for the shuttle.

"Van, I'm going to say it again. Don't do this," Perry said.

I studied the schematic, trying to match the point Netty had highlighted on it to the actual shuttle, a meter away from me. "And I'll say it again, noted."

I drew the Moonsword.

"Okay, let's see just how sharp you really are."

One hand on the MU's control, I raised the Moonsword.

Right about—there.

I slammed the blade point-first into the hull. At the same time, I fired a burst from the MU, to counteract the inevitable rebound force from the impact.

Honestly, I expected it to not work. Or, if it did work, to only sink a short distance into the hull, maybe even poke all the way through, and then have to stab and hack at the power conduit inside. But the Starsmith had said the sword was sharp enough to cut through hull-plate, and he was right. The Moonblade slid neatly through the hull-plating, then kept going, through the conduit. At about two thirds of its length, it finally stopped.

"Well?"

"A moment," Netty said.

I was mindful of the fact that this shuttle would quite likely explode, and quite possibly do it soon. "Netty, talk to me."

"Huh. Mission accomplished, Van. The shuttle seems to have gone into safe mode."

"I did not think that was going to work," Torina put in. "Van, you're one lucky asshole."

"Hey, whatever works. Anyway, the candle is snuffed. Can we take this thing home now?"

"Sure, just as soon as we deal with the Arc patrol ship heading toward us at high sub-light, probably to find out what happened to their shuttle," Netty replied.

"No rest for the wicked, is there?" I tugged on the Moonsword. It was stuck. Holding it, I planted my feet on either side of it.

"Van, coming aboard sooner would be better than later," Torina called out.

"Yeah, yeah. But I'm not leaving my spiffy sword stuck in the side of this thing." I heaved, yanking until the blade came free and I tumbled off into space. This time, I was ready for it.

22

THE ARC PATROL cutter was nimble and as almost as heavily armed as the *Fafnir*.

The key word is *almost*. He came at us in a high-speed pass, pouring out laser fire, but we sent twice as much back his way, along with a missile for good measure. Perry clicked his mechanical tongue at that.

"The chance of a hit on something that small and fast is pretty low, Van. And do you know how much missiles cost?"

Our return fire did persuade the Arc pilot to quickly veer away, though. He took up station at a distance, shadowing us for a while.

Torina grinned at that. "There's probably all sorts of comm traffic flying back and forth, with the Arc asking certain parties why their bribes didn't stop this."

Perry offered a more sinister warning. "Some of those parties might very well be Peacemakers, Van. The Guild tries to root out corruption, but it's there."

"You're telling me to watch my back, even around other Peacemakers."

"No, I'm telling you to never *stop* watching your back, no matter *where* you are."

———

THE ARC CONTINUED to petulantly shadow us as we removed incriminating cargo from the shuttle, all of it thoroughly documented by Perry. Then we handed custody of the shuttle, and the case, over to the Ceti Trans-Belt Authority, in whose space our intercept had occurred. Their reception of it was pretty lukewarm, suggesting that there were more bribes in play.

But I didn't care. We returned to Anvil Dark with the evidence, handed it over to the Magistrate Department of the Guild, and claimed our admittedly impressive reward.

"That's a lot of bonds," I'd said, eyeing the various denominations stacked on the table in the *Fafnir*'s tiny galley, which also served as a crew-lounge and general work-space.

Torina nodded. "It is. But almost all of it will have to go to the Arminsu-el Syngergists. That is, if you're still willing to help me with that."

I raised my eyebrows at the question, but I guess it wasn't a surprising one. Lots of people make promises to do things once they get the means. But lots of them then renege on those promises when they actually *have* the means.

But I wasn't one of those people.

"Of course I am," I replied, and she smiled brightly. But I had to frown back at her. "Once you're able to access your estates and they aren't in the hands of some money-grubbing usurpers, that is."

Her bright smile got even brighter. "See, now I get to give you this as good news, instead of having to use it to try to convince you to help me and my family out. I heard from my uncle this morning. The local authorities back at Van Maanen's Star finally woke up to the fact that our holdings had been illegally seized. They seized them back, and have returned them to my family."

"Hey, that's great!"

"I sense the involvement of The Quiet Room," Perry said.

I shrugged. "Said it before, I'll say it again. Whatever works." I looked back at Torina. "Well, let's go get you some Synergists to restore your lands—especially that spot where you first—" I filled my deliberate pause with a suggestive smirk. "—*kissed* a guy."

———

ARMINSU-EL WAS the fourth planet orbiting Epsilon Indi, a strange trinary star system consisting of a Sol-sized, albeit much more orange primary, orbited by two brown dwarfs. Eight planets swung around the trio, the inner four in erratic, interweaved orbits, thanks to the varying gravitation resulting from the movements of the three stars. The outer four planets were much more stable.

Arminsu-el itself was almost Earthlike, with a surface gravity a little lower than Earth's, but less ocean and much more land-mass. It was also only sparsely developed. It probably resembled Earth in roughly the Middle Ages, but that wasn't because it was backwards. Rather, through some complex web of agreements involving several star systems, Arminsu-el had been given over to the custody of the Synergists in perpetuity. In return, they developed and provided sophisticated terraforming expertise, and biosphere recovery services to worlds damaged by war or natural disasters. They also oversaw a wide range of species risking extinction on other worlds from things like industrial development.

It turned out that included a few from Earth, including the passenger pigeon, wiped out over a hundred years ago. It had joined a plethora of other flying species, which seemed to make up most of the fauna on Arminsu-el.

I craned my neck up at the massive, bluish-green trees towering over the landing site. The planet had only a single starport, nestled amid lush, rainforest-like vegetation near a tropical coast. According to Torina, the space for the port hadn't been cleared, but rather every tree and plant had been carefully transplanted to other locations. In other words, Arminsu-el was an environmentalist's dream.

Once Netty had set us down, a complex maneuver requiring a controlled vertical descent for its last thousand meters, while being buffeted by strong winds off the nearby sea, we walked the short distance to a terminal building made of wood and stone. Dozens, maybe hundreds of platforms ranging from a few meters square to hundreds of meters across, loomed among the leafy treetops. They were connected by bridges, as well as a complex web of terrifying-looking contraptions made of rope and sticks. As soon as I saw the Synergists, though, I realized why the idea of falls from their treetop homes didn't bother them.

They were birds.

Or bird-like, anyway. Tall, slender, almost ephemeral, with long, narrow faces, deep set and penetrating dark eyes, and wings. They were resplendent with decorations of beads and feathers, and dressed in layers of coarse, homespun fabric woven, embroidered, or—and this was the clincher—tie-dyed in a riot of colors.

While Torina stepped forward to introduce us, I just shook my head. "Well, shit."

"What is it?" Perry asked.

I released a long sigh of resignation. "I thought I'd seen everything. But here we are, dealing with space hippies."

We spent much of the day with the Synergists, Torina doing most of the talking. She provided imagery and other data and details about the natural state of her homeworld, and the damage subsequently done to it. By the time the orange sun was setting, the Synergists returned to the meeting room in the terminal building. Apparently, they didn't like off-worlders leaving the starport unless it was absolutely essential, to reduce the risk of contamination. When they ambled back into the building, all beaded and tie-dyed, I almost expected a cloud of weed smoke and sitar music to follow them.

"We can do this work for you," their lead representative, a Synergist named Sellon said, then handed over a data slate. "Here are the details of the pricing."

I peered over Torina's shoulder at the slate. *Ouch.*

She turned to me. "Are you sure about this, Van? It's your money."

"No, *we* earned it, so it's *our* money. But once your family fortunes are unfrozen and restored, some future considerations would be nice."

She gave me a hug and babbled her thanks to me. I have to admit, it made me feel surprisingly good, taking the money earned from someone doing something criminal and using it to do something positive.

Torina thumbed the contract, and that was that. The Synergists told Torina they would arrive and begin work in six of their days, which worked out to eight standard days.

"We will see you in six days, then, with our team and the materials needed to bring your lands back from the brink," Sellon said. "We will come prepared to sing. It is one of the things we do best."

They were going to sing. I imagined sitars again, and bongos.

Perry must have caught my eye-roll, because he murmured, "Not a word, Van."

I couldn't resist but kept it to a sidelong whisper.

"They're space hippies, and they sing, because of *course* they do."

THE *FAFNIR* HAD no room to spare, but I still wanted a place to work out, practice my sword and unarmed combat skills.

I settled on repurposing the cargo bay into a training room. It offered just enough space to swing the Moonsword or spar with Torina without hitting the bulkheads too often. It annoyed Netty because I did score a few gouges into the ship's structure with the sword, which Waldo had to repair.

Two days after meeting the Synergists, I was in the *Fafnir*'s training room, working through a series of sword-moves in a sequence reminiscent of the *kata* practiced by Asian martial artists on Earth. The sequence had been programmed into me with the memory installs, so I knew it well but didn't have it down to muscle memory yet. That was the goal. And it wasn't actually a fighting routine but a stylized series of movements intended to help me control my body and, by extension, the Moonsword.

Netty interrupted. "Van, I have an incoming message for you from Sil Vradas. She's a Peacemaker, requesting a parlay."

I stopped in mid slow-motion strike. A parlay was just a fancy term for a meeting between two Peacemakers, intended to swap information or equipment, transfer evidence or prisoners, or just generally shoot the shit. I was actually an exception among Peacemakers, especially Initiates, in that I had an actual living being on board, in the form of Torina. Most Peacemakers traveled with no one but their combat AI for company. I toweled off the sweat and got dressed while talking to Sil on the comm. We agreed to meet the next day on the outskirts of Wolf 424, midway between our current locations.

Sil and her *Dragonet* were already waiting for us when we arrived. Netty and her ship's AI collaborated to neatly dock with the *Fafnir*, locking UDAs together and forming an airtight seal between the two ships. I stepped across and entered Sil's *Dragonet*.

"Van Tudor, welcome aboard," she said—or, actually hissed, since she was an Ixtan, a species native to one of the planets in the Tau Ceti system.

"Pleased to meet you, too, Sil," I replied. Perry, in the meantime, had exchanged flickering eye-glows with her combat AI. It was another bird construct, a little smaller than Perry and darker overall. Her name was Rav. I wondered if Perry had learned anything useful from her. Or if it had been good for him, in an AI-bonding sort of way. I figured I'd ask about it later, though.

I introduced Sil to Torina, and we spent the next hour or so swapping stories and case leads, and generally making what amounted to Peacemaker small talk while drinking a liqueur Sil had brought along.

"Don't worry, it's rated safe for human consumption. It's distilled from berries on my home planet," she said, pouring me a glass of the murky brown liquid.

I gave it a suspicious sniff but just got a smell of berry, like taking a whiff of an open jar of raspberry jam. When I tasted it, though—

I've never been much of a drinker. But the next words out of my mouth were, "I want a bottle. Maybe a dozen of them."

Sil hissed and fluttered her eyelids, which my memories told me was the Ixtan version of a laugh. "Did I say rated for human consumption? Maybe I should have said rated for human *addiction*."

I licked my lips, then I saw Torina was enjoying it just as much as I was. "Yeah, I can believe that."

While I was draining the glass, Sil produced an envelope from a pocket on her uniform harness and slid it across the galley table to me. Again, she laughed.

"Almost lost my ass getting this one. Your grandfather was owed a small debt by some traders out in the Pleiades. Here's partial payment—they're good for the rest. We work with them. But you might have to wait a while. I'm staying away from that region until shit cools down a bit, and I recommend you do, too."

I was happy to receive unexpected money, but I frowned at Sil's ominous warning. "Why? What's happening out in the Pleiades?" Even as I asked it, I found myself marveling at how much I wasn't marveling at the question. I mean, *what's happening out in the Pleiades?* is a question *very* few humans will ever ask and expect a serious reply.

"The Stillness," was all Sil said.

My frown deepened. The Stillness was a strange, largely opaque hybrid of criminal syndicate and large corporation, Al Capone crossed with a multinational. And that's about all I knew about them. For some reason, the memories I'd been given about the Stillness were pretty thin.

"That's standard procedure. The Stillness is an opponent way beyond anything pretty much any single Peacemaker can take on. And that includes the Masters. So we don't want Initiates getting themselves enmeshed in things that are going to end up with them very dead, very quickly."

"They kill Peacemakers?"

"It's almost a line of business for them. Or it was." Sil picked up her slate, tapped at it, and called up an image that she turned to me. "Recognize this?"

"Yeah, it's the Wall of Remembered Honor. I saw it on Anvil Dark. It's a monument, right, listing all the Peacemakers that have died in the line of duty?"

"It is. And about a quarter of those names were killed by those Stillness bastards." Sil's good humor was gone, replaced by taut anger.

"Okay, if they're so bad, why haven't they been shut down?"

"The Peacemakers have tried, believe me. But the Stillness is too strong, and their leader, a shadow named Paress Kohl, too smart. The only time the Guild made any headway was by deploying the biggest Cohort they could muster, which included troops from the Knights Resplendent and a bunch of mercenaries. Even then, it was an inconclusive fight."

"That explains that big Cohort that no one wants to talk about."

"You can't blame the Masters. To assemble that much force and still not manage to land a decisive blow against the Stillness —it's frustrating and a little embarrassing. What we need is an entire navy, with at least *some* military-grade ships and firepower." She looked at me with her dark, glassy eyes. "Your grandfather was involved in that Cohort. He was one of the main drivers behind it, in fact. For some reason he never divulged, Kohl and the Stillness got to him in a pretty personal way. I think the losses from that escapade really bothered him."

I sat back. Gramps had been close-mouthed about most of

what I'd assumed had been an ordinary military career—an extraordinarily stressful and demanding one because he was spec-ops, but still *ordinary*, in the sense I never imagined it involved leaving freakin' Earth. But close-mouthed was, as I came to understand, his way of dealing with the impacts of some of the things he'd had to do. It seemed reliving them in his memories was enough. He didn't need to be reliving them aloud, too.

Little did I realize that some of his trauma had been incurred in outer space. But trauma was trauma, and silence was how he'd coped with it.

I briefly wondered how I'd cope with things like that. But only briefly because there was only one way to find out, and I was sure the time would eventually come.

———

WE RETURNED TO ANVIL DARK, and I made a specific point of visiting the Wall of Remembered Honor and spending a few minutes there. Perry and Torina told me they'd meet me in a popular bar on the Concourse. As I studied the lists of names, I particularly noted every fourth one. I had no idea, of course, if these particular individuals had been killed by the Stillness, but it didn't matter. It was enough to make it clear that Paress Kohl and the Stillness had a *lot* of blood on their hands.

I found Gramps' name and ran my finger across it. He might have died from some wasting disease, but the Peacemakers still considered him to have done it while on duty.

"You started something with the Stillness, Gramps. I'll see if I can finish it for you."

I left and headed for the bar to meet the others. My step bounced a bit. I'd always had the feeling I'd let Gramps and my father both down when I washed out of the Army. But it seemed they'd both be at least a little proud of me now.

―――――――

I HAD the Stillness stuck in my mind, and both Torina and Perry could tell as I stared into my drink, a spicy and surprisingly refreshing beer-like concoction. Torina finally rolled her eyes.

"Would you spill whatever it is you're brooding over, Van?"

So I did. I told them about my thoughts regarding the Stillness and how I'd like to see through what Gramps had begun.

Perry had swiveled his head side to side. "Van, you are *not* ready to be taking on something like that. Your grandfather was a veteran Peacemaker and an experienced warrior when he tried it, and, well, that didn't exactly end in glorious success—something you're not even actually cleared to know about yet, I might add."

"You gonna turn me in?"

"Not yet."

Torina was more blunt. "Van, it's a stupid idea."

"No, no, don't hold back. Tell me what you really think."

"Okay, it's a damned stupid idea. The Stillness are bad, bad news. I have a cousin who owns a shipping company, and he won't route his freighters anywhere near where they operate."

A new voice cut in. "Listen to the lady, my friend. She speaks wisely."

I turned to the speaker, a gruff alien resembling a big, astonishingly hairy man. Or maybe it *was* a big, astonishingly hairy man. He was a Peacemaker, and a seasoned one, wearing the rank insignia of a Myrmidon, a pretty senior appointment.

I smiled at him. "She usually speaks wisely, although not normally for strangers to overhear."

The man, or creature, or whatever, boomed out a laugh. "If conversations in bars were considered private, we Peacemakers would lose about three quarters of our leads." But he turned almost instantly serious. "Be annoyed with me if you want to, but I can't let you go off half-cocked without offering a bit of advice. If you can't hit them head on with a navy, then do what they do and pick them off one at a time."

The man, or creature or whatever, drained his drink and left with a grin and a wink. I turned to Perry. "Is that possible? Is there some place we might be able to find Stillness ships stuck with their butts out in the wind somewhere?"

"I'm not sure."

"Really?"

"Yes, really, Van. I'm not omniscient, even if it might seem like it at times. A lot of the information about the Stillness is classified or kept in offline archives for extra security."

"Offline archives?"

Perry bobbed his head. "Maybe it's time you took a trip to the Library."

"So to get bonafide, operational intelligence about the Stillness, a major and implacable enemy of the Peacemakers, I have to give the Librarian this?" I brandished the thing in my hand, a battered old copy of a sci-fi book titled *King of the Galaxy*. It was one of the few personal effects I'd brought from home, mainly because it seemed to fit the sudden theme of my life. It was also one of my favorite reads, which was why, apparently, it was my key to getting access to data about the Stillness. The Librarian, the Peacemaker that ran the Library, demanded *tokens of personal significance* and meaning from their patrons.

It was dumb. It was like some senior military planner consulting with their intelligence branch but having to compose a poem about their grandmother or hand over their dad's vintage cigar box before they could receive an intel briefing. I said so, and Perry shrugged his wings.

"The Peacemakers are an old organization, Van. Some of the things they do are rooted in ancient traditions. They don't have to make sense. You just have to learn to roll with them."

The Librarian, named Bester, was an alien from a race with an unpronounceable name that didn't translate into English. He loomed almost seven feet tall and looked like a big, anthropomorphic sloth. When I offered the book, he accepted it gladly.

"You're Mark Tudor's grandson, aren't you?" he asked.

"In the flesh."

"I knew Mark pretty well. A good Peacemaker and an even greater person. I was sorry to hear about his Return."

I glanced at Perry, and he said, "Bester's people believe that all beings come from, and return to, a single, universal intelligence."

"And by Returning to it, Mark enriches it with his memories, his beliefs and values."

I nodded at that. I actually liked it. It was a comforting idea.

I explained to Bester what we were looking for. He nodded sagely and gestured for us to follow him. He led us through compartments filled with a dizzying and haphazard array of data modules, reams of paper, dusty old books, rolled scrolls and maps, and even some stacks of 3.5" floppy disks and CD-ROMs. Bester and his assistants apparently knew where and what every single thing was, though, acting as living—and unhackable—catalogs. Anything stored here was truly inaccessible to someone who wasn't prepared to come to Anvil Dark and physically retrieve it.

He brought us to a rack holding thin sheets of photo glass standing upright. He considered them for a moment, making a deep *hmm* sound as he did, then selected one and gingerly placed it against a backlight. It was a star chart.

"This one here. It's where Stillness and that scum Kohl do their skulking," Bester said, pointing to a lonely gap between two twin star systems. "The place is known as Afterthought. The only thing there is an observation post staffed by androids."

"So, there. Afterthought. That's where we jump them," I said, and Bester nodded, his thick head bobbing, flat teeth shining in the dim light.

"Go get 'em, Peacemaker."

23

TORINA WANTED to confirm the arrival of the Synergists on her homeworld and their beginning the task of rejuvenating the place. That left us a few days to ponder the problem and come up with a plan. I brainstormed it with her, Perry, and Netty and was going to solicit help from some other Peacemakers, like Sil maybe, but Perry advised against it.

"Honestly, Van, when it comes to the Stillness, you have to assume that they could be anywhere. The Peacemakers are as much a thorn in their side as they are in ours, so you can especially bet that if they've infiltrated anywhere, it's here. Their agents, Shadows, are very, very good."

The idea that the Stillness had stuck their insidious hooks into the Peacemakers was a disturbing one, but it raised another question—had we done the same to them?

"If we have, Van, it's not something you or I will know

anything about. That sort of operation is controlled at the highest levels, and all due respect, but—"

"I'm not exactly highest-level material."

"Well, not yet, anyway."

"I'd point out that if you score significant successes against the Stillness, then you might attract more attention from those senior levels, though, who might be more willing to bring you some ways into the circle of knowledge," Netty pointed out.

But Torina just sniffed. "If he attracts attention from them, then he's going to attract it from other, less friendly places, too." She smiled sweetly at me. "Not saying you'll *actually* have a target on your back, but don't take it the wrong way if I start keeping a few paces away from you."

We eventually settled on the classic bait and switch. If we could convince a Stillness ship that there was easy prey available, maybe we could lure them into our reach. And the Afterthought was the place to do it. A lonely, empty expanse of space, it was a tough crossing between the stars surrounding it because of the presence of a small black hole nearby. Black holes and other supermassive objects, like neutron stars, played hell with twist dynamics, apparently. Netty tried to explain it, but I'd struggled with high-school calculus, and she was referring to flavors of mathematics even Earthly experts knew nothing about. What it came down to, though, was that the Afterthought couldn't be crossed in a single twist. Unless you bypassed it completely, you had to twist to the android-crewed observation post, get a navigational fix, then twist the rest of the way.

Most traffic avoided it. Unless it was necessary to cross it, it was generally easier, and often cheaper, to just go around it. It was for that reason that the Stillness liked it—it gave them a way to discreetly move their ships around with little chance of being detected. This was especially true for their covert agents, the Shadows.

We didn't want to run afoul of the observation post, a legitimate installation doing a legitimate job. So we selected a point almost a light-year away where a rogue planet, surrounded by a small constellation of asteroids, was on a multi-million year journey from whatever system it had been cast out of, toward some unknown fate. The trick was going to be getting a Stillness ship to bother twisting there.

"We could use the *Fafnir* herself as bait. If the Stillness thought a Peacemaker *Dragonet*, on some covert mission, had gotten into trouble in the Afterthought, they'd be all over that," Perry suggested.

Torina nodded. "They would. Maybe with overwhelming force. I think some sort of bait that would attract the Stillness, that we can monitor at a distance, would be a better idea, no? So if a dozen ships show up, we can just quietly cower out of sight."

"Hiding among the asteroids surrounding the rogue planet would be a viable strategy," Netty suggested. "What little data we have about them suggests they're pretty rich in things like iron and nickel, so they'll throw back all sorts of strong scanner returns."

I nodded. "Good idea. So, we just need bait."

Torina and I frowned in thought. I was sure Perry and Netty

would have, if either of them could. After a moment of thoughtful silence, it was me, surprisingly, that broke it.

"Hey. Hear me out... "

ONCE TORINA WAS SATISFIED the Synergists were settled in on her homeworld and getting to work, we made the trip to the Afterthought. Per Netty's recommendation, we took up station among the asteroids, switched to lower power mode, and waited, watching our bait.

It was a lowly, generic navigational beacon, no different than thousands scattered through known space. It had the combined advantages of being reliable, simple, and most of all, cheap.

"I don't know, Van," Perry said as we slouched around the *Fafnir*, which was waiting for something to tug on our fishing line, as it were. "I appreciate your reasoning, but it's pretty convoluted. Maybe it's because I'm an AI, but why the layers of obvious deception?"

"It's not that obvious, and that's the point," I replied, flipping the page on the book I was reading, feet up on the galley table. It wasn't *King of the Galaxy*, unfortunately, which I'd only gotten about halfway through. I'd read it about a dozen times before that, but that didn't matter. I missed my tattered old copy of the thing. Of course, that was the point too, wasn't it? It wouldn't be a *token of personal significance* if you didn't miss it.

Perry's concern revolved around the particular hacks I'd made to our nav buoy bait. With Netty's help, I'd wiped away all but the absolutely essential functions of the thing, such as power distribution. Then I copied and installed the transponder data from the *Fafnir*—an interstellar crime—and locked it behind a firewall. Then I created a fake transponder profile, based loosely on that of the robotic freighter we'd used as cover to reach Torina's homeworld at Van Maanen's Star, and uploaded that— another crime. And then I altered *that*, inserting a few hints that it was a fake profile. The point was to make the buoy appear, at a distance, as the *Fafnir*, inexpertly hidden behind a fake transponder profile.

It was a classic breadcrumb trap, a common trick used by hackers. Leave a breadcrumb or two where someone can see them and lure them into looking for the whole loaf that was hidden somewhere nearby. I'd lured more than a few of my hacker opponents into virtual places I wanted them to end up in and hoped the same would work with the Stillness. I'd also broken some laws back on Earth doing that, but omelets and eggs and all that, right?

Sure enough, about an hour later, Netty spoke up. "The buoy has just been illuminated by somebody's scanners."

I exchanged a glance with Torina, then we both headed to the cockpit. The buoy was just outside the asteroid field, hopefully looking like a ship trying to obscure its scanner signature— another breadcrumb. The trick was to not make it too obvious, which made it a finicky balancing act.

I settled into the pilot's seat and studied the tactical overlay. I saw a single ship, running with no transponder, just an anti-collision beacon. Military ships did it, it turned out, broadcasting essentially nothing but their location while on operational service —and that *was* legal. But from the data Netty was able to pick up passively, this was no military vessel.

"It corresponds to class two standard shuttle in size, but it's obviously not. The fact that I can't discern much more than that hints that it's probably stealthed pretty well. And by stealth, I mean some military grade stuff," Netty said.

I scowled. This was going to make things more difficult. Just as we had with the Arc of Vengeance cutter, we wanted to hit this ship hard enough to disable it without destroying it. But it was a small target, at long range, and protected by stealth systems. The surest targeting would, therefore, be manual, literally shooting at the ship based on visual reference.

And that was, I had to admit, beyond me. I turned to Torina.

"So you can fly like a pro and kick ass like a ninja. How's your shooting with spaceship weapons?"

She shrugged. "Let's find out."

She took control of the *Fafnir*'s fire control on the copilot's side, on manual mode. And then she waited.

I watched on the pilot's repeater as the little ship grew in the image. It was sleek and ominously dark, with a faint shimmer to it that made it hard to make out against the stellar background. Fortunately, there was one universal constant, a problem no ship anywhere could ever really work around.

That was heat.

Spaceships used energy to power their systems and keep their crews alive. Thermodynamics declared that this would produce waste heat. You could store it in heat sinks or cover it up with fancy cooling systems, but ultimately every ship would end up radiating heat. It was the reason we'd effectively latched ourselves to the robotic freighter to reach Torina's homeworld undetected. The *Dragonet's* heat signature was buried in the much larger one of the freighter. This guy, though, didn't have that luxury, nor could his stealth system, as good as it was, conceal him in the infrared spectrum.

Torina kept watching and waiting. I frowned in her direction. The Stillness ship had probably gotten close enough to the buoy by now to know it was a ruse. If he just twisted away—

Without any preamble, Torina fired.

Almost two full seconds passed, then the Stillness ship blossomed in infrared as though it had been lit with a floodlight. Two seconds of that, and it faded. But part of the ship still glowed brightly, recording Torina's hit.

She sat back. "My work here is done."

"What were you waiting for?"

"For him to turn. He was coming straight at us so our shot would have gone right into his cockpit. When he realized something was wrong, he immediately turned away so he could open enough distance between him and that rogue planet out there to twist. That exposed his back end, including his drive."

The planet. Right. I'd been fixated on the asteroids around us, but there was a whole super-Earth sized planet out there with enough gravitation to make it harder and more fuel-intensive to twist away.

"In that case, good shooting, my dear."

"Thank you, good sir. Now, shall we go say hello to our new friend?"

THE STILLNESS SHIP had no UDA, just a flat hatch. They probably didn't care if their people ever got rescued, which Perry confirmed by noting they typically scuttled their ships when they'd been disabled. That was a concern with this guy until we were able to see the damage Torina had done. She'd slammed a laser pulse straight through his drive, knocking it and his reactor neatly offline. A couple of meters one way, and she'd likely have breached the reactor and blown the ship apart anyway. A few meters the other, and the ship would probably have still been able to maneuver. So she'd landed a shot on a roughly three square-meter target from almost five hundred thousand klicks away.

Good shooting indeed.

We breached the outer hatch, but the inner was locked. This time, Perry had accompanied me, attached to a short tether and pulled along behind me as I crossed to the Stillness ship.

I couldn't resist as I clipped the tether to him. "Walkies, Perry! Time for walkies!"

He gave me a flat amber stare. "Van, have I ever shown you *why* I'm called a *combat* AI?"

Now, in the other ship's airlock, we hooked Perry into a data port with an adapter, so I could essentially use him as an intelligent terminal. He transferred data to my armor, portrayed it on my heads-up and, in turn, transferred my inputs back to the ship.

It took time. Torina and Netty, back in the *Fafnir*, were keeping an eye out for more bad guys. There were none so far, but it stood to reason the pilot of this ship would have at least sent back a message describing his contact with our bait-buoy, and that he was going to investigate.

I finally unraveled the firewall keeping me out of the ship's systems and found the inner airlock door controller. Before I opened it, though, I sent another command to a different system.

"Environmental lighting? What's that about?" Perry asked.

"Just watch," I said and opened the door.

We were greeted by a brief rush of air as the airlock filled with gas from inside the ship. The outer door, which we damaged while breaching it, had lost its airtight seal, meaning the ship was slowly depressurizing. But the other thing that came flooding through the open inner door was a barrage of light pulses, firing strobe-like thanks to the command I'd given. It had been enough to distract the armored figure standing just inside the airlock long enough for me to shove The Drop into his visored face. His own weapon, a nasty, short-barreled boarding shotgun, was aimed just off to my right.

"I'd suggest not even breathing, my friend," I said over both comm and external speaker. "Because—"

It was all I got out before he hit the muzzle of the shotgun against my side. It slammed me against the hatch coaming and made my snap-shot from The Drop strike the bulkhead behind him instead of blowing his head apart.

Well, shit. And now that same muzzle was swinging around,

right into my face. It was, I thought, like looking down a very deep, dark well.

This is awkward.

But something flashed past me and slammed into him, knocking him backward. His shotgun went off with a throaty boom, skittering flechettes off the deck inside the airlock. Perry kept up his attack, raking at the Shadow's dark armor with his claws, leaving deep gouges. There was no way I'd get a clear shot without risking hitting Perry, so I let go of The Drop, swept out the Moonsword, and slashed the Shadow across the upper right arm and chest. He went down.

Perry peered up at me. "Next time, spare the monologue and just shoot the bastard."

"I thought we were supposed to, you know, arrest people? Or are *judge, jury, and executioner* somewhere in the fine print on the contract?"

"When it comes to the Stillness, Van, *judge, jury, and executioner* is pretty much the *title* of the contract."

WE SEARCHED the ship and retrieved an encrypted data-slate and a couple of just as encrypted data modules. Perry had also done a thorough sweep with his scanners, and he got a ping from something located behind a bulkhead. We looked for a way of removing it, but I was keenly aware of time ticking past. The Shadows were, as Bester, Perry, and Netty all told me, intensely paranoid—probably understandable, considering the line of work they were in—and did things like set scuttling charges. If they didn't win the fight, then they'd force everybody to lose it.

"Screw it," I said and drew the Moonsword.

"Uh, Van? There could be live power conduits behind there. High-pressure coolant lines. A booby trap, courtesy our friendly Shadow."

"Yes, and this ship might go poof any second, as you yourself made clear. Shall we stand around and debate the merits—"

"Less talking, more cutting," Perry said.

I did get him to confirm, as best he could, that there were no dangerous spaceship components back there whose cutting would lead to our being irradiated or vaporized or whatever. Then I cut away at the alloy plate with the Moonsword, carving out the smallest possible piece to get access to whatever was behind it. It wasn't easy, a hot-knife-through-butter thing by any means. I had to strain and push the sword, point first, into the plate, then drag it out, move a few centimeters, and do it again, over and over. Perry assured me that future overlays to the blade would make this much easier.

"I can hardly"—I pushed, grimacing as I applied force—"wait."

We eventually retrieved the thing behind the plate. It was a small comm device. We didn't bother hanging about to study it, though, and hurried back to the *Fafnir*, which Netty had moved to just a few meters away from the Shadow's ship. It let us just push ourselves from one open airlock to the other, making the crossing in seconds. Once we were all safe back aboard the *Fafnir*, Netty prepared to seal the lock and back us off.

"What about our friend over there?" Torina asked, pointing past me to the Stillness agent still sprawled inside his own airlock.

I glanced back. "Oh. Right. I guess I'm supposed to take him in. He's probably worth interrogating."

"Actually, Van, he's probably not. The Stillness are so compartmentalized, and their Shadows are so conditioned, that we'd never be able to trust anything he told us. He'd probably cough up a thousand useless leads, and we'd need to chase a whole bunch of corroboration to know if any of them were even true," Perry said.

I glanced back at the still bulk of the Shadow. I'd never had the power of life and death in my hands before. At least, not directly. I'd done things back in Earthly cyberspace that might have gotten some very deserving people killed. Once, for instance, I discovered and handed over the identity of a mole that had infiltrated a particular intelligence agency that was—let's just say it's not unknown for its ruthlessness. But I literally had this Shadow's life in my hands.

"Meter's running, Van. If that ship blows with you guys standing in the open airlock—" Netty began, but I cut her off.

"Understood. Perry, am I not obligated to take that Shadow into custody and bring him back to Anvil Dark?"

"Assuming you could take him alive, yes, you are."

Perry might have been a machine-bird with glowing amber eyes, but I got the subtext from him as well as I would from any human. "So you're saying I could just kill him? And you'd be okay with that?"

"Would I be okay with you flagrantly violating interstellar law regarding the provision of aid to those who need it? Of course not. Would I stop you from doing it to that asshole over there? Absolutely not."

"I'm surprised your programming allows you to be so morally, um, *flexible*."

"If this had been five hundred years ago, sure, I'd have had an enforcement lock in place to prevent you from doing anything but following the letter of the law. But those days are long gone."

"And the Peacemakers have had much more of a positive impact on the galaxy since then, and, oh yes, by the way, tick tock, people!" Netty put in, her tone urgent.

I understood Netty's mounting concern, but this seemed like a watershed decision. I looked at Perry. "Do the Shadows kill?"

"Constantly. That and espionage is essentially what they do. Our friend over there wouldn't be a Shadow if he didn't have a sizable kill count."

"To which he wanted to add you, remember?" Torina put in.

"How do they kill?" I asked.

If Perry could have smiled, I was sure he would have, and it wouldn't have been a pleasant smile, either. "By any means necessary. But they do like to disable ships and leave people to die adrift in them. Everyone who travels through space has a particular fear of that, and the Shadows use it to up their ruthless reputation. It's basically their signature."

I stared at the fallen Shadow for a few more seconds. A ruthless killer who wouldn't have hesitated to kill me. Part of an organization that the Peacemakers considered their most bitter foe.

An organization that Gramps had tried and failed to stamp out, allowing them to continue being ruthless assholes.

I made up my mind. It wasn't an easy decision by any means, and I was sure I'd be second-guessing it for a long time.

I handed the comm device to Torina and prepared to return to the Shadow's vessel.

"We'll take his ship once we're sure it's not going to blow up. We'll leave him here, where he belongs."

Perry cocked his head. "Where he belongs?"

I smiled. "Yeah. As an Afterthought."

24

"WELL, THAT'S PECULIAR," Perry said.

I glanced back at him. We'd actually rigged a perch for him behind and between the pilot and copilot's seats that could fold aside when not needed. I couldn't help feeling, sometimes, that this must be what it felt like to be driving a family car with the kids in the back.

If your kids were hyper-advanced AI mechanical birds, that is, which I suspected was a situation pretty much unique to me, of all humans in known space.

"Saying *that's peculiar* aboard a spaceship powered by what amounts to a continuous thermonuclear explosion, carrying anti-matter suspended in magnetic containment fields, is a little unnerving, Perry," Torina said.

"Okay, not *we're about to blow up* peculiar. What's peculiar is that we've been told not to return with the comm rig we retrieved from the Shadow's ship to Anvil Dark. Instead, we've been given a set of rendezvous coordinates. And I transmitted our case summary with level five encryption, and the reply came back in level seven."

"So, instead of taking a million *million* years to break, it'll take a million *billion*," I said. Which actually wasn't true. In an era of massively parallel quantum computing, just the stuff of nerdy dreams on Earth but par for the course out here, no encryption scheme was truly safe. But level seven was far, *far* harder to crack than five, which suggested something big was up.

I shrugged. "Well, we got our orders. Netty, if you please?"

We'd already dropped and registered the Shadow's ship with a bonded salvage broker—after Perry, with Waldo's help, swept it for every possible dust mote of useful intelligence—and received our payout. Moreover, we were able to refuel the *Fafnir* from the Stillness ship's onboard supply, which meant the bastards were effectively paying for our gas. Accordingly, Netty reoriented her twist calculations and took us to the designated rendezvous, a random spot on the very edge of Gacrux, Anvil Dark's home system. We met another ship, one of the massive *Leviathan*-class ships owned by the Peacemakers, and generally only used for particularly complicated and far-reaching cases. The Leviathans were about five times the *Fafnir*'s mass and very heavily armed and armored. They were more warships than law enforcement vessels. And this one was lurking in the lee of a massive, grimy comet relative to the Peacemaker station. The comet was big and rocky enough that it would readily block comms and scanners, suggesting that this was a meeting about which Anvil Dark was supposed to remain ignorant.

So, a clandestine meeting with a very senior Peacemaker, aboard an extremely powerful ship. The mystery just got a *whole* lot deeper.

"The *Foregone Conclusion?*" I said, eyeing the other ship's transponder code.

"That ship belongs to Lunzemor Nyatt. She's the Keel's Emissary, a formal liaison position on behalf of the Masters," Netty said.

"It essentially makes her a Master-in-waiting," Perry put in.

That raised my eyebrows. I'd actually expected it would turn out to be Groshenko.

The mystery went from *deep*, to *black-hole gravity well*.

I shrugged. "Well, let's go see what the good Emissary Nyatt wants out here in the middle of nowhere."

LUNZEMOR NYATT TURNED out to be another human, a small, sturdy woman, late middle-aged, with a quick and infectious smile. As I stepped through the airlock, she greeted me and Torina warmly. When she saw Perry, her smile widened.

"Perry, you adorable old bucket of bolts, you. How's your new boss treating you?"

"Brutal. He's ruthless."

"Good!" she said, then leaned toward me and hissed a stage

whisper. "You gotta keep these AIs in their place. They think they run the Peacemakers."

Perry cocked his head. "What do you mean, we *think* we do? Netty, back me up, here."

"Well, since I could fly us all into a star if I wanted, and I choose not to, I'd say that's a *foregone conclusion*. See what I did there?"

Nyatt laughed and turned back to me. "So, just like Netty, you can call me Lunzy. All my friends do. As do a few of my enemies, though it's usually accompanied by a few other words. And that's enough talk for now. It's time for beer."

Lunzy led us through the sprawling interior of the *Foregone Conclusion*, which was kind of like stepping off a yacht and onto a cruise liner. She actually had a crew, four Peacemaker Deputies, a legal and political advisor, and four more crew who helped operate the ship. I nodded to those we saw as we passed by. We eventually arrived at a room that seemed strikingly out of place aboard a spaceship. It could have been the library or study in any Earthly mansion, complete with wood-grain paneling, overstuffed chairs, shelves of books, and even a crackling fire.

"I gather that's not real," I said, staring at the dancing flames.

"Nah, all the air tends to rush out through the chimney," Lunzy said, then handed over a mug of something the color of a thunderstorm, purplish-blue with a foamy head. I took a sip and uttered an involuntary *mmmm* sound. Torina lowered her mug with a delighted smile.

I licked my lips. "That's... amazing."

"Heaven's Nectar, it's called. Premium stuff."

"More than Premium," Torina replied. "There's a waiting list about a thousand years long to get it—and everyone on it is super rich." She ended on a look at Lunzy that clearly wondered how she'd come into some of the stuff.

Lunzy shrugged. "Contraband. I seized it, then completely messed up the paperwork and declared the wrong amount when I turned it over to Evidence. Careless of me, I know," she said, cutting herself off with a sip that was more than a little smug.

I was starting to realize that the Peacemakers were the good guys, sure, but also that they'd come to develop a rather *pragmatic* approach to their duties. I made a mental note to ask Perry exactly why the Masters had, five hundred years ago, taken away the AIs' rigid adherence to the law.

For a while, we lounged in the butter-soft wing chairs, sipping extraordinary beer and soaking up that warm, cozy feeling that typified studies and libraries and the like. Lunzy had me give her a summary of everything that had happened since I'd pressed the button on that remote back in Iowa, then put her mug down.

"Well, much as I'd like to say that this was just a social visit to welcome you to the Peacemakers, Van—and, by the way, welcome to the Peacemakers, Van—that's obviously not what this is about."

"No kidding. These sorts of meetings only happen when they involve something big, something sensitive, a lot of money, or more likely all three," Perry said.

"Well, believe it or not, it's not number two or three on Perry's list. Or, at least it isn't yet." Lunzy looked at me. "A

Legacy from Earth showed up at Anvil Dark, driving a *Dragonet* that he claims to own with what seems to be spotty provenance."

"Okay. That's interesting, I guess, but does it really rate this sort of secret squirrel meeting?"

Torina glanced at me, her mug just short of her lips. "Secret squirrel?"

"I'll tell you later. Anyway, I'd have thought getting this comms unit we recovered back to Anvil Dark would be a way higher priority, since Perry says it might help us crack open the shell of secrecy around the Stillness."

While I was speaking, Lunzy had tilted her head, her gaze locked onto me like lasers. I couldn't help thinking she was taking my measure, which immediately raised the question, *why?* Clammy fingers of unease tapped my spine. I took a quick sip of beer.

"That's all quite true. But this new arrival gave us some serious cause for concern, first because he's an asshole, and second because I don't trust him." Those eyes turned, if anything, even more attentive, more appraising.

"Oh, and he's also your cousin."

I'D ALWAYS ASSUMED SPIT-TAKES, where someone hears shocking news and literally spits out something they were drinking, were made-up bullshit for TV comedies.

Turns out, I was wrong.

Okay, I didn't spit out much, and it was more because I'd

sucked in a breath at the words *your cousin* and almost inhaled beer. As I wiped my mouth with a napkin, I realized that Lunzy, Torina, and Perry were all staring at me.

"The probability that a cousin of yours on Earth would also become a Peacemaker is small, Van, but not really spitting-out-stuff small. I take it there's more to it than just surprise," Perry said.

"I think it was the combination of *he's an asshole* and *he's your cousin*," Torina replied.

I straightened myself in the big chair and looked at Lunzy. "Let me guess. Carter Yost."

Lunzy put a finger on her nose and grinned. *"Ding ding,* we have a winner! *Quite* the asshole, too. Has that whole blue-blooded brat thing going on that really gets under my skin. I take it he's from a different branch of your family?"

"He's from a different species, as far as I'm concerned." I let my head sink back against the wing-backed chair. "His grandfather married into an old, plantation-style family in Virginia that made a fortune back in the US Civil War by selling food and supplies to both sides. They had both Union and Confederate flags and flew whichever was most expedient. So if there's any genetics involved in morality, that's what Carter's starting with. Anyway, his grandfather was my great uncle, so that makes him my second cousin."

Lunzy's grin hadn't changed. "Huh. So Mark—your grandfather—had a brother who was—"

"An asshole. And so was his son, and so's Carter. Like I said, it's genetic assholery."

Torina gave me a quizzical look. "There's more to it than that, though. He's not just an asshole, Van. He's the kind of enemy you take personally."

I considered just not wanting to talk about it because I never wanted to talk about Carter Yost. But the circumstances really did demand some explanation.

"Yeah, he is. Back when we were kids, we used to have these big family things once a year. Carter and I are close in age, so we got jammed together to—I don't know, be besties, I suppose."

Lunzy rolled her eyes. "Because children of the same age always get along." She smirked. "The adults just wanted the two of you to be one another's distraction."

"Oh, he was a distraction alright. He had to be right in everything, all the time. He was petulant, whiny, and just generally a miserable little tool. Somehow, that led to him and I becoming family rivals. The two of us got compared to one another all the time. *Oh, Van, Carter did this at school. Oh, Van, good for you for winning an award at computer camp, we'll have to let Carter know.*" I sighed. "Eventually, we parted ways when I joined the Army. He's allergic to things like *discipline* and *work*, though, so he went off to some Ivy League university, joined the Alpha-Bravo-Charlie fraternity, and partied his way through an MBA."

"Well, Van, I hate to say it, but he's back," Lunzy said.

"An event so dire that apparently it had to be revealed to you on the dark side of a comet orbiting a star a dozen light-years from Earth," Torina put in.

"Yeah, that sounds about right for Carter." I turned back to Lunzy. "But—*how*? How did he get his grubby hands on a *Drag-*

onet? How was he able to fly it? How was he——?" I shook my head and gave Lunzy a look I admit was pleading. "*How*?"

"Have you heard of Loyal Retainerships?"

I bit my lip and thought. I had. My implanted memories informed me that Loyal Retainerships were auxiliary positions that could be granted to individuals by the Peacemakers—not Peacemakers themselves, but working in support of the guild. Technically, Torina held a Loyal Retainership, making her my Chief Deputy. But the term Loyal Retainership was an archaic one and had been replaced by more specific terms, describing more specific jobs.

But the provision of Loyal Retainerships was still on the books—first, because no one had bothered to get rid of it, and second, because it was still occasionally used to temporarily draft people in Peacemaker service, sort of like the posses hastily assembled to track down outlaws in the Old West.

"Okay, so he got himself a Loyal Retainership. That still doesn't explain how——" I stopped. "Wait. He somehow bought one, didn't he?"

"Technically, it was a donation, but yes. Somehow, he managed to hook up with another Peacemaker on Earth and buy a Loyal Retainership," Lunzy said.

I slumped back again. "So there are other Peacemakers on Earth?"

"Just a few. Anyway, the Peacemaker in question was looking to retire, so they brought your cousin on as Loyal Retainer, then hung up their uniform. It probably means they owed a crap ton of bonds to somebody, which means that your

347

cousin is in for a nasty surprise if and when they ever come to collect."

"Good. Can we find out who they are to speed that process along?"

Torina put her mug down. "Somehow, your cousin must have found out about the Peacemakers. Your grandfather must have let something slip to him."

"Or the other Peacemaker involved just had it out for your grandfather and saw this as a way to hit back at him—send the asshole cousin of Mark's chosen successor into space, then sit back and eat popcorn." Lunzy shrugged. "Your grandfather had powerful friends among the Peacemakers, but he also had powerful enemies. This might all just come down to a plot to discredit him."

"Even after he's dead. Wow, that's some next-level douchebaggery right there," Perry said.

"The good news is that, as a Loyal Retainer and not actually a Peacemaker himself, your cousin has extremely limited powers. He can't be assigned or accept Peacemaker jobs or appointments. Technically, he's more of a passenger aboard that *Dragonet* than its pilot. But it doesn't stop him from swaggering it up around Anvil Dark. Or, at least the parts of it he can access, which isn't much."

I just shook my head. "Doesn't matter. Carter has no scruples. His moral compass has a needle that points any way he wants it to. He'll lie, cheat, steal, undermine, blackmail, extort—hell, he'd probably even kill to get what he wants. And if it's at my expense, so much the better. The bastard hates me, hated my dad, hated Gramps, probably even hates himself."

My voice dripped bitterness like those sprayed droplets of beer.

"Which brings us to this meeting way out here in the lee of this comet. Since I had a feeling that your cousin would be the moth to your flame, I wanted to intercept you before you got anywhere near him and he found out about that comms unit you recovered from the Stillness. He just struck me as the type of guy who'd try to personally profit from it, even if it compromised the investigation."

She sat back and laced her fingers together, elbows resting on the padded arms of her chair. "And I'm not going to let that happen. Van, you've done a great job already of filling your grandfather's boots. This comms unit might be the biggest break we've had against the Stillness in a long time. The last thing we need is some yahoo like your cousin screwing it up, so I don't want him anywhere near this."

"You, ma'am, are very wise."

I considered loosing another rant about Carter but forced myself not to. It was typical of him, dominating a conversation happening hundreds of millions of klicks away. He sucked all the oxygen out of a room just by entering it.

I thought about the last time I'd seen him, all wavy blond hair, over-whitened teeth that I swear made a little *ting* sound when he grinned, a cashmere cardigan hung over his shoulders, the arms tied together across his chest. He'd been saying something about winning an MVP on some lacrosse team. *Lacrosse.* That, and shitty poetry had been his shtick when we were teenagers, the latter inevitably targeted at girls lower down in the

social order that defined people like Carter. They loved the attention from the charming, good-looking guy with the too-perfect
teeth. They wrote him blank checks in return for his attention,
and he cashed them and then moved on.

What a piece of shit.

I looked back at Lunzy. "So what do we do? I don't mind
handing the comms thing over to you, but I can't stay away from
Anvil Dark completely—can I?"

Both Lunzy and Perry shook their heads. But then Lunzy
grinned again, her eyes filled with conspiracy.

"Well, while we work on breaking open Stillness, I might be
able to convince your cousin to take his first job."

"Something truly, profoundly shitty, I hope?"

Lunzy laughed, head thrown back in wicked delight. "Oh,
you have no idea."

25

WE MADE a quick stop at Anvil Dark, with Lunzy traveling there ahead of time to make sure there was zero chance of me having to interact with Carter Yost. When I did briefly see her again for a quick drink in *The Black Hole*, the biggest and most popular watering hole on the Concourse, she gave me a cryptic smile.

"Carter's busy."

"Doing what?"

Her smile just widened.

"Is it awful? Horrible, even? Does it carry a major risk of agonizing death?"

Her smile widened even more.

"Excellent," I murmured, and I meant it.

We handed the comms unit over to the Artificers, the fancy name given to the Peacemaker engineers and technicians who kept Anvil Dark running, oversaw the testing and development of new tech, and also provided maintenance and repair services to Peace-makers' ships—for a fee, of course. Lunzy herself escorted me into their particular part of Anvil Dark, a heavily guarded section of the bottom-most of three rings. She got us admitted past two imposing sets of blast doors, but that was as far as even she was allowed. Only Artificers with reason to do so or a Master could go any further.

I frowned my frustration at the sealed doors. It was like running into a directory or drive during the course of doing some hacking and finding it too heavily encrypted to access. All it did was make me want to know what was inside even more.

We handed the comms unit over to an Artificer Adept, who thumbed a receipt on the data slate Torina held out to him. She'd insisted on getting one, something I'd never thought of. When there was a moment of hesitation, she offered Lunzy a cool look.

"The chain of custody for evidence is important, right?"

"Ninety-nine percent of the time, it is. That one percent is those times when things like secrecy and security matter more."

But she just smiled, the offered data slate not even trembling in her hand. She was well within her rights to require an evidence receipt on my behalf, earning her an annoyed look from the Artificer Adept, a bemused look from Lunzy, and an appreciative one from me.

As we headed back to the *Fafnir*, we pondered what to do with the next two or three days, the time it would take the Artificers to crack the Stillness comms module. We considered taking on another odd job, but the only ones listed on the registry were either shitty, paying far less than the risk entailed, or were too complicated to complete in two or three days. And I did want to be around when that enigmatic device was finally cracked. If there was follow-up stuff that arose from it, I wanted to be in on it.

"You have a sudden urge to take on the Stillness?" Torina asked.

"Yeah, Van. Have to be honest, you're still technically an Initiate. The Stillness is one of the Peacemakers' five top cases, and maybe number one," Perry said. He waggled his head. "That's kind of like a toddler trying to start med school."

"I like to think I rate better than a toddler when it comes to Peacemaking," I said, fighting a scowl as we ambled into *The Black Hole*. There was a live band playing, an act comprised of Peacemakers who could play instruments and sing. They made good money on the side while hanging around Anvil Dark and were actually pretty good, even though their instruments included a glockenspiel-type thing that sounded like shattering glass in various keys and what looked like a sheet of drywall that vibrated with a thumping, catchy beat.

"You're right. Toddler's unfair. You've definitely made it past kindergarten," Perry said as we claimed a table.

"Thank you. Now hand me my pudding, sir, lest I wail," I said, sniffing with some dignity. "But seriously, snacks aside, what are we going to do?"

Perry flicked his wing out, then tucked it away, head tilting to one side. "You're kind of the boss now."

"I—well, shit. Okay, then with Torina's permission, I'm going to suggest we do something I've never even *imagined* saying out loud, let alone doing."

"Hit me, boss," Perry said.

Torina gave me a small wave, adding, "We're waiting. Boss. Heh."

I sighed with a small defeat. "We go visit the space hippies."

"Yesssssss," Torina said, pumping a fist like a dad at his kid's football game. "I mean, um, thank you. I know how difficult this must be for yo—"

"I'm going to tell the Synergists that Van is interested in hearing about crystals."

Torina looked like she was going to pass out from laughter. "It's not even my birthday, but this is truly a gift."

"If they ask me to join a sharing circle or sing, I swear I'll fly us into a star," I grumbled.

Torina patted my hand, and Perry let his beak hang open, the AI equivalent of a drunken guffaw. "I'll cover the fuel there and back. And food." She eyed me, then added, "Booze, too."

"Well... thanks. We can avoid that dickhead Carter, and you'll see your family," I said, which was a far better plan than hanging around Anvil Dark and sharing the air with my cousin, if he showed up.

Torina leaned close to me, and her smile was warm and genuine. "Van? Thanks, by the way."

"For what?"

"Taking me home," Torina said, then her grin grew wicked. "You sure you won't dance to a drum circle?"

I pointed to the nearest star while grimacing in resignation.

"Your destination just changed. Straight into the star with you, lady. And the bird goes too."

NETTY FLEW us in to Torina's homeworld, the moon called Helso. It was a different experience compared to last time, when we snuck in-system by hugging the belly of a robotic freighter. The flight this time was entirely uneventful, Netty depositing us close to where we'd landed the last time. We'd disembarked and—

Just kind of stared dumbly.

Part of it was the fact that the ravaged soil and bedrock, stripped and excavated by the illegal mining, was now covered with a carpet of wildflowers, a riot of colors up and down the spectrum. They sprouted from every available bit of soil, even the tiny amounts trapped in cracks and fissures in the bare, exposed bedrock. There were even a few saplings sprouting here and there. Counterpoint to this was a pair of robotic miners, repurposed to dig into the piles of soil that had been carelessly heaved to one side and carefully redistribute it across the naked rock.

But that was only part of what had struck us dumb. The other, much bigger part was the Synergists themselves.

They were literal flower children.

Some danced a stylized dance, accompanied by the thump, tap, and jingle of instruments that crossed a drum and a tambourine. One of them played a wooden flute, its high, clear notes slicing through the breeze like a knife. Many of the Synergists sang along, most just intoning a chorus like chanting monks, but a few more animated, projecting a bouncy tune. And one of them belted out songs like Pavarotti, the smoothly rich tones of his voice somehow both clashing and meshing perfectly with the rest of the racket. It was musical chaos that still managed to blend the parts of a symphony, resulting in something much bigger and more powerful than itself.

The dancers were likewise moving in a way that looked random but on closer inspection suggested a very specific sequence of moves. As they danced, some plucked up bits of wood and bark, dead leaves, and dessicated flowers, all debris from the time of the strip mining, and stuck them into their many, many voluminous pockets.

Now, take all of that and have it performed by big, anthropomorphic birds, and you'll understand why my very first thought was a flashback to that time I tried mushrooms in college.

Except this was even more surreal.

But my gaze was drawn back to the flowers and saplings. The Synergists were flighty and odd, but there was no doubt they were saving the land and starting to return it to its former glory. The thing was, no one was even sure how the Synergists did this. They used some tech but mostly seemed to rely on their singing and dancing. According to Torina, the popular opinion was that all these antics actually served as a collective focus for some latent psychic potential among the Synergists that interacted with plant life to spur it into growth that was unusually rapid but also healthy and sustainable. Nobody knew for sure. And if the Synergists knew, they weren't saying.

"Yeah. Me too," Torina said.

I glanced at her. "I didn't say anything."

"You were thinking it. So am I," she said, offering me a bemused smile. "They are all a bit... *theatrical*, don't you think?"

I snapped my fingers. "That's it. *Theatrical*. Like... like... members of the drama club, except giant birds, with planting devices and well-drilling machines. And skirts. They sure do like flowy skirts."

"I believe you called them *space hippies*," Perry said.

"I did, and I stand by it. If they start singing and holding crystals up—"

The Synergists closest to us chose *that moment* to do just that. They held up glowing crystals and began to keen in a high, sweet wailing note that should have set my teeth on edge. Instead, it just reminded me of a terrible wedding I went to once, where the entertainment was a quartet of experimental musicians who hummed for an hour while we drank tepid champagne. It decidedly did not blend with the rest of their music, not even remotely.

"You were saying?" Perry quipped, turning to regard me with a glowing eye.

Torina yanked her attention away from the flitting, singing, dancing bird people and their generally chaotic but obviously effective antics. "Actually, I have a question I'd like to ask before we adopt a habit of Skirt Life and begin dancing in a circle."

I snorted a laugh. "*Skirt Life* would be a great name for a ship. Or maybe a band. Anyway, what's your question, my dear?"

"When do we eat?"

"Hey, this is your world. You guys have pizza here? I could really go for a slice."

She pointed at a small village in the distance, in the general direction of her family's estate, huddled close to a river. The place reminded me of a ski lodge, giving off a vaguely alpine-vacation feel. I'd barely noticed it the first time we'd stood here, but my mind had been on other things, like not dying. "Actually, I can do better than pizza. We have *volask*. It's root vegetables, cheese, and sausage in a pie, drizzled with sweet luchat syrup."

My stomach grumbled at the idea. It obviously approved, so I did, too.

"Lucky us. *Volask* sounds like it could just be my new favorite thing."

OKAY, so *volask* didn't end up being my favorite thing, but it was definitely up there. It struck me that a big, steaming plate of *volask*, and some of Lunzy's premium beer would make for a premium meal. We actually brought a bunch of *volask* along with us, some refrigerated, the rest frozen in the *Fafnir*'s galley. The beer we most certainly did *not* freeze, because that would be alcohol abuse, an abhorrent practice in any star system.

And now, we were back at Anvil Dark to find out what—if anything—the Artificers had been able to dig out of the Stillness comms device.

It turned out to be a lot. The Shadows weren't just stealing ships, they were stealing wealth right at the source. And they had a way of doing it that I had to grudgingly admit was pretty clever because it was pretty simple.

Shadows-- Stillness agents-- would infiltrate a society, and take some time to tease out its pressure points. Was the population generally greedy and capitalistic? Money was the pressure point. Was it more altruistic and motivated by a desire to help others, like the Synergists? Then opportunities to do good was a pressure point. Was it militaristic? Then advanced military tech was its particular pressure point. Driven by sexual need? Okay, that one was obvious.

Anyway, for every society that wasn't just sentient crystals collectively forming a hive mind that took decades to complete a single thought—and, yes, there apparently was one of those—there was something. There was some place the Shadows could apply pressure so that wealth would come leaking out.

Once they'd identified the most promising ways of compromising people in their target society, they looked for individuals that were most susceptible to them—the greediest, the most generous, the most militaristic, the most sex-driven. They would then carefully engineer things to put those specific targets into the most vulnerable positions possible. The greediest would suddenly find themselves broke, or even owing money. The altruist would face a scandal, a real one, or even a manufactured one, that threatened to undo a lifetime of good work. The militarist likewise would find themselves suspected of leaking secrets to the enemy. And the sexually hungry, the—well, the sky was pretty much the limit when it came to them.

I knew this part of the scheme well, having been involved in gathering incriminating information on various subjects as fodder to use against them. And they'd all been pretty bad people, so there was no shortage of sleazy material to work with. I'd also helped block some similar operations targeting people who might get in the way of the bad guys, like prosecutors and judges.

Which made me wonder if any of my cyber opponents had been Stillness agents.

This point was where the Stillness added their most cunning touch. They offered some sugar to put in that bitter, bitter pill of extortion. Whatever wealth the targets managed to plunder on behalf of the Stillness, they got to keep a fifth of it. And with advanced tech provided by the Stillness to help them out, they could get very rich, very fast. Then there was no end to the money, the good works, the military might or the sexual satisfaction. It was a win-win. Or maybe more of win-*don't-lose-but-still-come-out-ahead*.

The real kicker for me? There were two Shadows on Earth, working for Stillness and walking among my people.

And one of them was my cousin, Carter Yost.

"*Unbelievable*. I mean, there are seven billion people on Earth. What were the odds that the Stillness would stumble onto *him?*"

The Artificer Adept who'd just described what they'd found on the comms module just stared at me with both eye clusters. Lunzy, Torina, and Perry all gave me equally flat looks. No one said anything.

I looked from one to the next. "What?"

Perry finally spoke. "Van, have you ever won millions in a lottery?"

"I—what? No. Why?"

"Have you ever been struck by lightning? Been in a plane crash? Been attacked by a shark?"

"No, once, and no."

"Wait. You were in a plane crash?" Torina asked.

"It wasn't as much of a crash, as the little tractor thing that backs planes away from the gate pushing ours into another one. It did force me to spend an extra night, though."

"Where?"

I muttered the answer.

"Sorry, where?" Torina asked, cupping her hand behind her ear.

"I said, at a resort in Acapulco. It was still technically a crash, though." I turned to Perry. "Anyway, what's your point?"

"The point, Van, is that the probability of all of those things is much higher than your cousin being selected at random from among seven billion people."

I'm a smart guy, but it still took me a moment to finally put together what Perry was saying

"It wasn't random," I said. "The Stillness *deliberately* picked Carter."

"Pretty much the only answer that makes sense."

"But why him, of all people? There's got to be at least a couple of billion better candidates…" My voice trailed off. "Oh. Shit. Because of Gramps."

"And probably because of you, too, Van," Lunzy said. "Your

grandfather was at the top of their hit list, so they were no doubt keeping tabs on him. They'd have known that he became your guardian."

"Which is why your grandfather never told you about the Peacemakers. By keeping you ignorant until he was gone, he was protecting you from the Stillness," Perry said. "They're ruthless, but they're not stupid. They knew they couldn't take Mark on directly, on Earth, without facing one hell of a fight."

Torina nodded. "Okay, yeah. And as long as it seemed that your grandfather had no intention of having you follow him into the Peacemakers, they didn't need to pick that fight and risk something major going wrong. But they also wanted to hedge their bets, just in case you did end up becoming a Peacemaker—"

"So enter Carter Yost, your cousin, a money-grubbing, narcissistic asshole, their perfect target, and someone already close to you," Lunzy finished.

Perry bobbed his head. "Your cousin is an insurance policy, Van, against *you*."

I NEEDED some time to wrap my head around the fact that Carter Yost, the snotty, self-absorbed jerk that had kept skipping in and out of my life like an especially unwelcome stone across a lake was a Stillness agent. I excused myself, returned to the Wall of Remembered Honor, and looked at my grandfather's name.

"Did you know about that, Gramps? Couldn't you have done something about it?"

But the answer was that if he could have, he no doubt would have. He either hadn't known about Carter, or, if he had, he'd decided it was better to keep that from me along with everything else. Like the invisible spaceship in the barn. Or the fact that the space around Earth was teeming with intelligent races, going about their business with about as much regard for Earth as a fishing boat gave to the fish it caught. Or that he was an interstellar Peacemaker and intended for me to follow him.

I sighed and returned to *The Black Hole* to meet Lunzy, Torina, and Perry.

As I joined them at their table and sat down, our robotic waiter, Bob, slid silently up beside me on nifty spherical wheels that let him move in any direction.

"Would you care for something to drink—"

But Lunzy cut him off. "He'll have a Misery Loves Company."

Bob swiveled an eyepiece toward her. "Are you sure?"

"I'm sure."

Perry did his laughing thing.

As Bob rolled away, I turned back to Lunzy. "What the hell is a Misery Loves Company? And why did Bob seem reluctant to bring me one? And why does Perry think it's so funny?"

"It's the drink of choice for Peacemakers right before, or right after, a tough mission."

"Sometimes during," Perry put in.

Bob returned with a glass containing a viscous-looking, slightly bluish liquid. "Please be advised that by consuming any or all of this drink, you are holding harmless this establishment and all of its employees for any resulting effects."

I picked up the glass. "It comes with a legal disclaimer?"

Lunzy waved a hand. "That only really matters if you have more than one. Oh, yeah, by the way—don't have more than one."

I sniffed it and got whacked with an especially alcoholic reek. I glanced around the table, shrugged, and slammed it back.

Afterward, the closest approximation I could give to what it was like was to imagine an entire bottle of bourbon, all of its flavor and alcohol content distilled down to a single shot. Now, add a small hammer, wrapped in velvet—but you don't drink that part. Rather, you take the hammer and strike yourself between the eyes with the delicacy of a Medieval blacksmith who has anger issues, and you've got something approximating how that drink landed in my gut.

When I'd mostly recovered, Lunzy patted my arm. "There. Feeling better?"

I shook my head and said what was supposed to be *No!* but all that came out was a strangled gasp. I finally found my voice.

"Smooth."

Lunzy laughed. "Really focuses the mind, doesn't it? Anyway, now that you're focused, how'd you like to go back to Earth, Van? In an official capacity?"

"What, to arrest Carter?" I was already halfway out of my chair.

Lunzy gestured me back into my seat. "No, he's still off on an assignment to keep him out of the way."

"But, wait. If he's flying around in a *Dragonet*, pretending to be a Peacemaker, and he's actually a Stillness stooge—"

"Way ahead of you. I've been in touch with his ship's AI and explained the situation. She's going to make sure he can't go anywhere where he can do any damage. And if it gets hairy enough, she's authorized to use extreme measures."

Perry leaned toward me. "That means she'll depressurize the ship, or even blow it up."

"So I gathered." I turned back to Lunzy. "If the chance comes, *please* let me be the one to push the button."

"Ah, the bonds of family," Torina said, grinning.

"Yeah, he'd push the button on me just as fast. Faster, even. But okay, if I'm not going back to Earth to deal with Carter, then what?"

"Remember I said that there were two Stillness operatives on Earth? We want you to deal with the other one." She produced a data chip and handed it to me. "Everything we've been able to glean about this agent is on there. It's not much, though. He—or she—works out of some place called Vancouver."

"British Columbia or Washington? There are two of them."

"Uh, the British one, I think. Anyway, it's on the chip. The agent's code name is Cosset. He, or she, or they, anyway, are siphoning something off Earth by means of an orbital transfer shuttle that meets up with a space-going ship in the lee of the Earth's moon, Luna, about every twelve to fifteen weeks. There's another rendezvous scheduled four or five days from now."

Perry cocked his head at Lunzy. "Are you authorizing Van to conduct the seizure? Because, as a Peacemaker Initiate—"

"Yeah, about that," Lunzy cut in. She produced a paper envelope from inside her jacket, which was actually sealed with red wax, of all things.

"In there, you'll find the Masters' Edict declaring you a Peacemaker Acolyte, the lowest rank of full Peacemaker. You'll find the insignia in there, too. Congratulations, Van, you just made one of the quickest trips through being an Initiate in history."

I accepted the envelope with the gravitas that seemed due, even though I still had Misery Loves Company fumes lingering in the back of my throat.

Torina raised an eyebrow. "One of the quickest? It took Van just a few weeks."

"It did. But I did it in three days fewer," Lunzy said, smiling, finishing her drink, then standing. "Anyway, enjoy Earth, Van. Just don't let anyone find out you're a starship pilot. Wouldn't want your life to get awkward."

26

"THE LAST TIME I traveled to Vancouver, I didn't fly quite so high," I said, crossing my arms and staring out the *Fafnir*'s canopy.

Earth sprawled below us—thirty-six *thousand* klicks below us. Netty had put us into a geostationary orbit over a point on the equator due south of Vancouver. Southern British Columbia, including the city, was hidden beneath swirls of white clouds. Coming back along the curving sweep of the planet, the western United States was having a much sunnier day, with only a few clouds sweeping around an adorably tiny hurricane—or typhoon, I guessed, since it was over the Pacific—far to the west of Chile, over the open ocean. I could pick out Iowa, too, including the approximate location of the farm. I'd told Miryam I was going to be traveling for a while and asked her to keep an eye on the place.

Which was true. I was traveling. The fact that I was traveling light-years at a hop was beside the point.

"Van, it's a bit crowded up here," Netty said. "How long do you think this is going to take?"

I glanced at the tactical overlay. Geosynchronous space was getting pretty crowded indeed, with constellations of GPS, communications, photo and radar imaging, and military and spy satellites sweeping around in lockstep with the Earth's rotation. Netty had found a clear spot for us between what was obviously a military satellite and a comms satellite with the corporate logo of a major telecom company emblazoned on it. I amused myself by having Perry leach a signal from the latter, and watched some YouTube videos.

"Are we in imminent danger of collision or something?" I asked her.

"Not really. But that spy satellite off to starboard is pretty sensitive, and we do give off *some* signatures, especially heat."

"Well, that next shuttle launch should happen sometime later today. So—some hours yet, I guess."

"Van—"

"Netty, don't worry about it. If we get detected, it'll just be another UFO thing."

"No, it's not that. I was assessing our heat signature and doing some background scans for the data. As a result, I detected this."

As she spoke, a new contact appeared on the tactical overlay. It was a faint but distinct heat signature in geosynchronous orbit about a thousand klicks spinward of us.

"What the hell is that?"

"Something that's stealthed up," Netty said.

I tapped the intercom. "Perry, Torina, you guys better get up here. It turns out that we're not alone."

"It's a weapons platform," Netty finally announced. "Standard hull design, produced by a shipyard at Tau Ceti for non-military users."

"Non-military users can buy weapons platforms?"

Torina answered. "Absolutely. The Stillness are a pain, but they're far from the only ne'er-do-wells in space. And if you've got a few million bonds tied up in a gas-mining venture or some zero-g fabricating facility, you're going to want to protect your investment."

I shot her a bemused glance. "Your family owns some, don't they?"

"Three. But they're small ones."

I leaned back in the seat. "Recommendations?"

"Destroy it."

Torina, Netty, and Perry all said it more or less at once. It left me a little surprised.

"Really? Isn't something invisible suddenly exploding into debris going to be, um, a little conspicuous?"

"You said it yourself, Van. It'll be fodder for the UFO and conspiracy theory enthusiasts. It's not like the Vela Incident back in '79. We really had to scramble to cover that one up," Perry said.

"The Vela Incident? I thought that was a test nuke that some country who wished to remain nameless detonated out over the ocean."

"And you just go right on thinking that, Van."

"But—"

"Van? Missile platform. Focus," Torina said.

"Uh—yeah, right. Okay, so if we open fire on it, don't we risk it just shooting back?"

Torina shrugged. "Would you rather let it shoot first?"

"Good point." I confirmed that we had a missile armed and that it was locked on the fitful signature of the platform. I kept waiting for the damned thing to suddenly come to life and open fire, but it didn't seem to have detected us.

I hovered my finger over the firing key, then pulled it back. "If we blow that platform up now, whoever's down there might know it and scrub that shuttle launch."

So we waited.

We spent a tense twenty or so minutes just sitting there, keenly aware that a missile platform loaded with ordnance was, by space-travel standards, close enough to touch. If it fired its entire load-out—six missiles—we'd be in trouble. Netty had already worst-cased it and figured that we'd almost certainly be hit by at least one of them. Worse, if they had nuclear warheads, their detonations would wreak havoc on everything in orbit on this side of Earth. Military satellites were generally hardened against EMP and might survive, but there was no way the civilian birds would.

It would take a lot more to cover up than the Vela Incident had.

The terminator dividing day from night scrolled over Vancouver, fading it into darkness and leaving it a fuzzy patch of light. A few moments later, Netty detected the signature of a launch. The shuttle was on its way.

We let it climb close to orbit. Only then did I fire the missile. It streaked away, and we waited. It was point-blank range for a space battle, but it still seemed to take forever. And all we could do was wait for return fire—

"Bingo," Netty said. "Direct hit. The missile platform is scrap."

There'd barely been a flicker, but it had been a conventional warhead detonating almost a thousand kilometers away. I nodded and turned my attention to the shuttle.

It was just making orbit. As soon as the platform had been destroyed, Netty started sending a signal to mimic it to whatever was receiving it down on the surface. The ruse might not have worked, of course, and the owner of the shuttle might try to quickly deorbit it, or even just make it self-destruct. But it settled sedately into orbit, prior to starting its journey toward the Moon.

"Okay. So far, so good. But we can't just nuke this thing, right? So I guess we need to board it."

Torina smiled. "Good. I'm in the mood for some boarding and looting and stuff. All due respect to the, um, space hippies, but I need to cleanse my palate with a little violence."

I started out of my seat to suit up. "Right? They were a bit much, weren't they?"

"That's one way to put it. So, swords? Or guns?"

"Both, just in case."

I MADE the final cut with the Moonsword. The shuttle didn't incorporate the same tough alloy components that the Stillness ship had, so the blade slid readily through the metal with a faint, squealing hiss and the occasional spark. The section I'd carved out of the interior hatch drifted away into the compartment behind it.

A light danced on the bulkhead as Torina joined me. "Perry and I have confirmed it. There's no crew. This ship's automated."

"You sound disappointed."

"I wanted to beat someone up."

"Well, you are very good at it."

Perry had pushed his head inside the sealed compartment and scanned around.

"Oh, for—"

"What? What is it?" I asked, alarmed, imagining he'd found —I don't know, viruses, or snakes, or something clearly displeasing. He answered by simply leading the way into the cramped hold.

"Well, this sucks," Torina said, opening a crate and hefting an object from inside. I did the same and nearly brained myself— things might not have weight, but they still had mass.

I stared at the gleaming brick. "It's gold."

"Right? It's just gold. *Bor*-ring," Perry replied.

I glanced around, doing a quick calculation of the cargo's value, assuming it was all gold. Tens of millions of dollars, easily. "Perry, we need to talk. Our concept of boring is—really quite different."

WE RETURNED TO ANVIL DARK, where I turned in the seized shuttle for a decent reward, and the gold for a much less decent one. To me, gold was gold, but Perry had explained that that was really an Earth thing.

"We can manufacture gold, Van, in elemental assemblers—basically, industrial particle beam reactors. It's really more valuable out here for its industrial properties, like ductility and resistance to corrosion than because of that human, *ooh, shiny* attitude about it. The only reason this stuff is worth anything is because it's a *little* cheaper than fabricating it."

But I still got some bonds for it, which, along with the other prizes we'd taken and a generous reward from the Guild for seizing the Stillness comms device, meant I was suddenly flush with cash. Or, more flush than I had been up until now.

"Want to upgrade the *Fafnir* to *Dragon* class, Van?" Netty asked.

"I don't know. Do I?"

We spent the next hour or so with me learning what the *Dragon* upgrade entailed, and its pros and cons. We finally concluded the upgrade wasn't really feasible yet, nor even really necessary. One of the big advantages of the Dragon, aside from its mass and potential for bigger and more powerful engines and weapons, was that it could accommodate a crew. I still wasn't there yet. We finally settled on adding an armor package and sticking a new weapon-system, a rail gun, onto one of the open hardpoints I'd added earlier. The rail gun was a vicious weapon, able to punch completely through a freighter's hull, but its projectiles were unguided, so it only worked at close ranges. We also upgraded the missile launcher, adding rotary magazines to speed up the reload time and configuring them to take a second type of missile, called *Starfires*. Starfire missiles were smaller, more nimble, and had powerful, directional warheads that flung depleted uranium spheres at their target in a lethal cone. They could easily take out a ship ten times the size of the *Fafnir*, but they were also *really* expensive. We'd reserve those for high-value targets only.

Torina and I were in the middle of learning how to bolt on applique armor modules from Netty and Perry when a call came from Lunzy, inviting us for a beer.

"Don't need to ask me twice," Torina said as we put away our tools and headed for the *Foregone Conclusion*, which was docked on Anvil Dark's upper ring.

We settled into her opulent study. Sadly, Lunzy didn't grace us with the really good beer this time, but the brew she poured out for us was still damned good. I was suddenly taken by some spirit of mischief and offered some to Perry, then made a dismayed face.

"I'm sorry, Perry, I forgot you don't, you know, drink anything."

He returned an amber scowl. "Ha ha. That joke never gets old. Not when you use it, and not the thirty-nine times your grandfather used it."

"Thirty-nine?"

"Thirty-nine. And yes, I counted."

Lunzy got right to the point. "We've finished stripping that comms unit for every glimmer of intelligence we can get from it. It seems the next big thing Kohl and the Stillness are planning is an attack on the 17 Tauri system in the Pleiades, a star better known as Electra. There's one sort of habitable planet, with a really profitable rare-earth element mining operation underway. Pretty much all of the mining is done robotically, though, then the concentrated ore is lifted to a shielded station in orbit for transshipment out of the system. It seems that Kohl intends for the Stillness to raid the place and seize some of the concentrate. He's especially interested in osmium, which has spiked in price lately."

"I saw that," Torina put in. "Something about a new industrial process for making more efficient power cells."

Lunzy nodded. "Anyway, Van, we've done a tactical analysis and figured that eight Peacemakers, in the right time and place, can head off the Stillness and even give them the bloody nose they deserve. You in?"

I glanced at Torina and Perry. "Any reason I shouldn't be?"

"Well, you could take a missile to the face and die," Perry replied.

"Is that a yes or a no?"

"How worried are you about taking a missile to the face?"

Torina leaned toward me. "Van, you need to start building some bridges with other Peacemakers. You've been pretty successful so far, so others are probably starting to take notice of you."

"Listen to the young lady, Van. She speaks wisely. More and more Peacemakers are hearing about this new guy, Mark Tudor's grandson, who's making a big splash. Not all of them are happy about it. More Peacemaker allies wouldn't hurt," Lunzy said.

I glanced around again, then nodded. "I'm mindful of the missile to the face thing, but yeah. I'm in."

"So the question is, where do we go, and when do we need to be there?" Perry said.

"I can answer that," a new voice said. Bester lumbered in, ducking under the hatch coaming to enter Lunzy's study. Once he was inside, it became a *lot* more crowded.

He gave a slow nod. "Or at least I can answer part of it. The timing's up to you. But as for the location, you can leave that to me."

WE MET LATER that day with seven other Peacemakers, a motley assortment of races, none of them human. And we had to do it in a secure portion of Anvil Dark that also had facilities to allow one of the Peacemakers, a creature resembling a big jellyfish with tentacles that were actually quite dexterous, to join in. It seemed to need an atmosphere of mixed methane and ammonia, meaning we spent the briefing with only a few millimeters of transparent window between us and a horrifically toxic atmosphere. Of course, we were also only a few meters away from hard vacuum, and I'd gotten pretty used to that.

The operation would be led by Alic, a squat, enormously muscled humanoid with a jowly, whiskered face that resembled a walrus. Alic had apparently come to the Peacemakers from a military background, his people, a race known as the Eniped, apparently being one of the more militant in known space. As Alic explained it, though, it wasn't that the Eniped were aggressive or expansionistic. They simply considered militarism to be a sort of artform, their martial culture focusing not on taking territory or seizing resources but rather emphasizing battle as something to be perfected within itself. It meant that some of the most prized and best-paid mercenaries in known space were Eniped. Lunzy was quite pleased that he was available to lead this mission.

In fact, Alic, and the other Peacemakers involved were all firm allies of Lunzy's. Perry pointed out that I was now as well. That actually made me glad, because I didn't feel quite so alone as a Peacemaker. It was nice to have the connection I did to the Master, Groshenko, but Perry had cautioned me about that, too.

"Groshenko was your grandfather's friend, yes. But he didn't become a Master just based on his charm and good looks. There was a reason your grandfather wasn't interested in becoming a Master himself. Masters are creatures of politics. Don't let yourself forget that."

We spent the next two days preparing, Torina and I working overtime with Waldo, Netty and Perry bolting on the armor upgrades to the *Fafnir* and getting the rail gun and new missile system installed. It made for long days, lots of sweat, and more than a few cuts, banged heads, and injured fingers. I learned about a dozen new profanities from Torina, a couple of them truly hair-raising. She'd seemed like such a nice girl, too.

We finished up with a few hours to spare before our scheduled start time. It gave Torina and me time for a quick bite to eat, so we treated ourselves to a pub-style dinner at *The Black Hole*. When we got back to the *Fafnir*, Netty informed me there was a message waiting for me.

"From who?" I'd assumed it would be either Alic or Lunzy, but Netty's answer was an unpleasant surprise.

"It's from your cousin."

"Shit."

"I can just delete it."

I sighed. "No, go ahead and put it on."

The comm screen switched from the Peacemaker logo to an image I long ago came to know and loathe. Carter Yost stared out of the screen at me, all wavy hair, ridiculously white teeth, and general mannequin-esque good looks—perfect, and plastic as hell.

"Hey, cuz. Notice you haven't made any effort to find me, invite me for a drink or anything. Anyway, you'll probably hear that I screwed up the mission I was given—"

Netty had to pause playback and rewind it back to the

moment before I crowed out loud and let it trail off into an evil laugh.

"—the mission I was given, but it was designed to make me look bad. I mean, I just know it. Now, I wonder who could have been responsible for that?"

His expression hardened, and I saw something on Carter's face I'd never seen before. It was genuine anger, mixed with shame. Carter wasn't used to failing. It was mainly because he'd pretty much been given everything he ever wanted and hadn't had to work for any of it. But no one could just give him success as a Peacemaker, and it stung him.

Which was damned good news, but it also meant that, in true narcissistic fashion, he'd find a way to make it someone else's fault. After all, he was Carter Yost. If he wasn't perfect, then someone must be to blame. And that someone was obviously going to be me.

"Anyway, cuz, just wanted to drop you a quick hello and say I'll be seeing you." He sneered. "Be seeing you real soon."

The screen flicked back to the logo. Torina immediately began brushing her hands over herself. I gave her a puzzled look.

"Something wrong?"

"Yeah. I've got asshole all over me."

I laughed, but it was more than a little grim. "Welcome to my life."

We did the last pre-flight prep on the *Fafnir*, then Alic called us on the channel assigned to this op. He spoke while transmitting the final operations plan, including flight parameters, to Netty.

"Okay, everyone, grab your rifles and hands off your gun, 'cause the first is for killing, the second's for fun."

Torina rolled her eyes. "What is with guys, anyway, and your fixation on your—"

"Dental hygiene? Good dental hygiene is important for overall health."

Torina grinned. "Yeah. Dental hygiene. That's totally what I was going to say."

27

Despite his sophomoric humor, Alic was a wizard when it came to fighting a battle. His years of military experience showed. He'd surmised that the Stillness would establish an outer cordon of picket ships to cut off approach to and departure from the mining platform orbiting the Electra system's sole rocky planet. He'd also assumed they'd count on being able to obscure themselves against the searing, blue-white background of the massive star. So he had us twist into the system in two groups of four ships each, one high above and one well below the system's ecliptic plane, and so close to the planet that we ended up poised almost right above its poles. It meant burning a lot of extra fuel, but Lunzy had already approved the additional expenditure and paid for it out of some operating budget she maintained.

"Van, the external antimatter pod is empty. Did you want to eject it?" Netty asked.

The *Fafnir* couldn't actually carry enough fuel for such a deep twist into the system's gravity well and then return to Anvil Dark without refueling. So we leased an external antimatter pod and stuck it on one of the free hardpoints, kind of like the drop tanks military planes back on Earth carried to increase their fuel load. In theory, we should be able to drop it, then recover it later. But if we lost it, we'd be on the hook for the cost—and antimatter pods weren't at all cheap.

The only reason to drop it would be to trim the *Fafnir's* center of mass, making her a little more maneuverable. I decided we'd hang onto it, at least for now. In the meantime, we started our high-speed run into the system.

Sure enough, the Stillness had deployed three ships in a picket cordon, all of them scout class, small and fast. If we came in using a conventional approach, they'd have been lost in the glare from the big blue star.

Alic came on the comm. "Okay, all ships, safeties off, weapons tight. Lethal force is authorized."

Weapons tight meant that we could return fire if threatened. Normally, that would require an actual shot taken or a missile launch, but when it came to the Stillness, Alic had been clear that even being lit up by their fire control systems was sufficient. And, sure enough, we hadn't been in-system for more than thirty seconds before that very thing happened.

A warning that we were being tracked chimed from Netty's defensive suite, and the point-defense gun came online. That was all I needed to hear.

"Firing now."

We snapped out two starfire missiles, which streaked away. Torina handled the laser, pumping out bursts with deft skill. The three Stillness ships, caught in a crossfire from more than twice their number, were quickly battered into submission. Two blew apart, while one began broadcasting a surrender code from its transponder. They did manage to loose five missiles, one of which locked onto the *Fafnir*. The point-defense gun spewed out projectiles, shredding it about fifty klicks away.

"Well, that was surprisingly easy," I said, veering the *Fafnir* onto the new course transmitted by Alic. But Torina and Perry both shot me warning glances. I half-expected one of them to say something like, *Don't get cocky, kid.*

Instead, Perry simply shook his head. "You can go from winning to dead in a space battle really quickly, Van. One rail gun slug in the right place, and you get to see a fusion explosion from the inside."

"Hey, just let me enjoy it for a few seconds," I replied, but I also got the point and gave Perry a nod of understanding.

Five more Stillness ships had closed on the mining platform. Four of them were, again, scout class, but one was a big bastard, corvette class. As we charged in, Alic sent a command from his ship's AI, linking it to Netty and the others. The result was a single, networked AI overseeing the details of the battle. It freed the Peacemakers from having to deal with the subtle nuances of thrust and momentum and the like, and allowed them to concentrate on fighting. Essentially, all I had to do was tell Netty where I wanted to go, and she'd take us there. Moreover, the other ships would collaborate, refining our courses to optimize our attacks and fields of fire. It was a nifty feature that I knew about Peacemaker ships but hadn't yet seen in action.

A Stillness missile streaked past us a few klicks away. Our ECM had confused it with an electronic ghost, prompting it to attack a piece of empty space. Torina kept up her deadly accurate shooting with the laser, while Perry interfaced with the defensive suite. When we started attracting laser fire from the corvette, he fired the glitter caster, shrouding us in a festive cloud of shimmering bits of reflective foil. Netty recorded two solid laser hits, but the glitter diffused them enough that they only scoured some of our new armor. Torina sat back and blew out a breath. With the glitter in place, she was momentarily out of a job.

It didn't last, though. A Peacemaker named Foros took two solid missile hits in rapid succession, knocking his *Dragonet* out of the fight. Alic took damage as well from a laser barrage. I was tempted to keep hiding in the cloud of glitter, but we were the only ship equipped with one, meaning the Stillness ships just shot at everyone else. I had Netty accelerate us out of the cloud to give them another target.

"Starfires away," I said, firing two more of the vicious little missiles at the corvette in a focused attack by six of our ships. By now, the range was down to hundreds of klicks, and the fire was coming and going thick and fast. The fusillade of missiles and laser shots overwhelmed the corvette's point defenses, and I had the satisfaction of watching one of the starfires detonate a few hundred meters from its flank. The corvette's hull shredded from a cloud of depleted uranium slugs, and another, bigger missile fired by one of the other Peacemakers sealed the deal, slamming squarely into the corvette's forward hull and detonating inside, blowing the bow off. The crippled ship went dark.

But we didn't have it all our way. While we focused on the corvette, the remaining scouts got in some solid hits. Foros had to eject before his ship blew apart, but his Second didn't make it and died with the ship. We were bracketed by two missiles, one of which punched a fragment through our hull just aft of the galley. Wind and fog gusted around us as the *Fafnir* depressurized. The wisdom of sealing ourselves in our armor and helmets before the battle was suddenly clear. Waldo plugged the leak, and Netty began repressurizing the ship from its reserve air supply.

And then it was over. One second, there'd been torrents of fire flying back and forth, and the next, nothing. We actually fired the last shot of the battle, a rail gun slug that slammed into one of the scouts and passed cleanly through it, blowing debris out the other side.

And that was it.

I slumped back. I felt like I'd just run a marathon or two. Torina did likewise, turning and grinning at me.

"We having fun yet?"

I grinned back. "Well, except for the possibility of dying a horrible death in space part, yeah, I kinda am."

A new voice cut in. It was Alic. "We aren't done yet, folks. The scouts are all down and out, but there's still a big chunk of that corvette intact, and it might have some valuable stuff aboard. So it's party time!" A dramatic pause. "By which I mean boarding party, of course."

"Is he always like that?" I asked Perry.

"I don't know about Alic in particular, but the Eniped are known for two things. One is military acumen."

"And the other?"

"They're famous for what, on Earth, you'd call *dad jokes*."

UNLIKE THE STILLNESS ship we'd seized in the Afterthought, this frigate had two UDAs, both of them still usable. According to Perry, it was to allow for boarding actions—just not boarding actions going *into* the ship. Alic docked his ship at one, and we took the other. The remaining Peacemakers fanned out to scour the remaining wreckage for useful intelligence, rescue Foros, and take the sole surrenderee from the initial engagement into custody.

Once we'd achieved a hard dock against the corvette's flank, I drew the Moonsword and reached for the airlock control. Torina backed me up with a handgun and what I knew to be her sweet, deadly moves. Perry led the way, doing the *combat* part of his job as a combat AI. Again, tension thrummed in the air. Netty had already confirmed that the corvette's reactor had gone dark, but the ship could still carry scuttling charges. We needed to get in and secure the wreckage fast.

As soon as we entered the Stillness ship, another problem hit me in the face—as in, literally hit me in the face when I turned a corner and clunked my visor into a fallen structural beam. The interior of the corvette was a maze of twisted conduits, cables and components, loose pieces of debris, and some astonishingly gory scenes where crew members had been hit by pellets from our starfire missile. Being hit by a two centimeter depleted uranium slug traveling at a couple of thousand meters per second apparently just caused a body to explode. We didn't find body *parts* as much as we found body *spatters*.

Perry offered a coolly clinical explanation. "Hydrostatic shock. The fluids inside the body just can't get out of the way of the projectile fast enough. Pro tip: don't get hit by a high-velocity slug."

I eased myself around one of the gross little displays smeared across decks and bulkheads. "Yeah, I'll keep that in mind, thanks."

We met up with Alic just forward of the corvette's ruined engineering compartment. He and his Second had found and retrieved a data core, which his second had taken back to his ship. We joined forces and worked our way into engineering, stumbling right into two Stillness crew frantically trying to rig a pair of missile warheads into makeshift scuttling charges.

Perry pulsed out his broadband stun flash, momentarily dazzling the two. Alic immediately launched himself at one of them. Torina was behind me, still negotiating a buckled bulkhead, so I took a breath and kicked off, then sailed through the zero-g vacuum toward the other. This time, I deliberately tried not to think about what I was doing and just let my body take over with its muscle memory.

I'd learned during my initial memory training back at Cross-roads that zero-g fights tended to go one of two ways—very fast, or protracted and drawn out. The two combatants tended to do things that pushed them away from one another, so a drawn-out combat involved something almost like old time jousting, striking, bouncing away, then closing for another pass. Protracted fights by far favored the more experienced and skillful of the engaged parties, and I was pretty damned sure that wasn't me. I needed to win as fast as possible.

So I didn't make any attempt at subtlety. I slashed out with the Moonsword, just as the Stillness agent stabbed at me with the pointed side of a boarding axe. Pain flared low in my right side. The Moonsword hit something, but the combination of my own momentum and the force of being hit spun me off toward a reactor component glowing cherry red.

"Fuuuu—"

I tried to jackknife, to get my feet in front of me and kick away from the overheated component. But a nova burst of pain in my right side almost knocked me out, leaving me sailing inexorably toward painful, and quite possibly fatal injury. But something slammed into me, knocking me off course and away from thermal nastiness.

It was Perry. He'd deliberately crashed into me, saving my ass. I hit a generator housing with one foot behind me, so I gritted my teeth and pushed off with it, straight back at the Stillness agent. He'd recovered and was in the process of drawing a sidearm. I could tell instinctively that he'd get a shot off at me before I could reach him, so I let that instinct keep going and threw the Moonsword at him.

I'd thrown the blade with a bit of turning force, meaning it rotated as it traveled. I cursed, imagining it harmlessly bumping pommel-first into my opponent. But it hit edge-on, which, for the Moonsword, was enough. The blade sliced through the suit and into the flesh beneath it. My opponent spasmed and reached for the blade, by which time I'd arrived. I crashed into him, started to rebound, then caught the blade by its hilt and swung it, all while practically whimpering around the pain tearing up my right side.

It was a solid hit, nearly decapitating him.

Gasping, I looked for Alic. He'd already taken his opponent down and was yanking cables away from the makeshift scuttling charge. Perry had found a systems interface and was busy hacking his way into what remained of the ship's computer, making sure there were no more nasty surprises in store. I bumped into a bulkhead with a groan. My armor's self-sealing system had worked, maintaining air-tight integrity, while also flooding my wound with a combination of antiseptic and pain deadener. Still, it hurt like a son of a bitch.

Torina deftly stopped herself with a foot against a conduit. "Aw, you guys didn't leave anything for me."

"Tell you what, Torina," I hissed. "Next time, *you* go first, and have all the fun you want with it."

PERRY, Torina, and Alic searched the ruined corvette and found three data cores, a few dozen miscellaneous documents, and a dozen weapons, including a nasty-looking antimatter gun. I dragged myself back to the *Fafnir* and got to find out just how good Waldo was at first aid. With Netty controlling him, he turned out to be pretty good, neatly cleaning, stitching, and bandaging my wound.

"I've had lots of practice. Your grandfather had a penchant for getting himself cut, stabbed, bludgeoned and burned," she said, as Waldo finished up. "Oh, he also nearly drowned once in a wave pool, but that was more due to enthusiastic—you know what, let's save that story for later." Her tone was apologetic as she directed Waldo to expertly snip the end of a wayward suture.

I thought about my grandfather's many scars. I'd always assumed he'd got them in combat, just not combat somewhere that wasn't Earth.

Unfortunately, none of the Stillness ships were worth more than their scrap value, plus whatever useful components could be salvaged from them. Missiles and fuel were the two big ones, and while I rested, Netty and Torina ensured we collected our share. In the meantime, I told Perry to prepare a message, to broadcast on the three comm channels he'd discovered the Stillness were using.

"Send it to Kohl himself. Tell him that his little raiding party is now interstellar toast," I said.

Perry cocked his head at me. "You sure want to do that, Van? You might be *poking the bear*, as your grandfather used to put it."

I smiled. *Poking the bear.* Yeah, I'd heard Gramps say that more than a few times myself.

But my smile fluttered away. He'd wanted to end the Stillness and their reign of terror, but had never managed it. Looking back with the benefit of my new perspective on him, and the things

Perry, Netty, Lunzy and Groshenko had said about him, I knew it had been a crushing disappointment.

So I nodded. "Yeah. Yeah, I do, Perry. Let's poke away."

"GOTTA ADMIT, those space hippies did damned good work," I said, shading my eyes against the midday sun.

The area ravaged by the illegal stripmining of Torina's homeworld now looked anything but ravaged. What had been nothing but barren, muddy bedrock was now a lush riot of trees, shrubs and wildflowers. Talus and scree were covered with soil and turned into rolling hills covered in grass and more flowering shrubs. And the worst area, where the miners had chewed their deepest into the bedrock, was now a placid pond, its edges rimmed with deep blue blooms not unlike lilies.

Torina smiled and nodded. "Yeah, I'd say we got our money's worth."

We wandered for a while, me occasionally wincing at dull flickers of pain in my side. The accelerated healing I'd received had done in a few days what would have taken weeks of recovery on Earth, but it would be a while yet before the wound was completely undone. Perry, meanwhile, wheeled overhead and transmitted images back down to a data slate, to let Torina see the reclamation from the air. It was as though there'd never been any illicit industrial plunder—as though the landscape had always looked like this.

"It's definitely different, but I like it. No, I love it," Torina finally proclaimed as we stood on the bank of the pond. A few water bugs had already moved in, and I could have sworn I'd seen something fishy flash briefly beneath the surface.

I turned to her. "Torina, I just want to say thanks, for everything you've done."

She narrowed her eyes at me. "Are you firing me?"

"I—what? No! I just assumed that, well, with your homeworld fixed up, that you'd—" I stopped, shaking my head.

"Well, I *could* stay here, I guess. Unless, that is, you'd like to keep me on as your copilot and Second."

"Are you serious?"

She shrugged. "I'm not really into the *idle rich* kind of thing."

"You don't really seem like a farmer, either," I said, smiling.

"Nah, I never was good at working the land and—well, I'm good at *eating* things, just not so great at *growing* them. But if you'll have me in your copilot's seat, I *would* ask that we come back here, now and then."

I grinned. "Deal."

"You should go home, too."

"To Iowa?

"If that's home, then yes. It's important to know where you came from."

"She's right, Van. There's a reason your grandfather lived on Earth," Perry added, landing nearby. His eyes glittered with mischief, but his words were wise ones.

"Okay, then. Home, and away. Whenever the galaxy gets a bit big, we'll make it small again. By going home."

"I like it," Torina said, nodding.

I glanced around, then looked back at her. "Well, I've seen your home, so how about you come see mine? Lunzy tells me that Kohl's busy licking his wounds. We could take a few days now."

She smiled and shrugged. "Sounds good. What's in Iowa, anyway?"

"Torina, let me tell you about something we call *corn*."

28

"This has Carter Yost all over it," I snapped, as Netty completed twisting us to UGPS 0722-05, a system so isolated and unimportant that that was its name—UGPS 0722-05. In fact, calling it a 'system' was giving it too much credit, because it was just a single object, a dim, cold brown dwarf star that Netty said was most likely a rogue planet, rather than a standalone star. It had no satellites, aside from a few tens of thousands of rocks swirling chaotically around it, all of it probably the pulverized remains of some moons destroyed by whatever had kicked it out of its origin system millions, and maybe billions of years ago.

Aside from serving as an occasionally useful nav fix and reference point, no one had any reason to come here at all. It was uninteresting, of little use to anyone, and given an importance it really didn't deserve.

Which brought me right back to my cousin, Carter Yost.

Lunzy had asked us to meet here, and not simply because it happened to be the easiest place for us to both get to. Yes, there was an element of that, but we could have twisted to many other places for the same amount of fuel consumption, and many more for even less. She didn't even want to be near Anvil Dark, this time.

Shortly after we arrived, we got a directional ping from a tight-beam comms transmission, which led us to a random spot about a million klicks away from the brown dwarf. Lunzy's ship, the *Foregone Conclusion*, hung a few hundred klicks, in turn, away from some of the outermost rocks accompanying the rogue planet on its lonely passage from wherever it started, to wherever it was destined to end up.

"She's concealing herself in the scanner-clutter of those rocks," Netty said.

"And she used a tight-beam comm transmission, in burst mode, and only as a locational fix. This is about as secret-squirrel as things get," Perry put in.

Torina and I both turned to him, perched between the *Fafnir*'s cockpit seats. She gave a blank look, and me a bemused one.

"Secret-squirrel? Is that a Peacemaker codeword or something?" Torina asked.

"No, it's a cartoon from the 60's, about, well, a secret squirrel —a squirrel who's also a spy. He wears a trench coat, and a fedora, and—"

I stopped. Torina was looking at me like I'd just started speaking in tongues.

I shrugged. "It was entertainment for kids, from about fifty years ago."

"What has that got to do with *any* of this?"

"For reasons not clear to this day, it became popular to refer to very sensitive, highly classified material as *secret-squirrel stuff*," Perry said. "So, uh—that. This is all very secret-squirrel—" He stopped. "You know, I regret bringing it up, now."

I laughed and tapped his head. "Don't. It taught me something valuable."

"What's that?"

"That you, my super-smart AI friend, have been watching kids cartoons."

"I was stuck in a barn, Van, sometimes for days at a time. It's not like I had much else to do. Oh, and in case you're interested, I can tell you the plot to every soap opera, the punchline to every joke on every sitcom, and if you're interested, I can figure out how to save a bundle on your car insurance, and why certain medications might be right for you."

"Why do I have visions of you wearing a dingy bathrobe and fuzzy slippers, parked on a ratty old couch and watching, I don't know, *Days of Our Lives* or something."

We rendezvoused with Lunzy, docked, and crossed into the Foregone Conclusion, back into her sumptuous, paneled study. She didn't offer much preamble, or any amazing beer this time. Instead, she got right to the point.

"Van, a Peacemaker has been taken hostage by a group of mercenaries that seized an orbital comm platform at Wolf 424. The Lupine Agglomerate, the outfit that runs the asteroid mining operations in the system, have made it clear they have no intention of getting involved."

"So it's not their platform, then," Torina said.

"No, it's not. It's a long-range relay booster owned by Interlink Enterprises."

I frowned in thought. Right. Somewhere among my implanted memories was a rough outline of how long-range civilian communications worked in known space. Military organizations, and bigger paramilitary ones like the Peacemakers, could afford to invest in long-range tech of their own, using systems that incorporated a function similar to a low-power twist drive. It was enough to allow real-time comms between points light-years apart, albeit by burning fuel to do so. That added overhead was why such systems tended to be reserved for important traffic only.

Such systems were priced far beyond the means of the non-military masses, though. Interlink was the biggest provider, operating long-range relay boosters like this one, allowing for long-range civilian comms for what amounted to a long-distance fee.

Questions tumbled through my head. Why would mercenaries seize such a facility? Why didn't the Lupine Agglomeration want to get involved? How did a Peacemaker get mixed up in it, and get themselves taken hostage? What was the ransom?

But one incandescent question burned through all of it, like a blowtorch through a jumbled stack of papers.

"This is about Carter Yost, isn't it?" I asked.

Lunzy gave me a wry look. "Do you two have a karmic bond, or something?"

"No. And if it ever looks like one's starting to form, just heave me out that airlock—please."

Torina rested her elbows on the arms of her chair, steepled her fingers, and looked past them at Lunzy. "I notice that your answer wasn't a *no*."

"No, it wasn't, because it's a yes. The Peacemaker who was taken hostage was, indeed, your beloved cousin, Carter Yost."

I stood. "Well, let me know how it turns out then. And if it turns out horribly, with him dying a gruesome death, make sure you send along some pictures, too—"

"Van, the Keel wants you to deliver the ransom," Lunzy said.

I just stood for a few seconds, staring. Then I shook my head, hard.

"No. No way. I refuse—"

"Van."

"—to pull that idiot's ass over whatever—"

"Van."

"—mess he's gotten himself into—"

"Van, sit down."

I stopped, surprised at the sudden, hard intensity in Lunzy's voice.

So I sat back down.

She sighed. "I'm the first one to admit that this whole situation is—a mess just scratches the surface. But there are several things at play here, and some of them are of vital interest to the Peacemakers as a whole."

I sighed right back. "I'm listening."

"Okay. First, Carter Yost is an idiot. He's muddled through

several jobs, none of them terribly difficult. He's blown one, and done okay on two more. Moreover, he was never properly recruited into the Guild, the way you were. And although he did go through indoctrination at Crossroads, like you did, his results were, well—"

"Shitty?"

"You might say that. From a strict technical knowledge perspective, he did alright. He even beat the standard in—" She picked up a data-slate from the table beside her. "Unarmed combat, and zero-g operations."

Torina raised an eyebrow. "But?"

"But, both Gus and Gabriella rated him as high in terms of narcissism and sociopathy, with a little psychopathy thrown in there just to spice it up." Lunzy looked up from the data-slate at me. "Bet you didn't know you were being evaluated psychologically while you were there, did you?"

"Uh—no, I guess not. I was just kind of overwhelmed by finding out that Earth isn't this lonely island of life, unique in the universe, but is actually kind of a backwater, like an out of the way bus stop that rarely gets used."

"Poetic, Van," Perry said. "Chills. Again."

"Unlimited horror brings out the poet in me."

"Well, Gus felt pretty much the same way. And that's his specialty, by the way, the reason he's in charge of the Induction Center. His race is extremely sensitive to emotions, so much so he can instantly conform to the psychology of whoever he's talking to. Did you notice how he came across as casual and easy-going?"

I remembered the big alien, and his ready charm. "Yeah. You mean that was just an act?"

"Not at all. He just automatically adapts to his audience. If you'd been from some stiff, stuck-up and highly regimented race, he'd have dealt with you accordingly. Anyway, all this is to say that Carter Yost should not be a Peacemaker."

"So why the hell is he, then?" I asked, standing again, because I had to pace. "I don't get it. If he's such a narcissistic asshole that even Gus and Gabriella had their doubts about him, then why wasn't he just shown the nearest airlock? One with, or preferably without a ship attached to it?"

"That, Van, is the big question here, isn't it? And that's why I asked you here, because I know a small part of the answer, but only a small part. And even that just raises a whole armada of more questions."

I turned back to her. "So what's the part of the answer you know?"

Lunzy looked at me squarely. "Your cousin wasn't summarily drummed out of the Peacemakers because the Keel intervened on his behalf. The Masters, or at least some of them, *want* Carter Yost in the Guild."

She paused, then shrugged. "Carter Yost has friends in high places. That's the part of the answer I know. I'd like you to find out the rest of it."

AGAIN, I just stared for a moment. Torina looked lost in thought. Perry was the one that finally broke the stunned silence.

"How much?" he asked.

Lunzy turned to him. "How much what?"

"How much are we being paid for this?"

I stared at Perry, incredulous, but Torina caught my eye and shook her head slightly, warning me off.

"I'll cover your costs," Lunzy replied flatly.

Perry nodded. "I knew it."

"You knew what?" I asked him, not sure what he was getting at.

"There's an old adage in the Guild, Van. The hardest jobs either pay a bundle, or nothing at all. Lunzy just said that *she* would cover your costs. So this whole op is off the books, which means it's probably way, *way* into the hard category."

"Lunzy, what the hell is going on here?" I asked.

She sighed. "That's what I'd like to know. I'm the Keel's representative, but I don't get to sit in on their meetings unless I'm specifically called to. So I don't know if he's just got the backing of one Master, or several, or even all of them. Nor do I know why, since there seems to be no advantage whatsoever to having that man around in the Guild. And I especially don't know why the Guild is prepared to pay a ransom to these merce-naries for his safe release, or why you're the one that's supposed to carry it out."

Her eyes turned hard in a way I wasn't used to in the normally affable Lunzy. "But I do want to know the answers to these questions, particularly since there's evidence that Carter Yost is somehow hooked up with the Stillness."

"I was going to ask about that. Do the Masters even know about that?" Torina asked.

Lunzy nodded. "I reported it to the Keel. But I have no idea if it ever made it to all the Masters."

I held up a hand. "Wait. You reported it? To whom, exactly?"

"To Groshenko."

"Shit."

"I know what you're thinking, Van, but it's a little premature to assume that your grandfather's friend is somehow involved in a conspiracy, especially one involving the Stillness. That would be *very* out of character for him."

"But it's possible," Torina said.

Lunzy shrugged. "Anything is possible."

Another moment of brooding silence passed. This time, I broke it.

"You can tell the Keel that I refuse to do this. I probably wouldn't piss on Carter if he was on fire, so I'm certainly not inclined to risk myself, Torina, Perry and Netty to—I mean, shit, to pay a ransom for him. And the fact he might be a stooge for the Stillness doesn't even factor into that—that's just the miserable cherry on top of my big, fat no."

I was adamant, too. The Peacemakers could fire my ass back to Earth if they wanted. There were so many things wrong with this whole situation that I wasn't about to put people—well, beings—that I'd come to consider friends in jeopardy for it.

But Lunzy stood and faced me. "Van, I get it. I don't just

understand, but I knew that's what you were going to say. But before you put your signature on that no, hear me out."

She turned and looked into the amazingly realistic flames flickering away in her fireplace. "Van, the Peacemakers have a long history of noble service. It's not a stretch to say that known space would be a very different place without us. It would be more chaotic, more unpredictable, and more dangerous. Even with us around, might still often makes right."

She turned to me. "Often. But not always. And the reason for that is us. We bring order to a galaxy whose natural inclination is to be a perilous, unforgiving place. I guess what I'm saying is that known space would be much worse off without us. At the risk of sounding melodramatic, Van, the Peacemakers Guild is bigger than any of us, in a lot of different ways."

I waited for Lunzy to get to the point.

"Having said all of that, the Guild is vulnerable. The way it works can tempt some people to put their own interests ahead of those of the good citizens of known space, whom we're supposed to serve. So, the protectors need protecting."

"You think there's some corruption at the top, and you want to use me to root it out," I said.

Lunzy shrugged again. "*Mea culpa*. But it's not because I want to throw you to wolves, Van. Quite the opposite. It's because I think you've got what it takes to resist the, um, baser sorts of instincts that afflict people like your cousin. I also think you have a good head on your shoulders, you've already proven yourself— oh, and if anyone can resist your cousin's bullshit, it's you."

I sighed. "Yeah. He is as charming as hell."

"Most narcissistic sociopaths are. And that may be why someone on the Keel has decided to make their—not sure if protégé is the right word, but they're definitely looking out for him. And that means that Carter Yost might be our best way of getting at the heart of whatever's going on."

I sighed. "Yeah, but not if he's dead, as appealing as that sounds. I get it."

"Can I say something?" Torina put in.

We both turned to her.

"Is it possible that this is a trap? Van shows up with the ransom, and he gets grabbed? Or attacked?"

I had to give Lunzy credit for her honest answer. "Quite possibly, yes."

She turned back to me. "If you're adamant about that earlier no way of yours, Van, I'll understand. And I'll find another way to get to the root of what's going on."

Now I stared into the fire for a moment. There was no good reason for me to do this. I was still new to being a Peacemaker, and being sucked into some conspiracy that went right to the top of the organization was just dumb.

On the other hand, though, I could see it from Lunzy's point of view. I had no baggage, aside from Gramps' reputation, which was apparently one of general respect, even reverence among the Peacemakers. And she was right about one thing—there was nothing Carter could offer me that I'd accept, nor was there anything I'd accept from anyone else involved with him.

And I could put Carter into a position where he owed me, big time. Which gave me an idea.

"Lunzy, how much is the ransom?"

"One hundred and fifty thousand bonds."

"And that's entirely off the books?"

"It'll be buried in some discretionary line-item in the budget, something like lavatory supplies for the Keel's office suite."

It was a lot, but it also wasn't. It was enough to buy some nifty ship upgrades, but not really enough to make someone what would be considered 'rich'.

"I'll do it," I finally said to Lunzy. "But, we're going to do it my way."

Lunzy gave me a curious look. "And what's your way?"

So I told her. It wasn't much of a plan, just the best I could come up with. I could see Torina and Perry would be doubtful, but Lunzy just gave me a slightly evil smile.

"Hold that thought, Van. I think I can help you out."

29

"THIS IS VERY COOL. How do I get one?" I asked.

Lunzy tweaked the *Foregone Conclusion's* flight controls, then leaned back. "Find a vendor somewhere who has one, which took me about five years, then spend a million bonds, then another couple of hundred thousand getting it adapted and installed on your ship." She smiled beatifically.

"So, easy peasy then."

Lunzy had liked the plan I'd cooked up, so much so that she'd offered some serious help with it-- by participating in my insane little scheme. But with her participation, desperately hopeful that it might somehow work out had become, hey, we have a shot at this—and it all came in the form of the device buried somewhere in the Foregone Conclusion's engineering section. It had the innocuous name of *stealth enhancement*. What it was, though, was something truly marvelous.

The device she was going to loan us-- I hoped-- was a *stealth enhancement* in that it made a ship virtually invisible. It was similar to the device Gramps had installed in the barn to hide what would become the *Fafnir*, but far smaller and less cumbersome, and generally more efficient. It used the scanner emitters to surround the ship with a distortion field that wrapped electro-magnetic and particle energy completely around it. In other words, while active, the device made the *Foregone Conclusion* invisible.

It wasn't perfect, but even active scanners, running at high power, would have trouble registering anything more than a fitful, flickering ghost. That wasn't uncommon on active scans. A tumbling piece of ice, rock or other debris showed up much the same way. Scanner systems were, it seemed, normally set to a minimum threshold sensitivity to weed out such weak, sporadic returns, so they didn't clutter the picture.

In other words, it would allow the *Foregone Conclusion* to fly into close proximity to the comm relay platform where Carter was being held, without being seen.

"It's Progenitor tech," Lunzy had said. "And I think it's just the thing you're looking for to carry out this scheme of yours."

Progenitor tech. It was a term for ancient tech recovered from long-gone races, locked away in sealed vaults, scattered among the wreckage of ships that crashed while my ancestors were still figuring out stone tools on Earth, or buried in the ruins of forgotten cities under the light of lonely, nameless stars. The stuff was highly prized just for its archeological value and whatever information could be gleaned from it. Working examples, like Lunzy's *stealth enhancement*, were rare almost beyond measure.

Now, we coasted through the outer margins of the Wolf 424 system, towards the comm platform, entirely unseen—or so we hoped, anyway.

The *Fafnir*, on the other hand, flew about ten klicks to our starboard, conspicuously pounding away with her active sensors and generally making a show about approaching the platform to deliver the ransom. The mercenaries, who'd turned out to be once more linked to the elusive Pevensi, would be focused on her, and have no reason to start studying scanner ghosts that might occasionally glimmer on their displays.

Or so we hoped, anyway.

It was a lot of hoping, I know.

Torina, sitting beside me in the Foregone Conclusion's cockpit in a jump-seat, stretched out her legs and stretched luxuriously. "I could get used to this. Van, you need to upgrade your ship. I have to step out of the cockpit to—"

"Change your mind?"

She smiled. "You've heard that one before."

"Uh, yeah. Did it just make it to your homeworld or something—*OW!*"

"Oh, I'm sorry, Van. Did I kick you in the shin?"

Lunzy looked back from the pilot's seat. "Hell hath no fury, Van."

I rubbed my shin. "Tell me about it."

Perry was piloting the *Fafnir*, ostensibly to make the ransom drop, whereupon Carter Yost and his semi-stolen ship, an unnamed *Dragonet*, would be released. Our first concern, that this might be a trap, had been mostly put to rest. There was no evidence of any other ships nearby, only Carter's, and a sleek, dark, arrowhead thing that must be the mercenary's ship, both docked at the platform. The platform itself was armed with a pair of point-defense guns and four one-shot missile launchers, intended to discourage anyone from making casual visits to an extremely expensive array of hardware. It's real protection, though, was its own—Interlink. It was probably one of the dozen largest corporations in known space, and spared no expense tracking down anyone who wronged it. Interlink contracts occasionally came up on the Peacemaker job slate, were always lucrative, and were correspondingly always the subject of fierce competition among the more senior Peacemakers.

"I wonder if Interlink even knows these guys have taken over their platform," I said, watching it slowly grow into view ahead of us.

Lunzy nodded. "They've been informed. Where do you think the ransom came from?"

"Really? They're just prepared to pay off some bad guys? Doesn't that risk setting a precedent you don't want to face down the road?"

This time, Lunzy shrugged. "Interlink probably dug these ransom bonds out of their couch cushions. They actually deal with shit like this all the time, consider it the cost of doing business. It's when people get greedy and genuinely piss them off that they get serious." She nodded towards the platform. "Those mercenaries? They've quite likely worked as problem solvers for Interlink before, and will probably do so again."

Torina was nodding as Lunzy spoke. "It's all just business to these people, Van."

"Okay, you kids better get yourselves saddled up. I'm going to have to burn pretty hard here, soon, to stop relative to the platform. And those mercenaries might be intrigued by a fusion exhaust plume that suddenly comes out of nowhere."

The plan was relatively simple. The mercenaries had already told us they were going to meet the *Fafnir* a hundred klicks from the station, and accept the ransom there. Only then would they release Carter, who was almost certainly still aboard the platform. Torina and I were going to take advantage of the distraction to board the platform, and retrieve Carter. We'd then all haul ass to get out of there. We'd likely have to leave Carter's *Dragonet* behind, but I was more than okay with that.

Sure enough, the mercenary ship had detached from the station, come about, and now powered towards the *Fafnir*. Perry and Netty would do their best to stall and keep whoever was aboard the mercenary ship busy as long as possible.

Or—and again—so we hoped.

Lunzy deftly brought the *Foregone Conclusion* to a stop relative to the platform, just a hundred meters away. Torina and I were already in the airlock.

"We've got zero delta-v relative to the station," Lunzy said. "You kids have fun now."

"Keep the motor running," I said, as we cycled the lock open and kicked out, sailing across the gap towards the platform's airlock, the closest of three. A monofilament tether connected us, and trailed behind us.

I studied the platform as we approached it. It wasn't all that big, a cylinder maybe fifty meters long and ten around, bristling with a variety of protrusions and antennae. We could see Carter's ship about halfway along its length, snuggled up against a second airlock. The mercenaries aboard their ship were just over a hundred klicks away, about to be disappointed by the absence of any ransom. That was actually the part that worried me the most. Perry and Netty were sitting in front of a heavily armed mercenary cutter, crewed by some unsuspecting bad guys. I just had to trust—

A sudden, searing flash, accompanied by a crash of static across the comm. I actually yelped out loud.

"What the hell was that?" I shouted, but my voice rang flat in my own ears.

My comms were down. In fact, my suit's systems had all gone offline, and were now rebooting. Torina pointed at her helmet. I pointed at mine.

Ten meters. We braced ourselves.

The hull of the platform loomed just ahead. I picked a likely hand-hold, the base of an antenna mount, and—

OOF.

I swung around the mount and banged against the hull. Torina had grabbed a stanchion, and pulled herself towards the airlock. I followed her.

I still had no comms. When we reached the airlock, Torina stuck her helmet against mine.

"I think that was an EMP," she said, her voice a muted buzz.

"Yeah, I know!" I checked my heads-up. My suit's environmental systems were back online, but most other functions, including comms, weren't. I wondered if the EMP had been the mercenary's doing. It might have been Perry and Netty, too, firing one of our spanking new EMP missiles, although why—

I shook my head. Didn't matter. Focus, Van. Focus.

Torina punched the code we'd be given by a friend of hers at Interlink into the airlock panel. She did it again. A third time. Then she shook her head at me through her visor.

Dead. Probably knocked offline by the EMP.

I swept out the Moonsword and went to plan B.

We didn't want to decompress the platform, but had no real choice. We'd brought along a crash suit, a flimsy suit designed for emergencies, in case Carter wasn't suited up. I glanced at Torina, who managed a facial shrug, then turned and sliced into the airlock's outer door.

This wasn't a military installation, nor was it even designed for human habitation, just periodic access for maintenance. The hull, including the airlock doors, were just relatively thin metal, through which the Moonsword slid with ease. In less than thirty seconds, I'd carved open a gap big enough for us to enter.

I faced the inner door, and took a breath. Torina braced herself. Only about a third of the platform's interior volume was pressurized, but that was still a lot of air to vent. Fortunately, we knew from the interior schematics, which we'd also obtained from Torina's Interlink buddy, that the platform was divided into three pressure zones, each of which could be independently sealed off.

But it was *still* a lot of air.

Again, I took a breath, and cut.

Nothing. No rush of air, no sudden, vaporous clouds. For some reason, the interior of the platform was depressurized.

I didn't pause to dwell on it, and just cut open the inner door, while Torina aimed her sidearm through it, ready to shoot.

We pushed into the platform's interior. As we did, Torina's voice suddenly crackled in my headset.

"Suit comms are back online," she said.

"Ouch, yeah, you don't have to shout."

We crept down the corridor. We weren't sure where the mercenaries were keeping Carter, but there really weren't that many places. Most of the interior of this place was filled with equipment, conduits and structural members.

"I guess our mercenary friends never bothered pressurizing the place," Torina said. "My Interlink contact did say it's normally not, since there's no one—"

A shower of sparks erupted from the bulkhead beside me. Up the corridor, I saw a suited figure that had just stepped into view, armed with a nasty-looking weapon.

Torina immediately double-tapped some shots back, driving the figure back around the corner.

I'd already switched the Moonsword to my left hand, and pulled out The Drop. Now, I banged out a succession of shots, while charging forward. Torina trailed just behind me.

My fire kept the bad-guy suppressed enough that he only managed a couple of shots as we closed. One hit the overhead above me, while the other ricocheted off the deck and hit Torina, but without penetrating her armor. I flung myself at the mercenary—

Who immediately dropped his weapon and stuck up his hands.

I stared at a gruff human face, male and bearded, behind the other visor. "Really?"

He shrugged. "This job doesn't pay enough that I'm willing to die for it."

"Oh. Uh, okay. Where's Carter Yost?"

"Sorry. This job *does* pay enough that I ain't gonna help you."

I opened my mouth, but Torina pushed past me. She'd pulled a pair of five-thousand bond tokens out of her suit. "How about this—"

"Third compartment along, on your left," the mercenary said. "Oh, and for the record, you can have him. He's a whiny, miserable little shit."

"Yeah, that's Carter alright. Believe it or not, he's my cousin."

"My condolences."

We took the mercenary's weapon, a handheld mass-driver. Torina gave him one of the tokens. "You get the other one on our way out. So I'd suggest not suddenly deciding to be a hero," she said, her voice flatly menacing.

"The only heroic mercenaries are the dead ones," he replied, sitting down on the deck and making himself comfortable.

We pushed on.

"I'm starting to think we can just buy our way past most of our problems," I said to Torina.

"You're only *starting* to think that?"

We reached the compartment the mercenary had indicated. I glanced at the security panel, saw it was still dead, then shrugged, swapped The Drop for the Moonsword in my right hand, then raised the blade.

"Uh, Van? It might be pressurized in there. It might be how they're keeping him secure, surrounded by vacuum with no suit."

I sighed. "Even when he doesn't intend to, Carter makes my life difficult." I jammed the blade through the door, and extracted it. Sure enough, a plume of air and vapor came streaming out of it.

Perry's voice suddenly rattled in my ears. "Van? That mercenary ship is probably just minutes away from recovering from our EMP. If they do, they are *way* more heavily armed than we are."

"What Perry's obliquely asking you is for permission to destroy the mercenary ship while it's helpless," Netty put in.

I glanced at Torina, who shrugged. These mercenaries would have been quite happy to kill us. But just blowing them out of space when they couldn't defend themselves seemed, I don't know—

"I'm beginning to realize I'm not a very ruthless guy," I said.

"That's what I like about you. But, sometimes…" She trailed off.

I nodded. "Yeah—"

Lunzy cut me off. "Don't worry about it, Van. I've shut down the stealth enhancement and made a big show of locking everything I've got onto our mercenary friends. I don't think they're going to want to take on me *and* the *Fafnir*."

I relaxed. A bit. Air continued to gush out of the compartment apparently containing Carter.

I glanced at Torina, watching the plume of vapor spilling out of the cut. "You know, we could just leave now."

"You won't blow up a bunch of mercenaries intent on killing you, but you *will* let your own cousin die a slow, agonizing death from asphyxiation?"

"Naturally."

She just gave me a look.

"Fine," I sighed, and readied myself to cut open the door, while Torina prepared the crash-suit.

CARTER ALMOST GOT *HIMSELF* KILLED. He panicked as the pressure dropped, making it hard to stick the hood over his head so he could breath. Torina finally pinned him in a nifty hold I needed to get her to teach me, I got the hood in place, then cajoled him into pulling on the rest of the suit. To be fair, I'd probably have panicked, too.

Still, seeing it, and then having Carter depend on me to save his ass, gave a dark thrill of satisfaction. I wasn't proud of it, but I wasn't going to lose any sleep over it, either.

We bundled Carter back to Lunzy's ship. By then, the mercenaries had called a truce, so they could recover the man they'd left on the platform, then quickly take their leave. We unfortunately never did find out what they'd been doing on the platform in the first place, but that was just going to have to be a question for another day.

Anyway, it left us in possession of the platform, a Carter Yost recovering from the effects of brief exposure to vacuum, and his ship. And we'd managed all of it without hurting anyone except Carter himself.

It was a good day.

I called Perry once we were back aboard the *Foregone Conclusion* with Carter, to get a status update. More to the point, I was wondering why Perry and Netty had decided to fire one of our EMP missiles.

"Because, Van, it was the most logical thing to do," he replied.

"That's it? Just like that? It was logical?"

"Uh, yeah. Neither Netty nor I have any particular desire to be blown to bits."

"Okay, and what if the EMP hadn't worked? If the mercenary ship had been able to withstand it, without going offline?"

"Well, *then* we would have blown it up."

I really couldn't argue the point. Firing the EMP might have complicated things for us, but it also temporarily disabled the mercenary ship, which effectively allowed us to carry out the rest of the operation without interference. I did have one question, though.

"Tell me, Perry, did you plan to fire that thing all along?"

"Nope."

"Really?"

"Yes, really. What Netty and I had actually intended to do was just blow them up. We figured we had a pretty good shot at it, too."

"Ah. And were you ever going to tell me this ahead of time?"

"It's easier to get forgiveness than permission, Van. Besides, we fired the EMP instead of live warheads, right?"

I didn't bother arguing the point. It did drive something home for me, though. I might interact with Perry and Netty as though they were people, but they weren't—they were machines, driven by logic, not emotion. It gave them a ruthless streak, and that was a valuable lesson.

We then went to check on Carter.

I grinned broadly at him, still looking bruised and swollen from his exposure to vacuum. "Carter, hey, long time no see! How's your mom and dad?"

He peered back at me through puffy eyes. "Save it, Van."

"You should thank your cousin," Lunzy said. "He did rescue you, after all."

"You could have just paid the damned ransom, and I wouldn't have had to feel like I was dying, sucking on vacuum."

"You actually *were* dying, until Van got that hood over your head," Torina said. "Oh, by the way, I'm Torina, Van's Second. Nice to meet you."

Unbelievable, he tried to look charming, flashing her a grin. "Yes, the pleasure's all yours."

She just rolled her eyes.

I leaned towards him, trying to look menacing. "Carter, there's some things—"

"That can wait for now. Carter needs some time to recover," Lunzy said, ushering Torina and I back towards the *Foregone Conclusion's* cockpit. I gave her a puzzled look, but went along with it.

"Sorry, Van, but I didn't want to jump into interrogating Carter. Not yet. I've put a covert data-tap on his ship, so we can see where he goes, who he talks to, that sort of thing," Lunzy said.

"So, what? We're just going to let him be on his way? I thought the whole point was to use him to flush out whatever's going on, find out if there really is a conspiracy involving the Keel, that sort of thing."

"We are, Van. Just not yet. Right now, this just looks like an elaborate way for us to keep the ransom—which, by the way, is waiting by the airlock for you to take back to the *Fafnir* with you. When the time comes to move, I want to make it decisive."

"So I don't get to make Carter's life miserable for the trip back to Anvil Dark?" I put on a pouty face.

"Oh, sure, if you want. Let's just keep it to shallow, personal misery, though, and save the deeper stuff for later."

I shrugged. "Eh, I can live with inflicting shallow misery on Carter for a while."

I turned to Torina. "Care to accompany me back to spend some quality time with my cousin? And by quality time, I mean making him squirm with the idea that he now owes me his life?"

Torina cracked a fiendish smile. "I've got nothing else planned."

30

I WINCED at another burst of chatter over the comm. It came out translated as occasional words laced with some truly shocking curses and profanity that referred to body parts I didn't even have. I glanced at Torina.

"These guys could make damned good money writing erotica for folks back on Earth."

"Really? It's a bunch of alien sexual references," she replied.

"Yeah, that doesn't matter. There's someone who'd buy it. Hell, there's someone who'd buy it *because* of that. What's... what is *nurling your glaccus sideways*, anyway?"

Torina winced. "Um... "

I held up a hand. "Forget I asked."

We were racing along, a class five or six ship in hot pursuit. We'd surprised them lurking near a space lane leading toward

Crossroads, where they were apparently intent on something nefarious. Outright piracy would be unusual that close to a major port like Crossroads, which suggested they were up to something else. Perry's bet was on waiting to conduct some clandestine rendezvous, probably to shift illicit cargo.

"With them powered down, the odds of us stumbling into them like that were astronomically small," Netty observed.

"But they're not zero, and sometimes even the most improbable things *do* occur," Perry replied.

While I went on the air and broadcasted our Peacemaker identity, Perry took the controls and accelerated the *Fafnir* away from the unknown ship. It powered up and began spewing fire at us the moment they'd realized we'd detected them, and finding out we were a Peacemaker ship just seemed to make them that much more determined to blow us up.

Any second now, I expected Perry to turn and do battle. But we just kept powering along in a straight line, the bad guys chasing us, hurling epithets and occasional laser shots. I finally turned to look at him.

"Uh, Perry? Did you open the range to do some maneuvering, or are you actually running from these guys?"

"Running. Why do you ask?"

"Why do you want to run from a pipsqueak like them?"

"Habit?"

"How much is that ship worth?"

"That class, in that shape, maybe two hundred thousand bonds, give or take."

"So *why* are we running from them again?"

Torina leaned dramatically toward Perry and hissed a stage whisper. "I think he's saying he wants to take these guys on."

Perry leveled his amber gaze on me. "We're roughly an equal match for these guys, weapons-wise, Van. And we have no advantage of surprise. A straight, toe-to-toe slug-out is iffy at best."

I scowled at the tactical overlay. Aside from the value of the other ship, we had no idea what it might be carrying, other than something valuable enough that they were willing to chase off a Peacemaker.

And we weren't exactly flush with cash. Torina had already sunk ten thousand bonds of her own into the *Fafnir*, and I didn't want to keep going back to that well. Our last few jobs had been profitable, but not much. Basically, we were keeping the *Fafnir* going, making a little on the side, and that was it.

I put on my helmet and sealed it. "To hell with it. Perry, my ship."

"Your ship," he said, relinquishing the controls. I could hear the resigned sigh in his tone.

While Torina sealed her suit, I burned the *Fafnir* through a hard turn, firing a single standard missile as I did. It was meant to prevent our pursuer from just cutting inside our turn. I could have just flipped our ship around and decelerated hard, but that would leave us momentarily dead in space until we finally reversed course. This kept us moving and maneuvering.

I watched on the overlay as the pursuing ship started to turn inside us, then it braked hard when it detected the missile. It bought me the few seconds I needed to complete the *Fafnir*'s turn.

"You're getting pretty good at this, Van," Torina said.

"Why thank you. I have good teachers."

Netty got tenuous target locks, but I refrained from firing. Our respective maneuvers had opened us to pretty much maximum effective range, and I wanted to keep our opponent guessing what our weapons loadout was. Two minutes, I figured, maybe three, and we should have good firing solutions again.

I smiled. I actually *was* getting pretty good at this.

But my smile vanished when something big and ugly appeared not far away. It was another ship, a massive one, that had just twisted into existence nearby.

"Who the hell is that?" I snapped.

Netty answered immediately. "Class twenty-three, so destroyer-class. Remember our little discussion about probabilities? Well, if this is a bad guy, then our probability of defeating him is—"

"Slim to none," I muttered, already applying braking thrust.

The big ship ignored us, though, and immediately closed on our original pursuer. They ruthlessly overpowered the smaller ship and disabled it with precise laser shots into its drive, then came about to board it.

"I guess we should do something about this," I said, though I wasn't sure what.

"You mean save the guys who were just trying to kill us by attacking the vastly larger and powerful ship now attacking them?" Perry asked.

I glanced at him. "Well, when you put it like that, it just sounds stupid."

We were still closing on the two ships. I dithered about whether to keep trying to intervene or not, but the ship made up our minds by loosing a missile at us, a big, fast one. Netty identified it as a firestorm, a potent piece of military ordnance.

"It's a message as much as an attack. That's a ten-thousand bond missile easily, which means they're telling us that they mean business," Netty said.

I hurled the *Fafnir* into a series of tight and hard evasive maneuvers. The missile burned hard to match us. Netty brought the defensive suite online, the point defense cannon trying, and failing, to get a lock.

At the last moment, the missile's engine cut out and it coasted, detonating about twenty klicks away in a powerful blast. A few seconds later, fragments pinged against our armor, and a few found gaps and punched through the hull. One even passed cleanly through us with a loud bang, blowing an entire hull plate out of the other side of the ship. A howl of wind and fog as we decompressed, then it faded into the silence of vacuum.

The next few seconds consisted of me cursing over the comm. We'd just taken at least a few thousand bonds in damage and expended a missile with nothing to show for it. The big ship seemed content on letting us withdraw and continued claiming its prize.

"Next time I decide to do some damn fool thing like that, kick me in the ass and tell me to smarten up," I snapped as Waldo got to work restoring airtight integrity to the *Fafnir*.

Torina gave me a bemused glance through her visor. "Do you

really mean that, Van? As in, we're to never let you charge into battle again?"

"For the next five minutes, yes, I do mean that. After that, I'll think about it." I spent a moment glaring at the tactical overlay and feeling stupid, then turned to the others.

"Who were those guys, anyway?"

"If I had to take a guess, I'd say Salt Thieves," Perry replied.

Torina nodded. "It has their decidedly malodorous pong to it, yeah. They specialize in raiding other bad guys, reasoning that no one really cares if thieves steal from other thieves."

"Yeah, well, they just stole from me. Add the value of that other ship they cut out from under our noses, plus the missile we wasted and the damage to the *Fafnir*, and I put it at something like—what, two hundred and fifty thousand bonds?"

"More like two sixty-seven, but you're close."

I cursed again.

Torina grinned. "Ooh, a thirst for revenge. And over money. I love it!"

"THERE GOES another couple of thousand bonds," I hissed, thumbing the pad on the terminal just inside the hangar on Anvil Dark. We'd planned to do the repairs outside, avoiding the hangar fees, but one look at the damage where the fragment from the Salt Thieves' missile had blasted out of our hull put paid to that. One entire hull plate was simply gone, and all those around it had been buckled and deformed. There'd also been some serious spalling damage to internal components. Torina, though, pointed out how much worse things could have been. She beckoned me around the *Fafnir* to look at the side of the ship that had been facing the missile-blast.

She pointed. "See that gouge in the applique armor right there? If you hadn't added that armor package a few weeks back, that would have gone right through the cockpit."

I sighed. "Born lucky, I guess."

"Not that lucky. Use the bolt shears, Van. Save your knuckles and time," Torina said, pointing to the damaged hull plates.

I gave a thankful nod, then turned my attention to the mayhem before me, getting lost in the job. I'd been immersed fully, snipping at a shattered strut piece when Perry and Torina returned.

"I know you'd like to make some money, Van," she called up to me. "And, to that end, I found a job you might be interested in."

I sat on the edge of the scaffolding, taking a break and looking down at Torina. "You said something about a job."

"I did. You're familiar with Spindrift?"

I thought about it. Yes, it turned out I was. Located in the Earthly constellation *Canis Majoris*, the Greater Dog, Spindrift orbited *alpha-Canis Majoris*, better known as Sirius. Also called the Dog Star, Sirius was a familiar sight in the terrestrial night sky, being one of the closest big stars to Earth.

Like Anvil Dark, it was an ancient station, almost a thousand years old. Unlike Anvil Dark, though, Spindrift had nothing to do with law and order. In fact, Spindrift was what Crossroads and Dregs were both aspiring to be—the epicenter of freewheeling lawlessness in known space. But Spindrift had hundreds of years of headstart on both, leaving the newcomers as wannabes at best.

But I also knew that Spindrift was considered a high-risk location for Peacemaker ops, and was technically out of bounds for Peacemakers below the rank of Myrmidon. However, that only applied to casual visits. The job Torina had found listed on the roster was a specific one, carrying a specific exemption to allow any Peacemaker above Initiate to take it.

I studied the data slate Torina had handed me. "So a snatch-and-grab, huh? Some criminal who's dealing in—human memory chips?"

"Just what they sound like," Perry said, soaring into view over the *Fafnir* and lighting on the edge of the comms array. "Recorded memories, or even synthetic ones, that can be played back. It's sort of virtual reality inside your own head. It works particularly well with the human brain, which is the biggest market for them."

"Do I want to know what sorts of memories we're talking about?" I asked.

"Use your imagination."

"That's the problem. I am."

Perry hopped down onto the scaffold with a metallic clatter of talons closing around the safety railing. He interfaced with the data-slate, then made a sound like he was clicking his tongue.

"The target's a Yonnox. This just gets better and better, by which I mean sleazier and sleazier."

Waldo handed me a water bottle. "Not very nice people, are they?"

"Oh, they're perfectly nice. But they're also greedy, manipulative assholes who consider cheating, stealing, and exploiting all perfectly fine because, hey, if you weren't careful or smart or observant enough to stop them, that's your problem not theirs."

While he'd been talking, Perry put an image of a Yonnox onto the slate. It showed a tall, reedy, three-legged creature with a long, narrow face, a tiny mouth, and a band of several eyes set around the top of its head.

"At the risk of coming across as alienist, I don't find that appealing at all," I said.

"And yet, the Yonnox are some of the most successful crooks in known space, and they manage to do it almost entirely without violence," Torina said. "Some big corporations and trading guilds even keep a few on staff to protect themselves against *other* Yonnox."

"Because there truly is no honor among thieves," Perry said.

I read over the details of the job, shrugged, and thumbed the acceptance pad on the slate, locking us into the task of finding this Yonnox and stopping his little stolen memory chip venture by taking him, his ship, and anything else relevant into custody.

"Done." I glanced back at the partial repairs to the *Fafnir*, sighed, and levered myself back to my feet. "If only this were done, too."

Torina pulled off her jacket, tossed it aside, and clambered up the scaffold with me. "Here, Van, let me show you a shortcut."

"Let me guess—besides martial arts pro, expert pilot, and dead-eyed gunner, you also know everything there is to know about fixing spaceships."

She stopped and grinned back. "Yeah, but I'm a lousy cook."

31

SPINDRIFT HAD, at one time, been a grand venture, an early attempt at establishing an entirely space-based habitation, with no support from a ground facility. The idea was that planets weren't necessary, so people could ultimately live anywhere. The consortium that had undertaken to build the place had poured vast sums of bonds into the effort, and had built a completely self-contained, artificial environment. Intended to house one hundred thousand, the orbital, as it was called, had been built in less than ten years—another remarkable achievement.

Unfortunately, things went disastrously wrong three years after its completion. Roughly two-thirds populated by then, Spindrift had been hit by an entirely unforeseen blast of incredibly intense radiation from Sirius. Several thousand people died as a result. It turned out that a previously unknown interaction between the big main-sequence star and its white dwarf companion periodically triggered huge mass ejections from its corona, which scoured the system with hard radiation. Desperate attempts were made to find ways of shielding the orbital and hardening it against the recurrent bursts, but all proved impractical, far too expensive, or both. Spindrift was finally evacuated and abandoned.

Enter the sleazier elements of society, who saw the derelict orbital as a terrific opportunity. Criminal enterprises of all sorts quickly moved in and set up shop. For almost four hundred years now, they'd been squatters aboard a facility whose ownership was *still* not clear. The avalanche of court proceedings and liability assessments had tangled the place in light-years of red tape, which no one today could be bothered trying to unwind. Bureaucracy and crime had found a point of peaceful coexistence, and here we were.

The obvious question, of course, *was what about the radiation?*

Well, the new residents of Spindrift had a novel way of dealing with that, which cost virtually nothing—they ignored it. It turned out that every twelve point four years, plus or minus two or three weeks, the Storm, as it was called, erupted from the dual stars. And, while it raged, Spindrift was simply abandoned again. Almost thirty thousand people, its rough population, simply fled, waited the storm out, and then came right back.

"Imagine the rats fleeing the sinking ship, except the ship rights itself again, so all the rats turn around and go right back aboard," is how Torina explained it.

I shook my head in wonder. "I don't get how they can *all* be thriving. How much crime *is* there?"

"Ah, well, there's probably whole books written about it—" Torina started, but Perry cut in.

"There are, and many. There are people that have spent their lives studying it."

She nodded. "It's not just about crime. These places are either under only nominal authority of some larger entity, like the Eridani Federation supposedly administers Dregs, or they're under none at all, like Spindrift here. These places become havens for refugees from war and natural disasters, people fleeing brutally oppressive governments, and anyone who generally wants to be free of interference in their lives by the state or large corporations."

I studied Spindrift as it began looming through the canopy. The original station had been a rotating cylinder almost five kilometers long, and one across. Since then, a motley collection of new construction had spread across its gigantic hull, including everything from purpose-built structures to old, repurposed spaceship hulls. It even *looked* freewheeling and anarchic.

No place like this would ever exist on Earth. Someone would end up imposing some sort of regulation on it. But this wasn't Earth. True freedom reigned here, with no regulation at all. Any little Spinner, as the residents were called, could grow up and become a superstar—as long as they survived, anyway.

THERE ACTUALLY DID TURN out to be a regulatory body of sorts on Spindrift, though. Called the Cloaks, they generally oversaw the big-picture operations of Spindrift. Someone had to make sure the air and water was recycled, the power stayed on, that sort of thing. They also operated an emergency force that combined police, fire, and rescue into one.

"But they're as corrupt as the rest," Perry said as we stepped out of the airlock and into a long, dim corridor leading into Spindrift's interior. "For that matter, all they *really* are is a criminal syndicate that happens to have a bit of a unique status. People pay them to keep the lights on and the air breathable."

"And if they don't pay?"

"Then the lights go out, and the air starts getting really stale really fast."

"So they're a protection racket."

"But an essential one. See how that works?"

We finally reached the end of the corridor. Vivid hazard markers striped yellow and black marked a GRAVITY TRANSITION ZONE. Perry had already warned me about this. We essentially had to maneuver ourselves around a ninety-degree change in the direction of down. The corridor incorporated a smooth curve to try and facilitate it, but there were still numerous handholds to help. The sensation was a truly bizarre one. It felt like I kept walking normally along a passage that curved downward ahead of me but nonetheless continuously flattened out as I walked it.

"This is weird," I said.

Perry bobbed his head. "You should try it drunk."

"How would you know what that's like?"

"Your grandfather told me all about it."

I snorted. "That I can believe."

The corridor finally opened onto a gantry-like gallery stuck onto the interior of a vast, cylindrical space hundreds of meters across and over a kilometer long.

Perry hopped up on the railing. "Welcome to Spindrift, Van."

My first impression was noise, an endless commotion that was part mechanical, the station's vital engineering functions rumbling away, and part organic, the incidental noise of its thousands of inhabitants. And it came from every direction because there were people in every direction, including up.

I craned my neck. There were people standing on the other side of the vast cylinder, directly above me. More people bustled around between us and them. Thanks to the station's spin, no matter where you stood inside the cylinder, your feet were always down. Even so, the gravity was a little on the light side, about three-quarters of Earth's one g. I let my body take care of it, though, my implanted muscle memory immediately adapting my movements and gait to the lower gravity. It worked fine until I actually thought about it, whereupon I'd find myself stumbling, or sailing a couple of meters into the air before falling, slowly, back to the deck.

The bustle and clamor of the place now engulfed us. Noise, smells ranging from delightful to eye-wateringly vile, shifting crowds, flashing lights—it was like wandering through some vast, perpetual carnival. I had to keep sidestepping, stopping, backing up, and finding another way to proceed. Neon holograms flickered and danced around us, advertisements for bars, restaurants, and sex clubs. A stunning woman wrapped her arms around my neck and began whispering in my ear, promising things that were probably felonies in at least a few states back home. I pulled away and she simply shimmered and vanished.

"She wasn't real? But I felt her touching me," I said—actually, yelled—to Torina.

She shrugged back. "Force fields. That's how you know a tech has come of age, when it gets used for advertising."

I ENDED up momentarily separated from Perry and Torina by the shifting crowd, but I saw them and made eye contact. Torina nodded and started back toward me. As she did, a gruff voice sounded from nearly right beside me.

"Can I see your entry visa?"

I turned. A hairy, humanoid alien, similar to Bester back on Anvil Dark but more compact, stood glaring at me. It wore a short, crimson cloak, which marked this as one of the Cloaks, the group that ran Spindrift. At Perry's suggestion, I'd bought a loose duster coat along, and wore it over my Peacemaker outfit. Apparently, the sight of a Peacemaker made half the residents of Spindrift clam completely up and sent the other half hurrying the other way.

"An entry visa? What's that?"

"A visa, for entry. You're supposed to have one to enter Spindrift. You don't?"

"Uh—no. No one ever told me I needed one."

The alien shrugged. "Not my problem. You need one. I can issue you one, but there's a fee."

I smiled. Of course there was. A fee that I could pay for made-up bullshit, right here, in bonds. As shakedowns went, it was a *little* more clever than just walking up to someone and demanding money.

"If you can't pay, you're gonna have to come with me," the alien said, looming toward me.

"Hey, Van, what's up?" Perry asked, stopping beside me.

Torina smoothly moved to my left and pretended to be interested in something laid out in a nearby kiosk.

"This gentleman was just explaining to me that I needed to pay him a fee for an—I'm sorry, an entry visa? And that I'd have to go with him if I didn't."

"Tell him to send an invoice to Anvil Dark, attention the Commissary Department."

The alien looked from Perry to me. "Wait. You're a Peacemaker?"

"Yeah, I am." I looked down at myself. "Oh, wait, you probably can't tell because of this old thing that I threw on at the last minute," I said, tugging on the lapels of my baggy duster coat.

"Yeah, well—Peacemakers are exempt, of course. Have a nice day," the Cloak said, then hurried off into the crowd.

I smiled after him. "Prince of a guy. I'm gonna like it here, I can tell."

THE DUSTER COAT served another function. Actually, two more functions, one of which was to make me look as cool as hell. The other was that it did a good job of concealing The Drop and the Moonsword hanging from my harness. I now checked both as we approached the docking port currently being used by our Yonnox quarry, named Gur-Malik. It had taken some doing, including a little hacking, but we'd managed to track him down to this port, where his flight plan said he was going to be docked for another few hours.

"Not that flight plans filed with the Cloaks mean much. Ones that are actually true and accurate are cheap, but for the right price, you can have them say anything you want," Perry said.

"I'd come back with something like, that doesn't sound very safe, but I get the sense that safety isn't job one around here."

"It's probably not jobs two through ten, either," Torina added.

We reached the port. Torina, who looked far less like a Peace-maker than I did, went ahead and scouted it. She vanished up the corridor, while Perry and I waited, pretending to be interested in a ramshackle storefront selling miscellaneous electronic components. Actually, I wasn't pretending. There was some interesting stuff here—

"Uh oh."

I turned at Perry's mutter and saw Torina beset by two people, a scruffy human and a big alien that resembled an anthropomorphic badger. They were both using hostile body language, looming over Torina and obviously trying to menace her for—some reason, but we were too far away to overhear what they were saying to her.

I reached to unfasten my duster coat and get ready access to my weapons, but Torina just smiled sweetly—then delivered a quick, precise flurry of blows and kicks that dropped both of her confronters to the deck. The crowd parted while it happened, then stopped to cheer and clap. Torina actually took a bow, then carried on to join Perry and me.

"What was that all about?" I asked.

"They thought I was cute."

"Cute?"

"Well, they said it in a way that was a lot more skin crawling, but that's what it amounted to. So I rebuffed their advances."

"Rebuffed 'em real good," Perry said.

"Anyway, Gur-Malik's ship is still docked. The hatch is sealed, though, so I don't know if he's onboard or not."

"If we just walk up and announce ourselves, he's going to undock and run," Perry said.

I nodded. "Yeah. If he's in there, we need some way of getting him to at least open up, and ideally come right out of his ship."

Torina grinned. "I have an idea."

"She is one attractive woman," Perry said.

I glanced down at him. "You're a machine, Perry."

"Doesn't mean I can't appreciate the human form. Based on

her biometrics, degree of bilateral symmetry, facial and cranial structure, and lack of skin lesions, blemishes, and imperfections, she'd reasonably be classified as *hot*."

"I have never heard a less sexy description of someone, but it still somehow gets the point across." I held up a finger. "Quick note for future reference—don't use the term *lesions* when listing her qualities, okay? Trust me on this."

"Noted. I still think it's a damned fine quality."

"And that's why you're single."

Perry turned, looked me up and down, and managed to raise one eyelid in a way that said *that makes two of us*. I called the discussion a draw and looked back at our subject of interest.

We were peering around a girder protruding from the bulkhead, just inside the gravity transition zone in the corridor leading to Gur-Malik's ship. Torina had gone ahead, theatrically putting a little sway into her walk, pouting her lips a little and tightening and tucking in her tunic behind her, to emphasize what Perry would probably call her *anterior anatomical structure* or something equally sensual. It was all intended to appeal to the natural sleaziness apparently endemic to the Yonnox. Despite resembling a tripod that had bought it's eyes on sale, in bulk, the Yonnox had a libido that was truly keyed into the concept of *opportunistic*.

And it worked. After just a few minutes of pouting into the vid pickup beside the airlock, it rolled open, and Gur-Malik came striding out.

I felt my lip curl. "Ouch. The picture didn't do him justice."

Gur-Malik moved with a slithery sort of sinuosity, like

watching something viscous and gooey being poured down a drain. And yet, the Yonnox apparently considered themselves highly desirable, even among other races. Either an entire species was completely deluded, or the Yonnox knew something we didn't.

We let Torina play out her little act for a few minutes. Her cover story was that she was looking for someone to carry a shipment of goods of questionable legality, and unquestionable immorality, to Crossroads. As they spoke, Torina slowly and subtly backed away, drawing Gur-Malik a little further from his airlock with each almost imperceptible step. I waited until she touched her hair in a particular way, the signal that her ruse was played out, and it was time for the next step.

I stepped around the corner with a purposeful stride. "Hey, babe, you lined up a ship for us yet?"

The Yonnox leveled several eyes on me. "You never said you had partners," he said. His voice came out nasally and petulant. Was there *anything* about this race that wasn't douchey?

Torina smiled sweetly. "Does it matter?"

"Depends who those partners are. And this one smells bad."

I kept approaching. "I smell bad? Watch it, twigs. I don't care for rudeness."

Gur-Malik let me get a few meters closer, then stepped back. At the same time, one of his long limbs flickered out as he jabbed something into Torina. She yelped, went rigid, and slammed back against the bulkhead.

I cursed and yanked out The Drop. Gur-Malik turned and dashed back into his airlock, reaching for the control to close it.

Before he could, though, I jammed the muzzle of The Drop into his face.

"Solid slug or energy blast, I can do both. Your choice."

The Yonnox uttered nothing less than a pathetic whimper and tried to jab me with what was clearly a short shock rod. It slammed into my Peacemaker armor, the sharpened electrodes barely making a dent. I swung The Drop, clubbing Gur-Malik across the—face? Head? The uppermost part of his body, anyway. He staggered against the side of the airlock, and I again stuck the twin muzzles of my weapon right in his—I was *pretty* sure it was his face.

"You know, when I think back to the Peacemaker job listing, I honestly can't remember if it said that I had to bring you in alive or not. Perry, do you recall?"

He flew up the corridor and neatly flared his wings, then dropped to the deck beside me. "Alive, unfortunately. But it doesn't say anything about healthy or *in one piece.*"

"Good enough for me."

Gur-Malik slumped. By then, Torina had recovered from her stun and moved in beside me, her face as hard and cold as some ancient comet.

I offered her The Drop. "Can you cover this asshole for me?"

"Oh, with pleasure." She aimed The Drop at Gur-Malik, who slumped even more. "Now, did I hear Perry say something about *removing limbs?*"

THE SITUATION very quickly escalated from gross, but kind of amusing, to horrifying. It turned out that the memory chips Gur-Malik was trafficking went well beyond kinky sex and into truly vile territory.

They recorded humans being murdered.

Perry interfaced with two, after sweeping them thoroughly for viruses and other malware, and decided he'd seen enough. "If you ever want to know what it's like to be murdered, Van, Gur-Malik can hook you up. Or, for added fun, you can play the part of the murderer instead." I'd never heard him sound quite so disgusted before, and he'd been dealing with interstellar scum for decades.

Torina didn't mince words, either. "We've got the chips, and we can probably get the details of whoever supplied them from his ship. So *why* are we keeping this piece of shit alive again?" She still had the Yonnox pinned to the bulkhead of his ship's airlock, and I saw her finger on the trigger whiten slightly.

I took the weapon from her. "Yeah, I get it. But I want to drain every last drop of criminal intel from this scumbag that we can. So we won't blow his head, or whatever this part of his body is, apart—at least, not *yet.*"

Perry slapped a Peacemaker seal on Gur-Malik's ship, registering it as *proceeds of crime*, and helped me bind the Yonnox for transport as a prisoner. We then headed back into the station to return to the *Fafnir*. I made the situation as clear to Gur-Malik as I could.

"This is the part where I would normally say something like, I don't want to kill you. But you know what? I *do* want to kill you.

You're nothing but a dealer in misery, and the universe would be better off with you not in it. So please, *please* make a scene, or try to escape before we get back to my ship."

But Gur-Malik did what all Yonnox apparently did when backed into a corner.

He began to beg, to plead, and to do it in the whiniest, most pathetic way possible.

"Please, I have a wife and children—"

"Yonnox don't form any sort of pair bonds, and you reproduce by asexual budding. To the extent you have any concept of family at all, you consider them your closest rivals and competitors—oh, and a source of spare organs and body parts," Perry said flatly.

Gur-Malik changed tack as we walked back into the gravity transition zone. "I can offer you bonds. Many bonds. Thousands. Tens of thousands. Hundreds of thousands—"

Torina suddenly slammed him against the bulkhead. "You know, being electrocuted has really spoiled my day. So I'm going to go a step further than Van. If you say another word, any other word, I'm going to twist your tentacles off one at a time." She smiled so frigid it made *me* pull away from her. "So please, *please* keep talking."

Gur-Malik said nothing. For once, he was smart.

We seemed to have everything we needed. We had the Yonnox, his ship and its contents, and the chips. I figured we were home free, at least until we stepped back into Spindrift and found a dozen Cloaks waiting for us.

ONE OF THEM, human and hard-looking, with a patchy beard sprouting amid smooth, shiny scars, stepped forward. "We understand there was some trouble here," he said.

I narrowed my eyes. "Define trouble."

"Two complaints of assault." As he said it, he glanced off to his right. I saw the two who'd tried to press themselves on Torina —and who she had, indeed, assaulted as a result, because the bastards deserved it. They tried to look tough about it but wouldn't quite meet my gaze.

"It's another shakedown, Van. They think you've scored something valuable on Gur-Malik's ship, and they want a piece of it," Perry said.

"Really?"

I stepped forward. "So you have complaints of assault. Let me guess—there's a fine, payable in bonds right here on the spot."

The man grinned a grin that was half gold teeth and half missing ones. "We call it streamlined justice."

"I call it illegal," I said, and in a move that I thought would have made Sergio Leone proud, I flipped my duster coat open, revealing my Peacemaker uniform underneath.

I'd expected a dramatic pause, then a ripple of consternation and fear. I got the first but only part of the second. Instead of fear, the Cloaks all began to curse and roll their eyes. The man talking to me groaned in ripe disgust

"A Peacemaker? Really? What absolute shit luck."

"Uh—sorry to disappoint you."

The man sighed. "Okay, how much?"

"How much what?"

"How much do you mean to take? We know you Peacemakers always want to take the biggest share—" He stopped, apparently at my blank expression.

"Wait—are you one of those *honest* Peacemakers?" He actually made air quotes around that *honest*.

"Well, if by that you mean, am I on the take, then no. I'm not."

"Shit."

One of the other Cloaks spoke up. "It's just him, the woman, and his bird. Why don't we—"

"Van, do you know how long it's been since the last major Peacemaker raid on Spindrift?" Perry said loudly, cutting him off.

"Why no, Perry, I don't. How long has it been?"

"Four years, five months, seven days, nine hours."

"That long?" Torina said. "Perry, prep a message to send back to Anvil Dark. Tell them that we'd like a full cohort sent here to investigate excise irregularities reported by The Quiet Room—"

"Loud and clear, you bastards," the Cloak who'd done most of the talking said. He nodded to his fellows, and muttering, grumbling, and shooting us dark looks, they all dispersed.

"Well, that could have been ugly," I said, relaxing a notch or two. As we started back to the *Fafnir* with our prisoner, I realized that I was sweating. Everyone in that little standoff had been armed with something deadly. So yeah, it could have gotten very ugly indeed.

Perry hopped along beside me with his now-familiar metallic tap-tap-tap. "Better get used to it, Van. Ugly is pretty much what Peacemakers do."

"It also describes their customers," Torina added, with a pointed glance at Gur-Malik.

The Yonnox rotated several eyes toward her. "I'll have you know that I'm considered quite attractive for a member of my species. Not that you can appreciate it."

We took a few steps in silence as Torina studied the Yonnox. She finally shook her head.

"You're right. I can't appreciate it at all."

GUR-MALIK VEHEMENTLY INSISTED he knew nothing about the content of the chips we'd seized—which was patently obvious bullshit since he'd paid for them and intended to sell them at a profit, a sordid, evil little venture he wouldn't have undertaken if he didn't know what he was peddling and its value. He also insisted he had no idea where the chips originated, which wasn't necessarily bullshit and actually had a ring of truth to it. The repugnant sorts of supply chains that would record a human murder, then sell the resulting horrifying experience, were typically chunked into pieces completely independent from one another. I'd encountered it often enough while chasing leads into and through the dark web back on Earth. My ratio of sudden dead-ends to actual, useful leads was probably ten to one.

So before we left Spindrift, Netty, Perry, and I stripped and studied every particle of data we could find aboard Gur-Malik's ship. It took us about a day and left us with some encrypted data the Yonnox claimed must have been on the ship when he bought it, and piles of utterly uninteresting stuff mostly related to the operation of his vessel. It looked like yet another of those dead-ends until I had a flash of inspiration that, in hindsight, was a pretty obvious one.

"Perry, look for references to Earth, no matter how obscure." I looked at Torina. "We've been kind of assuming these human memories were coming from people like you, not—and I don't think I've ever used this unironically before—Earthlings."

She nodded. "Worth a try—"

Perry's eyes flashed amber. "Done. I've found ninety-six references to Earth. Ninety-two of them are just listings in navigational data or mentions in reference data. The remaining four are listed in a comm log that was supposedly deleted."

I sniffed. "Yeah, that's not suspicious at all."

"It was also really careless. You'd think someone in Gur-Malik's sleazy line of business would be more diligent about wiping out incriminating files," Torina said, shaking her head.

"You'd be surprised how often criminals end up helping us catch themselves just by being dumb," Perry replied.

We reviewed the recovered logs, or what survived of them, since some data had been lost. Two of the four contacts originated at a set of coordinates we finally nailed down as Naperville, a suburb of Chicago.

I shook my head. "I leave the farm in Iowa and travel hundreds of light years, just to end up a few hundred klicks from the farm in Iowa."

We transported Gur-Malik to Anvil Dark, which was itself a trip that couldn't end soon enough. The Yonnox bitched and complained, whined, simpered, repeatedly tried to bribe us, and even tried threatening us a few times. When we were finally able to dump him off the *Fafnir*, I took a moment to enjoy the silence.

After finishing up the inevitable paperwork, I informed Lunzy about our progress and what we planned to do next.

"Chicago, eh?" She sniffed. "It's never somewhere like Florence, or Paris, or Istanbul, is it?"

I liked Chicago myself, but Lunzy did have a point. Given that the Midwest was now sliding into early winter, a place like Rio or Kuala Lumpur would have made for a nice change of pace.

Fortunately, it was never too cold for steak. "Torina, we're going to dinner while we're there."

"I like dinner," she said. "Go on."

I held my hands about a foot apart. "Imagine, if you will. A steak. This big—"

"Light the drive, Van. I'm in."

32

IT FELT strange to be back on Earth. We'd reentered the atmosphere over the Pacific, burning a lot of fuel to decelerate without creating too much of a lightshow. Our stealth system could make the *Fafnir* undetectable but wouldn't do anything to dim the trail of fire we'd leave across the sky if we just coasted, aerobraking as we descended in the way something like the Space Shuttle had. I thought of all the times the media carried stories of fireballs flashing across the Earthly sky and wondered how many of those were actually meteorites.

"Most of them are, in fact," Netty informed me. "Which is good because it makes it easier to pass off the occasional ship as a hunk of space rock."

We landed in a wooded ravine not far from our target in Naperville, Netty expertly nestling the *Fafnir* among some trees that leaned over a small rivulet of a creek. Snow swirled around outside as we waited for dark.

"We'll keep the lights on," Torina said as Perry and I prepared to disembark. I wore my trusty duster coat over my Peacemaker outfit again. It had nothing to do with the weather, because the armor would keep me comfortably warm. It was about covering up, especially The Drop and the Moonsword. Since we had no idea what was waiting for us, I wasn't prepared to go unarmed.

I got hit by a gust of icy wind as we stepped out of the ship. What I hadn't brought was my helmet, so I did catch the unpleasant weather right in the face. Perry flew ahead, scouting the way, while I clambered out of the ravine.

I eventually found myself looking into the backyard of a house that backed onto the ravine. I thought back to the map. Our destination was one of six possible houses further up this street, which the ravine turned into a cul-de-sac. I hoped Perry might be able to narrow our search down at least somewhat, since investigating six houses offered six times the chance of being discovered—and I really didn't want to have to contend with the local police.

I drew the Moonsword but kept it hidden under my coat. I didn't intend to use it as a weapon if I could avoid it but rather took advantage of its comm-suppression effect. Every wireless security camera in my line of sight should be knocked offline. As for the ones hardwired into their systems—well, life was risk, wasn't it?

I made my way through the backyard using a shed as cover,

then wended my way between a swing set and an old trailer. Frozen grass crunched under my feet. I eventually made it to the street without incident and fell into a slow amble, trying to look like someone who belonged. It was an affluent neighborhood, all huge, sleek houses on tiny lots, most with at least two or three vehicles in every driveway. There were lights on in most of them, but the only other person I saw was an older guy walking his dog on the opposite side of the street. We actually exchanged a wave.

"Psst, Van, over here."

I followed the voice, which had come from above me. Perry perched on one of the bigger branches of a leafless elm. Fortunately, the night was dark enough, and the matrix of branches and twigs thick enough, that no one was likely to see him.

"Any idea where we're going?" I asked, now trying to stand in one place under a tree, at night, in the cold and snow, without looking suspicious. I just ended up feeling awkward and conspicuous.

"Actually, yeah. Look at the house directly across the street, then look at the one to the right of it. There's a power signature inside it that's not coming from a home entertainment system, if you get my meaning."

"What do we know about—"

I cut myself off. Someone had appeared from a driveway two doors down, on my side of the street, and was heading straight toward me. I considered ducking behind Perry's elm. But if this person had already seen me, that would only put a neon sign over my head. On impulse, I pulled my data slate out of my belt. It was a little too big for a cell phone, but that shouldn't be obvious in the dark.

I raised it to my ear and began talking.

"Yeah… uh-huh. I know. You told me to turn left at the lights. No, you said left. You did too, Carol. I'm not going to argue, I'm —look, my mother has nothing to do with this. Hey, that's uncalled for, dammit, now—"

I rambled on like that as what turned out to be a teenager with earbuds wandered by. I just kept up my one-sided conversation as he passed; he barely even spared me a glance.

When he was gone, vanished into another house back the way I'd come, I put the slate away.

"Nice bit of subterfuge, Van. You're a natural at this," Perry said.

I shrugged. "I've been lying online for a long time now. Just a matter of applying all that shady experience to the real world."

The target house looked no different than the others—a newish, two-story, single-family detached, with a two-car garage and a postage stamp yard. I studied it while Perry continued to scan it, but both of us came up empty.

"There's something generating power inside that suggests a small fusion generator, but that's all I can tell."

"A fusion generator. Huh. Wonder if that conforms to code."

"I'm gonna say no, it probably doesn't," Perry replied.

And that underscored a problem. If we made a scene here, up to and including a thermonuclear explosion in a Chicago suburb, it would have… implications. It didn't take me long to decide on plan B, which involved putting a bug in place to monitor what went on here, then discreetly withdrawing and coming back another day when we had a better picture.

"Doctor Emil Hoffsinger, fifty-six years old, unmarried, currently an adjunct at the University of Chicago," Perry said.

I did a bit of hacking while we were waiting for the sun to set and was able to access property tax rolls for our six potential targets. As hacking went, it wasn't exactly rocket science—a subject I now happened to know quite well, mind you. I considered what we'd learned about the good Doctor Hoffsinger.

"Wasn't he the guy fired from NYU for some sort of ethics thing?" I asked Perry.

"He was. It was recorded in the campus blog but had no details, remember?"

"Yeah, I do."

Ethics violations. And now he was implicated in trafficking of human memory chips. Doctor Hoffsinger sounded like a fine piece of work.

Perry flew from his elm tree to another across the road on the property adjoining Hoffsinger's. He planted our monitoring device there, a strictly passive bug with a low power signature. Unless someone went specifically looking for it, it wasn't likely to be found.

Once Perry confirmed the bug was collecting data, we made our way back to the *Fafnir*. And, for the third time in my life, I lifted off of Earth and headed into orbit.

I wondered if Gramps had ever gotten used to casually flying off the planet. Because I sure hadn't. Not yet, anyway.

WHEN WE ARRIVED at Anvil Dark, we had a courier message waiting for us. Whatever it was, the sender had been concerned enough about its contents to send it as a sealed and encrypted message on a hand-delivered data chip rather than just transmitting it to us. And considering that there were heavily encrypted comm channels available, it suggested something even more sensitive than our standard Peacemaker information.

That made my radar power up a little. I accepted the chip from the courier bot that had been waiting outside the airlock, then returned to the *Fafnir*'s cockpit and plugged it into the dataport with more than a little trepidation.

"Why do I have the feeling this is bad news?" I said, my finger hovering over the playback control.

"Your cousin?" Torina asked.

I shrugged. "Let's find out." I touched the control.

It wasn't Carter Yost, though. It was Groshenko.

"Van, come to my ship, docking port Alpha Five. There's something I need to discuss with you."

The screen flicked back to the Peacemaker logo.

I leaned back. "Not quite as dire as I'd feared."

But Torina narrowed her eyes. "Actually, it might be worse. Groshenko doesn't want to talk about whatever it is he wants to talk to you about—not even on a secure, encrypted chip."

That made me grimace. "Okay, Netty, I'll let you take care of getting the *Fafnir* fueled up and ready to fly while we go and find out what's going on."

"You've made quite the name for yourself, even among the Masters, Van," Groshenko said as we settled into his particular take on a lounge aboard his *Dragon*, the *Murmansk*. Named, apparently, after his hometown back on Earth, Groshenko's ship looked more like a warship than something involved in law enforcement, with multiple banks of lasers and missile launchers and two twin proton-cannon batteries.

I settled into a deck chair and looked across an expansive rolling field dotted with small copses of trees. I had to squint at a bright, early afternoon sun. It was pretty remarkable, actually, considering we sat in a compartment aboard a ship docked at Anvil Dark.

"Looks real. I swear I can smell the grass," I said.

"You can. This is about as good as virtual reality gets," Groshenko said, smiling and offering Torina and I a drink—vodka, of course. "One of my last active cases involved a pretty big payout, so I decided to splurge and indulge myself."

I wasn't a hard liquor drinker, and that especially applied to vodka, which to me always just tasted of hangovers and broken dreams. But the stuff Groshenko handed out was actually quite good, smooth and with a hint of something citrusy.

"Van, I'll get right to the point. You've stumbled into something potentially big here."

"With the memory-chip trafficker on Earth?"

Groshenko nodded. So did Torina.

"I'd *hope* it would be considered big, considering it represents Crimes Against Life," she said.

I frowned a bit at that. The fact that she'd said it in such a specific way, Crimes Against Life, made it sound like something distinct—and it was. A subset of intergalactic laws, treaties, and other conventions and agreements specifically named some crimes as so heinous that they fell into a category all their own. Murder, on its own, was a crime, and a very serious one, of course—a literal crime against life. But murders perpetrated for some profit-oriented goal, like making torture and death porn, were considered especially egregious and were lumped in with things like genocide, forced genetic and other sorts of medical experimentation, development of bioweapons and pathogens, and a dreary handful of others. These got the sinister distinction of those capital letters, not just crimes against life, but Crimes Against Life.

Groshenko nodded to her. "Indeed. But if that doesn't make it complicated enough, we have another layer to it. And, Van, that would be you."

"Me."

"Yes. You. The fact you're Mark Tudor's grandson has already painted you onto a few scanners. Combine that with your scores against the Salt Thieves and the attempted force buyout of Ms. Milon's homeworld against the Stillness, and now against the memory-chip traffickers on Earth, and you're making some people distinctly uncomfortable."

I put my glass down on a small table beside the deck chair. "Who, exactly? And what does *uncomfortable* mean?"

"He means you're starting to make some other Peacemakers look bad," Torina said.

Perry bobbed his head. "More than that, some of those same Peacemakers might be worried that you're going to turn up some things that make it clear *why* they're looking bad."

"They're on the take, in other words," I said, then glanced at Groshenko to see his reaction.

He just smiled. "I would never presume to implicate a fellow Peacemaker in anything... untoward." He glanced into his vodka, then back up. "But yes, Ms. Milon and Perry are right. There are some Peacemakers who would rather not see this investigation happen quickly. Or thoroughly, for that matter."

He held up a hand. "Although to be fair, in a couple of those instances it's because you risk compromising other investigations, at least one of which has been going on for several years."

"So is this your way—and by *your*, I mean the Masters collectively—of telling Van to back off?" Torina asked.

Groshenko shook his head. "Not at all. My message to you, Van, is twofold. First, you're going to have to carry out this investigation pretty much alone. If you need help, you'll need to forge your own alliances with other Peacemakers. And if you *really* need help, both Lunzy and I will do what we can. But we've both also got our own interests to protect."

"Of course," I replied.

"Second, you need to proceed *very* carefully. Make sure you dot every *i* and cross every *t* before you move on from a lead. Your best defense against any sort of *interference* is a rock-solid case. Just be prepared to run into resistance anyway."

"What about money? If Van's going to take on something involving so much risk, he should be compensated for it," Perry said bluntly.

"I agree. I'm going to transfer twenty-five thousand bonds to you as a special stipend. That's the maximum amount I can offer without having to submit a detailed, fully costed proposal."

"All due respect, but even I know that's not very much," I said.

"No, it's not. But you're potentially onto solving several cases here, with a total payout that should keep you flush with cash for quite a long time. Plus, if I subsidize you any further, I'm going to start attracting attention I don't need."

Torina leaned forward, her gaze keen. "Are some of the other Masters... less than happy about Van's achievements?"

I widened my eyes at Torina's insightful—and blunt—question. Groshenko, though, didn't hesitate.

"That, Ms. Milon, is a most inappropriate question."

"To which the answer isn't no."

Groshenko sipped his vodka and said nothing.

I FOUND myself lost in my own thoughts as we headed back to the *Fafnir*. Torina picked up on it and just left me to it. So did Perry, whose empathy might be as artificial as his intelligence, but it came down to the same thing.

I stopped just short of the *Fafnir*'s airlock. "What do you guys think?" I asked.

Torina and Perry exchanged a look.

"About Groshenko? The case? The Masters?" Torina asked.

"All of it. I can't help feeling that maybe things are rushing along a little too fast." I crossed my arms. "I ran down quite a few bad guys on the internet. Quite a few of those were just overconfident. They were smug, showy, maybe even narcissists. They *wanted* to attract attention to themselves even though it gave people like me a hook to find them. Is that what's happening here?"

"No, it isn't," Torina replied.

I looked at her in surprise. "You sound pretty sure of that."

"I am sure of it. Or, at least I'm sure of the why of it. It's not because you're a narcissist, Van, and that you want to attract attention to yourself. It's because you're your grandfather's grandson. Like it or not, you're following in his footsteps as a Peacemaker. The people who loved him, hated him, or were indifferent to him are naturally going to be predisposed to looking at you the same way, at least until you prove otherwise."

Perry bobbed his head and picked up the thread. "Most Peacemakers start from relative anonymity, Van. They arrive at Anvil Dark as nobodies, recruited into the Guild one way or another, but ultimately, they're just more initiates. But the moment you docked here, in that ship, with that name, you were Mark Tudor's grandson, and everyone knew it."

"So what you're saying is, if I want to go on being a Peacemaker, I just have to suck it up."

Perry nodded again. "How does that bit of Earthly wisdom

go? Grant me the serenity to accept the things I cannot change, the strength to change the things I can—"

"And wisdom to know the difference," I finished. "Yeah, I get it."

"Van, if your grandfather didn't think you'd be able to do this, he'd have never left that remote in your desk drawer back in Iowa."

We carried on into the *Fafnir*. It was more than a little unsettling that there were others out there who might be taking a dim view of me and not just Carter Yost. Gramps had apparently turned down the title of Master, which meant he'd been moving in those circles with Groshenko. He had friends and enemies, and now, so did I.

I found Perry's words unexpectedly comforting, though. He'd known my grandfather as well as anyone probably ever had. If he thought Gramps believed in me, then I should, too.

———

I HADN'T EXPECTED to return to Earth for at least a couple of weeks, and perhaps a couple of months. But given Groshenko's implication that we were nudging up against some major Peacemaker cases, I wanted to check the data tap we'd placed on Hoffsinger sooner rather than later. Stealthed up, we slid into orbit and uploaded the tap's contents. While we did, we were able to watch a supply mission launch from Baikonur, heading for the ISS.

Watching the rocket rise on a tiny tongue of flame, I shook

my head. "You know, when I was a kid, I went through an *I'm gonna be an astronaut* phase."

"And you succeeded," Torina said.

"Yeah. I just never imagined space would involve so much paperwork."

Netty parked us in a high orbit, away from any possible collision hazard with the cloud of space junk whirling around Earth, so we could examine the data. To all of our surprise, we hit paydirt almost immediately.

"We have a hit. And it's two of our favorite people," Perry said.

The tap on Hoffsinger's place picked up encrypted conversations between him and a ship in orbit. The encryption was pretty good, three different schemes being used for different transmissions. Between them, Perry and Netty were able to crack two, but the third was really strong stuff—military grade, and by military I mean outer space military, not the Earthly sort. The two AIs eventually concluded they just weren't breaking that one.

"There are resources back on Anvil Dark that could probably do it. Bester can hook you up."

"For another treasured memory?"

"That's his usual fee."

The encryption we did break, though, was paydirt enough. Hoffsinger was working with another Yonnox named Kuthrix, who owned a ship called the *Lawful Windrunner*.

I glanced at Perry. "Lawful?"

"Hilarious, right?"

Kuthrix was high on the Peacemaker's most-wanted list, as

was his collaborator, who was also implicated in Hoffsinger's transmissions. Her name was Jeanette Ruiz-Rocher.

I sat up straight in the pilot's seat. "Holy shit. I know her."

Torina's eyes widened at me. "You *know* her?"

"Yeah. Or no, I don't *know* her, as in know her personally. But I know who she is. She was all over the news, oh, twenty years ago. I was just a kid, but I remember her because she just vanished into thin air."

Perry cut in. "In 2003, yeah. She was up for charges for fraud, racketeering, and our favorite crime, ethics violations, all stemming from her time as COO of a big biomedical company."

"Right. She disappeared right before the trial. It was big news. She was believed to have either skipped out and gone off the grid in some tropical locale, or been killed to keep her from revealing things in exchange for a plea deal. It still comes up on the internet from time to time, but I mostly remember it because of some talking head on TV who claimed she'd been spirited away by aliens." I had to smile wryly at that.

"Well, she's very much alive," Perry said as Netty put an image of her on the screen. I blinked at it.

"Is this an old picture?"

"Taken about four years ago, on Crossroads," Netty replied.

I just stared at the stunningly beautiful woman caught in the frame. She looked to be twenty-five, *maybe* thirty, at the most.

I shook my head. "She has to be in her sixties, though."

Torina smiled. "Amazing what bio-regenerative work can do, isn't it?"

"So how come everyone's not using this to stay young?"

"Remember those ethics violations of hers? They pale in comparison to the ones involved in these sorts of treatments."

"How?"

Torina's smile became thin and hard. "Tech has obviously come a long way, especially compared to Earth. But one thing it can't do is recreate actual living tissue."

"In humans, that's especially true for nerve cells and the various cells that make up the brain. Even if you have some to start with, they're really hard to grow," Perry stated.

I glanced from one to the other. "I don't like where this is heading."

"You shouldn't. Because not all of the people who've disappeared from Earth have gone on to live opulent lives as major criminals," Torina said.

"Or, they have—or at least parts of them have." Perry glanced pointedly at the image on the screen. "You're probably looking at a few of them right now."

"Holy shit. And she looks... normal."

"Well, she's not," Torina said, her voice flat and hard. "We tolerate shit from people because they're beautiful. That's a mistake with this one, Van. Her heart is a place of permanent midnight, and she does it all with a smile."

I stared at this strikingly beautiful and profoundly evil woman. To think that some of those UFO abduction stories weren't only true, they were far more horrifying than just some especially intimate probing.

"If you listen very carefully, you'll be able to *hear* my skin crawling," I said.

"There's a *reason* she's one of our most wanted, Van. But she's smart, maybe even almost as smart as me," Perry said.

I glanced at him, expecting to see him doing his laughing thing, but he was just staring at the woman's image.

"No one's ever been able to make anything stick to her," he went on. "The best the Peacemaker's have ever managed is some minor bullshit that led to fines. And for her, any fine we can levy is pocket change."

He turned to me. "And now we know why Groshenko was all but outright warning you off this case. Even your grandfather stayed clear of Ms. Ruiz-Rocher. It was mainly because his main target was the Stillness—but not entirely."

"You're saying Gramps was afraid of her?"

"Afraid? Hell, I don't think your grandfather would have been *afraid* of an exploding star." He glanced back at the image. "He just knew that taking this woman on was probably a lost cause. And at least a couple of other Peacemakers proved him right."

"How?"

Perry's amber gaze swung back to me.

"By dying."

33

AFTER MUCH DISCUSSION, we finally settled on trying to track down and seize the *Lawful Windrunner*. The encrypted data, which we'd managed to get cracked by Bester and his Librarians, only further implicated Kuthrix and Jeanette Ruiz-Rocher in the vile trafficking of human memory chips. It had cost me another of the books I'd brought with me, a well-thumbed copy of *The Hitch-hiker's Guide to the Galaxy*, which my father had managed to get signed by Douglas Adams himself. That was a hard one to part with.

But it was worth it, in its own way. The data, a comm-log, implied pretty clearly that Ruiz-Rocher had been colluding with Hoffsinger, not only in killing people and recording their memories of it, but also hauling the corpse off-planet to be harvested for its tissues. These were then sold into a burgeoning black market for bio-regenerative therapies.

"Waste not, want not, I guess," I said, glaring at the unencrypted comm log.

Torina shot me a glance. "This is just the human side of the business. There'll be similar things going on with other races. After all, you can't install human parts into Yonnox, or vice-versa."

I sighed. "In other words, all of this amazing technological advancement has enabled even more suffering and... " I wasn't sure what other awful thing to add because there were so many to choose from.

It was horrific stuff, but it was also enough to make the *prima facie* case against Kuthrix and Ruiz-Rocher, the bare minimum required to justify proceeding, and to apply for things like warrants. But we were a long way from a conviction yet. We needed more and harder evidence, and the *Lawful Windrunner* was the logical place to start.

And that led us to our next mystery. Netty, through querying traffic control databases, was able to establish where the *Lawful Windrunner* had recently been. Her last known stop was in the Tau Ceti system, and from there, she'd proceeded toward Spindrift. The mystery, though, was a ping from her transponder in the AD Leonis system about sixteen light-years from Earth.

"There's nothing there," Perry said.

But Netty spoke up. "That's not quite true. There is an automated fuel processing facility there, located on the second planet. It draws feedstock from three gas giants in the system and refines it for helium-3, deuterium, and a few other valuable gases."

I studied the entry for the system that Netty put up on the

screen. The gas mining was conducted by a consortium of corporations, and the Eridani Federation, who for some convoluted reason exercised jurisdiction over AD Leonis. But the gases were only bulk refined to a certain grade, then were shipped out of the system in bulk for further processing and refining at facilities scattered throughout known space. They weren't really usable as fuel or anything else as-is. So Perry and Netty were both right—there was something there but nothing that would interest anyone except a bulk gas-refiner.

So why had the *Lawful Windrunner* stopped there?

"A navigation fix, maybe?" Torina suggested.

But Netty shot that idea down immediately. "The twist route from Tau Ceti to Spindrift is so simple it might as well be burned into the nav processor of every ship in known space. Unless they somehow got their nav wrong, there was no reason they couldn't have made that trip the same way about two hundred other ships do every day."

"Okay, so could they have screwed up their nav?" I asked, expecting I knew the answer but wanting to be sure.

"You mean could they have accidentally entered the twist data for AD Leonis instead of Spindrift? Sure, they could have."

I didn't even need to ask Netty how likely that was.

"Okay, then. I guess we need to make a stop at AD Leonis and find out what prompted the *Lawful Windrunner* to spend some time there."

Torina raised an eyebrow. "Wouldn't it make more sense to go straight after the *Lawful Windrunner* while that trail is still relatively fresh?"

I rubbed my chin. "I get your point, but I don't know. There's just something about that detour that really piqued my interest."

I pondered it a moment longer, then decided this just *felt* right. "Netty, let's head for AD Leonis and find out just what makes gas refining so interesting to Ms. Ruiz-Rocher and company."

"There are a lot of red dwarf stars out here, aren't there?" I said.

"It's one of the most common star types," Netty agreed. "Granted, the vast majority of them aren't very interesting, but I think the universe offers more than enough excitement to make up for it."

AD Leonis was an unremarkable star, a dull, ruddy point of light that was actually hard to pick out against the starscape behind it. Its trio of gas giant companions were much more evident, all of them showing visible, albeit pretty dim disks. The only permanent facility in the system was on the second planet, a rocky world about the size of Mars. It had once apparently been Earth-like, but the death throes of its star had scoured it down to barren bedrock. The facility located there, a purely robotic gas refinery, really didn't care.

We detected no other ships in the system aside from the robotic collector ships shuttling between the three gas giants and the processing plant, and a single massive gas hauler on its way out of the system, bound for a refinery somewhere. All of these ships, like the plant, were robotic, which meant that Torina and I were the only living things in the system. Well, the only biological ones, anyway.

"Welcome to the lovely AD Leonis system. Please keep your hands inside the spaceship at all times," Netty said. "That is, assuming you want to go somewhere in particular and not just drift here, taking in the splendor."

I glanced at Torina. We'd already discussed the possibility that the *Lawful Windrunner* had just come here to rendezvous with another ship. But Netty couldn't find any traffic control logs to suggest that had been the case. The data could have been altered, but then why leave evidence that Kuthrix's ship had been here?

"The gas-processing plant seems to make the most sense," I said.

Torina pursed her lips. "Why would Kuthrix or Ruiz-Rocher be interested in visiting some smelly old industrial facility?"

"Maybe she's got a thing for heavy machinery?" I shrugged. "Only one way to find out. Netty, if you please."

The *Fafnir* accelerated, starting in-system toward the Leonis Gas Processing Facility.

WE LANDED on a pad assigned to us by the plant's traffic control AI. Even though we were valid traffic, the AI tried to warn us off, but Netty had invoked Peacemaker privilege. The AI, not wanting to implicate its corporate masters in obstruction of an ongoing investigation, grudgingly complied, but admonished us against breaching traffic control protocols.

"I think I can avoid smashing into a bulk gas carrier the size of a middling asteroid, thanks," Netty snapped back at it and brought us in for a neat landing on the blast-scarred expanse of bedrock.

We stepped out of the *Fafnir* and stared at the processing plant, a cluster of buildings at least a klick away.

"I can't help but notice there are some empty landing pads a hell of a lot closer than the one we were assigned," I noted as we made the walk.

"That would be the traffic control AI giving us the proverbial middle finger," Perry replied.

"Yeah, I assumed that."

It wasn't a difficult walk. The planet was essentially frozen in the moments following the stellar cataclysm that had blown away its atmosphere. Without air or water, the only weathering came from micrometeorites, which had left a thin layer of fine dust on the surface. There simply were no larger pieces of rock, aside from some massive boulders as large as the *Fafnir*, and a few even bigger. It made for a lonely and somewhat creepy walk under frozen silence.

That changed as we approached the gas-processing plant, though. Even a hundred meters away, I could feel a faint vibration through the soles of my feet. We reached an airlock that was prominently labeled.

CLOSED INDUSTRIAL SITE

DANGER – NO ENTRY TO UNAUTHORIZED PERSONNEL

I glanced at Perry. "Correct me if I'm wrong, but we count as authorized personnel, right?"

"You're the Peacemaker, Van. If you think we need to check this place out as part of an ongoing investigation, then you can invoke Interstellar Supplemental Protocol 4, Article 3, Section—"

"Perry, is that a yes?"

"Yeah, it is."

"Thank you." I stepped forward and tapped the airlock control. The outer door cycled open, then closed behind us and the airlock pressurized. The inner door remained closed. A sign on the bulkhead explained why. Since the exterior was airless, the airlock was a refuge station for personnel in emergencies. It contained access to comms and water, plus enough food to last six people up to three days. The inner door was sealed with a security lock and plastered with more signs warning of sundry hazards, including MOVING INDUSTRIAL ROBOTS and EXTREME HEAT.

I flashed my Peacemaker ID at it, and it slid open, while petulantly informing us that CONSORTIUM SECURITY WILL BE INFORMED, so there.

We stepped into a roaring, hissing world of industrial grunge. I didn't understand the details of how atmospheric gases from gas giants were processed, but it seemed to involve a lot of noise, pressurized gases rushing through massive pipes and tanks, and heat— lots of heat. It explained the EXTREME HEAT warnings. The temperature shown by my armor's heads-up shot from nearly minus two hundred Celsius outside to over seventy degrees here. The atmosphere was breathable, but not for long at those temperatures.

We wandered away from the airlock, taking in a soaring sprawl of massive tanks connected by a spaghetti-tangle of pipes and interspersed with pumps and other machines. Bots of various types rumbled purposefully about on balloon tires, although a few maintenance versions actually climbed amid the pipes like massive mechanical spiders, checking for leaks. All of it was lit by searing work lights that threw everything into either dazzling glare or deep shadow.

"This is like a steampunk version of Dante's Inferno," I said, taking in the automated grunge-scape.

"Yeah. Which leads to the question, why would Ruiz-Rocher and company have come here in the first place?" Torina said.

"And where do we even begin to start looking to find out? There are, by my estimate, three-point-three cubic *kilometers* of interior volume to this place," Perry put in.

"How many airlocks are there?" I asked.

"Six," Perry replied.

"Well, logic suggests that whatever they were doing here, they'd be doing near an airlock, right?"

"You've got no way of knowing if—"

Perry stopped.

Torina and I both tensed, and I reached for The Drop. "Perry? Something wrong?"

"There's a person here somewhere."

I exchanged a puzzled look with Torina. "Where? How can you even tell?"

"I routinely filter acoustic inputs by frequency, just to stay on top of things. Listen to this." He paused, then a new voice came through our ear sets, thin and ragged thanks to its isolation from the industrial racket. It sounded the way old time radio often did on Earth, scratchy and full of static.

"Help me!"

There was no doubt about it, though. It was a decidedly non-mechanical voice in a place that should only be populated by robots.

"Please, please *help* me!"

Perry started flying around, trying to localize the voice. He got the direction, and we headed that way. The voice, shared by Perry through our ear sets, got louder. Eventually, we found a bot about twice the size and bulk of a refrigerator working on a fuel transfer unit, switching feeds back and forth between pressurized tanks. Now Torina and I could hear it.

"Is… is someone here? Please? Anyone?"

Again, I glanced at Torina, then turned back to the bot. "Um —hello?"

"Yes! Yes! I'm here! Please help me!"

"I'm Van Tudor. I'm a Peacemaker. And you are—?"

"Fostin! My name is Fostin!"

"Okay, Fostin. And how can we help you?"

"By saving me from this! Please!"

I glanced around. The bot continued its back and forth operation of the transfer unit, but that was it. "Sorry, Fostin, saving you from what, exactly?"

"From this! What's happening to me! I'm trapped!"

Torina stepped forward, her eyes locked on the bot. "Van, you're not talking to that bot. You're talking to someone inside it."

I frowned. I hadn't seen a cab or any place for an operator—

Then what Torina was saying hit me. Fostin was literally inside the bot.

He was a memory chip, effectively enslaved to work in this dreary, pounding, infernal hell.

"IT MAKES A HORRIFYING SORT OF SENSE," Perry said. "Fostin's mental processes have been repurposed to run this machine, a sort of AI, except one that's far more adaptable and capable of problem-solving than your typical industrial version. An equivalent AI programmed from scratch would cost a hell of a lot more."

For a moment, I just stared at the bot. Fostin continued to implore us to help him.

This was—I'm not sure horrifying really even began to describe it.

"Why would they keep his personality intact, though?" Torina asked. From her tone, I could tell she was as viscerally revolted by this as I was.

"They probably had no choice. His higher-level thought

processes are too deeply and intimately integrated into the lower-level ones they wanted. So they co-opted the ones they wanted to use to run this bot and just left the rest in place."

"Meaning this poor bastard is stuck inside this machine." I shook my head. "And he has no conscious control over it. He's just—"

"Trapped. That's right. He might not even be aware of where he is."

I looked at Torina. She'd actually gone pale.

"Please tell me that this isn't a common thing around known space."

"It's not. This is—" She stopped and swallowed. "I've heard about some pretty terrible stuff, but this now sits on top of the pile."

We spent the next while having a really awkward conversation with the virtual version of Fostin, trying as gently as we could to tease out information about him. Apparently, he was a Wu'tzur, a member of a humanoid race largely involved in farming and exporting food from a planet nearly a hundred light-years away. Fostin himself was an engineer. He described how he'd been lured into a meeting over his planet on board the *Lawful Windrunner*, how he remembered meeting Kuthrix and Ruiz-Rocher, and that was it. His next memory was being here, operating this fuel transfer system.

"Except I'm not operating it! Or, I am, but not because I want to. I *have* to!"

"Fostin, that's okay," I said, trying to head off another collapse into babbling panic. "We understand. Look, we're going to talk about our options here, okay? We'll be right back."

"Please, no—!"

"We'll be right back, I promise."

I gestured for Perry and Torina to step away from the bot. "Is there anything we can do for this poor bastard?"

"I interfaced with the bot's maintenance system, the only one I can get into without doing some hacking," Perry said. "I also accessed the plant's production log. This bot isn't supposed to be here. It should be working in a different part of the plant entirely."

"Okay. And?"

"And, this bot has been co-opted to siphon helium-3 in small increments off of the main production circuit. Each time it does, the pressure in the system drops slightly. But before it drops below a certain minimum threshold and triggers a shutdown, it stops and lets the pressure return to normal. And that's it. That's what it does, over and over. The siphoned-off fuel is being stored in that big tank off to your left, which is meant as a backup reservoir for any production overflow."

"They're stealing fuel," Torina said.

"Yeah. And they're doing it really, really slowly. At this rate, it takes about two weeks to fill that tank. Presumably a ship comes along, drains it, and the process starts all over again."

"Yeah, well screw that," I said, turning back toward the bot. "We're going to put a stop to this right now—"

"Van, before you launch yourself into a noble mission of mercy, it's not going to be that simple."

I glanced back, curling my lip. "Of course it isn't," I snapped, then caught myself and sighed. This wasn't Perry's fault. "Why not?"

"Because whether Ruiz-Rocher and company intended to or not, they've created a situation in which there's a harmonic echoing through the pressurized gases throughout the main production circuit. If it's suddenly stopped, there's a risk of inducing failures through the system. At best, it could damage the circuit and force a shutdown."

"And at worst?" I asked, although I knew what he was going to say.

"The failures could cascade, and this place could go *kaboom*."

OKAY, so the chances of a *kaboom* were actually pretty small. Perry estimated them to range from five to ten percent. But that was still much higher than I was comfortable with. And even if it didn't, there was a fifty to sixty percent chance of serious damage to the system. Although we could argue for immunity from the cost of repairs, since we were in the performance of our duties. But it was by no means certain we'd get it.

"Surely we can claim we're rescuing someone here. That should take precedence over any property damage," I said.

Perry did his shrug. "The law's grey on whether Fostin, in this state, would legally constitute a person, in which case you're right, or an AI, in which case you're not."

"Shit. Well, I'm not just going to leave him here like this."

We batted around possible solutions, but it was Netty, who we'd linked into the brainstorming, who came up with our best solution.

"Waldo's AI is more than capable of operating that bot. If we replace Fostin's chip with Waldo's, and we do it carefully enough, we should be able to let it keep running uninterrupted."

"But we'll lose Waldo?" I asked.

"You might have noticed, Van, that Waldo isn't much of a conversationalist. His AI is about as interactive as an Earthly lizard. I keep a backup of it anyway, so all we'd need to do is get a new chip and reinstall him."

Perry and Torina both nodded. While they went to get Waldo's chip, I stayed with Fostin and explained to him what was going on.

"So what's going to happen to me when you... unplug me?"

"I don't know. I guess it will be like going to sleep."

"Or dying."

I could only agree with that. What happened when we closed our eyes for the last time was still a big unanswered question, and maybe the biggest.

"Can you bring me back to life? Install me in your bot, Waldo?"

"We can try."

"Please do, Van. This is—"

He didn't finish. He didn't have to.

Perry and Torina returned with the chip. The process of stealing the fuel didn't require the bot to move, so we were able to open it up and compare chips. They were mostly standardized, but there were some proprietary ones. Fortunately, one of the adapters we had aboard the *Fafnir* would allow Waldo's chip to replace Fostin's.

Perry interfaced with the bot and downloaded its essential programming, then used it to reprogram Waldo. That left only the actual transfer, which was the tricky part.

"We've got just over six seconds to make the switch," Perry said. "If we don't, and the system doesn't fail wholesale, then we've got just over six more, and so on. But each time we miss the mark, we run the risk of catastrophic failure—or the harmonic will just die out. As an added wrinkle, the robot will shut down after fifteen seconds if it loses communication with its AI chip."

"I kind of hope the harmonic just fades away and we can leave it shut down because I'd really like to stop this whole fuel-theft scam going on here," Torina said.

I glanced at her. "Yeah, that, and not being blown to bits would be nice, too."

She nodded. "There is that."

I locked my gaze onto hers. "Torina, look, why don't you—"

"If you say *go back to the ship*, there's going to be a catastrophic failure alright," she snapped. I knew better than to press the issue.

I turned and peered into the bot's open chassis. Amid components and cabling, the AI chip was prominent, mounted near the center of the bot for maximum protection and shielding. Replacing it looked easy enough, particularly since I'd fiddled with more than a few chips in my time, and that included soldering chips onto boards, not just plugging them into sockets.

"Okay, here goes nothin'." I popped open the clip holding the

AI chip in place, then gingerly grabbed the chip. I paused before removing it.

"Fostin, I'm about to unplug you."

"Do it. Whatever it takes, please. Even if I never come back."

I took a breath and tugged on the chip. It popped out, and a shrill alarm sounded. The bot flashed up a failure warning on its maintenance monitor, announcing it would go into safe mode and shut down in fifteen seconds.

I handed Fostin's chip to Torina, then slid Waldo's chip, nestled in its adapter, into place. It went most of the way in, then stopped.

It didn't fit.

"Shit! Torina, let me see that chip!"

She held it up, and I compared it to the adapter on Waldo's. I could immediately see the problem. Waldo's chip had two extra pins.

A second later, an ominous rumble shuddered through the pipes and tanks around us. The plant's control system had just over-pressured the entire circuit to compensate for the expected minor drop. Warning buzzers sounded.

My mind raced as I pointed. "Those two pins on the end, right there, we need to get rid of them!"

It was barely out of my mouth before Perry's head darted toward me and his beak snapped closed. When he pulled back, the two pins were gone, neatly sheared off at their base.

I didn't ask any questions, just turned and slid the chip into place. I had to resist the urge to hammer it in, because if there were any other mismatches, I might just bend pins and damage it irreparably.

It slid neatly into place and seated with a soft click. There were a few anxious seconds as the bot's maintenance screen continued to insist there was an error—

Then it cleared, and the bot happily returned to stealing gas.

"Well, that was fun," Torina said.

I glanced at Perry. "That was some pretty nifty biting you did there, considering my fingertips were just a few millimeters away from those shears you call a beak."

"Hey, super-sophisticated AI bird, remember? Accuracy is what I do."

When we'd confirmed that the plant was stable, we made to head back to the *Fafnir*. But Torina hesitated. I opened my mouth to ask her what was wrong, but she suddenly drew her sidearm. I flinched and grabbed for The Drop, and Perry flung himself in the air, both of us looking for whatever threat she'd seen.

A single shot rang out as Torina put a hole in the overflow tank. With a shrieking hiss, it began venting helium-3 gas.

I gaped at her. "What the hell?"

She cleared and holstered her weapon. "Like I said, I really didn't want those assholes to get this fuel. It's helium, so it's not volatile, and it's just going to keep venting through that little hole, then escape—well, probably into space, right, Perry?"

He dropped back to the floor. "Yeah. Probably. Being so light, it'll just diffuse away from the planet. It was a great idea, too, which would have been made even more awesome with some, you know, *warning*."

I re-holstered The Drop and scowled at Torina. "Yeah, what Perry said."

Torina just grinned and didn't look sorry at all.

34

WE TRIED PLUGGING Fostin's chip into Waldo and were pleasantly surprised that not only did he boot, but he did it intact.

"This is so much better," he said through Waldo's external speaker. "I don't know how to thank you for saving me from that."

I glanced at Torina, who shrugged. Honestly, I had no idea what Fostin's legal status was. Was he evidence? A witness? A victim? AIs were normally exempt from the rights afforded to what was, per interstellar convention, considered a person. But Fostin had been killed, ending his biological life. So was he legally dead? Or did his effective resurrection as an AI effectively mean he wasn't? Did he still own Fostin's home? Have access to his bond accounts? He had an insurance policy—was he entitled to a payout on it?

"Whether they know it or not, Kuthrix and Ruiz-Rocher have just created an entirely novel legal situation," Perry said.

"This is probably going to have to go before the interstellar courts to be resolved, which means we might get an answer during our lifetimes," Torina put in.

But I had to shake my head. "I think it's going to get more urgent than that. If they did this to Fostin, how many others are out there? Hell, we don't even know if there are others like Fostin in that gas processing plant."

They both nodded, which was all they could do.

In the meantime, we had a passenger. Waldo was no longer an idiot savant maintenance remote. He was a full-fledged engineer. Moreover, he was more than happy to help with chores around the *Fafnir*.

"I don't know that I want to stay in this body, but for now, it's like stepping out of a fire box into the cool night air," he said, sounding almost serene.

I cocked my head at him. "A fire box?"

"We Wu'tzur enjoy temperatures that you'd find decidedly uncomfortable. By cool night air, I mean as low as fifty degrees Centigrade."

"That's probably why Kuthrix and Ruiz-Rocher picked him for that fuel-theft job. He wouldn't be put off by the high temperatures," Torina offered.

"Indeed, I wasn't. The enslavement was my main concern. Well, that and having my physical body converted to profit, and the leftovers flushed down a drain," Fostin said, and for being fresh out of a terrible situation, he sounded rather relaxed. I quite liked him.

We lifted off, then set course for Spindrift to catch up with the *Lawful Windrunner*. We sent a status update to Lunzy as we did, fully encrypted, but also using some veiled speech to further conceal what we were doing. The message consisted of little more than, *We've obtained something of interest and are now going to secure that target we discussed.*

A short while later, we got a reply. Lunzy was sending Alic, the Eniped we'd worked with during our raid on The Stillness, to help. The subtext to it was just as important. If she trusted Alic, then so could we.

Not long after that, we twisted into the Sirius system and started our inbound run to Spindrift with one big question in mind.

Was the *Lawful Windrunner* still here? Or would the chase continue?

Netty gave us our answer.

"The *Lawful Windrunner* has just cleared the Spindrift control zone and entered the traffic pattern. She's on her way out of the system."

"Any sign of Alic?"

"He's inbound."

"Perfect. Let's get him on the comm, and we'll run these bastards down."

Perry stuck his head forward between the seats. "Spindrift is going to take a pretty dim view of a spacebattle right in the middle of the traffic pattern."

I shrugged.

"Tough. They can file a complaint."

"Wow, didn't take you long to start flouting the rules."

"Is that a complaint of your own?"

"Not at all. Merely an observation."

I shrugged again. "Well, Perry, my friend, rules are meant to be broken."

Perry paused, then spoke in a warm tone of respect. "Your Gramps would love to hear that."

WE COORDINATED CAREFULLY WITH ALIC, trying to take advantage of traffic heading in and out of the system to make our approach to the *Lawful Windrunner* less conspicuous. I had a nagging feeling it wasn't going to work, though, the same way I got a tickle of doubt when I knew some cyber target I was stalking was going to get away. People like that developed fine tuned senses to any sort of potential threat and would simply bolt. The number of times I'd *almost* run down a cyber crook or foreign operative, only to have them abruptly go dark—

Let's just say it happened a lot, and it was frustrating as hell every time.

And, sure enough, when we and Alic were nearly in position to make our final run and close the jaws of our trap on the *Lawful Windrunner*, Kuthrix must have noticed us. His ship abruptly accelerated hard, at the same time broadcasting a confusing blur of electronic countermeasures that turned its scanner returns to fuzz. Alic had a potent countermeasure suite he used to burn through the interference, then repeat the data to us, but it cost precious time reestablishing contact. And the *Lawful Windrunner* could theoretically twist away at any time as long as they had the fuel and a drive capable of it. Perry was pretty confident they didn't, and that we still had an opportunity to catch them, so we kept up a dogged pursuit, closing in on the ship from two directions. It dramatically limited their ability to maneuver without letting at least one of us close the distance fast.

I was just thinking we might get the bastards when Netty did something she didn't normally do—she swore.

Torina and I both sat back in surprise. The string of profanity Netty loosed must have been stuff she'd picked up from dockworkers and the like. It matched everything I'd heard in the Army, that's for sure.

"Uh, Netty, you okay?" Torina asked.

"Fine. I'm just pissed off."

"Why?"

"Because I've been plotting the performance curve of the *Lawful Windrunner*, and it abruptly changed during that minute or so we lost her in that ECM fog she generated."

I glanced at Torina, who shrugged. "Okay, and—?"

"And, the only way to account for it is sudden loss of sixteen tonnes of mass. That's almost exactly the loaded mass of a standard class two escape boat, which is just what a ship of the *Lawful Windrunner*'s class would be expected to carry."

"Wait—are you saying they launched their escape boat? They bugged out?"

"Bingo. Class two is twist-capable, too."

Now it was my turn to cut loose with a string of profanity. We consulted with Alic, and he and his AI confirmed Netty's calculations. But he insisted on running down the *Lawful Windrunner* anyway, because his AI had probably been commanded to twist it to some predetermined place so Kuthrix and Ruiz-Rocher could just rendezvous with it again.

Which is just what we did. For added certainty, Alic fired a tarpit missile, a drone that would catch up with the *Lawful Windrunner* and fly on station with her. It would then generate strong gravitational pulses, disrupting her ability to twist. A tarpit missile was on my wish list for the *Fafnir*, but the things were fantastically expensive.

After a brief chase, we were finally able to catch up to the *Lawful Windrunner* ourselves. Torina and I boarded her, while Alic flew overwatch in case anything unexpected came along.

Sure enough, the *Lawful Windrunner* had been abandoned, the docking recess for her escape boat empty. We had the satisfaction, at least, of seizing and impounding her as a prize, which was going to make for a nice payout for Alic and me. But it was an empty victory, and we all knew it. The real targets had eluded us and could be anywhere in known space by now.

"HAVE TO ADMIT, these assholes have good taste," Torina said, eyeing an intricately embroidered wall-hanging. "This is from Faalax, in the Teegarden's Star system. It has to be worth at least ten thousand bonds." She gripped it between thumb and forefinger. "Beautiful work."

I turned around, taking in the common cabin area of the *Lawful Windrunner*. Aside from Torina's pricey tapestry, there were paintings, a few of them holographically 3D, furniture made of wood the color and consistency of smoke, and a carpet so plush I was afraid I might lose a boot in it.

"You know, there's a lot more wall-to-wall carpeting in space than I'd imagined," I said. "I always envisioned spaceships as kind of utilitarian. But between Lunzy's ship and Groshenko's, and now this one—" I shook my head. "I'm starting to think the *Fafnir* is a little on the austere side."

Torina shrugged. "Even criminal scum can be comfortable, right? If you're going to live aboard a spaceship, you might as well make it home."

Perry hopped into the compartment from forward, where he'd been analyzing the nav data, comm logs, and anything else he could glean from the ship's systems. "Needless to say, virtually everything has been thoroughly wiped. They probably had a one-button way of doing it right before they left. This ship's computers are as fresh as if she'd just come off the showroom floor. Oh, and her AI's an a-hole, too."

I sighed. "So we got nothing?"

"I didn't say that. As usual, the bird outsmarts the bad guy. They wiped their data-storage modules, but not the buffers. Those were just overwritten again and again. Your grandfather had the brilliant idea to procure an application for me that can read and extract layers of data. It's not perfect, and more and more data is lost with every overwrite, but there's still a lot of stuff there."

"Huh. I had no idea Gramps had that kind of computer knowledge."

Perry leveled his golden gaze on me. "He didn't. He said he got the idea from you. Something about a job you did involving some arms sales in Africa. You were excited and told him all about it."

I stared back at Perry. I knew the job he was talking about, one during which I was able to extract some key data from a buffer in one of the bad guys' computers. I'd probably rambled on at length about it, assuming Gramps was just kind of nodding along. Turned out he was listening to me, and pretty closely it seemed.

I swallowed against another of those hurtful lumps and cleared my throat. "Okay. Well, anyway—what did you learn? Anything useful?"

"Bottom line, I was able to retrieve a list of fourteen different clients of our friends Kuthrix and Ruiz-Rocher, who are apparently using human memory chips to control robotic systems."

Torina and I were silent for a moment. I exchanged a horrified glance with her.

She finally broke the silence. "So there's a whole underground market for this."

Perry bobbed his head. "Uh-huh. Some of the chips are sold to sickos for their, uh, entertainment value. But a lot more are sold as cheap alternatives to complex and expensive AI operating systems for all sorts of things. One of them purchased a chip to use to run the air, water, and waste recycling and reclamation systems on an orbital platform in Tau Ceti. Another bought one to run an industrial-scale molecular-printing operation for spaceship parts. And one is using one of the damned things to operate an entertainment system."

I shook my head. "An entertainment system? Why would that require a complicated AI?"

"It doesn't. Which tells you something about that particular customer."

Torina pressed her lips into a thin line. "Yeah, that they're a sadistic asshole who just likes having an enslaved human mind running their collection of porn."

"Give the lady a prize," Perry said.

I clenched my teeth. This was—it was monstrous. I thought of some of the stomach-turning bullshit I'd encountered on the Earthly internet. It was bad. This was worse.

"Do we know who any of the poor bastards are that they've done this to?" I asked.

"Only one that I was able to extract from the data I had available. Her name is S'tila. She is—or was—a younger princess of a desert race, the Srall, who was famously in the media for her, uh, rebellious ways," Perry replied.

"Yeah, I remember her. She was a party girl from a culture famous for their traditional, theocratic ways," Torina said. Her face darkened. "She supposedly died in a spacecraft accident about two years ago. It was big news across the infosphere."

"Emphasis on *supposedly*. In fact, it seems she was actually stripped from her body, and put to work piloting a family pleasure yacht up and down a flowing river of sand unique to her home-world, presumably by her own family. There was a note appended to her file that no copies of her were to ever be made for any purpose since her family considered this chip to actually be her *ka'ja*, a vessel embodying her soul. Apparently, they were purifying her ka'ja with menial labor, in service to her family, to cleanse it of her wicked ways and prepare her for apotheosis, etc."

"Nice people. Remind me not to go to their family picnics," I said.

Torina was shaking her head. "*Copies?* They're making *copies* of these poor people?"

"I guess it's cheaper and easier than making new ones from, you know, scratch," Perry replied.

"Okay, great, just when I thought it couldn't get any worse." I gripped the hilt of the Moonblade and imagined jamming it through Ms. Ruiz-Rocher's skull. "We need to put a stop to this" —I hunted for a word but finally gave up with a shrug—"I don't even know what to call it. I can't think of a word that even starts to fit. Anyway, we need to stop it, permanently."

"We need to do more than that. We can't just stop with their network. We have to free the people they've stolen, too, and it's going to take some time. We have no idea how many lives have been taken."

I nodded. "We start with a list, we get help, and we cut this shit off at the root. Simple, if you ask me. So it takes months, or even years. Isn't that why I'm here? To do good-guy stuff?"

"I've got nothing better planned, aside from being a rich

heiress. And that's really boring." She said it with a grin, but I could see the fierce determination in her eyes. I wanted to give her a massive hug. She was right, she could just return to a life of idle luxury. Instead, she was going to see this through.

"And I'm immortal. You'll both be dead before my batteries run dry," Perry said.

I couldn't resist a laugh. I tapped Perry on his beak. "And that's why we'll always be friends, Perry. You're always so upbeat."

35

THE PEACEMAKERS as a Guild had no better idea than we did regarding Fostin's status. We hung around Anvil Dark for two days while the Masters interviewed him, then conferred behind closed doors. They finally rendered a judgment that Fostin was, from a legal perspective, too sentient to be merely evidence, so he was considered both a victim and a witness. Groshenko confided that the whole situation had sent the Peacemakers' legal arm into overdrive.

"After all, we know of two unfortunates in the same situation —Fostin and the Srall princess. And there seem to be more— maybe many more. It's quite likely this could become an entire subset of interstellar law, in fact. We've already got inquiries coming in from a dozen systems," he said.

Lunzy showed up at the *Fafnir* while Netty and I were pondering how to cable in an enhanced scanner suite we'd claimed as our share of the prize from the *Lawful Windrunner*. It was military-grade stuff, technically not even available on the open market. It would give us better scanner resolution at longer ranges, an improved ability to see through stealth systems and countermeasures, and better fire control, especially for the point-defense battery.

The trouble was, as I was finding out, that space inside a *Dragonet* is at a premium. I'd built a few laptops from components in my time, and it reminded me of that—sort of the electronic version of building a ship in a bottle.

"You need to upgrade to a *Dragon*, Van," Lunzy said, wearing a bemused smile as I cursed through the process of trying to get a torque wrench seated around a bolt that just happened to be on the far side of a structural member.

I had to do it by feel alone. It was a chore that Netty would have normally employed Waldo to do, but Waldo was busy being Fostin, off giving statements to the Masters' legal staff.

I sighed and yanked the wrench out of the narrow space between the inner and outer hull-plates, then placed it gently down on the floor of the scissors lift. I lowered the platform back down and joined Lunzy on the hangar deck.

"I'd love to upgrade to a *Dragon*. I just need a bazillion bonds to do it," I said, wiping my hands on a shop rag.

"Well, I don't have a bazillion bonds to offer you, but I do have a job that'll earn you some pretty good money, especially considering the actual amount of effort involved," she replied.

"What's that?"

"We'd like you to take Fostin home. His people are apparently anxious to have him back and are actually engaging some experts in bio-robotics to build him a permanent, android-style hybrid body. They'd also like to thank and reward the people who rescued him."

Well, this was a no-brainer. "I'd be honored and delighted to take him home."

"Good. Now, put your ship back together because his people are anxious to welcome him back. They're very community-oriented."

We got most of the new scanner suite online but had to give up, at least for now, on the improved point-defense fire control. Groshenko and Lunzy escorted Fostin back to the hangar bay a few hours later, by which time we were ready to fly.

"So it sounds like your people are going to have a new body for you by the time we get there. Just think, it's going to be like being a baby all over again," I said.

Fostin groaned over Waldo's speaker. "Better than being this clanking robot, I suppose, but still—I hate *plustinarek*."

"What the hell is plustinarek?"

Perry answered, projecting an image of wriggling, yellowish grubs in some kind of blue gravy.

"This is plustinarek. It's the Wu'tzur equivalent of baby food," he said.

Fostin groaned again. "Please stop showing me that."

Perry killed the image, and I turned back to Fostin/Waldo.

"You know, I don't say this lightly, but… are you *sure* you don't want to remain a robot?"

THE WU'TZUR HOMEWORLD was far too hot and arid for humans without the protection of at least an environmental suit, which meant Torina and I would be stuck wearing our armor. Instead, they invited us to dock at an orbital platform that maintained several atmospheric and temperature environments, including one designed around humans. We therefore arrived at the designated airlock, docked, and stepped into a steamy rainforest.

I took a breath of the sultry air. "Reminds me of some time I spent in Malaysia during the monsoons. I swear I was breathing as much water as air, kind of like this."

Torina nodded. "I guess this is their idea of a compromise, temperature-wise."

In their natural form, Fostin's people were vaguely apelike bipeds, with two sets of arms, the upper ones heavily muscled, the lower much finer and more dexterous. They were dark-skinned, covered in fine, downy hair, and had heads like flattened domes atop their shoulders. Their eyes, mounted high up on each side of the dome, gave them three hundred and sixty degree vision without having to move their head. The delegation that met us were adorned with gold and silver chains, medallions, and pendants, but wore no other clothes.

"Welcome to Wu'tzur," the one leading the delegation said, the translator rendering her voice smooth and melodic, more like a rhythmic chant than simply talking. "You are Van Tudor, the Peacemaker who rescued Fostin."

I nodded, then introduced Torina and Perry. The Wu'tzur

delegation head acknowledged us with formal bows, then introduced herself as Tsoan, First Rank of the Fourth Assembly—which made her pretty senior, actually, emphasizing the importance they attached to Fostin's return.

Fostin/Waldo rolled forward and immediately engaged the Wu'tzur in an animated dialog that amounted to a really convoluted *welcome home, Fostin.* I knew from the background reading I did on the Wu'tzur on our way here that the culture was extremely fixated on protocol and ceremony. Accordingly, Torina and I simply waited with suitably grave looks on our faces for the aliens to get back to us.

When they did, it was to invite us to a clearing in the artificial rain forest, where a feast had been prepared. I braced myself for another variation on squirming grubs, but the Wu'tzur either had experience with human cuisine or they'd researched it. Instead, we had, of all things, barbecued ribs—and good ones, too. Ribs of *what*, I wasn't entirely sure, nor was I entirely sure I wanted to know. But they were excellent anyway.

Perry, who simply waited patiently while we stuffed our faces with ribs, spoke up. "I'm curious—how was Fostin contacted by his, um, captors? And how did they gain access to him?" he asked Tsoan.

"We were wondering that ourselves, especially since we had no record of any ship corresponding to the period of Fostin's disappearance. Our intelligence secretariat investigated, and determined that they had help—we uncovered a small group of corrupt collaborators working in our customs and border protection services." Tsoan leered something that resembled a grin, but

I wasn't sure if it was that or she was just baring her teeth. "They have been dealt with."

She looked pointedly at the stack of ribs in the middle of the table.

I'd just bitten into one, my second helping, and froze. Silence descended over the proceedings. Out of the corner of my eye, I saw Torina slowly lower the rib she'd been eating.

The Wu'tzur suddenly erupted into raucous braying, like a group of mules had fallen into a wood chipper. It took me a moment to realize it was laughter.

"Ah, that joke never gets old. We haven't eaten anyone in years," Tsoan said.

I managed a half-hearted laugh at that. She just stared at me, and I fell silent.

Which made her start laughing again. "You humans are too damned serious. Life is too short to not fill it with laughter."

I glanced at Torina and shook my head, grinning. It was hard not to like these people.

But Tsoan turned serious again. "Anyway, we were able to determine that the movements of the ship belonging to those"—the next word didn't translate, but I got the profane gist of it—"that victimized Fostin had been concealed by the collaborators. Unfortunately, whether they knew it or not, they also managed to conceal the theft of several weapons from one of our armories."

"What sort of weapons?" I asked.

"Grand Slam anti-ship missiles. Ten of them."

Perry's eyes flashed. "Uh-oh."

I glanced at him. "Uh-oh?"

"Yes. Uh-oh. Grand Slam missiles are high-end military hardware. They're specifically designed for surface-to-space combat. Their manufacturer, a corporation based in the Tau Ceti system, has a spotty record for adhering to export controls, but they've been improving ever since an incident a few years back in the Wolf 424 system. An Eridani Federation battlecruiser was destroyed by one fired from an asteroid, which almost led to a shooting war."

Torina nodded. "The *Stardancer* Incident. I remember that. A whole bunch of commodity prices shot up when the Eridani threatened to impose a quarantine and blockade the system. That would have shut down a lot of interstellar trade, mostly in rare metals."

"So who destroyed the battlecruiser?" I asked. "Did they ever find out?"

"Yes and no. Everyone knew it was the Arc of Vengeance, but no one could prove it. It led to much tighter export controls on Grand Slams," Perry said.

"And now we've got ten of them out there somewhere." I turned to Tsoan. "Do you have any idea what happened to them?"

Tsoan replied by handing over a data chip. Perry accepted it and analyzed it's contents.

"Uh-oh."

I scowled. "Uh-oh again?"

"Yeah. It looks like the Wu'tzur intelligence services have traced the missiles to one of the five founding families of the Arc of Vengeance. They couldn't get Grand Slam missiles from the manufacturer anymore, so they found another way."

I raised a finger. "Wait. Kuthrix and Ruiz-Rocher stole missiles and sold them to the Arc of Vengeance?"

"So it would appear, yeah," Perry replied.

"And Kuthrix and Ruiz-Rocher are also implicated in dealings with our friend back in Chicago?"

"They are."

"So there's a definite line linking the Arc of Vengeance with Earth." I shook my head. "What an unsavory thread to find," I said, thinking of the damage that criminals like that could do to my home.

But it was worse than that. "There are—hell, there are millions of missing people every year. Earth alone could keep criminal assholes like this in business until the sun burns out."

Torina curled a disgusted lip. "And beyond."

"Van, given the nature of these crimes, especially the stolen Grand Slams, you can implement an emergency requisition, whereupon the Peacemaker's Guild will pay for fuel, weapons, and supplies on every successful arrest, and the recovery of every missile." He gave me an amber stare. "The operative word is *successful.*"

"What happens if we fail?" I asked.

"Then we owe a lot of money. Oh, and we all might die and be put into can openers in some vicious criminal's pool-house kitchen or something."

At one time in the not-too-distant past, that might have

deeply unsettled me. But the breathtakingly vile nature of the crimes here, explicit and implied, just pissed me off.

"Sounds about right. Where do we start, other than back at that fuel station where we found Fostin?" I asked.

"Right in this system. Out in their Oort Cloud, in fact, where the Wu'tzur intelligence services have detected ships operating without legitimate transponders. Want to guess as to what they're doing out there?"

"Something we can make money from, by grabbing them, melting their engines, or selling them for scrap?"

Torina smiled. "Attaboy."

WE TOOK A LONG, circuitous route to get to the ships lurking in the Oort Cloud. If we'd driven straight at them, they'd simply have cut and run. So instead we flew out of the system on an apparently unrelated and completely innocent course. Then—and this was the expensive part—we twisted away to the Crossroads system, before twisting right back and returning to the Wu'tzur home system just outside its Oort Cloud. And *then* we'd started our approach, working our way through the Cloud, using it as cover to confuse the scanners of the ships we were stalking. That was the same reason *they* were hanging amid the rocky, icy debris that made up the Cloud, after all.

Or, as Netty put it, "If the Cloud will do it with you, my friends, it will do it to you as well."

The hazardous and sometimes even harrowing part was navigating our long, arcing trajectory through the Cloud. We had to keep our velocity low enough that we could navigate without crashing into things, but also didn't want to spend days picking our way to our targets. It wasn't quite as exciting as outer space movies would have had me believe—the Oort Cloud really wasn't a swirling chaos of rocks flying about in all directions and smashing into each other. It was more a stately procession of lonely rocks and comets at least thousands, and often tens or even hundreds of thousands of kilometers apart. But a mountain-sized comet a few thousand klicks away gets really close and really big really fast if you aren't careful. So we spent almost a full day using the *Fafnir*'s thruster to gently veer our course to slalom around them.

But the convoluted approach paid off. By the time Netty was able to paint three targets on our tactical overlay, they were blissfully unaware of our approach.

"One is a container ship, class four, massing about a hundred thousand tonnes. The other two are workboats, roughly class two. I'm thinking it's a stop-and-drop operation."

I glanced at Torina, who shrugged. "Stop and drop?"

"The big ship is basically a depot for criminals, pirates, and the like to stop and drop off their ill-gotten gains. They get to empty their holds for quick cash—at awful prices, I might add, but they can't really afford to be choosy. The freighter, meanwhile, will haul ass once it's full, sell off anything illicit at places like Dregs or Spindrift, then sanitize the rest of the cargo and sell it back into the open market."

Torina made an impressed face. "Very efficient. There's a whole sleazy little ecosystem out here."

But Perry made a meh sound. "Kind of disappointing, actually."

I raised a brow. "Why?"

"It's just regular old thieves."

"Yeah, but we like stopping them, don't we?"

Perry didn't answer right away. Instead, he waited until our new scanners, which were liberated from the *Lawful Windrunner*, finished painting their output into the overlay. Then he lifted his head and wings slightly.

"When they've got cases of missiles aboard, with a huge reward? Yes, Van. Yes we do."

He gestured with a wingtip at the display. Sure enough, one of the items being loaded aboard the freighter was a rectangular case of the type used to transport missiles.

We discussed how to approach the situation, to take full advantage of the surprise we'd gained. I'd rather have disabled the freighter right away, but we finally decided we needed to take the two smaller ships out of the picture first—they were heavily armed enough to be a threat, while the freighter was really only equipped for self-defense. This risked the freighter making a run for it since it could twist away at any time. But Perry pointed out that with its holds open to receive cargo, it would need some time to get underway—at least fifteen or twenty minutes. We had that long, therefore to knock out the two smaller ships, and disable it.

"Okay, then, everyone, we have a plan," I said. "Netty, weapons-free, if you please."

The weapons came online, as did our targeting systems. The *Lawful Windrunner*'s scanner suite again proved its worth, easily burning through the dust and other detritus floating around in Oort space, giving us three very solid returns. I handled the helm, while Torina did the shooting.

The three ships immediately scrambled about, the freighter racing to shut holds and hatches, the two smaller ships lighting their drives to turn and face us. But Torina was ready and slammed laser fire into one, then the other. The first simply died, going dark when its reactor's safeties scrammed it to avoid an uncontained failure. The second wasn't so lucky and exploded in a dazzling flash that sent a crash of static across the comm system.

An escape boat powered away from the surviving ship. We let it go. Yes, they were criminals, but we had no evidence they were implicated in Crimes Against Life. More importantly, the big score was the freighter, and we wouldn't be able to take care of both. The freighter's crew had already started frantic efforts to get their ship configured for flight and would succeed sometime in the next five to ten minutes.

"I don't think so," Torina said and started snapping out laser shots, methodically shooting apart the freighter's engineering section. She tried hard to avoid hitting the fusion core itself, which showed up on the scanners as like a floodlight made of neutrinos. I eased the *Fafnir* in as close as I could without bringing us within range of the freighter's own point-defenses. The short-ranged weapons were meant to shoot down incoming missiles, but they could be deadly to ships at close range.

I tapped the thrusters, deftly bringing the *Fafnir* to a relative stop, then sat back. "Hey, I'm getting pretty good at this."

"You are, Van. Just remember the golden rule of flying a spaceship," Netty said.

"What's that?"

"Your first collision is probably your last."

"Words to live by."

Torina took advantage of the point-blank range—by outer space standards, anyway—to finish off crippling the freighter. She then demolished the two point-defense batteries. Now fully neutered, the big ship no longer posed a threat, so we moved in.

"Four airlocks, two of them damaged by our shooting beyond repair. A third might be usable, but there's probably significant structural damage inside it," Netty reported.

"Okay, so number four it is," I replied, touching the thruster controls and edging the *Fafnir* even closer.

We'd considered doing a hard-dock since the open airlock had a UDA but decided against it. Our scanners showed at least three life-forms still aboard, just inside it. Rather than risk having the *Fafnir* counter-boarded, we stopped about fifty meters off, then Perry and I launched ourselves across the gap for a contested boarding.

I glanced down as we sailed across the gap. That tug of vertigo that made my stomach want to flip-flop was still there, bubbling away inside me, but it wasn't anywhere near as bad. I put my attention back on the freighter, which was now looming like a wall ahead.

We both stopped ourselves against the scarred flank of the ship.

"Perry, are those three assholes still in there?"

"They are, yeah. And the ship's pressurized behind the inner airlock door. I guess you could say they're *lurking*, waiting for us to cycle through the lock."

"Lurking is bad. Lurking implies they have less than noble intentions. Time to introduce myself, I guess."

Since they'd decided to keep the ship, or at least the undamaged parts of it, pressurized, we decided to make things easier on ourselves. Perry hacked the outer airlock door, then I entered and planted a breaching charge on the inner door. I also drew the Moonsword and hacked through anything resembling safeties or emergency equipment inside the lock. I sliced away every handhold I saw, for good measure. Then I withdrew from the airlock and moved a few meters away along the hull. Perry did likewise. Torina eased the *Fafnir* out of the way.

I triggered the charge.

The effect was spectacular. A flash pulsed from inside the lock, then a cylinder of mist erupted from it and shot away from the freighter, carrying all manner of loose odds and ends. That included three suited figures.

Now, space is big. Very, very big. Netty's witticism about collisions notwithstanding, the chances of one happening were miniscule.

But miniscule wasn't zero, as these three poor bastards found out. They'd suited up but hadn't taken any precautions against a deliberate explosive decompression of their ship. The venting atmosphere swept them out of their ship, across over a kilometer of empty space, until they each slammed into the slowly spinning wreckage of the smaller ship that had survived our initial attack. I winced as all three rebounded and drifted off in random directions.

"Um, I find you three guilty of serious crimes. Best of luck out there."

"Great speech, boss," Perry said. "Really gave me chills."

"I COULD GET USED TO THIS," I said, counting my bonds. "That is, until we disconnect from the fuel barge and pay the docking fees, and hangar fees, and navigation fees, and holy shit are there ever a lot of fees. I'll never get used to that."

Torina shot me a mischievous grin. "Okay, dad. What are you going to complain about next? The cost of lunch?"

It was a good score. We handed over the remains of the two ships and their cargoes to the Wu'tzur for salvage costs and also returned eight of their ten stolen Grand Slam missiles. Two had been destroyed in the fracas, but I was quite happy to simply return their property. The Wu'tzur had insisted on paying us a reward, though, and I only objected enough to make a show of it.

As we backed away from the Wu'tzurs' orbital platform, I frowned at the navigation display. "So, where to next? Back to Anvil Dark?"

"Actually, we just received a Guild Edict, Van. The Masters want us to crack open another fuel station at Alpha Centauri.

They've got reason to believe there might be more like Fostin there, working as slave labor," Perry said.

"Huh. Alright, then." Guild Edicts were rare because they entitled Peacemakers to full compensation for their costs, plus a stipend, on completion of the assigned task. I'd already come to learn that the Guild tried to download most routine operating costs onto individual Peacemakers—hence the constant need for paying jobs. But while enforcing the Edict, our costs were covered.

Perry leaned in between Torina and me. "Actually, Van, I have a suggestion. Since you're currently flush with cash, I think it's time for you to put the Moonsword back on the anvil and make another upgrade." His amber gaze met mine. "Frankly, you're getting involved in some increasingly hairy stuff, and I think you're going to need it."

I nodded in the face of Perry's ominous wisdom.

"Starsmith, here we come."

36

"OKAY, just keep in mind that this blade is now razor sharp. With this upgrade, it has a virtually monatomic edge, reinforced by a structural integrity field energized by a power cell in the hilt," Linulla said, handing me the blade fresh from his forge.

I cast a critical eye over the blade. It had a shimmer to it, and indeed the edge had a slightly translucent quality to it, as though the blade didn't stop as much as it simply seemed to fade away.

"So do I have to change the batteries from time to time?" I asked.

"Actually, no, you don't. Or at least not unless you leave it sitting somewhere for more than a week or so. The power cell is recharged by the act of moving the sword around."

I gave the blade an experimental swing, being careful not to let anything—including parts of me—get in the way. "It actually feels lighter."

"That's because it *is* lighter. About a quarter of the blade's mass is removed with this overlay. Oh, and in addition to suppressing comms around it, you'll notice it also has a slight diffusion effect on light, meaning that while it's drawn, you'll be a little harder to see. The effect isn't as pronounced going the other way, so your own vision shouldn't be inhibited." Linulla raised a claw. "But don't expect too much from that. You are a long way from being invisible. It just might give you an edge in low-light situations."

I nodded and sheathed the blade, again being careful not to inadvertently cut my own hip open. "Thanks, Linulla. I appreciate it." I gave him a wry smile. "I guess I *should* appreciate it, considering how much it cost."

"Remember—good, fast, or cheap. You can have any two of those."

Perry spoke up. "I'm going to give you the same lecture I gave your grandfather when he had this upgrade done, Van. The Moonsword was lethal before, and now it's doubly so. You should only draw it if you intend to use it, and by use it, I mean to kill someone."

I gave him a curious glance. "You say that as though there have been problems with Peacemakers and their swords in the past."

"Let's just say that more than a few wanted criminals have bled out after being slashed by a Moonsword. If that's the outcome you want, fine. But if it isn't, then don't draw the thing. We've lost more than a few sources of potentially valuable intelligence to Peacemakers who get overly enthusiastic with their very, very sharp blades."

"Duly noted," I replied.

"Now, as for your vambraces, they're completed, too," Linulla said, scuttling over to his workbench. The vambraces were reinforced forearm pieces incorporated into my Peacemaker armor. Perry had recommended them, since even after the Moonsword's upgrade I still had enough bonds for more discretionary spending. The vambraces were one of the less expensive upgrades to the armor but also one of the most useful.

He handed them to me, and I slid them over the sleeves of my armor. They fit securely, locking themselves into place on small mounting grommets just below my elbow. In addition to giving me dramatically improved protection for my forearms, they could be used actively, blocking both impact blows and slashing attacks with edged weapons. The Moonsword could probably cut through them, but anything less wasn't likely to. They also incorporated touch pads to control future upgrades to the armor.

"You're definitely looking the part," Torina said when we'd said our farewells to Linulla and returned to the *Fafnir*. "Spiffy Moonsword and those vambraces, it's all coming together."

I glanced down at my bulkier forearms. "I feel like Popeye."

"Who?"

"Popeye. You know, the cartoon character with the grossly enlarged forearms, eats spinach to get super strong, laughs *yuk-yuk-yuk*—" I stopped at her blank look.

"What the hell are you talking about?" she asked.

I smiled. "I can see you have some woeful gaps in your education, my dear. I'm going to have to introduce you to Earthly cartoons, one of the highest artforms in known space."

As we accelerated away from Starsmith, Netty spoke up.

"Well, that's interesting."

I glanced at Torina, who just lifted an eyebrow.

"You know, Netty, that's just a variation on asking me to come take a look at something. Which I'm perfectly willing to do, of course, but——"

"There's a Yonnox ship, a class nine fast freighter, calling for assistance just over two light-years away."

I smiled. "Aw, yeah. It's our time to shine."

Perry cocked his head at me. "Touch theatrical, Van, don't you think? And by theatrical, I mean like a high-school production of King Lear the Musical".

I frowned. "King Lear isn't a musical."

"No, it isn't, is it? That's because some things just shouldn't be done, like saying *it's our time to shine*. We're lethal agents of justice, not——"

"I get it. I'll glower more," I cut in, scanning the display to verify our course. "You know, make it very *High Plains Drifter*. That should be suitably badass."

Perry bobbed his head. "Sullen glowering is appropriately badass, I agree. After all, our brand is important."

"Torina, can you glower?" I asked.

"I was thinking more of a cold, indifferent stare. That way, we can do *bad-ass cop, uncaring cop*."

I had to laugh. "So you are familiar with Earthly culture—just not cartoons, huh?"

"You've intrigued me, Van Tudor, enough that I've decided to start studying your quaint little planet in my off time," she said.

"Quaint? Really?"

"Really."

I shrugged. "Could be worse things to be called than quaint. Anyway, shall we race to the rescue of our Yonnox friends?"

"By all means. Just make sure you count your fingers—and your toes, for that matter—after you're done shaking hands with them."

WE DID a slow pass around the Yonnox ship. It had been badly damaged in a clearly deliberate attack, judging from the blast marks and laser scars gouged into its hull. Debris drifted around it in a cloud, while a fitful leak of atmospheric gas shimmered in a long, meandering trail.

We actually hadn't been the first on the scene. The first arrivals had been a bulk carrier hauling ore to Tau Ceti, and an Eridani Federation diplomatic cutter. The first had been sniffing around salvage rights, but since the Yonnox ship was still technically underway, it didn't qualify. They moved on when we arrived. So did the cutter, which had stopped to lend emergency assistance if necessary, as interstellar commerce law required.

When we arrived, though, they were quite happy to make it our problem and move on.

"Yonnox ship, this is Peacemaker Tudor aboard the *Fafnir*. Prepare to be boarded so that we can render assistance."

"This is the part where they say they don't need help," Perry muttered.

"That's okay, Peacemaker, we don't need help."

I glanced at Perry, who shrugged his wings. "Can I call 'em or what? No doubt they've got all sorts of contraband on board and would rather take their chances limping to a safe port."

"Can I legally force the issue?"

"Yes and no. Yes, insofar as they did broadcast a distress signal. That means they could be the subject of a hijacking. No, because they've specifically declined our help."

I looked at Torina. "I don't know about you, but I heard Perry say *yes*."

"So did I," she agreed.

We announced our intentions, then I maneuvered the *Fafnir* in close to one of the Yonnox ship's UDAs. I let Netty make the final maneuvers and establish a hard docking.

We cycled the airlock, and I, complete with vambraces and preternaturally sharp Moonsword, strode through it. Torina and Perry followed. We were walloped by a stink of burning insulation and hot electronics. Grey smoke fumed the air. A Yonnox in a pressure suit greeted us, and by greeted us, I mean blocked our way forward.

"It really isn't necessary for you to come aboard, Peacemaker," he said. "We've got the situation well under control."

I touched my comm. "Netty, can you give us a status report on this Yonnox ship?"

"Certainly. Its drive is offline, as is its reactor. It's running on fission-battery backup. Forty percent of the ship, including its engineering section, is decompressed. It has suffered some severe hull integrity degradation, and will be limited in its ability to accelerate or maneuver."

"Thank you, Netty." I gave the Yonnox a bemused smile. "You know, I'm not a spaceship engineer, but all that would seem to me to qualify your ship as—oh, what's the technical term? Oh, right. *Broken*."

"Even so, we're more than capable—"

I held up a hand. "Please, I won't hear of it. Leaving you here without rendering assistance would be unconscionable of me. Now, then, how many souls on board?"

I heard Torina suppress a laugh over the comm. The Yonnox variously blustered, pleaded, simpered, and even offered a bribe —a big one, too. All that did was make me more determined to see just what they had on board.

I started to politely, but firmly push past the Yonnox, one hand pointedly holding The Drop's holster, the other resting on the pommel of the Moonsword. In the middle of the commotion and waving Yonnox appendages, Netty cut in.

"Van, another Yonnox ship just twisted into the system, and is now heading this way."

We all stopped and went momentarily silent. I glanced at Perry. I wasn't sure what happened now. Technically, I didn't really have any probable cause to search this ship, aside from this

Yonnox's determination to not let me. And now that another Yonnox ship was here, I wasn't sure if I could still claim to be boarding to *render assistance*. My implanted memories didn't offer an answer, so I was about to pull back to consult with Perry and Torina, when the Yonnox themselves made the decision for me.

"Van, the newly arrived Yonnox ship is launching missiles," Netty said flatly.

I gaped at Perry and Torina for a moment. "They're attacking a Peacemaker?"

I realized, of course, that the Peacemakers were as liable to be attacked as anyone, but to do so without provocation, and openly, with other potential witnesses around, seemed pretty reckless.

Or—

I spun back on the Yonnox. "Who attacked you? Who damaged your ship?"

"I... don't know—"

I swept out the Moonsword. The Yonnox yelped.

"You know, I was just told not that long ago to not draw this blade unless I intended to use it. If you don't answer, and do it truthfully and right now, I'm going to assume you're in league with those other Yonnox out there, which makes you an imminent threat, which means I *will* use this thing." I brandished the blade right in the Yonnox's face. "Got it?"

"Yes. Fine. That other ship—it attacked us. It's an unfortunate... disagreement. A dispute over property, nothing more." The Yonnox began to flail several of its appendages. "So I'm requesting your aid! We need your help, to protect us from those —" Another word didn't translate. Apparently, the translation database didn't stock alien profanities, although Perry had informed me it was available as paid DLC, downloadable content.

I nodded. "Fine. Perry, can you access this ship's weapons?"

He answered by hopping to a nearby dataport and plugging into it. "This would go a lot faster if I didn't have to hack into the system. That's what we call a hint, you greedy wicker basket with eyeballs."

"Give him the password," I snapped at the Yonnox. He did, and Perry immediately accessed the ship's fire control system. While he worked, I asked Torina to go back and get ready to undock the *Fafnir*, and keep her finger hovering over the *Haul Ass* control.

"Ready to fire, Van," Perry said.

"Do it. Everything you can."

The Yonnox ship shuddered as missile launchers coughed out their ordnance. Perry put the single laser battery into continuous fire mode, then disconnected. As the laser fired, the lights and ventilation systems being powered by the backup fission batteries flickered and faltered.

"That laser is only firing at about one-third power, Van, just so you know," Perry said.

I tapped my comm. "Netty, any change out there?"

"Aside from missiles now flying in both directions, no. And the other Yonnox ship is—"

The deck thumped under my feet, and I heard a roar of escaping atmosphere from somewhere aft.

"—firing its lasers now."

"Shit. Okay, Perry, let's go."

The Yonnox grabbed at me. "Wait! You can't just leave!"

"I am not going to stand here while your cousins out there blast this ship apart around me," I snapped and hurried back toward the *Fafnir*. The Yonnox resumed his aggravating mix of begging, cajoling, threatening, and bribing, following us to the airlock with it. I actually had to threaten him with The Drop to prevent him from coming aboard the *Fafnir*.

"Don't you have a crew?"

"I've just resigned my commission. I'm now a private citizen, claiming refugee status—"

"Nice try." I shoved the Yonnox back into the airlock and sealed the outer door.

"Okay, Torina, we're—"

The *Fafnir* had already disconnected and accelerated hard away from the Yonnox ship. We had a few tense moments as we waited to see if any of the inbound missiles were targeted at us. But they weren't, which meant we had ringside seats to the destruction of the Yonnox ship we'd just escaped. The second Yonnox ship didn't escape without damage, though, taking several solid missile strikes.

And then, unbelievably, it *did* open fire on us.

"You know, I was about to say something about how this was just an internecine argument between Yonnox rivals, and then they went ahead and did that," Netty said, flashing the inbound missiles onto the tactical overlay.

"Probably because they knew that a Peacemaker wasn't going

to sit idly by while one ship destroyed another in a public space lane," Torina said. "Right, Van?"

Actually, I'd been going to do just that because, after all, we had more urgent business, such as the Guild Edict we'd been given. But Torina had a point. This had been what amounted to piracy. So I nodded.

"Yes, absolutely. This is entirely inappropriate and unacceptable," I said, prompting a wry grin from Torina. She wheeled the *Fafnir* around and we closed back on the Yonnox ship, shooting down its incoming missiles with a combination of laser and point-defense fire. The Yonnox kept up a steady laser fire as we approached, apparently having expended all of their missiles, but Perry urged caution.

"Sometimes clever bastards will try and lure other ships in by pretending to be out of missiles, then open fire with a salvo at point-blank range."

I nodded and redirected our laser fire at the two missile launchers mounted on the top and bottom of the Yonnox ship. I wrecked one, but we took three laser hits in return that scoured gouges into our ablative armor and damaged two of our maneuvering thrusters. Cursing, I fired the glitter caster, shrouding us in a shimmering cloud of reflective particles. Then I turned to Torina and Perry, opening my mouth to ask for recommendations—

When the Yonnox ship abruptly exploded in what was obviously an uncontained reactor failure.

We eased our way out of the glitter cloud and took stock. The first Yonnox ship was a battered wreck, breaking apart. The other was just a rapidly cooling cloud of plasma.

As we went weapons-tight, I sat back. "Well, that was exciting. Entirely pointless, but exciting."

"Not entirely pointless," Torina said.

I shot her a questioning look.

"We know that the Yonnox can turn on one another. That means the Yonnox can be *turned* on one another."

I had to admit that was right. Perry summed it up even better.

"This is one smart lady."

37

THE FUEL DEPOT we'd been sent to investigate turned out to be a sort of dreary jackpot. Not only did we locate eleven enslaved memory chips similar to Fostin's there, we were also able to bust open an entire underground operation. It turned out that at least seventeen different ships had been making clandestine visits there to fuel up, all of it happening entirely off the books. The depot had, in effect, become a gas station for bad guys.

"This list of ne'er-do-wells is going to keep us busy for a long time," Torina said, frowning at the data scrolling across the screen between the *Fafnir*'s pilots and copilot's seats. "Oh—well, damn. I went to school with her," she said, pointing at a name.

"Were you guys friends?" I asked.

Torina sniffed. "Hardly. She was a bitch."

"And she would have referred to you as…?"

"Nothing but charm and sweetness, of course."

"Naturally."

One name, though, stood out and brought us to a rendezvous with Lunzy on the outskirts of the Wolf 424 system.

"Emil Hoffsinger," she said as we sat drinking beer. Not her best stuff this time but still pretty good. "Mister Hoffsinger has now been implicated in enough sordid little affairs that the Masters have decided it's time to bring him in, charge him, then do some good, old fashioned plea bargaining for his testimony." She looked at me over her beer. "That's where you come in, Van. The Masters have decided they want you to bring in Hoffsinger."

I glanced at Torina. "Chicago, here we come."

"Actually, it's going to take a few days to get the warrants sorted out. Hoffsinger ain't dumb, and he has some powerful friends. The warrants need to be as airtight as a docking adapter. To that end, the Masters have Bester looking them over."

"And there's your few days. Bester and his people are known to carefully consider all of the implications of every word, every phrase, every comma and period. They just don't do it very quickly," Perry put in.

"But they do it thoroughly. No warrant verified by Bester and his people has ever failed a legal challenge. In the meantime, though, we'd like you to go to Earth and prepare to arrest Hoffsinger."

"So just go chill on Earth, waiting to grab this guy?"

"Something like that. It's of the utmost importance Hoffsinger be taken alive, though, Van," Lunzy said, giving me a hard look.

"Message received, loud and clear."

We landed in the wooded ravine we'd used for our previous surreptitious visit to Hoffsinger, when we'd planted the data tap. It was still working, still providing us with decent intelligence, and a quick walk through his neighborhood showed that nothing had really changed.

Aside from the season. I was a little surprised, actually, to find that during the weeks we'd been away, winter had passed, and spring was in full bloom. Since we had a few days yet to wait, I turned to Torina with a grin as we climbed back into space.

"Torina, remember when I asked you if you wanted to see corn?"

She looked at me with suspicion. "Is this some kind of mating ploy? Is corn hallucinogenic?"

Perry actually howled with laughter, a surreal and somewhat frightening experience given that he was neither human nor equipped with a mouth. When he finally stopped the raucous noise that was his version of a belly laugh, he actually put a companionable wing around Torina's shoulders. "I think you'll find just the opposite to be true. You see, Van is from Iowa. Iowa is in a region called the Midwest. And corn is grown in the Midwest."

"And you're telling me my virtue is safe because of this —Iowa?"

Perry managed to wink—again, quite a feat for the AI that seemed to consist of him dimming and then brightening one amber eye. "On the contrary. Midwesterners are as randy as any other variety of human. In fact, their birth rates are—"

"Excuse me, Dr. Love, but can we hold up on the reproductive tendencies of people in the corn belt? I'd like to show Torina my family farm, and share my history, you innuendo-spewing dullard."

"Dullard? Huh. Not the word I expected, but probably the one I deserved. Though not as much as the innuendo-spewing part. Where are you taking her first?"

I thought for a moment, staring at the broad, sweeping arc of blue and swirling white that was the Earth from thirty-odd thousand klicks up. We were looking down on the Indian Ocean, so I could make out western Australia to the right, Madagascar and Africa to the left, and the triangular spike of India across the top of the curve. Not for the first time, I had a real moment of, *holy shit, I'm actually in space*. Strangely, that only seemed to happen here, when I was looking down on Earth.

I rubbed my chin. "I think we'll start with the Cheese Castle in Kenosha. That's in Wisconsin."

Before Perry could laugh or wink or offer any other smart-assed responses, Torina smiled and clapped her hands twice. "I've got no idea what a Kenosha or a Wisconsin is, but I love cheese. All ahead full, please."

I gave Perry a look of triumph and kicked the drive, sending us hurtling back toward re-entry.

I LET Netty settle the *Fafnir* into the barn, whose roof slid silently closed. She powered down the ship, and Torina, Perry, and I disembarked.

The sun was just rising over, sure enough, fields of corn. A dawn chill hardened the air, just short of frost.

Torina stopped outside the barn and looked around. "It's really not that different than—" But she stopped and wrinkled her nose. "What is that *smell?*"

I breathed in, wondering what she'd smelled. All I noticed was the rich, earthy tang of—

"Fertilizer," I said.

"Really?"

"Yeah. You know, animal shit."

Her eyes widened. "What?"

I gave her a bit of a *duh* look. "Animal shit. Fertilizer. You know."

"Wait. Am I led to believe that you use *animal waste* as fertilizer?"

"Well, not me personally. But, yeah. Why wouldn't you?"

"Because it's nasty? Gross? I mean—ewww."

I laughed. "Farmers can use chemical fertilizers, but they cost money. If you've got animals, their poop is free, and it contains a whole bunch of soil nutrients—nitrates, phosphates, organics—"

"What about disease?"

I smiled sweetly. "Don't know about you, my dear, but we wash our food when it comes out of the ground."

We carried on into the farmhouse. It was just as I'd left it, aside from a note stuck to the refrigerator with a magnet embedded in a plastic apple. It was written in Miryam's flowing script, listing things she'd done in my absence, such as paying bills —and reminding her I owed her fee, less the friends and family discount. And speaking of fees—

"Shit."

Torina walked up beside me and stopped, both of us looking out the front window.

"Are you talking about fertilizer again?" she asked.

"Only indirectly." I pointed out the window at a car sitting in the driveway.

"Interesting. Some sort of ground vehicle, right?"

"Yes. A rented one. That I drove here from the airport in Des Moines. That I was supposed to return within two days." I glanced at her. "I forgot about it."

"Well, you had a lot on your mind. Like outer space."

"It does have a way of distracting you, yeah."

While I called the rental company to assure them that their car hadn't been stolen, and that I'd simply been called away on urgent business—and I was *so* tempted to add "off-planet" just for the hell of it—Torina spent some time looking around. It turned out that the rental agency was more than happy to take my money and call it all good, and I eventually found Torina in my bedroom.

I stopped in the doorway. "Wow, flashbacks."

She turned from a poster on the wall, one depicting the space shuttle atop the modified Boeing 747 that used to haul it around. It suddenly looked so… quaint.

"Flashbacks to what?"

"To every fantasy teenaged me had about having a beautiful woman in here."

She glanced from me, to the bed, then back, and made a face. "I don't need to know any more than that, thanks."

"No, you don't."

WE SPENT the rest of the day drinking coffee and wandering the farm, with me explaining Earthly lore to Torina. It struck me that the story of our planet was fantastically complex, which made me realize that every planet I'd encountered, dozens of them, had histories as rich, and complicated, and nuanced, and sometimes ridiculous or infuriating, as Earth did. When I thought about the sum total of all that stuff, I was quiet for a moment or three. The galaxy was... complicated.

Our fields were fallow, but Gramps didn't really own a lot of land, for reasons I now considered obvious—when would he possibly be able to find time to plant, maintain, and harvest them? That isn't to say he didn't grow anything at all, but it was never the main point. Gramps had clearly chosen the farm in Iowa for its solitude, not his life's work.

We eventually ended up down by the creek that meandered between our property and that of the farm next door. It was a sluggish little waterway, nestled between muddy banks lined with trees, elms and a few oaks. I watched a leaf making its lazy way downstream, and wondered if it would make it to the Mississippi, and how long that would take. We spent some time there, enjoying the peace and quiet.

"I could get used to this," Torina said.

"Really? You strike me as more cosmopolitan than that."

"You've been to my homeworld, Van. Did it strike you as a cosmopolitan place?"

I thought about the rolling fields, now restored by the Synergists to their former, wild glory, the forests, the orchards, and smiled. "So you're a farm girl, then?"

She shrugged. "I'm not exactly that, either. I like people and socializing, parties and clubs and the like, sure. But I also like sitting beside a slow stream under some trees, watching the clouds waft past—in a sky that's way too blue, by the way."

"Sorry, *blue sky* came with the place."

"I'm used to a touch of mauve, myself."

We'd been lounging against the trees; I sat up. "Torina, why are you here?"

"Because I followed you? I mean, you're the one who knows your way around the place."

"Not what I mean. Why are you here, aboard the *Fafnir*? Isn't it—I don't know."

"Beneath me?"

"Well, when you put it like that, it sounds bad."

She smiled and sat up. "You sound like my family. They are not happy that I'm zipping around space with you, instead of sitting in board meetings and socializing with clients, networking, that sort of thing."

"And what do you tell them when they ask why?"

Torina stared into the water for a moment. My leaf had barely drifted more than a few meters downstream.

She turned back. "Do you know what it's like being rich, Van?"

"I absolutely do not, no. Though it's not for lack of trying."

"Being rich is—it's work. And I know that sounds strange because everyone thinks that rich people live in idle luxury. And some do. But my family's wealth comes from a business empire, and business empires take work to run." She stretched out her legs. "Boring work. Tedious work. Detail-oriented, laborious work."

She shrugged again. "For reasons even I don't understand, I don't really want that. I don't want to sit in board meetings and rub elbows with clients and suppliers and investors. I want to—" She smiled. "I want to fly around the galaxy, fighting bad guys. Why do you think I became so adept at martial arts, and piloting a ship, and using its weapons? Those sorts of skills aren't in much demand for the CEO of a large corporation."

"Well, I have to be honest, I'm glad, Torina. I guess I don't quite get it—but then, maybe I do. I became very, very good at cyber-ops, but it wasn't my first choice. I wanted to follow in my father's and grandfather's footsteps. And, yes, I realize I have stepped into my grandfather's space-boots, but remember, I only knew of him as a very Earth-bound soldier until pretty recently. Anyway, that was what I wanted. What I got was hours and hours and hours of sitting in front of a keyboard and mouse."

"So we're both afflicted with some sort of wanderlust," she said.

"Wanderlust, with some combat built into it, yeah."

We eventually ambled off, crossing onto the neighbor's property to walk among the corn. It was newly planted in the black soil, and still barely shoulder-high.

"It gets a lot higher than this, easily way above your head," I said. "It can actually get a little scary. I got lost in this very corn-field when I was, oh, twelve, maybe? Or thirteen? Anyway, I ended up running blindly and crying, I got so freaked out by corn all around me, not letting me see more than a few meters in any direction."

Torina nodded. "We've got a crop like that back home. It's called *thryza*, a native species similar to, um, wheat, I guess. It grows pretty tall, too. And, yes, I got lost in it once."

"Did you cry and run blindly?"

"No."

"Really?"

"Maybe a little." She stopped and looked down. "Wait. Am I standing in animal scat?"

"There's a reason the soil's as black as space."

"Yuck—"

A sudden rush of wings cut her off. Perry wheeled over top of us, then plunked down amid the corn. His head poked above it, but the rest of him had vanished among the green stalks.

"We have it. The warrants came through. Time to go get paid," he said. "And to do some justice, of course."

38

WE CONSIDERED TRYING to land the *Fafnir* closer to Hoffsinger's house on the cul de sac, so when we snatched him, we wouldn't have as far to try and move him back to the ship. But the only other realistic place to ground the *Fafnir* was a small park on the corner, where the cul de sac met another street. The problem with it was that it was dotted with enough trees, swings, slides and other playground equipment that we couldn't set down without inflicting obvious damage to it—and, although unlikely, possibly to the *Fafnir* herself. I wasn't anxious to repair the damage done by having a teeter-totter get caught up in the *Fafnir*'s landing gear, so we considered just landing on the street in front of his house.

But that raised another issue that Torina pointed out. "Hoffsinger must know by now that at least part of his evil little supply chain has been compromised. I mean, we did snatch the *Lawful*

Windrunner from his contacts, right? So he's probably going to be on the alert."

"It's a good point, Van. He might have even acquired tech to detect the *Fafnir*," Netty put in.

We finally decided that a low, slow approach back into the wooded ravine was our best bet. Once we'd grabbed Hoffsinger and had him under control, Netty would bring the *Fafnir* in basically on his front lawn, and we'd load him aboard.

This time, Torina and I both went. Perry flew ahead, scouting and relaying information back. Aside from the season, he reported that nothing had changed around Hoffsinger's house.

"Except for his neighbors two doors down. They're putting in an in-ground pool. Do they know how little that adds to the property value? In some cases, it even reduces—"

"Perry, we're here as interstellar cops on a sensitive mission to arrest a dangerous offender, not as realtors," I said.

"Sorry, boss."

I wore my trusty duster coat over my armor, the Moonsword and the Drop. Torina had acquired a stroller coat that likewise covered her own armor and sidearm but left her legs free—and the uniform leggings didn't, at distance, look much different from cargo pants.

Despite it being nearly midnight, we were definitely overdressed for the weather, which was a lot warmer than the last time I'd been here. We reached the cul de sac and started a casual amble. Torina even took my hand and held it.

I glanced at her. "Something you want to tell me?"

"Uh, well, aside from something like, if you make any more

smart-assed remarks about me holding your hand I might accidentally break your fingers—no, I'm good." She smiled sweetly as she said.

I sniffed. "Romance is dead."

"And buried."

We walked past Hoffsinger's place. Torina studied a data-slate as though she held a cell-phone and was texting away on it, a trick I'm proud to say she learned from me. She shook her head.

"Our bug is still working up in that tree, and there's that anomalous power signature you and Perry detected last time coming from his house, but that's it," she said, tapping her thumbs randomly against the slate's case.

We'd already reviewed the data from the bug, but it was designed only to tap into data transmitted via comms, not conduct detailed surveillance. It didn't tell us much about the immediate situation.

We carried on just past Hoffsinger's front yard, then stopped where a hedge blocked the view back to his house. "So what do you think?" Torina asked me.

I touched my comm. "Perry, anything to report?" I glanced up, but Perry was wheeling somewhere a few hundred meters above, invisible against the night sky.

"Looks like his next door neighbors got themselves a dog. It's out in the backyard in a shockingly large, fenced-in run. Makes no sense to cage a dog. They're meant to roam. Like me."

"Damn. A dog?" I replied, then looked at Torina. "I really don't want to have to hurt a dog."

"I absolutely agree," Torina replied. "I have only one question. What's a dog?"

While I took a moment to explain the concept of canine pets to Torina, Perry did a few low passes over the house. The dog was the only complicating factor. If it weren't for that, we could pretty much walk into the backyard, right up to Hoffsinger's door.

I frowned into the darkness. Spaceships, twist drives that could move them lightyears at a hop, advanced AIs, and we had nothing to deal with a dog. Unless, that is, we wanted to vaporize or blow it to bits, which we could do several ways. But I didn't want to hurt the dog. For one, I loved dogs. In fact, I was a sucker for animals of all sorts. For another, the dog's owners probably loved their furry beast. And, of course, there was the practical side of it. Unless we could *silently* silence the dog, then the proverbial bark really *would* be worse than the bite.

"I can't believe we don't have some sort of weapon that can just, you know, stun something without hurting it. A non-lethal gadget would seem to be a pretty basic law enforcement tool," I grumbled.

"Uh, Van, you do. You've got The Drop," Perry said.

"The Drop? It's a massive gun. Do you have a different idea of what *non-lethal* means than I do?"

"Yes, the gun part is big and loud and very lethal. But the underslung pulse gun can be dialed back to a non-lethal charge. It even scans a target, up to ten meters away and configures the pulse for maximum stun effect with minimal injury."

"It can?"

"You didn't know that?"

"Well, it's not like Gramps left me a user manual for the damned thing, and it's never occurred to me to ask until now." I drew The Drop and examined it.

Torina glanced around. "Uh, Van, are you sure it's a good idea to brandish a gun like that?"

"This is Chicago. We're fine."

Perry talked me through setting the pulse gun to the lowest stun setting, something accomplished with a small, recessed dial in the butt of the hand grip. "Oh, and your grandfather did leave you an owner's manual, by the way. It's in that list of reading I recommended for you, oh, weeks ago."

"I've been busy," I said, holstering The Drop, then nodding to Torina. "Okay, let's go."

I drew the Moonsword, keeping it tucked under the duster coat, to disrupt comms and hopefully security cameras with it. Then we slipped along the far side of the hedge from Hoffsinger's house, creeping into the backyard of the neighbors without the dog, the ones building the pool. Their backyard was a sprawl of muddy grass and dirt piles around a big hole. An adorably tiny excavator was parked beside it. It actually worked in our favor, giving us ample cover while we worked our way into Hoffsinger's backyard.

I drew The Drop and very, very carefully made my way across the lawn, using some shrubs as cover. Torina followed, managing to be much quieter than I was—of course.

I stopped briefly as the unreality of the moment hit me like a slap in the face. Here I was creeping through the yard of a suburban Chicago house, intent on arresting a man for literal identity theft so he could be transported to stand trial dozens of lightyears away. If, while I was sitting in the driveway in the rental car reading my grandfather's will, someone had asked me to come up with the most wild and outlandish direction I could imagine my life going from there—let's just say that *interstellar cop* probably wouldn't have made the top ten of that list.

We reached the far side of the yard. I had The Drop in hand, ready to stun the poor pooch next door. But I hadn't seen or heard a thing from the other side of the fence.

Curious, I peeked over it, looked around, then down.

Right into a big, black nose framed by a pair of glinting eyes. I heard panting.

I froze. The dog stood, his tail wagging like a windshield wiper on high. I heard panting and slobbering and a faint whine of anticipation, and instantly recognized his distinct shape. He was an enormous mastiff, with a head like a bucket and extra skin everywhere. And extra drool. Actually, he was just plain *extra*.

"If you're supposed to be a guard dog," I whispered, "you're not very good at it."

I couldn't resist reaching over the fence and scratching the dog's huge head. Torina joined me.

"This is a dog?"

"In the furry flesh."

The dog turned to Torina, his tail becoming a blur. She wrinkled her nose. "Not to put too fine a point on it, but it stinks."

"What a thing to say. That's the smell of love. And damp dog. But mostly love."

Torina had tucked away a couple of energy bars in a belt-pouch, in case we got stuck on a lengthy stakeout. I asked her to produce one, and offered it to the dog. I think he managed to swallow it without it touching the sides of his gullet. His tale whipped back and forth so fast I swear we'd soon be hearing tiny sonic booms from its tip, and he followed his snack with a belch that would make a barfly applaud.

"Um, what is the beast's name?" Torina asked, casting a gimlet eye at our new friend.

"Dunno. He hasn't told me yet."

"Are you saying this monster can speak?" Torina asked, incredulous.

Which was a really bad thing to say out loud because the mastiff cut loose with a single bark that rattled my eardrums.

"Maybe don't use the s-p-e-a-k word, okay?" I said, opening my mouth to pop my ears.

Torina stared, dumbfounded. "Dogs are complicated."

At that, the mastiff licked her arm—or at least most of it—in one movement and then peered up at Torina with small, twinkling eyes.

"By all the stars, I've been—"

"Geezed. We call it geeze, and you'll survive," I told Torina. "You stay here, buddy. Stay. Okay?"

The dog, choosing that moment to exhibit excellent manners, sat down placidly. He stayed, and we began our stalk to the house once again.

Someone moved just inside Hoffsinger's back door.

I glanced at Torina. Her eyes had gone as wide as mine. We

both stepped back and pressed ourselves against the house on either side of the door.

A thump, and the inside door opened. A light snapped on overhead, and I snapped one eye closed to preserve my night vision, an old army trick. I could tell someone stood just inside the outer, screen door, peering into the darkness. The dog, for his part, kept up an erratic incessant barking, our unwitting ally in flushing out Hoffsinger.

I heard the door unlatch, and readied The Drop.

It swung open—right into my face. Oops. But Torina was ready. She grabbed the man, spun him around, and pinned him against the side of the house while wrapping her arm around his throat to choke off any shouts.

I let the door swing closed on its own, raising The Drop so Hoffsinger could see it.

Except it wasn't Hoffsinger.

"Who the hell are you?" I hissed.

"*Ack—guck—*"

"Uh, Torina, can you let the guy answer?"

She eased off the pressure.

"Bodyguard," the man gasped.

I heard movement inside the door again. I didn't hesitate, turning, sweeping open the door and stepping inside, The Drop leveled into the face of—

Another guy who wasn't Hoffsinger.

I glared at him over The Drop's sight. "How many more of you assholes are there?"

"Depends what you mean by assholes," he said, then snatched a gun protruding from a shoulder holster.

I fired The Drop, triggering the pulse gun. For about half a second, nothing happened, giving me only enough time for a bellow of rage—

The guy got his weapon clear of the holster and was just starting to raise it when he was enveloped in a bluish burst of light like a camera flash. He toppled straight into me, and I caught him, then eased him to the floor. As I did, I realized that the delay must have been the pulse gun deciding how best to stun this guy. It was a nifty feature, despite the fact it had nearly led to me having a heart attack thinking the thing didn't work.

Torina appeared, having incapacitated her man. We moved into the house, hunting from room to room. I was ready for Hoffsinger to be waiting for us with a leveled—I don't know, plasma cannon or something. What I didn't expect was opening a bedroom door, and hearing snoring from within.

I crossed the room, my feet silent on the carpet. I heard Torina behind me, but kept my focus on the snoring lump. I crouched, looking into the face, half expecting it to be yet *another* stranger.

But it wasn't. It was Hoffsinger.

I tapped his cheek with the muzzle of The Drop. He sputtered, then fluttered open his eyes.

"Mister Hoffsinger? Hi. My name's Van. I'm a Peacemaker, here with a warrant for your arrest." I flashed him my best smile. "Oh, right. Sorry, but I'm going to have to ask you to put on pants."

"Wha—? Why?" Hoffsinger managed, eyes gone wide.

"Because I have a pants policy on my ship." At Torina's polite cough, I added, "For people I don't know, anyway."

WE GAVE our canine ally the other energy bar, then escorted Hoffsinger around the house, toward the front, where Netty had just grounded the *Fafnir*. Torina had Hoffsinger in some kind of hold that caused him intense pain if he did anything but meekly walk ahead of her. I was going to have to learn that.

As we stepped around the house, a sudden flood of pulsing red and blue light engulfed us.

"Ironically, it's the police," I said.

An amplified voice spoke up. "Put your hands up, then lie down on the ground, your head toward us."

I could see the police car sitting at the curb, and two officers, both on the other side of the car, with their weapons drawn and aimed at us.

"I thought you said showing off a gun in Chicago wasn't a big deal," Torina hissed.

I shrugged. "To be fair, I've never lived here, so I was just going by the place's reputation." Which, when I thought about it, had been pretty shortsighted. This was suburban Chicago, which probably didn't see as much open gunplay.

Hoffsinger barked out a laugh. "You'd better let me go or —*ERK!*"

Torina had barely moved, but whatever she did cut him off.

"This is the police. We're warning you again, raise your hands and lie down on the ground. Failure to comply could result in you being shot."

I saw porch lights snapping on, people coming out of houses.

This was getting complicated.

I raced through my options, and decided to make it even more complicated.

"Netty?"

"Right here."

"When I say now, I want you to deactivate the ship's stealth field."

"Uh—"

"Van, that's against some pretty strict protocols," Perry put in over the comm.

"I don't care. Do it."

"Operator override accepted," Netty declared.

"This is the police. This is your last warning—"

"Now, Netty." I swept out the Moonsword and killed—I hoped—all Earthly comms around us.

An instant later, the *Fafnir* shimmered into existence, filling Hoffsinger's front yard.

"Let's go!" I said, and we hurried to the airlock, bundling Hoffsinger inside. As we entered, I heard someone, maybe one of the cops, shouting.

"What the f—?" was all he got out before the lock sealed.

"Okay, Netty, stealth us back up, and let's haul ass."

While Torina secured Hoffsinger, I clambered into the cockpit and glanced down, at the police car and the neighborhood around it falling away. Just for fun, I had Netty zoom an external camera onto the cops, who were gaping up stupidly at us.

"So worth it," I said.

Torina climbed in beside me. "Aren't you worried that's going to become, um, a significant incident?"

"I'm sure it will. It's probably already on YouTube and TikTok, in fact."

"I'll pretend I know what those are, and ask, doesn't that concern you?"

I smiled. "Nope. Half the world will think it's cool and all, *what if*, half the world will think it's a hoax, and half the world will declare it a government conspiracy. In other words, another routine day on planet Earth."

"That's three halves."

"I never was good at math."

"You're not good at something else, Van," Perry said over the comm.

"What's that?"

"Remembering to not fly away without picking up the AI bird."

39

I assumed we'd drop Hoffsinger off at Anvil Dark, and be on our way, while the wheels of the justice system creaked and groaned their way into glacial gear. And none too soon, either, because our prisoner was a gas giant-sized pain in the ass.

He bitched, constantly, though not about the fact he'd been arrested. He bitched about the temperature. About the food. About the way the *Fafnir* smelled. He bitched about his restraints being too tight and, at one point, too *loose*, so they were chafing him. For a rather plain, middle-aged guy, Hoffsinger was one hell of an entitled *prima donna*, as if being implicated in horrific Crimes Against Life didn't make him charming enough.

He tried spouting legalese at us, apparently hoping just blustering about it would be enough.

"According to Interstellar Convention Three, Article Two, Paragraphs two through four, I'm entitled—"

"Interstellar Convention Three, Article Two, Paragraphs two through four?" Perry cut in. "Certain conventions governing the use of fusion drives and similar systems with high-intensity exhaust plumes in proximity to other vessels and installations?"

"I mean Convention Four—"

"So Interstellar Convention *Four*, Article Two, Paragraphs two through four? Trouble is, Article Two only has three paragraphs, and they all deal with the procedure for issuing notifications for revision to docking and landing fees."

I shook my head. "Hoffsinger, Perry is literally a legal eagle. You're trying to trick a Peacemaker AI regarding interstellar law."

"Kind of like sticking your hand over the muzzle of a gun to stop the bullet. And then, when it doesn't work, trying it again with your other hand," Torina said.

So I was more than happy when I thumbed the data-slate handed to me by the Magistrate, a hulking brute with skin that seemed to be made partly of metal. It transferred custody, making Hoffsinger his problem. I was quite happy to amble off and collect the spoils.

But the Magistrate scowled at me—a pretty terrifying sight, considering he stood seven feet tall, and not much narrower across the shoulders. "Aren't you coming to the trial?"

"Well, yeah, once I get the date."

"The date? That would be today. Trial's in thirty minutes, in the Judgment Chambers, Hall Three, Justiciar Durthix presiding." With that, he clamped a hand the size of a basketball around Hoffsinger's arm and dragged him away. We could hear the man's complaints and demands fading away down the concourse.

I sniffed and shook my head, and started discussing refueling and other matters related to the *Fafnir* with Netty. But Perry interrupted me.

"We'd better hurry, Van. It's a fair hike from here to the Judgement Chambers," he said, and hopped away.

I glanced at Torina, then we both hurried after him.

"So this is, like, a preliminary hearing or something, I gather. Probably to read the charges out or something?" My implanted memories were pretty good regarding the process right up to handing off a prisoner to a Magistrate, and then they became kind of vague. It suggested that Peacemakers didn't have much of a role in the actual trial process, which now struck me as a little odd.

Perry shot me an amber glance. "It's the trial."

"The trial. Like, the actual trial."

"The actual trial, as opposed to—what? The practice trial? It's not like a wedding, Van. There's no rehearsals."

"You mean they're actually going to try him in, like, half an hour?"

"No sense waiting around."

Even Torina seemed a little surprised, and she'd grown up amid galactic policies. "What about evidence?"

"The Justiciar will have already reviewed it."

"Am I going to have to testify?"

"Only if the Justiciar calls you for it, and they probably won't."

"But—" I shook my head as we veered around two Peace-makers bickering over something—*division of spoils* from an operation was all I caught. "So, how long is this trial expected to take—?"

Perry stopped and looked up at me. "Van, I know why you're asking all these questions. But this ain't Earth, where trials happen years after the crime, and can take weeks, or even months. This is—" He stopped. "Let's just go attend the trial, and you'll see."

He hopped off.

"Torina, do you know what a kangaroo court is?"

"I don't even know what a kangaroo is."

I glanced at her, smiled and shook my head. "Never mind," I said, and we followed Perry to the Judgment Chambers.

IT MIGHT NOT HAVE BEEN a kangaroo court, but it did have the distinct smell of marsupial to it.

We arrived in the Hall to find Hoffsinger already there, standing in a dock that enclosed him in a soundproof barrier—he could hear what was going on, but couldn't speak unless the Justiciar allowed it. The only others present were me, the Magistrate, Torina, Perry, and a pair of bored and surly looking security personnel, one human, and one Yonnox, of all things. I mentioned my surprise at that, but Torina just gave me a bemused look.

"The Yonnox homeworld has a population of at least five

billion. It's probably reasonable to assume that there's at least a few among them that aren't unrelenting, criminal assholes," she whispered. "After all, your grandfather and Hoffsinger are both humans."

I nodded. "Good point."

And then there was the Justiciar.

If you envision something like an octopus, but with some sort of skeletal structure allowing it to sit upright, with several extra tentacles ending in clusters of eyes, you'll get the idea. The race apparently had an unpronounceable name, and came from a water world that was strictly off limits to all outsiders. This was backed up by a formidable array of interlocked defensive systems that would open fire, without warning, on any ship that came too close. Their only interaction outside their fortified home system was the Justiciars, which not only described their role, but had also become the informal name of the race itself.

As near as I could tell, the Justiciar somehow combined judge, prosecution, defense and jury all in one. I started to make a comment about how that seemed not only profoundly unfair, but also ground for corruption as fertile as black Iowa soil, but Perry cut me off.

"The Justiciars are incapable of deceit, have absolutely no emotions as we understand them and, by their nature, only evaluate things on the basis of factual evidence. That's what makes them so valuable as, well, Justiciars," he said. "They basically combine the dispassion of a computer with the judgement and free will of a sentient being."

"Why not just use an AI?"

"Someone has to create an AI, so it's going to reflect its creator in some respects, no matter how hard they might try to prevent it. Justiciars are as close to being truly impartial as any known living thing can get."

"So, if they're so xenophobic, how did this arrangement with them even start?"

"No one's really sure. The first Justiciars assumed office over nine hundred years ago, right here, with the Peacemakers. If anyone recorded how that happened, or why they decided to have this one, specific interaction with other species, it's hidden away somewhere."

I had more questions, but the Justiciar called for order in a voice the translator rendered as flat and utterly devoid of tone.

"This case is the preceding of the Peacemakers, under the auspice of Warrant 569-01L-6, against Emil Hoffsinger, human—

The Justiciar went on, quickly getting to the list of charges, which were presented in mind-numbing, bureaucratic detail, but were at least mercifully brief. I could see Hoffsinger ranting away in the dock, but thanks to the silence effect, I couldn't hear him.

"...fourth charge, an offense against Section Three-Point-Seven-Point-Two, Abetting the forcible confinement of unwilling subjects. How does the accused plead?"

The Justiciar dropped the silence effect, and Hoffsinger's whiny, nasally voice slashed through the Hall.

"—total sham! I have my rights! This court has no jurisdiction over me, as a citizen of Earth! I refuse to take part in this f—"

"The Court will enter a Not Guilty plea on behalf of the accused," the Justiciar said, smoothly cutting Hoffsinger off.

"The Court has reviewed the evidence against the accused, and will now—"

I leaned over to Perry. "Doesn't he even get to see the evidence against him?"

"He did. You know those memory uploads you had on Cross-roads? He had one injected into him, which means he knows every last detail of the evidence the Justiciar will be using to try the case."

"Huh."

"—the accused have any statement to make prior to the Court's ruling?"

"—bullshit! I demand a lawyer! A human one! You can't—"

"The accused has no statement to make prior to the Court's ruling. Accordingly, the Court finds the accused, Emil Hoffsinger, guilty of all charges. Sentencing to follow."

I shook my head. "Holy shit. How long until sentencing—?"

"This Court sentences the convicted party to serve, for one hundred standard years and in memory-chip form, to operate a sand-runner craft under the jurisdiction of the Srall, in accordance with the agreement numbered as—"

The Justiciar went on, but what it amounted to was that Hoffsinger was going to replace the Srall princess who'd been consigned by her own family to a life of mind-numbing tedium operating a sand-runner, a small, surface-skimming craft used by her people to traverse their arid homeworld. I leaned toward Perry again.

"What about her family? Aren't they just as guilty of Crimes Against Life?"

"Yup. And they're facing justice under Srall jurisdiction."

"Which entails what, exactly?"

"It *starts* with them being flayed alive. Would you like to hear more?"

"Not really."

The Justiciar declared the trial concluded. By my armor's chronometer, it had taken—

"Just under two minutes," I said, shaking my head. "The whole damned trial lasted less than two minutes."

"I know, right? It really dragged on," Perry said.

I shot him a glance, expecting to see him laughing.

He wasn't.

BACK ABOARD LUNZY'S SHIP, enjoying some more of her decent beer, I was still shaking my head.

"So you finally got to see the legal system at work," she said, lifting her glass to her mouth. Her eyes gave me a bemused look over the rim.

"Yes, and I blinked, so I almost missed it. I mean, holy shit. Hoffsinger's a vile piece of human garbage, sure, but how could that be considered fair?"

"Perry explained the Justiciars to you?"

"Yeah, he did. But, still. He didn't even have time to mount a defense!"

"The evidence was incontrovertible, Van. And he was scanned to ensure he wasn't suffering from some psychological or physical defect, and genuinely couldn't tell right from wrong. What more is needed?"

"But what if he wanted to challenge the evidence? How was it collected or handled, or—something, anyway?"

"He had an opportunity to make a statement. And, if he'd somehow come up with something compelling enough, the Justiciar would have considered it. Hell, a few years ago we had a trial go on for almost three consecutive *days*, because the accused had managed to point out some inconsistencies in the evidence. And good thing, too, because the Peacemaker involved was on the take. Guess who was in the dock next?"

"And that trial didn't take three days," Perry put in.

"Actually, our boy Hoffsinger is lucky. Crimes like his would normally get him spaced out of the nearest airlock. The Srall intervened formally, though, because they wanted to make an example out of everyone involved."

"The Srall are big on making examples out of things," Perry agreed.

"And that is the perfect segue into your next job, Van. And it's an easy one. Ten thousand bonds in stipend to carry some passengers," Lunzy said.

Torina sniffed. "We just carried a passenger all the way from Earth. I'm not sure ten thousand bonds would have been worth the aggravation."

"Well, this trip shouldn't be nearly as onerous. You're going to transport Hoffsinger, newly installed on his memory chip—which serves the evil bastard right—to the Srall homeworld. And you're going to be carrying another passenger from there, to Spindrift, also on a chip."

Torina lifted an eyebrow. "The princess?"

"Indeed. Princess So-metz of the Srall has elected to forgo remaining on her homeworld, for reasons that should be pretty apparent. The Srall Hegemony has arranged for her to receive a new body on Spindrift."

I leaned forward. "Are these actually the same, er, people? Is the Hoffsinger on the chip actually the same Hoffsinger we nabbed on Earth?"

"Yes," Lunzy said.

"Really?"

She smiled and shrugged. "Actually, I have no idea, Van, nor does anyone else. I mean, is all of this that you're experiencing real, or just a perfect simulation?"

"You could actually be standing in your bedroom back on Earth, Van, having just pressed that button on that remote. How would you know?" Perry asked.

I clapped my hands together with finality. "Well, that's my quota of existential philosophy filled for the day. Let's go do some flyin'."

"I HAVE TO ADMIT, Hoffsinger has been much better behaved on this trip, than he was on the one from Earth," Torina said.

I glanced at the case containing his memory chip, which had

been sealed in a blast proof container that only I could open. It was to ensure he ended up where he was meant to be going, and not just snatched, then given a new body somewhere so he could start his life of crime all over again, but in an entirely new guise.

It was too bad, too. I'd been kind of hoping to plug him into Waldo—with the speaker disconnected, of course—and put him to work doing menial chores around the ship. Like Lunzy said, it would serve the miserable old bastard right. I did have the opportunity to speak to him once, before he was sealed away, though.

The Magistrate had plugged him into a chip-reader, so that his new, chip-born existence as a sentient collection of data could be tested before we carted him off to Srall. Perry pointed out that the law that applied to individuals who'd been *chipped*—the new word for it, apparently—was still in its infancy. Hoffsinger represented a test case, and the Guild was watching it very closely.

Hoffsinger's contribution to the conversation was predictable and profane. He leveled especially vile curses at me and Torina. A moment of that, and I'd had enough.

"You should be dead, Hoffsinger. And if I somehow live long enough to see you serve this time out, watch for me, you bastard. I might be waiting."

WE ARRIVED at the Srall homeworld, also named Srall, which was the second planet orbiting the binary star system 61 Cygni. Consisting of two orange stars each slightly less massive than Sol, Srall orbited just zero-point-three astronomical units—the distance from Sol to Earth—from the two stars, meaning it skimmed the innermost edge of the system's Goldilocks Zone. The result was an arid, heat-blasted planet that vaguely resembled Mars, right down to being unrelentingly dusty red.

We landed at a spaceport called K'r'Tll, a name that was supposed to be pronounced with absolutely no vowel sounds. It was something that the Srall could apparently do, but no one else could, so everyone just called it Kirtil, rhyming with *turtle*. The port sat in the middle of a vast, dusty plain that offered variations on brick red, but that wasn't saying much, because most of the planet was a vast, dusty plain offering variations on brick red.

As soon as the airlock opened, I was hit with a wall of furnace heat so dry I swear I heard a tiny slurping sound as it sucked the moisture out of me. A group of Srall approached from a cluster of domes—all of them yet another shade of brick red—beyond which sprawled more domes, apparently a settlement. Flat-topped mesas with sheer, cliff-faced sides rose in the distance. A keening wind swept across the barren landscape, doing nothing to mitigate the heat and just raising a fine, stinging dust.

The Srall were humanoid and chunky, with tough, leathery skin. Their physiology had adapted them to the environment, so they retained water and lost it very slowly. They were also heat resistant to an insane degree. Their faces resembled those of a wild boar, complete with tusks, but flattened, and they wore goggles. Their only other clothing was a light robe made of something vaguely metallic, like something knitted from steel wool.

The lead Srall stopped a few meters away. He—and I could

tell it was a he only because males sprouted coarse pelts down both front and back—crossed his arms in a formal gesture of welcome. His tusks had been drilled through, and sported a variety of rings and baubles that apparently indicated his station, which was a pretty senior one.

"You have arrived."

I nodded. "We have."

"Give us the chip."

I glanced at Torina, who shrugged, then offered over the case containing Hoffsinger. Perry had warned me that the Srall were abrupt in a way that might come across as rude—and he was right.

The Srall accepted the case, and I thumbed it open. He extracted the chip and handed it to an underling, who plugged into what I assume was their version of a data-slate. After a moment, the underling grunted something.

"The miscreant is intact. Good."

As we'd been standing, squinting into orange sunlight that felt like sitting under a heat-lamp, I'd noticed feathery trails of dust wafting back and forth in the distance. I assumed they were vehicles of some sort, moving fast. I pointed at one. "Are those your sand-cutters?"

"Why do you ask?"

"Just curious. I've never been here before."

"Nor do you need to stay long." The Srall—who still hadn't even bothered to introduce himself—handed over a case containing another chip. This one wasn't sealed. I extracted it and Torina plugged it into her data-slate, confirming that it did, indeed, have an intact memory-ghost loaded into it.

"This seems to check out. Look—"

All but two of the Srall abruptly turned and walked away.

I stared after them. "A touch rude for my taste."

Torina shrugged. "I guess they're kind of xenophobic."

But Perry shook his head. "Nope. They trade and interact freely with other races. They're not xenophobes—just assholes."

The two remaining Srall stepped forward. They were both armed with wicked, curved blades that seemed to be made of glass, and strangely ornate sidearms.

"Before you leave, you must pay the tribute."

"The tribute."

"It is—customary."

I glanced at Perry, who returned a barely perceptible shake of his head. I saw Torina place the chip she'd been given into her belt pouch, then casually move to my left, giving her a clear path to the two Srall trying to shake us down.

I really didn't want this to devolve into a fight. For one, I didn't fancy turning our *departure* from this planet into an *escape*. For another, I didn't want anyone to get hurt.

"Van, this is a Srall show of force. They expect you to either demonstrate that you're even stronger, or back down," Perry said. His voice hummed through my translator's ear-piece, so only I could hear him. It was a nifty trick we'd tested, but had never used before.

I nodded, then glanced back at the *Fafnir*. A show of force, huh?

Fine.

"Netty, fire a missile at those cliffs off to your left."

"Van, that's not—"

"Do it."

I felt Torina tense and duck her head. Perry lifted his wings. I gritted my teeth and tried to keep a cool expression leveled on the two Srall.

A second passed, then an ear-splitting roar slammed into me, accompanied by a thick, choking cloud of dust. The missile flashed over the intervening barrens in maybe a second, then slammed into the cliffs with a massive detonation that flung chunks of reddish rock, some as big as a car, high into the sky.

"Would you like another donation, or is that good enough?" I asked, trying to sound as blase as possible. At least, I think I tried, because the shrill whine ringing through my ears made it hard to even hear myself.

The two Srall exchanged a look, then shook their heads and walked off toward their fellows, who'd all thrown themselves flat at the unexpected missile launch.

"I guess that was a good enough show of force for them, eh?"

Torina turned to me. "What's that? I can't hear you over all the stupid!"

"Van, when I said show of force, I meant something like drawing your weapon, the Moonblade, standing up to them. I did not mean the high-tech equivalent of walking up to the biggest, baddest guy in the yard on your first day in prison and trying to beat the shit out of him, to prove how crazy dangerous you are," Perry said.

We waved away swirling dust and made our way back to the *Fafnir*. "Worked, didn't it?" I said, then paused to spit what amounted to red mud out of my mouth.

"Yes, Van, it worked. You brought a weapon designed to blow apart spaceships to a gun-fight."

"And spent a few thousand bonds doing it," Torina pointed out.

"Worth it. Although, those things are a lot louder down here than they are in space, aren't they?"

Perry gave me a *look*. "Yes, Van. Yes, they are."

"Van, are you sure you want to do this?" Torina asked.

Perry gave a mechanical sniff. "After roasting us with the backblast from a missile, you even need to ask him that?"

"Tell me about it. I'm still picking sand out of my—"

"Yeah, I'm sure," I said, nodding. "She's been stuck in limbo long enough."

"She's Srall, Van. She's quite likely going to be—unpleasant," Perry said.

"Yeah, I know. But she's also a victim. She deserves better than this."

We plugged So-metz's chip into Waldo, and waited for him to reboot. Unlike Hoffsinger, her chip hadn't been sealed, because there'd been no need for it. It didn't mean we were under any obligation to bring her back to, well, *life*, but I felt sorry for her. Miserable bitch or not, she was entitled to be alive—

—ish.

Waldo came back online. "Where am I?"

Her voice was low and deliberate.

"You're aboard my ship, the *Fafnir*. I'm Van Tudor, a Peacemaker, and I've got Torina, my Second, along with my combat AI, Perry, and the ship's AI, Netty, with me."

"I am very pleased to meet you all," she said. I glanced at Torina, who gave me a, *so far, so good* kind of look in return.

It got better from there, and we soon learned why. So-metz was wholly unlike the other Srall we'd met. Torina had warned me not to judge an entire species based on the nature of a few individuals, so I'd tried to keep an open mind, and was glad I did.

So-metz was a delight.

She'd actually left Srall as the equivalent of a young teenager, thanks to an arranged marriage with a wealthy Yonnox merchant. And this represented the second decent Yonnox I knew of, because the man had apparently been a loyal and loving husband. For obvious reasons, they couldn't have children except by adoption, so the point of the marriage hadn't been to produce heirs. Rather, it was a crass attempt by So-metz's family to break into off-world commercial ventures they'd otherwise have to, you know, actually *work* to build.

The trouble came when So-metz's Yonnox husband died in a spacecraft accident. She'd been heartbroken, and returned to Srall—but not before relinquishing any claim to the Yonnox's business empire. Her family had been infuriated; after all, the whole point of marrying her off had been that, easy access to off-world wealth. She'd been bitterly declared *just another mouth to feed* and, shortly thereafter, had died of what had been officially recorded as natural causes.

I glanced at Torina. "Wow. Family, huh?"

"I think about my family often," So-metz said, somewhat sadly.

Torina nodded sympathetically. "I'm sure you do."

"And when I do, it's to hope that they are eternally drowning in the everlasting and infinite ocean of eternal punishment."

I liked this girl.

40

WHEN I'D BEEN TOLD we were bringing So-metz to Spindrift for a new body, I'd assumed that meant a new robotic body, something like the one his people had constructed for Fostin. But there were apparently Flesh-Merchants on Spindrift—yes, they were called Flesh-Merchants—who specialized in constructing so-called biologicals, normally replacement limbs and skin-grafts, using a complex combination of 3D-printing, genetic engineering and cellular regeneration technologies. They were constructing an actual Srall body for So-metz, a profoundly delicate and time-consuming job, but one that only the Flesh-Merchants of Spin-drift could pull off. Apparently, only they had the know-how to actually recreate the Srall nervous system, including a functioning brain. Still, it was a challenge they'd readily accepted—for a fantastic sum of money. When I'd asked Perry how much he thought it had cost, he'd just shrugged.

"Considering what they charge for a single limb, I'd say a whole body would be—" He paused. "Let's put it this way. You know how much it's going to cost to upgrade the *Fafnir* to *Dragon* class?"

"Yeah. A shit-ton of bonds."

"Well, this would be at least several shit-tons of bonds."

Say what you will about the Srall, but they were sparing no expense to right a horrific wrong.

There was no particular need for us to wait around, but we did anyway. I took the opportunity to get a better feel for Spindrift, a place to which Perry said we'd likely be returning many times.

"Your grandfather sure did. Walk into any bar on Spindrift, except for *The Black Star*, of course, and ask for Mark Tudor's *usual*. You'll get one."

"Why not *The Black Star*?"

Perry hopped up onto the back of a chair with a metallic clatter, and put a companionable wing around me. "Let me put it this way. Your money is no good in *The Black Star*. I mean, literally no good. You'll be dead long before you get to the bar. *The Black Star* is where crime *comes* from."

SO-METZ TURNED AROUND. "What do you think?"

I smiled. She'd been given a Srall body which, honestly, did nothing for me. But that was the point of the smile, which was genuine.

"You look fantastic," I said.

Torina nodded. "Absolutely lovely, So-metz. The Flesh-Merchants did an amazing job."

I had to nod at that. The only Srall I'd ever seen had been the ones on her home planet. But if you dropped her in among them, I'd never have known the difference.

"So what are you going to do now?" I asked.

"Return to Srall and take over my family's business. It's been held in trust by my uncle, the only surviving member of my family."

"Yeah, I'm so sorry about that."

"I'm not," she said flatly. "My family was horrible. The galaxy is better off without them."

I raised an eyebrow at that—until I thought about Carter Yost, my cousin. As soon as I did, I nodded back.

"Yeah, I've got family like that, too."

"Van, Torina—and Perry and Netty, of course—I want to thank you for all you've done for me," she said.

I shrugged. "All we did is carry your chip from Srall to Spin-drift. Just a courier job, really."

But So-metz shook her head. "I know how you discovered the trade in illicit memory chips, and the poor people who've been trapped in them, like I was. I also know that most of them will never be able to afford, well—" She gestured down at herself. "This."

She walked up to me, put her arms around my waist, and bowed her head. I heard her muttering something. I frowned at Torina, who just shrugged. Perry, though, perked up.

So-metz stepped back. "You are now my brother, Van Tudor. I welcome you into my family."

She moved to Torina and did the same thing. "And you as well, Torina Milon. You are my sister."

She looked at Perry. "Um—"

Perry shook his head. "That's okay. It's the thought that counts."

"If any of you are ever in trouble, or need refuge, my home is yours," she said.

She bid her final farewell to us, then turned and headed for a Srall ship that would take her home.

Perry shook his head. "Wow."

I glanced at him. "Wow?"

"Yes. Wow. That muttering you heard was her—I guess baptizing you is the best analogy. You and Torina were just reborn into the Srall and are now part of her family."

I stared for a moment, then shook my head.

"Space is both friendly and cruel. A mixed message, if you will."

As we were preparing the *Fafnir* to get underway, I noticed a commotion a few klicks off. Several small boats had swarmed around a bigger ship that had apparently been coming in to dock pretty much right alongside us. Something about the big ship immediately hit me right away.

"Netty, why does that ship look familiar?"

"Maybe because it exactly matches the class and configuration of the Salt Thieves' ship that we encountered near Crossroads," she replied.

"The one that snatched that pirate out from under us?"

"The very same."

"Well, well. I wonder what's going on? Something terrible for them, I hope."

"Van, I have a confession," Netty said.

Both Torina and I turned to the consoles in front of us with raised eyebrows. "Go on."

"I was testing the comm system's decryption subroutines, and inadvertently accessed privileged comms between Spindrift Traffic Control, and other ships waiting to approach and dock."

Torina smirked. So did I. "What did you do, Netty?"

"I overheard—entirely by accident, I might add—comms between Traffic Control and that Salt Thieves' ship."

I gave a theatrical sigh. "Well, now that you've made such a terrible mistake, Netty, you might as well unburden your electronic soul and confess fully."

"The Salt Thieves—or, as they brand themselves for everyday consumption by the masses, the Salt Merchants' Guild —apparently owe substantial docking fees. The Salt Th— Merchants—Captain claims he paid those fees last time he was here."

Perry leaned in. "Translation—they owe somebody, probably in Customs and Excise, kickbacks for overlooking past cargo *irregularities*."

Torina chuckled. "Even money on whether they actually paid,

and someone's trying to shake them down, or they really do owe. There truly is no honor among thieves."

"I've said it before, I'll say it again—if they'll do it with you, they'll do it to you," I said.

"Uh, Van, there's an external cargo pod attached to that Salt Thieves ship," Perry said.

"Not surprising. Considering how heavily armed it is, most of what would normally be internal hold space is probably taken up by weapons system infrastructure and storage for ordnance," Netty said. "They've got four external pods, two per side, to supplement their cargo capacity."

I knew what Perry was getting at. It was an insane idea, which was a big part of why I liked it. "Netty, do those pods use standard hard-point attachments?"

"They do. That way, they can be swapped out with any number of other attachments, modules and pods, including external weapons, scanner suites, instrumental arrays—"

"And we've got free external hard-points on the *Fafnir*," I said.

Perry gave me a head-bob. Torina rolled her eyes.

"You've got to be kidding," she said.

"Well, I'm thinking he's probably full of cargo, and low on fuel, right? Because he hasn't docked yet?"

"Stands to reason," Perry said.

"And all ships have their weapons locked-out by Traffic Control within a certain distance of the station, right?"

"You really don't want to have ships shooting at one another while they're docked, or close to it," Netty agreed.

"And these guys owe us money, right?"

"Van, do you really want to make enemies of the Salt Thieves," Torina asked.

"Uh, correct me if I'm wrong, but aren't they bad guys? Doesn't that make them our enemies by default?"

"Yes—but we're talking about you making specific enemies here."

I sat back. "Torina, you're my Second. I value your advice. If you genuinely think this is a bad idea, then say the word, and we'll be on our way."

"I think it's a terrible idea."

"Does that count as *the word?*"

A sly grin spread across her face. "Are you still here? Shouldn't you be suiting up to go steal a cargo pod?"

In theory, the job was simple. As we backed away from our berth on Spindrift, we'd pass within a few hundred meters of the Salt Thieves' ship. It was still keeping station a couple of klicks short of the station, still embroiled in a dick-waving debate over who owed what to whom. We could easily nudge ourselves to within a few hundred meters of our quarry, thanks to a clunky freighter approaching to dock at the berth on the opposite side of us from the Salt Thieves. It would be a simple matter of me crossing to their ship trailing a winch-line from the *Fafnir*, hooking it to the cargo pod, cutting it free of the big ship with the Moonsword, then winching it, and me, back to the *Fafnir*. We'd attach it to the free hard-point on the bottom of the *Fafnir*'s hull, then accelerate away. By the time the bigger ship came about and started after us, we should have enough of a head start that pursuit was pointless. Moreover, we had a full load of fuel to use to twist away, while the Salt Thieves were probably low.

Simple.

Well, except for all of the things that could go wrong. And there were *lots* of those.

I tried not to let the whole list of them trudge drearily through my head as I stood in the *Fafnir*'s open airlock. I'd already retrieved the winch cable, and attached it to my harness. The winch, whose tether was a bundle of tough, monofilament lines, was designed to pull things to the ship, or the ship to things, particularly when maneuvering thrusters couldn't or shouldn't be used. Netty had done all the calculations, and worked out that we could safely twist to destinations representing about forty percent of known space—which was still a lot of destinations. We settled on Torina's homeworld at Van Maanen's Star, reasoning that if and when the Salt Thieves came looking for us, they'd probably start their search at Anvil Dark.

"Okay, Van. When I give the word, we'll be starting our closest approach to the Salt Thieves' ship. It's going to take us about ninety seconds to complete it, and then we'll be pulling away from them again. That's your window," Netty said.

"Ninety seconds, huh? Not even exciting." I tried to keep my voice even as I said it. Watching the looming bulk of the Salt Thieves' ship towering over us, this suddenly seemed a touch reckless.

"Okay, Van. Time."

I took a breath—and a final second to ask myself if I really wanted to do this—then launched myself out of the airlock.

It would only take me a few seconds to sail across the two hundred meter or so gap between the two ships. As I made the crossing, I was only too aware of the weapons bristling from my quarry, the sinister, hulking shapes of laser-emitters and missile launchers, the gaping snouts of point-defense batteries. With each passing second, I expected them to suddenly come to life, spin, and blast me and the *Fafnir* to tiny bits.

But they all remained silent. Ominously so, but ominous silence was better than laser-blasts and streams of point-defense slugs. Nor was there any other response from the Salt Thieves' ship, suggesting that they were still arguing over their supposed docking fees—

Something slid into view, then started toward me. It was a Spindrift customs cutter.

"Well, this is suboptimal."

"Again with the speeches, boss," Perry said.

Technically, I was violating a rule requiring all extra-vehicular activities—EVA—to be cleared with Traffic Control. After all, having miscellaneous bodies drifting around the busy space surrounding Spindrift could be as much of a problem for navigation as other ships were. We'd seen the cutters withdraw earlier, but one must have stuck around, hanging about on the far side of the big ship.

It accelerated straight toward me. I was just over halfway to my destination, the cargo-pod. If the cutter's pilot ordered me to stand-down, I'd either have to defy them, or accede, and either way our little operation would be blown. Frantically, I tried to think of some way of getting them back to back off.

Torina rescued me.

"Spindrift Customs Cutter CL237, this is the Peacemaker ship *Fafnir*. Be advised that you are interfering in a legitimate Peacemaker operation. If you don't withdraw immediately, we'll have to treat this as—" She paused, and I imagined her consulting Perry.

"We will have to treat this as interference in an ongoing investigation, potentially obstruction of justice—"

A new voice cut in. "No one informed me about a Peacemaker operation underway."

"All due respect, but if you wanted to keep something secret around here, would you tell yourself about it?"

A pause, then the cutter pilot replied. "Point taken, ma'am. You have a nice day."

The cutter pitched up, yawed left, and accelerated away.

"Good job, Torina," I said, readying myself to stop against the cargo pod.

"Yes and no. The Salt Thieves' didn't miss that. They're demanding that the Spindrift Traffic Control Authority bring that cutter back to stop us."

I had to laugh at that. "So they want to call the cops? Quite the change of heart."

"Well, Spindrift isn't playing ball, because there's *still* the matter of those unpaid bribes—I mean, docking fees."

Perry broke in. "But there is an airlock on that ship starting to cycle at your one o'clock, high, Van."

I glanced up and to my right, and saw the airlock in question. Its external indicator was flashing red, meaning it was in use and depressurizing.

A few seconds later, I thumped gently against the cargo pod. I immediately unhooked the winch cable from my harness, and snapped it onto a stanchion, then realized how dumb that was, because it would leave me without a tether back to the *Fafnir*. So I reversed the process, costing me precious time.

"Sixty seconds, Van, then we have to pull you back," Netty said.

"Got it." I clambered across the surface of the pod, which fortunately was equipped with all sorts of stanchions and hand-holds to make it easier to move around, load and unload. It also had additional hard-points, so it could be hooked up in any orientation. I glanced down and saw that it wasn't attached to one hard-point, but two, spaced about five meters apart.

"Problem."

"Van, if there's a—" Torina started, but I cut her off.

"No *serious* problem. Yet."

I got as close to the first hard-point as I could, which required me to squeeze partway into a tight gap between the pod and the ship's hull. I moved the Moonsword into position.

"Time to find out if this blade is as sharp as advertised," I said, and swung it at the hard-point. It cut through the tough metal clamps that formed a collar around the hard-point, forming a female fitting that closed and squeezed around the male mating-point on the pod.

The Moonsword cut deep. It reminded me of chopping soft

wood with a sharp ax. It still took several blows before the hard-point finally failed and the pod came free.

One down.

I pulled myself out of the gap and headed for the second hard-point. As I did, I noticed a flash just to my right. I glanced that way and saw nothing, then noticed a shiny furrow plowed into the metal of the pod's hull.

It took me a second or two to realize what it was. That second or two almost cost me my life.

I was aligned parallel to the pod's hull, about a half-meter away from it. The Salt Thief's next shot passed just beneath my head and chest, struck the pod directly beneath my male mating-point, then ricocheted up to pass between my knees before starting its long journey to wherever it was going to end up. Fragments spalled off the hit spattered against my armor.

"Weapons!"

I glanced up to see the Salt Thief standing in the open airlock, the one that had cycled earlier, aiming his weapon at me. It was a rifle, less than thirty meters away; the fact he'd missed at all meant he was either a crappy shot, or his sights were off. I scrambled toward the second hard-point, then realized I'd be stationary, my hips and legs fully exposed, for a good ten seconds. He'd have to close his eyes and spin around a few times to miss me. Worse, even if the *Fafnir* winched me back, I'd be an exposed target for a good thirty seconds.

I swore richly and made a decision.

I wanted this cargo pod, but not badly enough to die for it. I was about to tell Netty to abort and winch me back, when the

Salt Thief suddenly spasmed, then drifted out of the airlock, limp, his weapon spinning off in another direction. I glanced back at the *Fafnir*, and saw Torina standing in its open airlock, aiming one of our Gauss carbines at the Salt Thieves' airlock.

"Don't tell me—you're an expert shot, too."

"I'm a complicated woman, Van. And you've got thirty five seconds left."

I scrambled into place, and hacked apart the second hard-point, while Torina gave cover. The pod was free. I snapped the tether back onto a stanchion, then told Netty to winch away, hanging on to the pod as it was pulled steadily back to the *Fafnir*. The Salt Thieves tried to get another sniper into position, but Torina kept them pinned inside the airlock with a withering fire.

By the time the pod reached the *Fafnir*, the Salt Thieves' ship was coming about. Netty deftly snuggled our ship against the pod and locked our own hard-point around one of the mating-points I hadn't sliced away. By the time I'd got back inside and started the airlock cycling, the Salt Thieves were in pursuit.

This was where being a much bigger ship was a *disadvantage*, though. She had more powerful engines, but also a lot more mass to accelerate. The *Fafnir* had the edge on acceleration, and were able to pull away.

The Salt Thieves knew they weren't going to catch us, and lobbed a petulant comm transmission after us.

"When we catch up to you—and we will catch up to you— you won't have a hope of surviving, you scumbag. Your badge won't always protect you, and the *Kondor* has you so outgunned that most of the crew's just going to be able to watch the pretty fireworks, since they won't need to bother shooting."

I settled into the pilot's seat, nodding for Torina to open the comm channel.

"Actually, my thieving friend, I think my badge will protect me just fine. Assuming you ever do have the balls to come looking for us, well, the *Fafnir* won't be this small for very long. So, don't bother coming for us. Just check your mirrors, because we'll be coming for you."

I shut off the comm.

Perry gave me an amber *look*. "Check your mirrors? Really?"

"Hey, I thought it sounded pretty clever."

"As long as it makes you happy, Van."

Torina stretched. "Well, that was quite a day. Adopted into a new alien family, made sworn enemies of the Salt Thieves, got into a firefight, stole somebody's undoubtedly stolen cargo..."

I grinned as Netty accelerated us, in preparation to twist away.

"Right? And it's not even dinner time yet."

EPILOGUE

"GOTTA ADMIT, those space hippies do damned fine work," I said, shading my eyes against the light of Van Maanen's Star and taking in the new splendor of Torina's family estate.

She nodded. "It's different than what I knew, of course, but it's still beautiful. A whole new region of wilderness to explore."

The Synergists had, indeed, returned life to her family's lands. The only evidence of the illegal strip-mining was the rolling character of the terrain, rounded hills rising from wooded low ground, a few of them wetlands, and one a large, placid pond. Moreover, this wasn't new growth, all shoots and saplings. The trees towered with years of growth coaxed out of them by the Synergists—magic? Okay, maybe not magic, but there was definitely something 'supernatural' about their achievement, in the sense that it surpassed nature. Their unique fusion of high-tech with what was probably some sort of psionic talent, expressed through the focus of their drumming and piping, singing and dancing, had turned barren lifelessness into thriving life. It all looked as though it didn't just belong here, but as though it had *always* been here.

We wandered off down the hill from the place we'd first confronted the Salt Thieves who were in the employ of the mysterious mercenary leader Pevensi, into lower ground. We stayed out of the most deeply wooded spots, sticking to humped ridges of higher ground that led us, eventually, to the bank of the pond. The light was starting to fade, the horizon purpling, the first stars appearing in the darkening sky above us.

"You know, except for the color of the sun, it kind of reminds me of your creek in Iowa," she said.

"Yeah, it does that—"

Torina pushed me into the water.

I landed in it with a heavy splash, an *oooooof,* and a gasp at the cold water. I came up shaking my head to clear away water, sputtering in shock and irritation. But it faded fast when I saw Torina laughing, then vanished altogether when she jumped in after me, fully clothed.

"What the hell, woman?"

She splashed over to me. We could actually stand on the bottom, and didn't need to tread water. "Sorry, Van. Don't know what came over me."

"Yes, that shit-eating grin of yours tells me that you're *sooo* sorry."

We clambered out of the water and started to strip down.

Perry arrived in the midst of it, stopped, and spread his wings again.

"I see you guys are busy getting naked. I'll come back when you're done—"

"Easy there, tin chicken," I said, stripping off my sodden socks and wringing them out. "We both just happened to fall into the water."

"Clumsy of us, I know," Torina put in.

Perry just stared for a moment. "Riiiiight. Anyway, Van, we just got a list from Anvil Dark of the latest names of missing people that are probably victims of Hoffsinger, Kuthrix, Ruiz-Rocher, and their evil, scummy company. Netty uploaded it to your comm." He glanced at my pile of soaking clothing, which included my belt and data-slate. "Whenever you've finished, uh, *drying out*, and are ready to review it, just dump the fish and pondweed out of it."

Perry flew off, heading back to the *Fafnir*. I pulled off my undershirt, but left my shorts on to preserve at least some degree of modesty. Torina likewise retained her undergarments. I draped my clothing over some shrubs, removing my data-slate from its pouch so it could dry out, too. As I did, I stopped and tapped the screen.

A list of names glowed back at me.

So many missing people.

Torina's hand clasped mine, and pulled it away from the slate. She plucked it from my grasp, and put it on a log—face down.

"We'll get to them soon enough," she said, as we settled

ourselves beside the pond and watched Van Maanen's Star set in a dramatic show of purple-orange glory.

"I hope so. And when we do—"

Torina smiled into the dusk.

"And when we do, I'll be right there alongside you," she said,

"Good, because victory's kind of like sunsets." I waved a hand at the horizon. "It's better when it's shared."

Torina leaned on me, and her sigh was agreement enough.

Van will return in RED BOUNTY in November 2021. Available to preorder now on Amazon.

For more updates on this series, be sure to join the Facebook Group, "J.N. Chaney's Renegade Readers."

GLOSSARY

Anvil Dark: The beating heart of the Peacemaker organization, Anvil Dark is a large orbital platform located in the Gamma Crucis system, some ninety lightyears from Earth. Anvil Dark, some nine hundred seventy years old, remains in a Lagrange point around Mesaribe, remaining in permanent darkness. Anvil Dark has legal, military, medical, and supply resources for Peacemakers, their assistants, and guests.

Cloaks: Local organized criminal element, the Cloaks hold sway in only one place: Spindrift. A loose guild of thugs, extortionists, and muscle, the Cloaks fill a need for some legal control on Spindrift, though they do so only because Peacemakers and other authorities see them as a necessary evil. When confronted away from Spindrift, Cloaks are given no rights, quarter, or considerations for their position. (See: Spindrift)

Dragonet: A Base Four Combat ship, the Dragonet is a modified platform intended for the prosecution of Peacemaker policy. This includes but is not limited to ship-to-ship combat, surveillance, and planetary operations as well. The Dragonet is fast, lightly armored, and carries both point defense and ranged weapons, and features a frame that can be upgraded to the status of a small corvette (Class Nine).

Moonsword: Although the weapon is in the shape of a medium sword, the material is anything but simple metal. The Moonsword is a generational armament, capable of upgrades that augment its ability to interrupt communications, scan for data, and act as a blunt-force weapon that can split all but the toughest of ship's hulls. See: Starsmith

Peacemaker: Also known as a Galctic Knight, Peacemakers are an elite force of law enforcement who have existed for more than three centuries. Both hereditary and open to recruitment, the guild is a meritocracy, but subject to political machinations and corruption, albeit not on the scale of other galactic military forces. Peacemakers have a legal code, proscribed methods, a reward and bounty scale, and a well-earned reputation as fierce, competent fighters. Any race may be a Peacemaker, but the candidates must pass rigorous testing and training.

Perry: An artificial intelligence, bound to Van (after service to his grandfather), Perry is a fully-sapient combat operative in the shape of a large, black avian. With the ability to hack computer systems and engage in physical combat, Perry is also a living repository of galactic knowledge in topics from law to battle strategies. He is also a wiseass.

Salt Thieves: Originally actual thieves who stole salt, this is a three-hundred-year-old guild of assassins known for their ruthless behavior, piracy, and tendency to kill. Members are identified by a complex, distinct system of braids in their hair. These braids are often cut and taken as prizes, especially by Peacemakers.

Spindrift: At nine hundred thirty years old, Spindrift is one of the most venerable space stations in the galactic arm. It is also the least reputable, having served as a place of criminal enterprise for nearly all of its existence due to a troublesome location. Orbiting Sirius, Spindrift was nearly depopulated by stellar radiation in the third year as a spaceborne habitat. When order collapsed, criminals moved in, cycling in and out every twelve point four years as coronal ejections rom Sirius made the station uninhabitable. Spindrift is known for medical treatments and technology that are quasi-legal at best, as well as weapons, stolen goods, and a strange array of archaeological items, all illegally looted. Spindrift has a population of thirty thousand beings at any time.

Starsmith: A place, a guild, and a single being, the Starsmith is primarily a weapons expert of unsurpassed skill. The current Starsmith is a Conoku (named Linulla), a crablike race known for their dexterity, skill in metallurgy and combat enhancements, and sense of humor.

CONNECT WITH J.N. CHANEY

Don't miss out on these exclusive perks:

- Instant access to free short stories from series like *The Messenger, Starcaster,* and more.
- Receive email updates for new releases and other news.
- Get notified when we run special deals on books and audiobooks.

So, what are you waiting for? Enter your email address at the link below to stay in the loop.

https://www.jnchaney.com/backyard-starship-subscribe

CONNECT WITH TERRY MAGGERT

Check out his website
http://terrymaggert.com/

Connect on Facebook
https://www.facebook.com/terrymaggertbooks/

Follow him on Amazon
https://www.amazon.com/Terry-Maggert/e/B00EKN8RHG/

ABOUT THE AUTHORS

J. N. Chaney is a USA Today Bestselling author and has a Master's of Fine Arts in Creative Writing. He fancies himself quite the Super Mario Bros. fan. When he isn't writing or gaming, you can find him online at **www.jnchaney.com**.

He migrates often, but was last seen in Las Vegas, NV. Any sightings should be reported, as they are rare.

Terry Maggert is left-handed, likes dragons, coffee, waffles, running, and giraffes; order unimportant. He's also half of author Daniel Pierce, and half of the humor team at Cledus du Drizzle.

With thirty-one titles, he has something to thrill, entertain, or make you cringe in horror. Guaranteed.

Note: He doesn't sleep. But you sort of guessed that already.

Made in the USA
Las Vegas, NV
17 February 2022

44111879R00331